# WITH ONE MORE LOOK AT YOU

## MARY J. WILLIAMS

# ABOUT THE AUTHOR

Writing isn't easy. But I love every second. A blank screen isn't the enemy. It is the opportunity to create new friends and take them on amazing adventures and life-changing journeys. I feel blessed to spend my days weaving tales that are unique—because I made them.

Billionaires. Songwriters. Artists. Actors. Directors. Stuntmen. Football players. They fill the pages and become dear friends I hope you will want to revisit again and again.

Thank you for jumping into my books and coming along for the journey.

# *HOW TO GET IN TOUCH*

Please visit me at these sites, sign up for my newsletter or leave a message.

http://www.maryjwilliams.net/

https://www.facebook.com/maryjwilliamsauthor/?ref=hl

https://twitter.com/maryjwilliams05

https://www.pinterest.com/maryj0675/

https://www.instagram.com/2015romance/

https://www.goodreads.com/author/show/5648619.Mary_J_Wil
liams

# MORE BOOKS BY MARY J. WILLIAMS

### Harper Falls Series
If I Loved You
If Tomorrow Never Comes
If You Only Knew
If I Had You (Christmas in Harper Falls)

### Hollywood Legends Series
Dreaming with a Broken Heart
Dreaming with My Eyes Wide Open
Dreaming Again
Dreaming of a White Christmas
(Caleb and Callie's story)

### One Pass Away Series
After the Rain
After All These Years
After the Fire

### Hart of Rock and Roll
Flowers on the Wall
Flowers and Cages
Flowers are Red
Flowers for Zoe

# TABLE OF CONTENTS

# CHAPTER ONE

"GET UP. WE'RE leaving."

Sophie kept her eyes closed, pretending she was actually asleep. In truth, it was too hot. The air in the tiny motel room was thick with humidity, stale cigarettes, and mildew. Sweat drenched her body, soaking through the scratchy sheet. She could barely breathe, let alone hope for a decent night's sleep. However, when her mother kicked the bed for the second time, Sophie didn't stir.

"If your ass isn't in the car by the time I've loaded our suitcases, I won't wait," Joy Lipton threw their meager possessions into a bag. "You can stay in this shithole of a town and fend for yourself."

When Sophie was younger, that used to sound like a threat. More and more, calling her mother's bluff sounded like a fine idea. Maybe this time, Joy would do both of them a favor and actually leave.

For all intents and purposes, Sophie took care of herself. With what little money Joy provided, she bought groceries. Every time they checked into a motel, she would ask the manager if he had any odd jobs that needed to be done. Cheap labor—paid under the table. That kind of work wasn't hard to find, and it provided Sophie with a little extra spending cash.

Sophie learned fast to keep her stash hidden. Joy had no problem stealing from her daughter. And no shame when caught red-handed. *It was little enough payment for all she had sacrificed—both personally and financially.* Sophie had rolled her eyes at the outrageous claim. That little gesture had earned her a slap across the face. Sophie didn't know which of them had been more surprised. For all her failings as a mother, Joy didn't hit. Verbal abuse was her specialty.

The slap was never repeated. Sophie didn't dwell on the incident. There was no point. She was fifteen years old and looked at her life with a pragmatic attitude. For now, she was legally

1

bound to a woman who ninety percent of the time treated her as though she were invisible. The other ten—filled with rants and crying fits—Sophie had learned to tune out. If Joy had a reason for keeping her daughter around, she wasn't sharing.

"What did I say?" Sophie's only pair of jeans landed on her head. "Move. Now!"

The little voice tempting Sophie to tell Joy to go to hell wasn't a match for the sliver of fear. Bravery was easy—in her head. In reality? The unknown was scarier than following her mother to another town. Sophie was a voracious reader. Since they moved so much, attending school was hit and miss. Books, magazines, newspapers. They had taught her most of what she knew—and provided her with a vivid imagination.

The stories—both fact and fiction—led Sophie to an indisputable conclusion. The world wasn't kind to fifteen-year-old girls on their own. No matter how smart she thought she was. Or how much savvy she possessed. Without some kind of protection—even the barely there sort her mother provided—things almost never turned out well.

Picturing herself in tattered clothes, freezing to death—quite a feat considering the mid-July heatwave—Sophie climbed out of bed. Chances were slim that she would perish as some kind of modern-day *Little Match Girl*. The perverts and/or murderers would probably get her first.

"Finally." Joy shut the last suitcase. "Take a pee and get dressed. We're out of here in under five."

Grabbing a pair of clean underwear and a t-shirt, Sophie took her jeans and shuffled to the bathroom. "What's the hurry?"

As if Sophie didn't know. They typically high-tailed it in the middle of the night for one of two reasons. Either Joy had pissed off her latest *boyfriend*—and Sophie used the term lightly—or they couldn't pay the bill. More times than she could count, it was both.

"There is only one reason that matters." Joy tossed her long, chemically enhanced red hair over her shoulder. "I'm your mother."

Sophie was glad she had her back to her mother. The expression on her face—major eye roll—might have earned her another slap. Joy trotted out the *'I'm your mother'* crap from time to time as if it actually meant something. The days of Sophie wanting Joy's love and approval were long gone. The spark of hope wasn't completely dead. However, she would need more than the occasional smile and a pat on the head for it to bloom into a full-fledged flame.

There was so much about her mother that Sophie didn't understand. One second, she seemed like the dimmest bulb in the box. The next, her mind was sharp as a tack. It changed depending on the situation—and Joy's level of interest. Men were the highest priority. Other women, not so much. Sophie did know one thing. Her mother wanted to be the center of attention. The best way to get information was to act as if she didn't care.

"Whatever," Sophie said with a shrug.

Perfectly mimicking Joy's hair flip, Sophie nonchalantly closed the bathroom door. She barely had the cap off the toothpaste when like clockwork, she heard Joy's raised voice.

"I've finally landed *the* big fish."

*Bigger than the plywood salesman in Topeka? Or the guy in Scottsdale who made a living selling bathroom fixtures?* Sophie spat into the sink. They had been nice enough—that was her impression from the short amount of time she spent in their company. She could say the same about most of the guys Joy hooked up with. Every man was *the one*—until he wasn't.

These once-in-a-lifetime relationships rarely lasted six months. Once, Joy actually managed to last a year before going off the rails. Sometimes things ended with a whimper. Mostly with a bang. But either way, end they did. Inevitably as the sun came up in the east.

Sophie used the toilet. Washed her hands and face. Combed her shoulder-length dark hair. All the while, Joy waxed on and on about her latest and greatest conquest. Her mother was like a battery-operated bunny. Once she started, she went on and on and on.

"We met at *The Tremont*."

The first thing Joy would do when they hit a new town was scope out every bar. The dives were for fun, the classier ones for business. Hotel watering holes were the best. Sophie had never been inside, but she knew *The Tremont* was the most expensive place in the area.

Technically, Joy wasn't a prostitute. Yes. Sex was involved. And money. But almost never on the first date. The random hand job. Oral when priming the pump became absolutely necessary.

The fact that Sophie knew all of this was disturbing on so many levels. That it no longer bothered her was just plain sad.

"His name is Newt. Newton Branson, to be exact. The edges are a little rough, but he is class all the way. Expensive champagne. Top-shelf whiskey. Do you know that he didn't even blink when I ordered the lobster?"

In Joy's world, not grousing over the dinner bill was a certified stamp of approval. Though she never ate more than a bite or two of her meal—a girl had to watch her figure—she liked when it cost as much as possible.

Joy Lipton was beautiful. Head to toe, she had the kind of looks that attracted attention. Male attention. The only thing average about her was her height. High cheekbones. Full lips. Wide eyes the color of dark chocolate. Sophie had seen her draw a man with nothing but a smile. Curvy and buxom, if she wasn't vigilant, her body tended to run toward fat. Petrified of gaining a single pound, Joy lived on little more than coffee and cigarettes. Add alcohol when somebody else was paying.

Personality wise, Sophie and Joy were miles apart. Physically, the difference was even greater. Other than their cheekbones and the color of their eyes, any resemblance between mother and daughter was harder to find than Waldo.

Sophie was a stick. That wasn't an insult, it was a fact. Tall—at fifteen she already topped Joy by a good four inches—and skinny without a trace of her mother's curves. Though she wasn't terribly worried that her breasts were non-existent. And her hips? Well, she didn't have hips. Or a waist for that matter. Her body was pretty much a straight line from top to bottom. As long as she remained healthy and able to stand on her own two feet, Sophie didn't care about the rest.

Leaving the bathroom, Sophie retrieved the paper bag she had saved from last night's takeout. When Joy saw what Sophie was doing, she stopped her glowing commentary of Newt Branson's stellar qualities long enough to shake her head.

"Forget that crap."

Without a pause, Sophie filled the bag with various toiletries strewn around the bathroom. The almost-empty toothpaste. The bottle of shampoo she had purchased the day before. The counter was filled with potions, and lotions Joy didn't think she wanted. In a day or two, she would change her tune. From experience, Sophie knew if anything was left behind, the fault would fall on her shoulders.

Ignoring the look of disgust, Sophie added the bag to the two suitcases sitting at the foot of the bed she and her mother shared.

"If you've found Mr. Wonderful, why the sudden need to leave?"

"Newt is headed back to his ranch in… I don't remember." Joy made a dismissive movement with her hand. "Somewhere west. He wants us to go with him."

"Us?"

By Sophie's calculations, the romance of the century wasn't much more than a weekend old. Joy never confessed that she had a daughter until much further into the relationship and only when it was absolutely unavoidable.

"Naturally. We're a team."

That wasn't how Sophie would have put it. A team conjured images of them working together toward a single goal. If Joy had an endgame in mind to their perpetual trek from one end of the country to the other, she certainly hadn't shared what it was.

Sophie wasn't a player in the game. She was a reluctant observer. At best, an afterthought. At worst? Who knew? Though they had scraped rock bottom a time or two, Sophie had the feeling they had yet to hit it. If that day ever came, she had no doubt it would be every woman for herself.

"Quiet," Joy warned. Picking up a suitcase, she cracked open the hotel room door. Peering right, then left, she motioned for Sophie to follow.

Great. Sophie sighed. They were skipping out on their bill. It wasn't the first time. Joy always looked for crap-hole establishments—with male managers—that were willing to take cash under the table. Flirting and a couple of bucks usually got them a room. Joy's ample cleavage allowed them to stay past the first night. After that, it was down to how much shit the manager was willing to swallow. The promise of sex went further with some men than others.

"Just a second."

Ignoring Joy's hissed warning to get in the car, Sophie sprinted back to the room. With a sigh, she dug thirty-four dollars out of her pocket, tossing it onto the bedside table. The manager was a nice guy. Stupid. But a lot of men fell into that category when it came to her mother. The money didn't begin to cover what they owed. Sophie found it a way to assuage her conscience. Her way of convincing herself that she was better than the woman who gave birth to her.

The second Sophie was in the car, Joy hit the gas. As always, their room was the last unit and the greatest distance from the office. It made getting away so much easier. No fuss. No muss. At least for Joy. She dropped her bombs from a distance. By the time the impact was felt, she was long gone.

"Where are we going?"

"Newt has invited us to stay with him for a little while."

*This was a new twist*, Sophie thought. Since it was the second time her mother had said they were both going, it might actually be true. Occasionally, Joy went away with her current man for a long

6

weekend. But *stay for a little while*? Sophie included? That didn't happen often. And if history were any judge, it wouldn't end well. The last time wasn't that long ago. Almost a year to be exact. After a few days filled with either heated arguments or pouting silence, they ended up stranded in Poughkeepsie. The gentleman friend stole their car *and* their clothing. The only reason he hadn't gotten away with their money was that Sophie followed her instincts hiding what little they had where neither adult could find it.

With a sigh, Sophie looked out the window. How could Joy learn from her mistakes when she never admitted to making any? According to her mother, the disasters were never her fault. So she kept repeating them. Over and over again.

"You said that Newt lives *out west*?"

"That's right."

"How far? We'll be lucky to make it to the county limits in this rusty bucket of bolts," Sophie warned.

Their current transportation had been little better than when Joy acquired it last month from a used car salesman one town over. Wisely, Sophie had refrained from pointing out that if a beat-up old Ford Escort was the best she could do, Joy had been grossly exaggerating her talents.

"We aren't driving. Newt is. He has a brand-new Escalade. That's a Cadillac. Top of the line." Joy practically vibrated with excitement.

"How do you know?" Sophie wasn't averse to a little luxury. She had never ridden in a new car of any make or model. However, Joy tended to exaggerate. A lot.

"He let me drive it. There is no mistaking that smell. Fresh from the factory."

For now, Sophie would take Joy's word for it.

"Any chance you can tell me where we are going. Other than west?" They were in California. There wasn't much *west* left. Unless Newt could magically drive them to Hawaii.

"I don't know, Sophie." Joy's tone was impatient. "You'll find out when we get there."

7

"Or I could simply ask Newt."

"No." Joy shot Sophie a warning look. "Don't start asking Newt a bunch of questions. Be polite. And keep your thoughts to yourself. Understand?"

"What's the problem with asking where he's taking us?"

"Once you start, you don't know when to quit. The last thing I need is for him to get annoyed and dump us a hundred miles from nowhere. "

Sophie frowned. "Didn't he think it strange that you wanted to meet him in the middle of the night?"

"Newt likes to get an early start. His son's birthday is tomorrow. Talking him into leaving *extra* early wasn't a problem."

"But—?"

"Newt is taking us to his home. That's all you need to know."

Sophie's heart leapt to her throat. *Home.* Just the word was enough to set her pulse racing. So many meanings. A million interpretations. For Sophie, the concept seemed like a dream. A place where she belonged.

There would be no more limping from town to town. Someplace permanent where Sophie could attend school on a regular basis instead of a week here or a month there. A chance to make friends who lasted beyond a tentative hello and no goodbye at all.

*Home.* Sophie didn't know what it looked like, but she knew what it represented. She held onto the dream—the only one she allowed herself—while her mother pulled her from town to town. The longer hopes and dreams remained unfulfilled, the heavier they became. Sophie's slight shoulders were strong, but there was a limit to everything.

She kept her dreams buried for a reason. It hurt to get her hopes up only to have them broken into a million pieces. Newt. His ranch. His *home.* Sophie couldn't let herself think of it as real. Not with Joy calling the shots. Her mother had the attention span of a gnat. Always looking past what she had. Certain something bigger and better was just around the corner.

Calling herself the biggest kind of fool, Sophie gave herself a shake. She was getting ahead of herself. Chances were high that something would happen to prevent them from leaving town—let alone reaching this so-called ranch.

Joy slowed the car, coming to a stop next to a deserted row of parking meters. Without a word of explanation, she exited the vehicle.

"I know what you're thinking." Joy kicked the temperamental trunk. Once. Twice. Third time's the charm.

"I doubt that." Sophie removed her suitcase and the paper bag.

"You think that I'm afraid to let Newt see the kind of car I drive."

"Close enough," Sophie muttered as they started their walk. Actually, for once, Joy was spot on.

"Trust me, missy. You are not as deep and mysterious as you want to believe." Joy wobbled down the uneven sidewalk in a tight skirt and five-inch heels. "One day you'll understand why I do the things I do."

That seemed unlikely. Sophie was happy in her sneakers and old jeans. No matter her age, Sophie couldn't see herself in her mother's shoes. Figuratively *or* literally.

"I'll let you in on a little secret. Men want perfection. Newt likes the idea of helping a woman who is slightly down on her luck. But I can't actually *look* like I need his money."

"It's better to trudge down the street in the middle of the night than roll up in a crappy car?"

"Yes." Joy set down her suitcase, giving herself a moment to catch her breath. "Besides, he won't see me trudging. When he comes down to the lobby, I'll be waiting. Fresh as a daisy."

"The sweat rolling down your face isn't very daisy-like," Sophie pointed out.

"That's what bathrooms and a change of clothes are for." Determined, Joy picked up the suitcase and her pace. "I've never let a man see me when I'm not at my best."

"What about in the morning?" Sophie had seen Joy when her eyes were rimmed with mascara, and her hair was standing on end. Before noon, Joy tended to look like a frightened raccoon.

"I make certain to wake long before he does. I sponge myself off—a shower would spoil the illusion. Brush my teeth. Put on new makeup. Fix my hair. Then I sneak back to bed before he knows I was gone."

"It sounds exhausting." And ridiculous. Sophie knew that her mother's boyfriends were less than rocket scientists. But only a fool would believe that Joy woke up looking like she stepped off a magazine cover.

"It's necessary."

Joy sounded so sure of herself. So superior. So worldly. So idiotic it was all Sophie could do not to burst out laughing. Perhaps if this were the nineteen-fifties and *Leave It to Beaver* ruled the television airways. Or maybe—just maybe—if Sophie had lived a sheltered life without the benefit of books and the internet. If all of that were true, she might buy the line her mother tried to sell.

By association, Sophie was forced to ride a rollercoaster of secondhand disappointment and frustration. The pity was all on her side. Not for herself. She could picture the day when all of this was a distant memory. On her own. Away from her mother's drama. Sophie pitied her mother because no matter what, Joy would never change.

This was the life Joy wanted. The sad part was that whether she ever admitted it or not, she fought a losing battle. Like the Wizard of Oz, her mother was so afraid that somebody would get a look behind the curtain, she had never learned to enjoy the here and now.

"Finally," Joy said as the hotel came into view.

Their walk was probably the most exercise her mother had in years. The heat didn't help. Though well after midnight, the temperature was still in the high seventies. Breathing heavily, Joy took a handkerchief from her purse, wiping her profusely sweating face.

"Are the rooms as nice as the lobby?" Sophie knew she was gaping, but this was the first time she had seen the inside of a place that didn't rent by the hour. Everything was so clean. And the air conditioning was a slice of pure heaven.

"For Christ's sake, Sophie, close your mouth. You're acting like an unsophisticated yokel."

"Because that's what I am." Sophie wasn't embarrassed. She took a seat in one of the plush velvet chairs and sighed. This was so much better than her imagination—and her imagination was spectacular. However, picturing herself in a place like this had nothing on actually being here.

"I'm going to freshen up." Joy took her makeup bag from the suitcase before setting it next to Sophie. "Don't move. Don't talk to anybody unless they work here. And then, what do you say?"

"I'm waiting for my father." Sophie knew the drill. Adults gave well-behaved children some leeway. Especially when the child claimed a parent was in the vicinity.

Though tall, Sophie looked her age. Maybe a little younger. When she spoke, the story was different. Her mental maturity far outdistanced her body. However, she was smart enough to tone down her intellect when necessary. If somebody wanted an innocent tween, that's what she gave them.

Today, Joy wanted invisible, so that was the illusion Sophie presented. Still but observant, she sat patiently, doing nothing to draw attention. Her feet didn't swing, her hands lay unmoving in her lap. But Sophie's mind was anything but quiet. She took it all in. Every sight. Every sound. It didn't matter that this was a small hotel. Or that the patrons weren't even close to celebrity status. All around her was a different world than the one she normally inhabited.

To pass the time—and amuse nobody but herself—Sophie made up stories. For example, the couple at the reception desk. Young. Attractive. Obviously in love. Newly married, they were running away from disapproving parents. She had a job waiting for her in San Francisco. He was a hopeful author. She would work while he completed his half-finished book. When it hit the bestseller list, she would go back to college. Perhaps they would start a family. The future was limitless as long as they were together.

Then on the opposite end of the happiness spectrum, the man waiting near the entrance looked uncomfortable. The man speaking earnestly to him was his lover. Married, they met on the down-low whenever possible. The smaller, animated speaker stated his argument for the umpteenth time. They should confess everything to their families. Didn't they deserve to be with each other—the person they loved? From the first man's reaction, it didn't seem that he agreed. Sophie didn't try to feel sorry for the men. Her sympathy lay with the deceived wives—not the cheaters.

Enjoying the game, Sophie looked for another target for her harmless musings. Dismissing several possibilities, her gaze came to rest on a tall, lean man who seemed to be looking for somebody. Handsome. Not too young. Not too old. Sophie wasn't very good at guessing ages. For her story, she settled on forty-five. Maybe a little younger. His dark-blond hair was worn short, and he was clean shaven. In his hand, he held a cowboy hat. That was interesting.

His boots were in the same vein. Blue jeans that looked like they were straight from the store. A crisp white shirt, tucked in, fastened with silver snaps. Neat as a pin, and a little nervous if the way his fingers clutched the brim of his Stetson was any indication. He had a kind face. Sophie hoped whoever kept him waiting was worthy of that kindness.

"Well? What do you think?"

Not exactly a miracle, but Joy had worked wonders on herself. In Sophie's opinion, the makeup was too heavy, and the dress was still too short, but Joy's long hair hung loosely around her shoulders softening her look considerably.

Knowing her part in this play, Sophie said her lines without a stumble or stutter.

"You look beautiful. Not a day over twenty-five."

Thirty-five was more like it. But Sophie wasn't supposed to mention her mother's real age. *Ever.* One of Joy's hard-fast rules.

Happy, Joy scanned the room. Slowly, her smile widened, and her body took on a sultry pose.

"There's Newt."

Sophie turned. She should have guessed. The cowboy with the kind face waved his hat. As he made his way toward them, her emotions were mixed. For her sake, she wanted Newt to be a good man. For his sake, she hoped his skin was thicker than it looked.

"One more thing," Joy whispered to Sophie out of the side of her mouth. "I'm your sister. Don't forget."

Sophie watched as Newt swung a laughing Joy into his arms. *Sisters.* Not the first time they had perpetrated that particular deception. Maybe it was his sweet smile or the warmth in his deep blue eyes. Something about Newt made Sophie want to tell him the truth. Damn Joy and the consequences.

"Is this your little sister?"

"That's right." Perhaps sensing Sophie's hesitation, Joy sent her a warning look.

"Hello, Sophie." Newt took her hand in his. "Are you ready to go home?"

That one word sent all others from Sophie's brain. She swallowed hard.

"Home?" she asked hopefully. When Newt nodded, his kind eyes crinkling at the sides, the hope in Sophie's heart canceled out her twinge of conscience. Taking a deep breath, she smiled. "Yes, sir. I am."

# CHAPTER TWO

"OH, FORBES! OH, Forbes! *Oh! Forbes!*"

"Shut the fuck up."

"What?" Aaron Green asked his best friend with feigned innocence. "I'm just recreating the sound everybody else at the party heard. Shelly's screams of pleasure—they were pleasure, right?"

"Fuck you."

"Why bother when you have Shelly Thomas at your disposal. She's hot. Willing. Able. Doesn't ask for a commitment longer than it takes her to get off. And those tits." As a visual reference, Aaron held his hands a good three feet from his chest. "Still. The way she screeched? Your bedroom is on the second floor, and we heard her like you were screwing three feet away."

Laughing like a madman, Aaron Green collapsed onto the sofa. Not able to prevent himself from getting in one more jab, he sighed loudly. "Oh—"

The sopping-wet sponge hurled at his face hit Aaron smack-dab in the mouth, effectively preventing him from finishing.

"I told you to shut up."

Forbes laughed—hard. The sight of Aaron's face covered in water, soap, and whatever grimy crap the sponge had picked up from last night's party almost made the pain in his exploding hangover-laden head worth it.

"Not cool, man." Aaron scrubbed his face with his shirtsleeve. "Isn't that the spot where Dwyer tossed his cookies?"

"And a half pint of cheap whiskey."

Feeling his stomach roil with protest, Forbes remembered to breathe through his nose. The only consolation was that the vomit hit the hardwood, missing the cloth-covered furniture. Knowing his friends, before the party started, Forbes had rolled up the expensive Persian rug that normally blanketed the living room floor, packing it away behind the locked office door. Along with his mother's crystal vase and anything else a pack of rowdy teenagers might destroy. In the end, all that was left was a coffee table, one old lamp, some chairs, and the sofa. The last was covered by an old blanket.

"What the hell did they spill on this thing?" Aaron's nose wrinkled. "It smells like a brewery—that somebody pissed on."

Returning to scrubbing the floor, Forbes shook his head. His friends were pigs. Worse than. However, he had known that when he invited them to celebrate his birthday. With his father out of town, it made perfect sense to get together here at the ranch. A few days early didn't matter. Saturday was their usual party night. Instead of meeting out at Tyler's Pond, they met here.

The only rule? If they drove, they left their keys at the door. Nobody got into their vehicle unless Forbes deemed them sober. As a result, it had been one huge sleepover.

Aaron picked the blanket up off the sofa, holding it at arm's length. "Remind me why we're stuck doing the dirty work?"

"Because the two of us are godless. Except for Wylie who is still passed out in the corner, everybody is at church."

"Listening to Reverend Stokes preach about abstinence?" Aaron shuddered. "No sex? No liquor? No fun? No thanks."

"It would have gotten you out of cleaning crap off the floor." From the smell, Forbes thought with disgust, the brown stuff might actually *be* crap.

"I've shoveled my share of shit. I'll take the real stuff to the made-up stuff Stokes hands out any day."

"Amen, brother," Forbes said. Picking up the bucket of soapy water, he stood. "It looks good. The smell on the other hand? Not so much."

"I have some cans of air freshener in my truck."

"Why didn't I think of that?"

"Because this is the first time your dad has left town long enough for you to host one of these shindigs."

Alone, except for Wylie Wilcox snoring in the corner, Forbes walked around the house, opening every available window. When he got to the set of French doors, he turned the knob. The cool, welcome mid-morning breeze drifted up from the Columbia River. Stepping onto the deck, Forbes leaned against the rail, breathing deeply.

The smell would be hard to describe to an outsider. Pine trees. Freshly cut alfalfa that in a day or two would be bailed into hay. His mother's prized roses that she used to tend with such care. Now the beds were kept pristine in her memory. To Forbes, the combination of scents blended perfectly. Better than the most expensive perfume. He knew that no matter where he went. No matter how long he was gone. It would always smell like... home.

The Branson Ranch. Forbes knew its history.

The first Branson had come from Ireland at the turn of the century. The twentieth century. Landing in New York, he had longed for a place to call his own. And land. Somewhere he could raise a family. A legacy. He wanted his family name to be remembered for generations to come.

Cyrus Branson's descendants weren't exactly world beaters. However, in their corner—Eastern Washington State to be exact— the family was doing fine. They were well thought of. Successful. Influential. If something needed to be done in this part of the state, the Branson family—or more precisely Forbes' father—was one of the first people contacted.

"Here you go." Aaron handed Forbes a bottle of beer and three aspirin.

"Hair of the dog?" Forbes downed the pills with two gulps from the bottle.

"That was hours ago. This is for old time's sake. Once your dad gets home, you'll be back on the wagon. At least until next weekend."

"Nope. Football practice starts the day after tomorrow." This would be their final season, and Forbes wanted that state championship. This year, the coach was king. His rules were to be followed to the letter. "If Riggins tells us to scratch each other's balls every hour on the hour, we scratch."

"My balls are off limits to you, son." Aaron stared at the view. "Now, if you want to send Shelly Thomas my way, *she* can touch any part of me she wants."

Forbes wasn't in the mood to discuss Shelly Thomas. It had been a drunken hookup. Not the first time, but he hoped the last. Shelly was a nice girl. And not nearly as promiscuous as rumor would have people believe. She was fun. And smart. Easy to talk to. The problem was, all of a sudden, she wanted more than he was willing to give.

The steady girlfriend thing didn't interest Forbes. Never had. When his friends started pairing up—around the seventh grade— he didn't follow along. Dating was fine. Fooling around. Making out. Transitioning into sex when the girl was willing. All those things were great. As his dad would put it, they were part of being a teenager.

However, when a girl started to cling, Forbes lost interest. Maybe something was wrong with him. Maybe he lacked the want—or the need—to have a special someone. His class ring stayed firmly on his finger. His letterman jacket on his back. No girl had ever worn a symbol of his affection. With one year left in his high school career, he doubted any would.

Though Forbes knew that Aaron was teasing, he quickly re-routed the conversation away from his personal life and onto that of his best friend.

"What about Cindy? Wouldn't she object to another girl touching your private parts?"

"Cindy and I are on a break."

Forbes turned his head, a frown marring his brow. "Since when? Just last week you were talking about taking her to the homecoming dance."

Aaron shrugged. "She's a kid. I need a more mature woman."

"She's a few months younger than you."

"Maturity isn't always about age."

It didn't take long for the light to go on in Forbes' brain. "Oh, for the love of— Sex? Is that what this is about?"

"Cindy wants to wait." Aaron worked his thumbnail under the label of his beer. "I don't."

"But you like her. *Really* like her. Since we were in the second grade, you've been crushing on the girl." Forbes couldn't imagine it. His longest crush lasted all of three months. His fourth-grade teacher seemed like the perfect woman. Until she took away his favorite fire truck as punishment for shooting a spitball into Marianne Palmer's hair. The love affair ended then and there.

"I'm aware of how long I've liked Cindy," Aaron muttered.

"It took you until last year to finally make your move. Now that you have her, you're going to break up over something so minor?"

"Says the man who got his rocks off less than twelve hours ago. Since your first time, how long have you gone without sex?" Aaron made it sound like an accusation. "That month you and your dad went fishing in Alaska?"

More like two weeks. Forbes had hooked up with the college-age daughter of their guide his father had hired to help them traverse the Alaskan wilderness. He quickly learned that there was something to be said for an experienced woman. Forbes smiled at the memory. That trip turned out to be educational in more ways than one.

"Son of a bitch." Reading his friend like a book, Aaron punched Forbes in the arm.

"Hey! Coach Riggins will have both our asses if I show up to practice unable to make a pass."

"Apparently, making a pass has never been your problem. Who was the girl? How did it happen? And why the hell didn't you tell me you scored more than some salmon while in Alaska?"

"I don't brag." Forbes cut Aaron off before he could begin. "Even to you."

Nodding, Aaron didn't look happy. "It's one of your most annoying qualities. Living my celibate lifestyle would be so much easier if my best friend shared a few juicy details about his many, many, many conquests."

Forbes liked sex. A lot. It was right up there in his top two or three all-time favorite things. However, he hadn't become sexually active at an unreasonably early age. Sixteen. And a half. That added up to just under eighteen months. He wasn't ashamed to admit that he was counting. Eight different girls. One certified woman. The number of times he had sex with each? Forbes had lost count. Perhaps he was a bit of a dog after all.

"Would you stop grinning like a satisfied loon?" Aaron flopped onto a piece of patio furniture, the frame groaning under his considerable bulk. At almost three hundred pounds, he was one of the best in the state at stopping running backs before they crossed the line of scrimmage. "Since I started dating Cindy, I've been in a sexual drought. My hand doesn't cut it anymore."

Laughing when Aaron gripped the bottle in a graphic example of his masturbation skills, Forbes drained the last of his beer. He felt for his buddy. Honestly. But he knew Aaron well enough to know that he would regret letting Cindy go. And if she started dating somebody else? Nope. He didn't particularly care about the fool who was stupid enough to ask Cindy out. Forbes was worried about Aaron. He didn't want his best friend to spend his senior year of high school—plus the next twenty years—in prison for murder.

"You love Cindy. Yes, you do," Forbes said when Aaron would have protested. "*That* is the reason to give her a break."

"Jesus. When did you go all Oprah on me?"

Taking the jibe in the lighthearted vein it was meant, Forbes shot Aaron a grin. "She knows her shit, man."

"Maybe." Aaron let out a hefty sigh. He closed his eyes, running a hand through his already tousled dark hair. "I *do* love Cindy. My mom says it is only puppy love."

Aaron's mom believed in keeping the apron strings tight. Though for once, Forbes didn't think she was far off base. "At our age, what's the difference?"

"People get married right out of high school." The fact that Aaron was looking at the ground instead of at him told Forbes that this wasn't the first time the thought of marriage had popped into his head.

"Cindy is holding out for a trip down the aisle? I thought she was better than that. Unless..." *Well, shit.* "*You* want to get married? Seriously?"

"Not today," Aaron said defiantly. "When we graduate. Maybe. But if Cindy is the one, shouldn't I sow my wild oats right now? If we get hitched, that's it for me. No cheating."

So many things chased around in his mind, Forbes didn't know where to start. Aaron wasn't the most complicated guy in the world. He liked things simple and easy. Because they had been friends for so long, it wasn't difficult to boil the situation down to its bare essence.

"You want to break up with Cindy now. Screw around for the next five or six months. Then get back together with her in time for graduation and a summer wedding?"

Aaron perked up. "Exactly."

"You're an idiot."

Forbes headed back into the house. For a person of his size, Aaron was quick to his feet, trailing right behind.

"Why?"

"What about Cindy?" Forbes handed Aaron two large garbage bags loaded with empties and fast food wrappers.

"What about her?"

"She may not like the scenario you've painted. And if she does, do you think she'll stay home every night, waiting for your oats to get sown?"

"Sure." Outside by the garage, Aaron smashed his bags into the already full garbage can before opening its twin for Forbes. "What else would she do?"

"Date? Screw around?"

"Cindy?" Aaron found it hard to grasp the concept. "Get out of here."

"Your problem is that you think of Cindy as a sweet, innocent girl. Take another look. She's hot. Long blond hair. A curvy little figure. And those wide blue eyes? If you weren't my friend—and didn't think of her as a sister—I'd be tempted."

"You think she would cheat on me?"

"It wouldn't be cheating if you broke up with her—for the sole purpose of screwing around."

"Name one guy who would dare—"

"I could name a half dozen."

"But—"

"That's it." Forbes stopped Aaron's forward progress with a hand to the big guy's chest. The fact that he could spoke volumes about Forbes' strong, athletic legs, and Aaron's instinctively gentle nature. "The aspirin isn't working on my raging headache. There is still some cleaning to do before Maeve gets back from her sister's."

"And?"

"I love you, man. But one more word on the subject of your love life and I will personally set Cindy up with Rick Billingsley."

Just the idea of his sweet girlfriend in the hands of the most notorious horn dog at Cloverton High School was enough to shut Aaron up. At least temporarily.

Forbes was halfway through his second glass of water when Aaron asked sheepishly, "You wouldn't really? Would you?"

"No."

"Okay."

And just like that, the conversation was over. Forbes and Aaron worked the rest of the afternoon in relative silence. Stopping to raid the refrigerator once their stomachs could handle the thought of food. By then, Wylie Wilcox was back among the living. Though for the life of him, he couldn't remember much about the party—or how he had gotten there.

"Since your car isn't out front, somebody must have brought you." Noticing that Wylie was still a little unsteady on his feet, Aaron took his arm. "Come on. I'll give you a lift home."

"It's a good thing football season is starting. It won't hurt any of us to go on the wagon," Forbes said, holding open the door of Aaron's truck.

"I'm the manager," Wylie muttered.

"If we don't drink, you don't drink. Got it?"

Forbes was team captain. Voted on by his fellow players, he took the position seriously. From water boy to cheerleader. If they were involved with the Cloverton Cavaliers, they were his to watch out for.

"Yah, I got it." Wylie didn't sound sold on the idea, but Forbes was confident he would come around. Especially when all his drinking buddies were no longer available to party on Saturday night—or any other day of the week.

As the last of his guests drove away down the long driveway, Forbes walked to the gate, letting himself into the backyard.

"I know you're in here," he called out as soon as the latch was back in place. "Pouting won't solve anything. If you won't meet me face to face, how can I apologize properly?"

Knowing it wouldn't take long, Forbes waited. A few seconds later, a large, dark-brown flash of fur barreled around the corner of the house. The animal—a mixture of Labrador, Great Dane, and Lord knew what else—skidded to a halt a few feet away. Quivering, he didn't jump at Forbes, barely containing his natural instincts. Understanding how this went, Forbes crouched until they were eye to eye.

"I'm sorry, Bailey." Reaching out, Forbes ran his hand over the gentle giant's head. "My human friends are a little rowdy at these get-togethers. Add in alcohol, and I thought it best for you to stay back here. I know you can take care of yourself," Forbes assured his four-legged pal when the dog tilted his head in a questioning manner. "But if anything happened to you, I don't think I could take it."

Never one to hold a grudge, Bailey closed the gap between them until he pushed Forbes to the ground and, despite his considerable size, climbed onto his favorite person's lap. Happy to oblige, Forbes wrapped his arms around the dog, burying his face in the familiar-smelling fur. Magically, the remaining fuzz cleared from his brain, his headache lowering to a bearable ping instead of an unearthly rattle.

Bailey had been a puppy when he became part of the Branson household. Abandoned, Forbes' mother found him on the side of the road, huddled in a ball during a raging rainstorm, leaving no question about bringing him home. Ella Branson had the softest heart in the county. She couldn't stand to see any living creature suffer. With plenty of room on the ranch, one more mouth to feed wouldn't matter—even if that mouth turned out to consume enough to feed a small army.

All it took was one look. Bailey belonged to Forbes, and he belonged to Bailey. Eight years later, that hadn't changed. A friend. A confidant who would lock anything Forbes shared in the deepest, most impenetrable vault.

However, if none of that were true, Bailey would always have a special place in Forbes' heart. The puppy was the last gift his mother gave him before her sudden death a few short weeks later. *God damned drunk driver.*

"I still miss her," Forbes said, his throat clogging with emotion.

Silently, Bailey commiserated. More than once, the dog had stood vigil while Forbes cried the tears he couldn't—wouldn't—show his grief-stricken father. It had been a dark, joyless time. Though things were better, the light had never fully returned. The spring was gone from his father's step, the happiness dimmed in his blue eyes.

"Dad needed some time away." Forbes got to his feet, brushing off the back of his jeans. "I hope he had a good time at the rancher's convention. Maybe I wasn't the only member of the family who got lucky this weekend."

On the way to the garage, Bailey sent Forbes a baleful look. "Sorry, fella. Having you fixed was the responsible thing to do. Blame Bob Barker, not me. Besides, unlike Dad, you never had sex. I suspect he's been with a few women in the past eight years, but not often enough for a man still in his prime."

"A man in his prime? Send him my way."

Forbes almost jumped a foot. And to his embarrassment, might have let out a sound reminiscent of a frightened little girl.

"Maeve. I didn't hear you arrive."

"Too busy sharing secrets with that horse masquerading as a dog." Bailey preened, certain he had received the finest of compliments. Laughing, Maeve took a large soup bone from the refrigerator. "Here you go, Mr. Ed."

Maeve Kincaid had been the Branson's housekeeper since before Forbes was born. Unapologetically vain about her looks, she kept a standing weekly appointment at the beauty parlor. Hair and nails. Without fail. Not a big believer in talking about her age, when pushed she would admit to fifty-five. Though sixty-five was more like it.

More than an employee, Maeve was part of the family. For years, she and Forbes' mother worked side by side, cooking for a rotating bevy of ranch hands, cleaning the big main house. Making it into a home. After Ella Branson died, Maeve stayed on. She took care of them.

For months, when Forbes' father was so wracked with grief he did nothing but work and sleep, Maeve was the rock Forbes leaned on. A boy missing his mother, she allowed him to grieve when he needed to. Consoled him when he would let her. Mostly, she was simply there. Carrying on when sometimes it seemed like nobody else could.

And? Maeve hands down made *the* best cookies in the world.

"How was the party?"

"Party?" Though acting wasn't his forte, Forbes did his best to pull off surprised and nonchalant. By the look on Maeve's face, he failed. Horribly.

With an indulgent smile, Maeve wiped her hands on a dishtowel, shaking her freshly coifed head. "You're seventeen. I'd be worried if you hadn't invited your friends over to kick up your heels."

"I'm eighteen," Forbes corrected. To him, it was an important point.

"Not until tomorrow, young man. Good Lord, where has the time gone." Lightly, with infinite affection, Maeve touched Forbes on the cheek. "What happened to that sweet little boy who constantly needed me to pull a sliver from his finger or bandage his knees?"

"I was never sweet." With a smile, Forbes popped a jam-filled butter cookie into his mouth.

"Rambunctious," Maeve admitted. "A scamp with so much energy your mother and I had to tag team each other to keep up."

That was another thing Forbes loved about Maeve. She was never hesitant to mention Ella Branson. Her references were casual. Natural. Delivered with gentle affection for a friend she would always miss and never left her heart. In stark contrast, his father never spoke of his wife. He held his grief—and his memories—close. Never sharing them with anybody. Not even his son.

Long ago, Forbes wished for his father to open up so he could do the same. It never happened, leaving an invisible wall that neither tried to breach for the simple reason that they didn't realize it was there.

"Time moves too slowly for my liking."

"You won't say that in twenty years. Or thirty." Maeve sighed. "Believe me. When you look back, it will seem like they went by in a blink."

Forbes dismissed Maeve's words with the blitheness of youth. He wasn't concerned about the future. Next week and football practice seemed like it was taking forever to get here. Beyond that, his senior year of high school, and picking the college he would attend, were as far ahead as he cared to look.

"Dad should be home this afternoon."

"I know." Standing in the doorway between the kitchen and living room, Maeve placed her hands on her ample hips. "You never did answer me about the party. I smell... Glade air freshener. Spring Morning, if I'm not mistaken." She took another sniff. "Stale beer, cheap booze, and a bit of vomit."

"Is it that bad?" Denial was useless at this point. Looking over the top of Maeve's much shorter head, Forbes tried to see the room from her perspective.

"No. You did a surprisingly good job of cleaning up." With efficient movements, Maeve straightened a few objects that only her expert eye could identify as out of place. "Who helped you? Besides Aaron?"

"Just him."

"Church?" When Forbes nodded, Maeve laughed. "Funny how devout some folks get when there's unpleasant work to be done. You should have held their lazy rumps over the fire and made them stay."

"It wasn't that bad." Maeve shot him a look that said she was unconvinced. "I covered the furniture before that party started. Locked some doors and restricted everybody to in here, the bathroom, and the kitchen. It worked. For the most part."

Forbes didn't see the point in telling Maeve about Jock Blanding using the vegetable bed as a urinal. What she didn't know wouldn't hurt her. Forbes, on the other hand, planned on taking a pass on zucchini for the rest of the summer.

"I won't ask you about the chores. I know you wouldn't let the animals go hungry."

"I had Mike and Jerry to take care of the horses before heading into town."

They lived on a working ranch. A successful one. The bunkhouse—renovated just last year—comfortably held four permanent cowhands. Depending on the season—winter was the only real downtime—there could be anywhere from ten to twenty on the payroll—not counting Forbes and his father.

Some were strictly cowboys, brought on to deal with the herds of cattle that ranged all over the far-stretching property. Branding. Vaccinations. Keeping the miles and miles of fence in working order. It was a never-ending cycle. Migratory, the men would travel wherever the work took them. The Branson Ranch had a well-earned reputation for treating workers with respect and proper compensation. Good pay. Good food. Good lodgings. By the end of fall, they always walked away with a nice chunk of money in the bank.

With the thoughtlessness of the typical teenager, Forbes didn't realize how lucky he was. His family had money. Though he loved riding horses and working cattle, he wasn't forced by necessity to be a slave to the life. Instead of having to rush home after school or spend his weekends rounding up strays, he was able to have an active social life that included playing football in the fall and baseball in the spring.

"Good boy." Satisfied that everything was just so, Maeve nodded. "The only reason we could talk your father into getting away was that he knew he could count on you not to burn the place down in his absence."

"I think I did a little better than that."

For all his carefree lifestyle, Forbes took what responsibilities he had seriously. Every morning since his father was away, he diligently did the chores. He worked side by side with the cowhands, whether riding the fence line or mucking out horse stalls. This was his summer job, and he did it gladly. One day, the ranch would be his. Learning the ins and outs was important. The men treated him as a friend, but if a decision needed to be made, they didn't hesitate to look to him.

Forbes had earned their respect—not by virtue of his position as the boss' son. He did it by pulling his weight. It was dirty, sweaty, sometimes bloody work. And he *never* shied away from doing his share.

Leaving Maeve to settle in, Forbes changed into his work clothes. Old, scuffed-up cowboy boots. Jeans that had been washed so many times, they were white around the rivets. The tear near the knee was new, caused by a run in with some barbed wire and an unruly steer.

Stuck in a mud hole the result of a sudden downpour, the animal stubbornly fought Forbes and his efforts to pull him to dry land. Finally, Forbes, a good, strong rope, and Chester—the best cow pony on the ranch—succeeded in extracting the four-hundred-pound animal. As a thank you, it butted Forbes into the fence. Hence, the torn denim.

"Ready to get some exercise?"

He didn't need to ask Bailey twice. He was game for anything Forbes threw his way. Always had been. Calling out to Maeve that he was headed to the barn, he and the dog set off down the road. Happy. With the warm Sunday afternoon. With their lives in general. And mostly, with the silence and each other's company.

# CHAPTER THREE

"ALL OF THIS belongs to you?"

The wonder in Joy's voice seemed to make Newt's chest swell with pride.

"As far as the eye can see, this has been Branson land for generations."

"How wonderful."

Sophie listened to her mother's response with half an ear. She had heard it too often to take any notice. Newt was another matter. He couldn't know that the patter had been practiced and perfected to the last ooh, ah, sigh, and batted eyelash. It wasn't up to Sophie to warn the man.

Newt Branson was an adult. From what she had been able to glean in the past two days, he seemed to possess a reasonable amount of intelligence. If he couldn't see past Joy's artifice, too bad. He would find out soon enough that while she bubbled with enthusiasm on the outside, she calculated how much of his wealth she could charm him out of. And how long it would take.

The timetable was the key. Joy was a city girl through and through. The suburbs were too rural for her liking. Though careful to turn her head from Newt's gaze, Sophie had seen the sneer on her mother's face—the look of disdain in her eyes—as they traveled through Cloverton. If they had been alone, the sharp-tongued comments would have filled the car from city limit to city limit. And beyond.

No. It didn't matter what Joy thought. Or how Newt heard only what he wanted to hear. Sophie was completely and utterly enchanted. From her vantage point in the backseat of the SUV, everything looked so... spacious. They drove for miles without passing another car. No houses littered the countryside. Just tree-lined hills and open fields. Sophie knew that such places existed. But she had never expected to see one close up. She wished they would stop so she could run. Nowhere in particular. The idea of so much nature and nothing else made her almost giddy.

Questions swirled through Sophie's head. What did they do on the ranch? Was it just cattle? Or did they have sheep? Llamas? Yaks? Whatever? Did they rise with the sun and go to bed before nine o'clock? Big breakfasts with lots of eggs and bacon and potatoes and...? Sophie wanted to start asking, not stopping until her brain was empty. She wanted to bounce with excitement. It felt as though they were going to an exotic location filled with the wonderful unknown and she couldn't wait to get there.

Breathing deeply, in and out, Sophie controlled her impulses. Staying perfectly still, she stared out the window, asking none of the questions that wanted to burst from her mouth.

"You're awfully quiet back there."

Newt had commented on Sophie's lack of conversations several times. As usual, Joy answered for her.

"Sophie isn't much of a talker."

The lies rolled off Joy's tongue with ease. If given a chance, Sophie could talk. And talk. And talk. She also knew how to keep her mouth shut. A definite difference. But Newt didn't know it. If Joy had her way, he never would.

Newt Branson really was a sweet man, Sophie thought with a twinge of regret. Too sweet for a barracuda like her mother. He was a lonely man. A widower still mourning the loss of his beloved wife. Ripe for the picking, Joy used that to her advantage, pouring on the sympathy. Coupled with her best asset—her sex appeal—poor Newt was putty in her hands.

"What do you think about my part of the country?"

Since it was a direct question, Sophie sighed, answering honestly. "It's beautiful."

"I think so too," Newt beamed with pride. "A few days in the country is exactly what you and your sister need. We'll get some roses in those cheeks of yours."

"I don't need the country to do that," Joy purred, her hand sliding along Newt's thigh. "You did that all by yourself when were in California. Every night. And again in the morning."

Newt blushed—*actually blushed*—at Joy's words. Sophie couldn't remember seeing such a thing. Not from a grown man. And especially not from one of her mother's men. They usually ate up her overt flirting, never concerned who was watching. The color on Newt's face—and the gentle way he patted the creeping hand before removing it from his leg—proved once more that he was a different breed from the kind Joy usually attracted.

"We'll be home in a few minutes," Newt sent Sophie a smile in the rearview mirror.

"I can't wait to meet your little boy," Joy gushed, drawing Newt's attention back to her.

"Hardly little. Like a told you, tomorrow is his eighteenth birthday."

"Honestly, I thought you were pulling my leg. There is no way you are old enough to have a son that age."

Sophie groaned. Quietly. Certainly not loud enough for her mother to hear. But for the love of Pete. What was wrong with men? Joy's line was older than dirt. Yet, again and again, she used it. To great success.

*I tell them what they want to hear*, Joy once explained. *Men want you to lie to them?* Sophie had wondered, keeping the question to herself. It seemed to be true. Puff up his ego. Lay on the lies—the thicker, the better. It made the men happy. Joy got what she wanted—at least in the short run.

With a sigh, Sophie couldn't help but think the whole thing was terribly... sad. There was no better word for it. Every relationship Joy had—no matter how brief—was built on a foundation that could be easily toppled by the simple act of removing a pair of blinders. There had to be a better way. Wasn't there? Sophie certainly hoped so.

"There it is. Home, sweet home."

Sophie sat forward, practically pressing her nose to the glass.

"Is that your house? It's so big," Joy said with the breathy glee of a little girl on Christmas morning who received the exact gift she wished for.

"It's been added onto a few times over the years. It *is* a bit large for three people."

"Three?" Joy's eyes narrowed. "I thought you told me it was just you and your son."

"Maeve lives with us. Our housekeeper."

"Oh." Joy nodded with a relieved smile. "She's a servant."

"No. Maeve is a part of the family."

"Of course," Joy gushed reassuringly. "I can't wait to meet her."

Joy didn't care about meeting *any* women. One that had any influence over Newt? Sophie couldn't see that sitting well with her mother. She could only hope that the drama that was bound to ensue—the inevitable blowup that saw them either thrown out on their asses or sneaking away in the middle of the night—didn't happen for a day or so. Long enough for Sophie to explore the ranch. And ride a horse. Just once. Wouldn't that be something?

Hugging the thought to herself, Sophie watched as Newt turned off the main road onto a long, L-shaped driveway. The first part ran alongside two fields tall with something green and lush.

"Alfalfa," Newt said as though reading her mind. "It's been a good summer. That's our third crop. One of my men will take the swather to it in a few days."

"What's a swather?" Sophie had to ask. If she didn't get out at least one question, her head felt as if it would pop.

"It's a big machine with a spinning cutter. See?" Newt pointed to Sophie's right. "There it is."

Fascinated, Sophie craned her neck to get a better look. It wasn't what she had expected. Most of her ideas about farming equipment came from watching old movies. This machine was modern and shiny with the driver's seat completely enclosed by glass and metal. Obviously, Newt's ranch was a far cry from *The Grapes of Wrath.*

"What's the other machine?"

"That bales the hay. We have a third one that picks up the bales, stacks them neatly, and deposits them in the barn. It's a lot easier than when I was a boy. We did a lot more by hand back then."

"Are those cabs air conditioned?" Sophie was enthralled by every detail. "Do they—?

"Sophie!" Joy's tone was sharp. "That's enough. Newt doesn't want to be bothered with your questions."

"I don't mind. Not a bit," Newt assured Sophie. "Would you like to take one for a drive?"

"Really? Do you mean it?"

"Absolutely."

Sophie couldn't remember the last time she cried. But Newt's promise made her throat tighten, and her eyes burn. She knew it probably wouldn't happen. Either he would forget, or Joy would talk him out of it. Still, for a little while, she could let herself do something she rarely gave into. Sophie let herself hope.

"I'm sure Newt is simply trying to be kind, Sophie." Though her lips curved upward, Joy's eyes held no answering smile.

"It's safe," Newt said, misinterpreting Joy's annoyed expression as one of concern. "There's no place to get into trouble in a wide-open field. Besides, somebody will be with her to make sure nothing goes wrong."

Joy didn't have a ready argument, but Sophie was certain she would come up with one later.

Unaware of the sudden tension between Joy and Sophie, Newt slowed the SUV to a halt. "Looks like we have a welcoming party."

"Is that a dog?" Joy asked, wary of the large animal that bounced excitedly on the cobblestone-covered area in front of the house.

"We think so." Newt seemed to find Joy's question funny. "Bailey eats like a mid-sized elephant. But don't worry. He's a pussy cat."

*A dog.* Sophie made no attempt to hide her grin. Things kept getting better and better. Right then and there she made up her mind. No matter how long this adventure lasted—an hour or a few days—she wouldn't spend it in quiet solitude. She would explore. And ask questions. And maybe even drive a swather. With a newfound sense of resolve, Sophie unbuckled her seatbelt, jumping from the vehicle.

Bailey was too much of a gentleman to jump on a stranger. But it was obvious he wanted to. Quivering, he looked up at Sophie. For a girl who had lived her entire life with a woman who doled out affection sparingly, and only when she expected something in return, the unabashed affection in the dog's eyes went straight to her heart. Despite the books she read, she had never believed in love at first sight. Until now.

"Hello." Sophie held out her hand, laughing when Bailey did more than sniff at it. His tongue slathered the back with saliva.

"Bailey," Newt chided. "Mind your manners."

"That's okay. He's just saying hello back, aren't you, boy?" Dropping to her knees, Sophie threw her arms around the dog. When he snuggled close, she felt that tightness in her throat again. Afraid there might be actual tears in her eyes, she quickly buried her face in his furry neck.

"I'm sorry, Newt. I don't know what's come over my sister."

Newt put an arm around Joy's waist, giving her an affectionate squeeze. "She's acting like a kid. Nothing wrong with that."

Sophie didn't wait around for Joy's response. Jumping to her feet, she took off, Bailey at her heels. Her long legs encased in worn jeans carried her toward the corner of the house and around. Looking over her shoulder to make certain the dog was with her, Sophie didn't see the large, solid object that blocked her path until it was too late.

The object didn't move an inch. Sophie landed flat on her ass.

"Are you okay?"

*No, idiot. You knocked me down. How can I be okay?* The response was the first thing that sprang to Sophie's brain. Hurt or not, she had learned long ago that she needed a tough exterior to survive. Pushovers and marshmallows didn't last long with a mother like Joy. The places they stayed. The people they met. It could be dangerous. Nobody had Sophie's back except Sophie. A sharp tongue wasn't the best weapon, but it kept a lot of weirdos at bay.

When Sophie looked up, ready to spew a little venom, what she saw made her eyes widen. His good looks didn't keep her silent. Guys with winning smiles and dimples didn't impress her. They were a dime a dozen—Joy had a particular weakness for them. The brawnier the body and dimmer the bulb, the better.

No, it wasn't his pretty boy good looks that left Sophie speechless, but the way the sun backlit him, producing a halo effect. A coincidence because of time of day and where he stood. Probably happened all the time. But not to her.

Though it seemed like time stood still, the clock continued to tick. When Sophie didn't respond, the young man smiled as if—for him—this kind of thing happened all the time.

"Arrogant," Sophie muttered under her breath.

"Excuse me?" He leaned closer, ruining the otherworldly effect. When Sophie shrugged, he held out his hand. "Here. Let me help you up."

"I'm fine." Sophie swatted him away, scrambling to her feet. Getting knocked down. Letting a little thing like an optical illusion scramble her brain. How embarrassing.

"Sorry." He stepped back, his hands in the air. The smile on his face didn't slip. Damn him.

Brushing off the back of her jeans gave Sophie a second to regroup. When she finished, she straightened her shoulders, sticking out her chin.

"Who are you?"

"Forbes Branson. Who are you?"

Newt's son. Great. "Sophie."

"Just Sophie. No last name? Like Cher or Madonna?"

"Ha, ha, ha. That's funny. A little polish and you could take that act on the road." Sophie had heard the line in a movie. Not the wittiest comeback, but it would do.

Looking slightly bemused, Forbes rubbed a thumb over his lower lip. "Let's start again. My name is Forbes," he held out his hand. "Sophie. It's nice to meet you."

"Okay." Tentatively, Sophie shook his hand. She wasn't a bitch by nature. It was a defense mechanism that she tended to fall back on. There hadn't been many opportunities to interact with somebody close to her own age. When she felt awkward—like now—she covered by acting tough. Rarely was anybody around long enough for them to figure out it was just that. *An act.* "It's Lipton. My last name."

Forbes nodded. His blue eyes—so much like his father's—were warm. Kind. It seemed to be a family trait. Sophie didn't know if she inherited anything from *her* father. She had never met him. Had no idea who he was. It must have been nice to look at somebody and see part of himself. She didn't see it in Joy. They were opposites in every way. Physically and psychologically. The only proof Sophie had that they were mother and daughter was Joy's word for it.

"It looks like you've met Bailey." The dog had plopped himself between Forbes and Sophie as if he were watching a show—and enjoying every second. "Are you here to see Maeve? She has so many nieces, I've lost track."

This was tricky. It wasn't Sophie's place to inform Forbes that his father had returned home with a *'friend.'* Or that she was the friend's *'sister.'* That involved too many air quotes. Let Newt explain. Boy, would she like to be a fly on the wall for that one.

"I don't know Maeve. Your dad is back, by the way." Sophie darted around Forbes. Running backward, she met his gaze. "I'm exploring. Do you mind if I take Bailey with me?"

"I don't mind if he doesn't."

Sophie patted her leg. Bailey hesitated, turning to Forbes for permission. "Go on. Make sure she doesn't get into trouble."

"Thanks," Sophie called out with a wave.

Lifting her face, she breathed deeply. All thoughts of Forbes, Newt, Joy, and any potential drama sailed from her consciousness. The river was to one side of her, Bailey—tongue lolling out of a grin that almost rivaled hers—to the other.

No doubt about it. Best. Day. Ever

Forbes watched as Sophie soared away. Soared. It was a good word to describe the way she ran, her feet barely touching the ground. It occurred to him that she had left without telling him who she was. Where she came from. Why she was here. He knew her name and that his father was home. That was it. He supposed he would find out the rest eventually.

With a chuckle, Forbes let himself into the mud room. Sophie was a funny kid. Bailey seemed to like her. Not much of a guard dog, he had a good nose for people. If the dog didn't like somebody, he kept his distance. The fact that he was happy to join Sophie while she explored, whatever that meant, was good enough for Forbes.

Toeing off his boots, Forbes neatly placed them in the row of other shoes next to the door. Knowing Maeve would check, he washed his hands, taking two pumps from the liquid soap dispenser the housekeeper always kept full. Splashing some water on his face, he didn't worry that a good amount of it ended up on the front of his sweaty t-shirt. He planned on hitting the shower—after a detour to the kitchen and a half dozen or so cookies. Hence the bother of stopping to wash his hands.

Forbes entered the kitchen, surprised to find it empty. Less than an hour until dinner time, Maeve could usually be found chopping or slicing or something food related. Perhaps she was unpacking his father's suitcase. Maeve had a thing about letting dirty clothes sit around for any length of time. The washing machine in the Branson household was almost always running.

The smell of something spicy bubbling on the stove made Forbes' mouth water. Lifting the lid, he breathed in deeply.

Spaghetti sauce. That meant garlic bread hot from the oven with plenty of melted butter and herbs. It was one of the things he loved most about Maeve. She didn't believe in *light summer meals*. The fact that outside the temperature pushed the mid-nineties was immaterial. Her job was to feed working men. That meant stick-to-your-ribs fare.

Forbes took a spoon from the drawer. Checking to make sure he was alone, he took a big bite of the sauce, his eyes closing in pleasure. For good measure—and since nobody was looking—he double-dipped. *So damn good.*

Not forgetting the cookies, Forbes grabbed a couple handfuls from the pinecone-shaped jar, sprinting up the back stairs as he popped one after another into his mouth.

Normally, Forbes would have taken the right hallway. The house had six bedrooms, three in one wing, three in the other. Today, he decided to delay his shower and veered left.

Until his eleventh birthday, Forbes had a room on this side of the house. Near his parents. After his mother's death, being near his father was nice—a comfort for them both. But a year later, he decided it was time to grow up. With Newt's blessing, he moved to the other wing.

Though Forbes would never admit it, the first month was tough. Every time the house creaked or groaned in the middle of the night, he was tempted to run to his father. But eventually, he settled in. Once he reached his teenage years, he learned to appreciate the privacy afforded by separate wings.

Once or twice—or three times—he snuck a girl into his room. Then snuck her out before daybreak. Whether his father knew or not, Forbes couldn't say. The subject had never come up, and that was fine with him.

Whistling softly, Forbes turned the corner. At the end of the hall, the door to his father's bedroom was ajar, the low mumble of voices reaching his ears. Figuring it was Maeve, he pushed the door open without knocking. What he saw—his father locked in a heated embrace with a strange woman—almost had him spewing cookie particles across the room.

"Whoops. Sorry. I thought—I mean, I didn't realize—" *Shit.* Red-faced, Forbes tried to retreat before he swallowed his tongue along with the rest of the cookie.

"Forbes! Wait." Newt said a few quiet words to the woman before chasing after his son.

Almost to his room, Forbes groaned when he heard his name called out again. Finding a woman in his father's bedroom was new territory. More than embarrassing. Awkward. Unsettling. And though his mother had been gone for a long time, it felt wrong.

"I was hoping to talk to you before you met my friend."

"Then maybe you should have shut the door before you started groping each other.

Forbes wasn't thrilled with the petulant tone of his voice. Then again, he wasn't all that thrilled with his father's behavior. He didn't consider his attitude a double standard. Sneaking a woman in and out of your room in the dark of night was one thing. Flaunting her in broad daylight was another.

Giving a fast look over his shoulder—as if he thought the woman might have followed—Newt pushed Forbes the rest of the way down the hall toward his room. Shutting the door, he frowned.

"I understand it was a surprise, but you will keep a civil tongue in your head when you speak about Joy."

Speak about Joy? Forbes was at a loss. How could he say anything about the woman when until a few minutes ago, he didn't know she existed? Who was this woman? Where had she come from? And what did his father plan to do with her? Besides the obvious.

Forbes didn't know how to ask. Didn't know if he wanted to.

"Dad." Moving to the row of shelves above the dresser, Forbes pretended to be fascinated with the placement of his old Little League MVP award. "It isn't any of my business. I was surprised, that's all."

"I met Joy in California. At the hotel where I was staying. In the bar."

"Okay." Jesus. Was his father saying he picked a woman up in a bar and brought her home? "You were at a convention. Nothing wrong with having some fun. But most people don't take the fun with them when they leave."

Newt looked almost as uncomfortable as Forbes felt. "Joy and I, we sort of hit it off."

"So it would seem."

"You can drop that tone right away, young man. Take a seat," Newt said, pointing to the bed.

"Yes, sir."

Forbes did as his father asked. The respect and love of a lifetime weren't going anywhere. He couldn't imagine anything— or anybody—that could change it. Not now. Not ever.

Newt took the old chair that Forbes used when doing his homework, setting it a few feet away. He straddled the back. With a sigh, he looked Forbes in the eyes.

"I don't need to tell you how it's been since your mother died. It took a long time for me to look up from the grief. When I did, do you know what I realized? I'm lonely."

"But—"

Newt held up a hand, staying Forbes' argument. "I know. There are women around here I could spend some time with."

"Plenty." Forbes could name a half dozen off the top of his head. "Let people know you're looking, Dad. The women will be lining up. You'll have to beat them off with a stick. One word and—"

"I get the idea, Forbes." Newt laughed. "Could be you're exaggerating just a tad. But my ego appreciates the thought."

It wasn't an exaggeration. Newt Branson was a catch. And not just in the little part of the world in which they lived. Handsome. Young by most standards. He had land, money with the brains and brawn to hold onto both. Since his wife's death, many women had made it clear they were interested. Some were bold, others subtle.

Either way, Newt didn't reciprocate. A date here or there. Never anything long term.

"Why now? Why this woman?" Forbes frowned. "You barely know her, Dad."

"I can't explain." The look on Newt's face—the frown—mirrored his son's. "Joy is gorgeous. The attraction—well, you don't need to know about that."

"That's the problem. You have an itch that hasn't been scratched nearly often enough. It's easy to be dazzled by sex."

"Is that so?" Newt's lips twitched. "I'll save us both the embarrassment of discussing how often either of us has been *dazzled*."

"Thank you," Forbes said with feeling.

Newt gave in and chuckled. When he spoke, the light in his eyes had a serious tone. "I appreciate what you're saying, son. But that isn't what this is. Joy makes me... happy? It's been so long; the feeling isn't easy to identify. I will admit that we don't have a lot of life experiences in common. And she is quite a bit younger than me."

"How much younger?" It wasn't a big deal—not really. Still, Forbes felt compelled to ask.

Newt shrugged. "Joy is twenty-five."

Closer to Forbes in age than his father. He knew it shouldn't matter. But everything was coming at him all at once. The age difference was really the least of the issues at hand.

"Tell me what's going on, Dad. Is Joy my new mommy?"

"No." Newt jumped to his feet knocking the chair over in his haste. "She and her sister are here for a visit. A few days. After that, I don't know. We'll see."

"Her sister?" Forbes had forgotten all about the girl he met outside the house. "Sophie? Tall? Smart mouth?"

"I don't know about the smart mouth part. She barely said two words on the trip north. But her name *is* Sophie. You met?"

"More like ran into her. Or she ran into me. Strange kid."

"Shy. Reserved. There's a story, but that's for another time."

Forbes wondered if they were talking about the same girl. Shy and reserved? Sophie? Hardly. Surly, with a major chip on her shoulder, was more like it. But like his father said, another time.

"What happens in a few days?"

Newt ran a hand through his thick, sandy-colored hair—another trait shared by father and son, though Forbes wore his longer, running toward unruly instead of neat.

"I promised to put Joy and Sophie on a plane to wherever they want to go. Unless..."

"You want Joy to stay."

"And Sophie. They are a package deal, and I'm just fine with that." Newt looked at Forbes, obviously worried. "I don't know what's going to happen, son. Joy might decide she doesn't like ranch life. How do you feel about all of this?"

It was a good question. One Forbes couldn't answer straight out. For a long time, he had hoped his father would find somebody special. A woman to share his life. Lover. Girlfriend. Wife. As long as it made Newt happy. But in his wildest imagination, he hadn't pictured this scenario.

A stranger—*two* strangers—invading their lives? Forbes found it a lot to take in.

"I'm not opposed to the idea. Exactly."

"You need time." Newt nodded, seemingly relieved. "You'll see. Joy is a wonderful woman. Smart. Fun. You'll like her in no time."

Forbes wasn't as certain as his father. If things didn't work out, it would be hard on Newt. He didn't want him to get hurt. For now, he would keep his doubts to himself. Hopefully, it would all work out.

"About Sophie."

"Yes?" Cautiously, Forbes waited, not sure what was coming. Not sure he wanted to know.

"There isn't that much age difference."

"How old is she?"

"Fifteen."

"Fifteen? Really?" Forbes would have guessed younger.

"It might be difficult for her to make friends right away. You're good with people. Draw her out. I don't think she's had much experience with people her own age."

"Why not?"

"Her mother kept Sophie isolated. Homeschooled. She wasn't given a chance to interact with other kids. Socially stunted is how Joy put it."

"Great," Forbes muttered. "Boo Radley incarnate?"

"Don't you dare say something like that to Sophie, you hear?" Newt tried to look stern as if he didn't appreciate his son's sense of humor. But in spite of himself, he chuckled. "You don't have to make her your new best friend. All I'm asking is for you to draw her out. You're good at that."

"Sure, Dad."

"Are we good? Any more pressing questions you need answering?"

"Not at the moment." Forbes was sure something would come to him. Perhaps a million somethings.

"Don't hesitate to ask, Forbes. This is new territory—for all of us."

Exchanging a gruff but affectionate hug, father and son parted. Newt—Forbes assumed—went back to Joy to continue what they were doing before the sudden interruption.

His father having sex. In this house. That was right at the top of the list of things Forbes had to get used to. Were Newt and Joy sharing a bedroom? His *mother's* bedroom? No matter how mature he considered himself to be, Forbes wasn't sure he was ready for that. It was too jarring. Too quick. He didn't know this woman. He wouldn't say it to his father's face, but he wasn't sure he wanted to.

As for Joy's plus one? Sophie? The sister? Forbes decided it was *way* too soon to tell about her.

43

His bedroom had a connecting bathroom. That was a plus, Forbes thought, turning the shower on full blast. He wouldn't be sharing with anybody. As an only child, he always had things pretty much his own way. As an eighteen-year-old heading into his last year of high school, he knew that—if push came to shove—Sophie would only be his problem for a few months. The length of a school year.

That was in his head. In his heart, Forbes was leery at the idea of anybody invading his territory. Joy might turn out to be an annoyance, but she was an adult. His father's territory. Sophie was a different matter. Obviously, his father had forgotten what it was like in high school. To a man in his forties, a three-year age difference didn't seem like a lot. Between an eighteen-year-old man and a fifteen-year-old girl? It was a chasm. Potentially a rift as wide as the Grand Canyon. Especially if Sophie turned out to be as socially backward as Newt said.

Forbes lathered his body, letting the spray of water rush over his face. What was the word his father used? Stunted. That was it. If Sophie's social development was stunted, that made the divide even bigger. It also meant he couldn't abandon her to the wolves.

*Shit.* Forbes scrubbed his scalp with more pressure than necessary. He didn't want to be responsible for some kid he didn't know. He knew himself pretty well. If—and at the moment that was a big if—Sophie was still here when the school year started, Forbes knew he wouldn't let her flounder.

Cursing himself, Forbes threw back the shower curtain, grabbing a towel from the rack. Sometimes having a strong moral compass well and truly sucked.

Hearing the words in his head, Forbes laughed. It was a good thing none of his friends knew what he was thinking. Aaron especially would call him out as a pompous twit. Or words to that extent. More graphic in tone. And he would be right.

Wiping the steam from the mirror, Forbes gazed at himself. He didn't see the strong jaw or handsome features. Not that he was unaware of how he looked. He knew that people found him

44

attractive. However, he didn't find the face in front of him anything special. He saw it every day. At the moment, his bright blue eyes were focused on whether or not he needed to shave before meeting his father's guests.

Forbes rubbed his chin, deciding to forgo the razor for another day or two. If he had his way, he would grow a beard rather than scrape off the accumulating stubble. Unfortunately, one of Coach Riggins's many rules included an aversion to facial hair on his players. If Coach had his way, they would all sport his perpetual crewcut. Thankfully, he didn't take his hardline quite that far.

Forbes tugged on the ends of his damp hair. Longer than usual, he had let it go over the summer. Sometime in the next few days, he would get to the barber.

Mindful of years of Maeve drilling it into his head about cleaning up after himself, Forbes automatically tossed his wet towel into the hamper before leaving the bathroom.

It would be an interesting week, Forbes thought, pulling a pair of clean jeans from the dresser drawer. His final year of high school loomed. Football practice was something to look forward to. Who knew what would happen on the home front with not one, but two new females to contend with.

For his father's sake, Forbes hoped it worked out. Newt deserved some happiness. But to be honest? With a sigh, he decided on the blue t-shirt over plain white. He wasn't looking forward to the unknown.

# CHAPTER FOUR

"THE NEXT FEW days are crucial, young lady." Joy crossed her arms, the toe of her high-heeled pumps tapping furiously on the hardwood floor. "This is my big chance. I will not have you ruin it by acting like a dimwitted teenager."

"Is this my room?" Having heard it all before, Sophie wasn't listening to her mother. She ran her hand over the polished furniture, breathing in the fresh lemon scent. "All mine?"

"Sophie!" Joy grabbed her arm, giving it a shake. "What has gotten into you?"

*Freedom*! It sang through Sophie's blood. Bubbly. Like carbonation times a thousand. It was amazing what a tiny taste could do. Ideas had always swirled through her head, but they had always been outside of her reality.

Imagining the smell of clean air and the feel of unrestricted sunlight on her face was one thing. It was another to run across a thick, green lawn without the sound of car horns in her ears. Or the smell of exhaust fumes clogging her lungs.

Sophie knew that Joy would never understand. She lived with dollar signs in her eyes. Occasionally, Joy let lust sidetrack her. A well-toned ass could turn her head temporarily. But eventually, she remembered what was important. Money. The more the better.

"Don't worry, Joy." Sophie had never called her mother anything else. Never Mommy. Mom. Or any variation of the word. "I won't screw this up for you."

"That's what I'm talking about." Joy jabbed a sharp red nail into Sophie's chest. "Lose the attitude, little girl. Now!"

*Or what*? Like so many times before in her life, Sophie swallowed her question. She left it unasked. But she couldn't help but wonder what the answer would be. What could her mother do? If Sophie chose, she could decimate Joy's fragile house of cards with the tiniest puff of breath. As always, it was built on lies. A

46

few words and poof. The light in Newt's eyes would turn from kindness to contempt.

Joy had no idea that the power in their relationship had shifted. Nor would she anytime soon. Sophie had spent too long lying low, doing what was necessary and just getting by to test her muscles right now. But it was exciting to realize she had them—just in case.

In the meantime, Sophie knew how to get Joy's attention off her and back where they both preferred.

"Newt can't take his eyes off you."

Joy preened, pausing to admire herself in front of the antique mirror that hung over the dresser. Sophie could almost read her thoughts. Joy leaned closer, dabbed at her perfect lipstick. Then lifted a hand to her hair before dropping it to her side, deciding she had no reason to mess with perfection.

"This is a big fish, and he is mine to reel in without breaking a sweat." Joy snapped her fingers. "It's almost too easy."

"Why didn't you spend the night with him on the trip here?"

Innocently—at this point in her jaded life, it had come as a surprise that Joy could still effortlessly pull off something so far from the truth—her mother had insisted on separate rooms. *For Sophie's sake*, she had whispered to Newt. Obviously disappointed, he had agreed. Two nights. It had to be the longest Joy had held a man at bay.

"Newt appreciates my motherly concern."

Motherly. That was a hot one. Sophie snorted. She hadn't meant to, it just came out. Joy was so caught up in admiring the way she was handling her *big fish*, she let it pass.

"We'll make up for lost time soon enough." Joy sighed, her lips curving slowly upward. "Newt is a surprisingly good lover. Energetic. Inventive. It's not a hardship having that man on top of me."

Sophie preferred the facts, but that was way too much information. Unfortunately, as far as Joy was concerned, there were no boundaries she wouldn't cross. It didn't matter that she was speaking to her fifteen-year-old daughter. She used the same candor when Sophie was ten. And seven. And five. It wasn't done out of spite or nastiness. It simply didn't occur to Joy that using frank, explicit language about her love life was inappropriate.

Sophie went from not understanding to looking things up, to tuning Joy out. After all these years, she should have been desensitized to sex. Instead, she found it embarrassing. Crude. And the last thing she ever wanted to try.

So many of the books Sophie read backed up her mother's words. They rhapsodized about it. On and on and on. Love equaled hot, can't keep my hands off you, lust-filled days and nights. The foolish protagonists were always ruled by their bodies—not their common sense.

If that were true? Sophie had one answer. A big no thank you. Love. Sex. Passion. Call it what you wanted. Joy was a shining example of where they got you. And Newt—who she really liked—hadn't done anything to change Sophie's perception.

"Have you met the housekeeper?" Joy said it with a sneer, carefully running her finger over the surface of the bedpost. She seemed disappointed when it came back clean.

"No." There hadn't been anybody around when Sophie entered the house. Before she could explore, Joy had herded her upstairs.

"I need to keep an eye on that one. Not that I can't handle her. Maeve." Joy added a scoff to her sneer. "What kind of name is that?"

"I think it's pretty."

Sophie looked around for her small suitcase. When she couldn't find it, she checked the closet. Hanging there were the few items she didn't have on her back. An extra t-shirt—plain, faded yellow. A cotton dress that she was supposed to grow into but still hung on her like a sack. An old jean jacket with a ripped sleeve that more than once had been rescued from Joy's attempt to toss in the trash. And a pair of shorts. Brand new, still sporting their tags.

Sophie knew it was silly not to wear them, but they were one of the few things she had ever owned that hadn't belonged to somebody else first. In a rare moment of generosity, Joy had picked them up a few weeks ago at a Wal-Mart. For now, she was happy to simply look at them.

Glancing over Sophie's shoulder, Joy shook her head. "My stuff has been unpacked, too. That housekeeper is quite the brownnoser."

Sophie didn't like the thought of somebody going through her meager belongings. She didn't care that they were old and worn—except for the shorts. She couldn't do anything about the number of things she owned or how old they were.

What she could control—and what she was fastidious about—was cleanliness. There hadn't been time to wash out her underwear. Since the three pairs of panties weren't to be found, she had to assume that Maeve had taken them.

After all the places Joy had dragged her and all the things she had seen, not much could phase Sophie. However, the idea of a stranger having possession of her worn panties had the heat of embarrassment creeping up her neck.

"I need to find Newt. Hopefully, he's finished speaking with his son." Joy paused at the door. "Remember, Sophie. Screw this up for me, and I'll make you pay."

The empty threat fell on deaf ears. Sophie might be only fifteen, but she was a seasoned campaigner when it came to dealing with Joy. There was no point in worrying about the things that came out of her mother's mouth. Her moods—and convictions—had the staying power of a feather in the wind. If Sophie worried every time Joy shifted gears, her stomach would be in a state of constant turmoil.

"Did you hear me?"

"Of course," Sophie said with an innocent expression—one she had learned at Joy's knee.

Joy, unaware that Sophie was playing her with one of her own well-worn tricks, nodded. "What are you going to do?"

"Keep my head down and my mouth shut."

Satisfied, Joy turned her thoughts to more important things—Newt to be specific. Shimmying, she carefully adjusted the fit of her dress. With practiced ease, she reached into the low neckline, tugging at one breast, then the other, until they were positioned right where she wanted them.

Sophie shook her head as she watched Joy's swaying hips leave the room. She had to give Joy credit. She put a lot of time and effort into her seduction routine. If she focused that energy on one thing for a sustained period of time, the woman could rule the world—or at the very least, a good chunk of it.

Sophie shuddered. *Wasn't that a scary thought?*

Doing a slow twirl, she surveyed the room. It was huge. And for as long as Joy kept in Newt's good graces, it was all Sophie's. Hugging herself with disbelief, she jumped onto the bed. It had to be queen sized—maybe king. Laughing, she bounced on the mattress that didn't smell of stale cigarettes. She noticed no stains on the bedspread, ones that Sophie usually had to ignore if she wanted to get a halfway-decent night's sleep.

Springing to the floor, Sophie rushed around, showing the enthusiasm she had tempered while Joy was watching. She opened every drawer, unconcerned that they were empty. Looking in the closet again, she was amazed by the size.

Sophie turned on the light, peering from one side to the other. Amazing. More than once, she had slept in smaller spaces that weren't nearly as appealing.

Crossing the room, Sophie opened another door. When she saw what it hid, her eyes almost popped from her head. *Holy crap, holy crap, holy crap.* A bathroom. And with no other way in or out save the window just above the toilet, it had to be hers.

All hers. Feeling slightly lightheaded, Sophie gripped the edge of the marble sink. Everything was so shiny and clean. She opened the window, filling her lungs. No wonder she felt faint. After years of breathing in grunge and garbage, it would take a while for the oxygen in her bloodstream to purge itself of a lifetime full of toxins.

Practically floating on a high of happiness and fresh air, Sophie turned toward the bathtub. It looked big enough to do laps in. Deciding to test the theory, she reached down, turning the taps on full force.

Several pretty glass bottles lined the side. Sophie took the lid off the first. Nice, but too flowery. The second fragrance was highly perfumed and reminded her of Joy. Scrunching up her nose, she set it down with a decided thump.

The last bottle claimed to smell like a summer rain. Not sure what that meant, Sophie took a tentative sniff. And smiled. It was lovely. She poured a generous amount into the steaming water, delighted when a mass of bubbles emerged, quickly taking over the surface.

Making sure the door was locked, Sophie stripped off her clothes, easing her body into the tub. Even with her long legs stretched as far as possible, her wiggling toes didn't reach the end. Bliss. That's what it was. Oh, yes. She could get used to this. With a sigh, Sophie closed her eyes and sank beneath the bubbles.

"IT'S A DISGRACE," Maeve whispered, furiously beating a bowl of cream into submission.

"Maeve..."

"A man of your father's age should have better sense. Bringing a stranger—and her sister—to your mother's home. It's all your fault."

Startled by the accusation, Forbes paused in the middle of taking a stack of plates from the cupboard. His mother's second-best china, to be exact. They were the dishes they used every day. Nothing special. Maeve's words had him thinking twice. As if using them to feed his father's friend was some kind of betrayal.

"What did I do?"

"You encouraged him to go to that convention. Practically shoved him out the door. Told him to bring you home a souvenir."

"I meant a t-shirt or a coffee mug." Forbes opened the silverware drawer. "Trust me, Dad wasn't thinking of me when he invited Joy Lipton to come home with him."

"What about the girl?"

"Sophie?" His voice squeaked, something that hadn't happened since he was thirteen. Carefully, Forbes set down the dishes, feeling the shock of Maeve's question tingle all the way to his fingertips. "Jesus, Maeve."

"Watch the language, young man. Eighteen isn't too old for me to take a switch to you."

Maeve had never taken anything to Forbes. Not even a swat to his backside. However, that had never stopped her from using it as a threat. And it still worked—more out of respect than the worry of actual physical pain.

"Sorry." Figuring the cream was sufficiently whipped—a few more beats, and it would turn to butter—Forbes took the whisk from Maeve's hand. "Sophie is a kid. And Dad is not a pimp."

"I misspoke." Maeve sighed, having the good grace to look embarrassed. "Aren't you concerned? I never thought of your father as a pushover for a pretty face. Or a big set of— well, you know."

Of course, he was concerned. Forbes wanted his father to be happy, but this seemed like an extreme solution to a case of loneliness. All he had to guide him was his trust in his father. It had never steered him wrong before.

"What did Dad tell you?"

Maeve's voice took on a sing-song quality, the lowered pitch a poor imitation of Newt Branson. "*Joy and Sophie are our guests for the next few days. Treat them accordingly.*"

"There you go." Adding paper napkins to the pile of plates and silverware, Forbes shrugged. "Dad knows best."

"This isn't a television show, Forbes."

"Huh?"

"*Father Knows Best*? Robert Young?" When Forbes simply shook his head, Maeve groaned. "Look it up on that fancy computer of yours. The point—and I had one before you sidetracked me—is that Newt isn't infallible. Even the smartest people make mistakes."

"We don't know that Dad has made a mistake."

"Yet."

Maeve had a point. Since no one else was around to hear, Forbes conceded. "Yet," he said. Then added, "It might work out. Let's wait at least until after dinner to decide. Okay?"

"Hmm."

"For Dad's sake?"

"All right." Maeve gave the bubbling pot of pasta a stir. "But I won't keep my mouth shut if I think that woman is trouble."

"I wouldn't expect you to. Neither would Dad."

As he set the table, Forbes wondered if what he told Maeve was true. His father was a man who appreciated the truth. Straight talk, was how Newt put it. This was different. When a woman was involved, the rules changed. Forbes knew that from personal experience. He had tried to warn a friend—Donny Priest—about a certain girl from a nearby town. She was a ball buster. A heartbreaker. Not hearsay, but a fact proven by her actions.

Donny hadn't listened. He accused Forbes of wanting the girl for himself. Jealousy. Spitefulness. Or something along those lines. When the inevitable happened, and Jerry paid the price with more of a bent ego than a broken heart, their once-easygoing relationship never recovered.

Kill the messenger, kill the friendship.

Forbes couldn't see his father going that far, but lesson learned. He wouldn't rock any boats unless necessary.

Placing the last fork, Forbes added drinking glasses. The room just off the kitchen was technically for formal dining, but they used it for every occasion including daily meals.

The table was oval, made from Brazilian cherry wood. It and the matching chairs had been a second-anniversary present. His father had it specially made with extra leaves they could add to accommodate what they planned to be a large family.

The large part hadn't worked out. Though his parents tried, they were never able to conceive after Forbes. Just one of those things, the doctors said. Ella and Newt considered fertility treatments. In-vitro fertilization. Surrogates. Even adoption was discussed. The reason none of the options were pursued was between them. His parents never discussed it. The result was that Forbes was an only child.

Forbes found it sad. Not for him. For his parents. Ella and Newt had so much love to go around. It seemed a shame that they hadn't been able to fill the chairs at the large dining room table.

Then again, maybe it was for the best. When Ella died, Forbes wasn't yet a teenager. His father would have been left with a houseful of small children and no wife.

"That's a mighty pensive look. What's the problem, Josephine? Water spots on the silverware?"

Mike Phillips laughed as if the joke was new—or funny. Forbes had heard it a hundred times. Josephine was the name Mike had assigned him the first time he caught him doing chores around the house. The long-time Branson ranch hand believed there was men's work and women's work. Washing dishes and setting the table fell into the latter category.

Forbes wasn't offended. The ribbing was good natured. In that vein, he gave as good as he got.

"Here," Forbes handed Mike a fork. "Shove that where the sun don't shine, old man."

"He's had stranger things than a fork up there."

"Fuck you," Mike gave Jerry Weber—his oldest friend, fellow cowboy, and bunkmate—a shove.

"I have a bar of soap in here, and I'm not afraid to use it."

Mike and Jerry exchanged pained, contrite looks. They didn't want to get on Maeve's bad side. Not only did they respect her as a woman, they didn't want to do anything that might cut off their main source of sustenance. With only a small cooktop stove and microwave oven in the bunkhouse that were only used in case of emergency, they took almost all of their meals at the main house.

Like Maeve, Mike and Jerry weren't just employees. They were family.

"Sorry, Maeve," Mike called out. "It won't happen again."

"Yes, it will." Maeve entered with a cloth-covered basket in each hand. The smell of garlic bread filled the air, making mouths water in anticipation. "You will curse again. And again. All I ask is that you refrain from doing so inside this house."

"Yes, ma'am." Mike and Jerry said simultaneously.

"You say that now. With the promise of spaghetti and meatballs moments away." Maeve laughed. For all her stern words, she was as fond of the men as they were of her. "Looks like you cleaned up nicely. At least I don't have to nag you to wash your hands."

Mike and Jerry had showered before leaving the bunkhouse. Slicked-back hair. Clean button-down shirts and jeans straight from the dryer. They did their own laundry by necessity. Which meant—Mike's opinion that tended to bend to the situation—it wasn't women's work.

"Forbes, call your father and his guests. Dinner in five."

"Guests?" Jerry asked Forbes. A good half foot shorter than Mike, his height, and slighter build didn't keep him from taking the lead on the range and off. He motioned for his friend to sit before taking his usual seat. "What kind of guests?"

"The human kind. Two mouths. Four feet. Hands. Heads."

"Funny kid." Mike eyed the bread, deciding to do the right thing and wait for everybody else. "Who are they? Anybody we know?"

"No. Dad will introduce you."

"But—"

"It's a woman. And her sister," Forbes said, exiting the room to carry out Maeve's instructions.

"A woman?" Jerry asked his question to empty air. He turned to Mike. "What do you think about that?"

"Can't be nothing romantic? Right?"

"Newt?" Jerry shook his head, a bit of the dark hair he so carefully combed back falling across his forehead. "Doesn't seem likely. Forbes said a woman and her sister. Why the distinction?"

"It's a mystery," Mike agreed.

"Hey, Holmes. Watson." Maeve set a large bowl on the table filled with greens, tomatoes, and various vegetables from her garden. She lowered her voice to a conspiratorial whisper. "The woman is a special friend. The sister is... To tell the truth, I don't know about the sister. It's the older one I'm worried about."

"Worried how?"

"She's after more than a few days of rest and relaxation. Keep your eyes peeled. And off her cleavage," Maeve added as a warning.

"Cleavage?" Jerry said in a lowered voice as soon as Maeve was out of earshot. "How much do you think we're talking about? I'm only human."

"Newt has always liked them classy. Maeve is probably overreacting."

"Mike. Jerry. I want you to meet somebody. This is Joy Lipton."

Mike and Jerry surged to their feet. One look was all it took for the men to realize Maeve hadn't exaggerated. And Newt's taste had taken a drastic detour. Joy wasn't trashy. She was flashy. From her hair to her makeup to her clothes. This woman would be noticed wherever she went.

Cleavage. Mike and Jerry did their best to keep from looking. But damn. They found it impossible not to sneak a side glance or two. Or three.

"Nice to meet you, ma'am." Jerry took Joy's hand, conscious of how soft it felt next to the roughness of his own.

"Pleasure." Mike simply nodded.

Joy's smile sparkled, her voice pitched somewhere between friendly and sultry. "Believe me, gentlemen. The honor is all mine."

"HEY." FORBES POUNDED on Sophie's door for the third time. "Are you deaf? Dinner. Is. Ready."

"I said just a minute. Are *you* deaf?"

Frowning as Sophie pushed past, Forbes wondered if this was how it would be as long as this little twit was in his house. For the second time, she came at him with an unjustifiably surly attitude. He hadn't done anything but deliver a message.

"My hearing is perfect. Better than." Forbes used his longer legs to catch up. "You didn't answer me."

"Yes, I did."

"It isn't necessary to lie. Just admit—"

Halfway down the stairs, Sophie rounded on Forbes. Caught by surprise, he stumbled backward.

"I never lie," she said, jabbing him in the chest with a pointy index finger.

Forbes didn't know anybody who told the truth one hundred percent of the time. No matter how inherently honest the person, it simply wasn't possible.

"Never? Come on."

Sophie met his gaze, the color of her eyes darkening to a deep caramel. "I keep my opinions to myself—mostly. That saves a lot of lying. So when I speak, the words that come out are the truth."

A blush rose to Sophie's cheeks. Combined with the way the focus of her eyes shifted off him, told Forbes that she had said more than she meant to.

"It doesn't matter." For some reason he couldn't pinpoint, Forbes felt the need to reassure her. "Maeve is the best cook in the world. Bar none. Tonight, it's all you can eat spaghetti and meatballs. Are you hungry?"

Sophie shrugged as if when it came to food, she could take it or leave it. But her stomach had other ideas, choosing that moment to growl with the ferocity of a bear searching for his first meal after a long hibernation.

Forbes laughed good naturedly. "I guess that's my answer."

Red suffused Sophie's face. Not a subtle blush but full-on heat. "Up yours, Forbes Branson.

Before Forbes could ask what the hell had crawled up her ass, Sophie zipped away. She took the rest of the steps two at a time, the skirt of the dress she wore—a garment that could have moonlighted as a circus tent—swirling around her skinny legs.

Odd. That's what the girl was, Forbes thought, following at a more leisurely pace.

"There he is." Maeve was just setting the steaming bowl of pasta and sauce on the table. "Are you hungry?"

"Starving."

Unable to help himself, Forbes looked for Sophie. Pulling out his chair, he found her where she sat quietly near the far end of the table. Her eyes and expression were neutral. Completely blank. The bright red was gone from her face. She held his gaze for a second, but he saw no sign of the feisty pain in the ass from just moments ago.

*What the hell*? Odd? Was that what he had thought? It didn't begin to describe Sophie Lipton. From hellion to zombie at the snap of the fingers. Who was she really? It was a freaking mystery that quite frankly, he had no desire to solve. Whatever her problem, hopefully, it wouldn't affect him—or anybody he knew—for long.

# CHAPTER FIVE

SOPHIE CHEWED EVERY bite slowly even though she wanted to shovel the plate of food into her mouth as quickly as possible.

This was her first experience with a sit-down family dinner. But she was pretty certain a modicum of manners was expected.

There was so much to eat. Mounds of it. Almost too much for Sophie's eyes, mind, and stomach to take in. It didn't seem possible, but according to Maeve, she had more in the kitchen, so they shouldn't worry about eating their fill.

The problem was, Sophie didn't know what that was. She had never *been* full. Not even close. One time she spent all of her money on junk food and proceeded to eat every bit until she was ready to burst. But it had come back up so quickly, she didn't think it counted.

Conversations went on around her, dominated by Joy. She flirted lightly with every man at the table but was smart enough not to take it too far. Obviously, Newt was enchanted, and it didn't take long for the ranch hands, Mike and Jerry, to fall under her spell. The three of them laughed uproariously as if every word from Joy's mouth was the funniest thing they had ever heard.

Sophie's mother was a good storyteller with a fair amount of wit. But honestly, watching the spectacle play out reinforced every prejudice she had formed about the intelligence of men. They were so easily swayed by a little attention, some not so subtle flattery, and a pretty face.

How the male of the species had ruled the world for so long was a confounding mystery.

Maeve made it clear she wasn't impressed. Her expression— narrowed eyes and a curled lip—told the tale. Nothing new. Women were not Joy's target audience. She had little use for them, and the feelings were mutual.

59

For a little while, Sophie felt a blooming of hope for Forbes. He seemed immune to the eyelash batting. However, it turned out to be inattention instead of immunity. All it took was Joy laying her hand on his arm. A gentle squeeze. A warm smile. Boom. Sophie's hope had died a quick death. And because she really didn't care, it was a painless one.

While Joy had the floor—or the dinner table—in her thrall, Sophie was busy cleaning her plate, wondering if she could snag another helping without drawing anybody's attention.

"That's what I like to see," Newt said, taking his eyes off Joy long enough to notice what Sophie was up to—damn him. "Would you like some more, Sophie? Bread. Salad. Spaghetti? Maeve always makes enough to serve several small armies."

Did she want more? Yes! Absolutely. Sophie almost got the words out. She had finished half of a nod. Unfortunately, Joy was faster.

"She's had plenty." Joy's smile seemed benign, but Sophie knew better. "Isn't that right, sweetheart?"

Sweetheart? Was Joy kidding? The unfamiliar endearment delivered in a sappy, sugary tone was almost enough for Sophie to lose her appetite. Almost. If Joy wanted to eat like a bird in the belief that men thought it charming, all the power to her. Sophie couldn't understand why she had to follow suit.

With a sigh, Sophie nodded, pushing away her plate. She knew the game, and though it was getting harder and harder to play along, for now, she did just that.

"Thank you, Mr. Branson. I couldn't eat another bite."

"I thought we agreed that you would call me Newt."

"I—" Sophie looked at Joy.

This time, Joy's smile was all for the man sitting to her right. "If that's what Newt wants, then that's what you should do."

"Thank you. Newt."

Newt scooped himself a second helping heavy on the moist, tender meatballs. Sophie knew he wasn't purposefully taunting her, but at the moment, that was how it felt. If Joy hadn't been staring daggers at her, she might have caved. But willpower was her middle name. Actually, it was Denise. She had never been fond of it so, given the circumstances, Sophie figured willpower was a good substitute.

"You're sure?" Newt asked, liberally sprinkling on the freshly grated parmesan.

"Positive."

So much for never lying. Under her eyelashes, Sophie sent a quick look at Forbes. He was listening to something Jerry was saying. She doubted he had heard the exchange between her and his father—or cared if she was telling the truth or not.

Sophie cared. Truly, she tried to be honest whenever possible. Unfortunately, circumstances weren't always under her control.

Living with Joy meant living with her conscience. Neither was easy. However, Sophie knew she didn't have a choice.

"I know today isn't the official day. But I baked you a surprise."

"My pre-birthday cake?" Forbes asked.

Standing, Maeve laughed. "Not much of a surprise, I guess."

"Not when you do it every year," Mike said, winking at Forbes.

Forbes hurried from his seat, wrapping Maeve in a hug. "Devil's food with marshmallow frosting?"

Pleased, Maeve patted Forbes on the cheek. "Don't I know my boy?"

"I hope everybody saved room for dessert."

"Are you kidding, boss?" In anticipation, Jerry started clearing away the dinner dishes. He gave Mike a shove on his way past, prompting the other man to help. "When have we ever turned down anything baked by Maeve?"

Pre-birthday cake? Sophie didn't know such a thing existed. Joy or no Joy, she wasn't missing out.

"I'll have a piece." Sophie anticipated her mother's attempt to abstain for the both of them. "Please."

"That's four yeses." Newt turned to Joy. "How about you, honey?"

"Maybe a sliver. I have to watch my figure."

"You leave that up to me. You're gorgeous. Top to bottom. A little piece of cake now and then won't change that."

Red lips parted in a coy smile, Joy laid her hand on Newt's thigh. The tablecloth hid what was going on, but the sudden flush on his cheeks and the way he cleared his throat indicated it was more than a friendly pat.

Forbes was in the kitchen. Jerry and Mike—laden with dishes—had followed close behind. Sophie was the only one left to witness the eye-rolling spectacle. She wished there was something left on the table to clear—any excuse to leave the room.

Which did she want more? Cake, or to get away from the weirdly oblivious couple at the opposite end of the table? Sophie gave a sigh of relief when the door to the kitchen swung open, saving her the choice.

Startled out of the spell Joy had weaved around him, Newt moved her hand from his lap, scooting closer to the table. Sophie had a good idea what he was trying to hide—though she wished to God she didn't. Out of the corner of her eye, she noticed Newt look her way as if suddenly remembering she was there.

Joy couldn't have cared less about a witness, but it appeared that Newt was different—when in his right mind. To save him any more embarrassment, Sophie pretended that the pastoral painting on the wall closest to her was the most interesting thing she had ever seen.

"The candles weren't necessary," Forbes said, blissfully unaware what his father had been up to in his absence.

"You'd be disappointed if I didn't put them on." Maeve set the cake in the middle of the table, standing back with a proud smile. "No Happy Birthday sing-along until tomorrow. But as usual, you get a bonus wish."

Grinning, Forbes put an arm around Maeve's shoulders, pulling her close.

"That's a tough one. I can't think of anything I want that I don't already have."

*What would that be like*, Sophie wondered?

Forbes couldn't think of a wish, she could think of a million. Just off the top of her head. At the moment, she would settle for one. And since Forbes wasn't using his, she didn't see anything wrong with borrowing it.

Closing her eyes, Sophie said the words to herself.

"There you go. Enjoy."

Holding her breath, Sophie raised her lids. Sitting in front of her was the biggest, most beautiful piece of cake she had ever seen. *Well, what do you know?* Sometimes wishes did come true.


THE HOUSE WAS quiet. Everybody was in bed—or back at the bunkhouse. Sophie opened the bedroom door, checking right, then left. In her head, she knew the odds of not getting caught were with her. With two separate wings, the house was huge. She was on the east side with Forbes way down the hall.

Newt lived on the other side. Joy in the same area. He had made such a production of making sure everybody knew there would be separate rooms. Different beds. Who he thought he was fooling, Sophie had no idea. She knew the score. As did Maeve, Mike, and Jerry.

That left only Forbes. If he believed Daddy and the new girlfriend were happy with holding hands and a chaste goodnight kiss, then his mind worked differently than almost every other eighteen-year-old in the world.

The lights were out, but Sophie had no problem finding her way to the staircase. Plush carpet lined each step, gleaming hardwood peeking out at the ends. Earlier, as she made her way up and down, there hadn't seemed to be any glaring squeaks. However, just to be safe, Sophie descended on tiptoes.

Though certain she was alone, Sophie opted not to turn on any lights, making her way by memory. Her night vision had always been excellent—a handy trait for somebody who spent so much time slinking from place to place under the cloak of darkness.

Dressed in the oversized t-shirt she used as a nightgown, Sophie kept to the side of the room. She hurried toward her goal, enjoying the way the cool wood felt under her bare feet. Smooth and clean. She found it a pleasure not to worry about stepping on gritty patches of dirt. Or worse, broken glass.

Aware that Maeve's room was toward the back of the house, yet uncertain which one she occupied, Sophie sent a furtive look in the general direction. Keeping her gaze low, she saw no sign of light filtering under any of the doors.

With a sigh of relief, Sophie let herself into the Branson kitchen.

The refrigerator had beckoned all the way from Sophie's room. Knowing the delights it contained was too much temptation for her to resist. Truth be told, she wasn't terribly hungry. The cake—which had come with the creamiest vanilla ice cream she had ever tasted—almost filled the hole in her stomach she hadn't thought fillable.

That was hours ago. The need for food wasn't gnawing at her. Still, Joy could always knock on her door at any minute, bags packed and ready to hit the road. Just in case they didn't make it to breakfast, Sophie planned on fueling up while she could.

It turned out that mooching some food wasn't as simple as she imagined. First, there was the refrigerator itself. Sophie had never seen anything even close. Like the biggest, shiniest, best toy ever. Taking a deep breath, she tugged on the handle.

"Holy crap."

For a second, Sophie's mind went blank. Fruit and vegetables and fried chicken and milk and juice—such a dazzling array that she didn't know where to start.

"The chicken is your best bet."

Sophie couldn't stop the yelp that escaped her mouth. Whirling around, she found a shadowed figure sitting at the counter. Though she couldn't see his face, his voice was unmistakable.

"What the hell are you doing here?"

"My house. My kitchen. My food." Forbes leaned right, his long arms easily reaching the light switch. Sophie squinted, raising a hand to shield her eyes. "I should be the one asking what the hell."

"Your Dad's house. Your Dad's kitchen. Your Dad's food," Sophie countered with a cockiness she didn't feel. "He said to make myself at home."

Forbes pushed Sophie out of the way. He grabbed the chicken, setting it on the counter. Several covered containers followed.

"Milk?"

"Okay."

"Or would you rather have orange juice? Lemonade?"

"Sure."

"Which one?"

Sophie frowned. Hadn't Forbes just offered all three?

"I have to pick?"

Forbes chuckled. He took two glasses from the cupboard. "Why not try one at a time. Milk is a good place to start."

As long as he wasn't stopping her from eating, Sophie wouldn't complain. She watched as Forbes poured the milk noticing for the first time what he wore. Or *not*, to be more accurate. A pair of shorts. Underwear, maybe? Nothing else covered his tall, surprisingly well-developed body. Moving with a sure kind of grace, Forbes filled two plates, the muscles of his back and arms flexing with each movement.

Sophie had two quick reactions. Both troubling, though she wasn't certain which worried her more.

First. Forbes was a pleasure to watch.

Sophie's thoughts wandered back to the time Joy's latest conquest had dumped them near a small artist's community in Colorado. While her mother gnashed her teeth over another sucker slipping through her fingers—while hanging out at the local watering hole, eyes peeled for her next victim—Sophie explored.

The streets were filled with artisans selling their creations. Though she had absolutely no knowledge of what made good art, instinctually, Sophie understood that most of what she was looking at didn't qualify. Not that the pottery and paintings and sculptures weren't made with passion and commitment. Simply put, they would never reach beyond the mundane.

Like it was yesterday, Sophie could remember with crystal-clear clarity the one exception. The painting depicted a woman holding a white flower. Not a complicated subject. But in that simplicity, Sophie found something that touched her to the core. It made her heart beat faster. Her breathing quicken. Emotions swirled that she neither recognized nor understood.

Confused yet unbelievably moved. That was how Sophie felt when she saw the painting. Though not as intense, she felt a touch of the same stirrings when she looked at Forbes.

That was her first reaction. Her second could be summed up in one word. Joy. For the moment, her mother was too busy dazzling Newt. When she came up for air—which always happened—Forbes would be the first thing she noticed.

If men were Joy's weakness, young, handsome ones were her addiction. There might as well have been a flashing neon light over Forbes' head. *DANGER. DANGER. DANGER.*

Thankfully unaware of Sophie's thoughts, Forbes set the plates on the counter. "There you go. Eat what you want. Bailey will clean up the rest."

"Hello." Sophie hadn't noticed Bailey. She smiled when he placed his head on her leg, his eyes filled with affection and hope. Knowing what it was like to want something that was out of her control, she broke off a piece of chicken.

"You don't have any problem smiling at Bailey. Why do I get nothing but frowns and growls?"

Sophie felt awkward around people her own age. Unsure of how to speak or behave. Though she had a longing inside her to reach out and connect, how to proceed was problematic. So, she fell back on the skills she had honed by necessity. A sharp tongue and a less-than-welcoming attitude.

Most of the time, Sophie couldn't afford to be prideful. That didn't mean that she lacked the emotion. Explaining herself to Forbes would have meant revealing a certain amount of vulnerability. And that wouldn't happen.

"Is it me?" Thoughtfully, Forbes chewed on a chicken leg. "We just met. I'm more than capable of pissing people off. But for the life of me, I can't figure out what I did to you?"

*Where to start?* The confidence Forbes exuded? The ease of his manner? Knowing he belonged? That Forbes was comfortable in his own skin when at times Sophie wished she could claw hers off and start all over again?

All of those things pissed Sophie off. Royally.

Conversely, Forbes was the kind of person she often wished she could have for a friend. If she made a little effort, would he help her find her way? Or would he laugh at her? Mock her insecurities?

One thing Sophie was certain of. She would never know unless she tried.

"I—" Sophie swallowed. "I'm a little nervous."

*Talk about the understatement of the century.*

Forbes snorted. "You're joking."

Sophie knew he expected her to laugh—or shoot him a smart-mouth remark. When she did neither—holding her breath—Forbes frowned.

"Why?" he asked.

A simple question. As for the answer? *Nothing* in Sophie's life was ever simple.

"Your father invited Joy. Not me."

"Dad knew you were a package deal. Right?"

The sequence of events was a mystery to Sophie. Maybe Newt knew from the beginning that Joy came with a plus one. Maybe he found out after he was already hooked. From the way he had treated her, she would guess the latter.

"Your father has been very kind."

"Why wouldn't he be?"

Forbes seemed genuinely puzzled as if the concept of offhanded cruelty was foreign to him. *Wasn't he lucky?* Sophie finished off the last bite of creamy potato salad. For all his alpha male bravado, Forbes had lived a sheltered life. In his world, kindness was easy to come by. In Sophie's, not so much. She wasn't looking for his sympathy or pity, so she kept that nugget of wisdom to herself.

Talking about herself was fraught with landmines. Sophie didn't know all the lies Joy had told. Because Forbes was filled with questions that she couldn't answer without a cheat sheet, she decided it would be safer to turn the conversation away from her and onto him.

"You don't want us here."

When Forbes flushed, his blue eyes darkening with what she interpreted as guilt, Sophie knew she had hit the bullseye.

"You and your sister were a… surprise."

"Not a good one."

Without asking, Forbes poured Sophie some lemonade then some for himself.

"Whatever you're going to say must be bad." Sophie raised her glass. "We've moved to the hard stuff."

That brought a slight smile to his lips. "Do you want the truth?" Forbes asked.

"Please." Real honesty was hard to find. And harder to achieve. But Sophie preferred honesty any day of the week.

"Dad is vulnerable. He hasn't dated very much since my mother died. It was a shock when he arrived with a woman he barely knows."

This was Sophie's chance to do the right thing. Forbes had a smile—an open demeanor—that almost made her want to confess all and damn the consequences. *Almost.* She had spent too much time worrying about what was coming next to jeopardize the cushy setup Joy had landed. Sophie knew herself well enough to know that it would be an ongoing battle between her conscience and her full stomach.

Sophie wasn't keeping silent to protect Joy. Never that. Her mother was all about self-preservation. Probably the only valuable lesson the woman had ever passed along. Take care of yourself because nobody else would do it for you.

Knowing that Forbes expected some kind of response, Sophie shrugged one shoulder. "Your father is a grown man."

"True." Forbes hesitated. "I want him to be happy. But I don't want him to get hurt."

*Good luck*, Sophie thought sympathetically. Newt had hitched himself to the *Joy Express*. The best he could hope for was a wild ride. Fun would be had by all. However, that never lasted. The worst? Sophie had seen everything from tears. To shouting matches. To outright depression. One man's wife showed up wielding a gun. Though to be fair, it turned out not to be loaded.

"There are no guarantees." Silently, Sophie laughed at herself. Spouting worn platitudes? Is that what she had come to?

"You're good at the one-line answers, Sophie," Forbes said.

"Yes."

With a bark of laughter, Forbes ran a hand through his dark-blond hair. "Every girl I've ever known talks my ear off—given half a chance. Getting *you* to say more than two words is like pulling teeth. Why is that?"

"Maybe you're hanging out with the wrong girls."

The deadpan answer brought Forbes up short. Tilting his head, he held her gaze. Sophie didn't blink. If staring her down was his attempt to get her to spill her guts, he would be bitterly disappointed. Sophie was a master of protecting her thoughts from prying eyes.

After several seconds, Forbes sighed. "You may be right. However, until I head off to college, there isn't much chance of meeting any new ones."

*You met me.* Sophie didn't know where those words came from. In her head, they sounded flirty. Like something Joy would have said. God forbid.

Sophie picked up her plate. Not a speck of food remained, just a bare chicken bone. Copying what she had observed after dinner, she dumped the bone in the trash before opening the dishwasher.

"Thank you for the food."

"And the company?" Forbes put his plate in the machine next to hers.

Sophie was confused. She had politely thanked Forbes. Wasn't that enough? They sat on a couple of stools, ate some leftovers, and exchanged a few words. Was she supposed to compliment him for deigning to honor her with his presence? Had she misread Forbes? Did he need her to stroke his ego?

If that were the case, he barked up the wrong tree. The only thing Sophie was willing to stroke was Bailey's head. Forbes, his ego—and anything else—would have to rely on one of his babbling girlfriends for gratification.

"Aren't you going to say good night?" Forbes called out.

Halfway out the kitchen door, Sophie stopped. Annoyed, she turned her head. Unable to resist, she had to take a shot. "For a kid raised like a prince, you're kind of needy, aren't you?"

Sophie knew she shouldn't have done it. She saw no logical reason to poke at Forbes. However, when she saw the flash of anger in his blue eyes, she received a burst of satisfaction. Sure, it was a petty emotion. But as she bounced up the stairs, Sophie knew she was just fine with that.

# CHAPTER SIX

"SHE'S A WEIRD kid."

"How so?" Mike asked, handing Forbes a pair of wire cutters.

With an expertise earned from years of doing the same task hundreds of times, Forbes grasped two pieces of broken barbed wire in his gloved hand. With the other, he twisted the ends together using the needle-nose end of the tool, then efficiently clipped off the excess.

They had found the broken fence near one of the lower fields by an outcropping of pine trees. Though the sun was up—had been for several hours—it was still early. Just after dawn, Forbes had met Mike, saddling Jubal—the horse he had received on his tenth birthday. Mike was on Prairie, his longtime mount. Together, they set out to ride fences, checking for breaks or downed poles. By mid-morning, the temperature would be pushing the mid-eighties, so they liked to get this kind of job out of the way before noon.

This kind of work was mindless, but Forbes enjoyed it. There was nothing like the open range. It provided a peacefulness that was impossible to duplicate.

Some of the best conversations Forbes could remember had occurred while riding. With his father or Mike. Or one of the other hands. They didn't have much else to do besides watch the scenery and talk. He never knew what the subject would be. Often, they began in one area, ending up someplace completely unrelated.

This morning was a perfect example. Mike opened. He went on and on about a fly that had gotten into his bedroom. To hear the cowboy tell it, there had been an epic duel, ending—naturally—in death. There were some forgettable exchanges in between, leading—somehow—to the subject of Sophie Lipton. She was weird. Period.

"She's antagonistic." Forbes tried to think of a way to explain. "For no reason that I can think of."

71

"Huh." Mike scratched the growth on his chin that never seemed to get any longer than a three-day stubble. "Seemed nice enough last night. Polite. Quiet. Didn't do more than nod when Newt introduced her. Jerry and I thought she came off as a little shy."

"Shy, my ass." Patting Jubal on the neck, Forbes grabbed the pommel, swinging onto the horse with one smooth motion. "The girl has a mouth on her. Plus a razor-sharp tongue." When Mike looked skeptical, Forbes rubbed his chest. "I have the painful cuts to prove it."

"I see," Mike chuckled, urging his horse to an easy walk.

"*What* do you see?"

"Since you were in the crib, every female in a fifty-mile radius has flattered and fawned over your every word. Sophie didn't follow suit?" The dirty look that Forbes sent him didn't stop Mike from laughing even harder. "Must kind of stick in your craw."

"There is nothing wrong with my craw. Stick-free," Forbes muttered.

"Must be up your ass then. Something's making you squirm."

Forbes knew from head-thumping experience that winning an argument with Mike was impossible. Facts and figures didn't matter even when they were shoved in his face. He had a comeback for everything—usually nonsensical—and staying power beyond the reasonable.

Mike believed that wearing his opponent down was equivalent to a victory. And nobody—*nobody*—could outtalk Mike Phillips.

"Forget Sophie." Forbes certainly wanted to. "With any luck, she won't be around for long."

"I wouldn't count your chickens, son. That Joy is a looker. And sweet. It's been a long time since I've seen your daddy smile that much."

"You liked her?"

"Sure. Didn't you?"

Forbes agreed with Mike. Joy was pretty. And sweet. The interest Newt showed seemed to go both ways. If his father was happy—not just temporarily infatuated—then Forbes would welcome the woman wholeheartedly. Even if she came with a sniping little sister in tow.

"Call me cautiously optimistic."

"Cautiously optimistic." Mike said it with an exaggerated accent somewhere between a terrible upper-crust British, and his natural southern-Texas drawl. When he chuckled, it was as much at himself as Forbes. "I love the way you put things. Drop the cautiously, Forbes. That woman has put a heap of bounce in your daddy's giddyup. That's all that matters."

When Mike put it like that, Forbes knew he was right. He would keep his fingers crossed that Joy was everything she seemed to be. As for Sophie? He would think of her like a gnat. Annoying, but easily shooed away and forgotten.

"It's almost noon. Let's get these ponies back to the stable and find out what Maeve has cooked up for lunch."

The idea of filling his belly put a smile on Forbes' lips. Giving a sharp whistle, he waited for Bailey to come loping from the stand of pine trees. The dog never lost an opportunity to explore the area even though he already knew the land like the back of his paw. He always found something new to see and smell.

Satisfied that the dog was with them, Forbes touched his heels to Jubal's flanks and headed home.


A WEEK HAD passed since Sophie had set foot on the Branson ranch. She went to bed each night happy, full, and wondering when it would end. But the time in between was pure magic.

Newt had kept his promise to let Sophie drive the swather. He let her take a full turn around the field—with the cutting blades engaged.

The vehicle shook as it moved along caused by a combination of the bumpy field, the chugging engine, and—Sophie was certain—her exuberant, vibrating excitement. Sitting in the air-conditioned cab with Newt standing behind her, Sophie held the steering wheel. For the first time in her life, she felt a real sense of power. That she was in control. She wanted to yell. Whoop. Pump her fists.

Sophie did none of those things. But she couldn't keep from looking over her shoulder, her eyes glowing, a grin on her face.

Newt grinned back. Her obvious enjoyment contagious.

"Want to make another round?" he asked when Sophie would have taken her foot off the gas.

"You wouldn't mind?"

"Heck, no. If you get expert enough, I'll gladly turn it over to you for good. This has never been one of my favorite jobs."

Sophie knew he was joking. But that didn't stop her from wishing it could happen. She discovered that she liked working at something with a purpose. That had a goal where the end product was tangible. In this case, it was cutting alfalfa that would soon become bales of hay.

"Have you ever ridden a horse?"

"No."

"Would you like to?"

This time, Sophie couldn't control herself. She pumped one fist in the air and let out a resounding whoop. The sound echoed through the insulated cab.

Laughing, Newt winced, shaking his head to clear the ringing caused by Sophie's exuberance.

"Should I take that as a yes?"

"Yes. Yes, please."

"Then it's a date. Tomorrow morning. Bright and early."

Sophie gripped the steering wheel even tighter. Newt could have no idea what this meant to her. It wasn't driving the swather. Or the promise of riding a horse. It was Newt. The small gestures of kindness that came so naturally to him were like a revelation to Sophie. She had never been around anybody like him. When he placed a guiding hand on her shoulder. Or sent her an encouraging smile. Sophie didn't know if she wanted to laugh or cry. Most of the time, she felt like doing both.

A good man. That's what Newt Branson was. Sophie had known it from the beginning. The last week had driven the point home. She wanted to be selfish. She wanted to stay on the ranch as long as possible. She wanted to stay forever.

But if Sophie stayed, that meant Joy was sinking her talons deeper into Newt's unsuspecting flesh. Maybe his heart. That was something she couldn't allow.

"One more week."

"What was that?" Newt leaned closer.

Sophie hadn't realized she spoke the words aloud. Thinking quickly, she raised her voice. "One more round?"

"Sure. Then we'll stop for lunch."

Turning the wheel, she kept her eyes on the field. The odds were still good that Joy would ruin this very good thing before Sophie had to shut it down. That would be the easy way. Easier for Newt—and Sophie. Mentally, she crossed her fingers that her mother would be good for seven more days—then do something that would make Newt break up with her. If Joy were the one to screw up, it wouldn't keep him from a bit of pain and embarrassment, but the fallout would be a lot less.

Sophie knew from watching Joy over the years that it was always better to be the *breaker-upper* than the *breaker-uppee* —or whatever you called it. Sad but true.

"You were great, Sophie." Newt talked her through shutting off the machine. Opening the cab door, he jumped out, turning to help her down. "Did you have fun?"

"It was great. Thank you, Newt."

"My pleasure." Newt gave her shoulder a brief hug. "Ready to eat?"

At the mention of food, Sophie perked up, letting go of her heavy thoughts—at least for the time being.

"What do you think Maeve made for dessert?" To Sophie's delight, Maeve *always* made dessert.

"I heard rumblings that there might be cookies. You haven't lived until you've tasted one of Maeve's chocolate chip specials."

Chocolate chip. Sophie's mouth watered. As much as she liked Newt. And the ranch. When the time came to leave, she knew without a doubt that it would be Maeve's cooking that she would miss the most.

*One more week,* Sophie vowed, as she hoisted herself into Newt's truck. Looking around, she felt a moment of panic. Seven days wasn't enough time. She had a lot more memories to make. *Two weeks. Three at the most.* That had a better ring to it.

Sophie sighed. She edged onto a slippery slope. One wrong step and boom—disaster. But damn it, didn't she deserve some fun? Joy was having a good time. So was Newt. He started each morning with a goofy smile on his face—one that popped up from time to time throughout the day. She would keep an eye on things. If that smile started to slip, she would act.

Until then? One month. Maximum.

FORBES GRIMACED. HIS muscles protested as he carried a saddle from the tack shed. Football practice was in full swing, and he suffered the consequences. Damned freshmen. One or two were always intent on impressing the coaches. Forbes knew that. But it hadn't stopped him from a moment of inattention just as a two-hundred-fifty-pound rookie linebacker decided to show off by plowing into the team's all-state quarterback.

The move had gotten the kid a chewing out from Coach Riggins—and an early trip to the shower.

Though gasping for breath, Forbes had popped right back to his feet. He had a reputation as a tough S.O.B., and no overeager freshman would keep him down for long. That said, today, he paid the price, with a bruise the size of Rhode Island down his back, ending at the slope of his right butt cheek. It made lifting a fifty-pound western saddle—a task he usually did with little effort—harder than it should have been.

With a grunt, Forbes settled the expertly constructed leather onto Dolly's back. The dapple brown mare placidly waited while he ran the cinch under her belly, leaving it loose for the time being. The horse was pushing fifteen years old and knew the routine. At one time, she was a pony tasked with cutting cattle from the herd or zipping after stray calves. These days most of her time was spent basking in the sun and eating. Her reward for years of loyalty and hard work.

On occasion—like today—Dolly was trotted out to initiate a newbie to the joys of horseback riding. She was calm, unflappable, and no longer had the energy or inclination for more than a leisurely walk.

Dolly sighed—long and heartfelt—telling Forbes that she was resigned to what she had to do. But not particularly looking forward to it.

"I'm with you, girl," Forbes said, patting the horse's rump.

Off the top of his head, Forbes could think of a dozen things he would rather do than spend the morning with Sophie Lipton. Hell, he would trade places with Hack Tredway in a heartbeat. A seasonal worker, Hack had been given the not-so-pleasant task of cleaning the horse stalls. It was sweaty. Backbreaking. Monotonous. But compared to an hour or two with the annoying Sophie? Forbes would have volunteered in a heartbeat.

"Hello."

The voice was barely more than a whisper, but it had Forbes jumping a foot.

"Jesus Fucking Christ." He grasped his chest, certain his heart had skipped a few beats. Taking a deep breath, he frowned at Sophie. "Where the hell did you come from?"

"That way." Sophie pointed to the side of the barn.

"There isn't a trail back there. It's nothing but brambles and brush from here to the main house."

Sophie shrugged. "I like to explore. The view of the river is beautiful."

"You can get the same view from the main road." Forbes looked Sophie up and down. "Your arms are covered with scratches. Ticks breed in those bushes. Check yourself tonight."

"How?" Frowning, Sophie tugged at the neck of her t-shirt, peering down the opening at her chest. By her side, Bailey, his dark coat covered with leaves and sticks, pawed at his ear in apparent sympathy.

"It serves you right," Forbes told the dog. "If you stayed with me—where you belong—instead of following Sophie to hell and back, you wouldn't be dealing with creepy-crawlers. Do you want another flea and tick dip at the vet's?"

*Vet.* Bailey knew the word. Acting accordingly, he shuffled behind Sophie's legs. Whether he thought he was now invisible, or that his new friend would protect him from a fate worse than death, Forbes didn't know. But the sight of the big dog cowering behind a girl he outweighed by a least twenty pounds was so ridiculous, Forbes had to laugh.

"Don't worry. You're probably safe." Forbes patted his leg. Without hesitation, Bailey trotted over, his eyes filled with love and trust. "I'll give you the once over this afternoon—just to be sure. As for you."

Sophie crossed her arms, her expression wary. "Keep your once overs to yourself."

"Trust me. You're safe from me," Forbes raised an eyebrow when Sophie snorted.

"Never trust a man who says trust me."

"Who gave you that stupid piece of advice?"

"My mother. It's one of the few smart things she ever told me."

Grimacing, Sophie unwound the rubber band that held her hair in a ponytail, her fingers running through the shoulder-length locks, checking for an infestation.

Forbes didn't comment. What could he say? According to his father—as told to him by Joy—Sophie's mother hadn't been a very good role model to either of her daughters. She alienated the oldest and kept the youngest isolated most of her life. What education Sophie had was done by hit-and-miss homeschooling.

It explained a lot. No wonder Sophie seemed socially backward. Her life before Joy took charge couldn't have been easy. Forbes took a deep breath, reminding himself to try a little patience. If that didn't work, he always had time to give the girl a swift kick in the butt.

Though Forbes knew he would never carry through on it, the image was enough to make his spirits lift.

"I expected your father."

"Dad sends his apologies. He had a late night out with Joy. He asked me to fill in."

Forbes went about tightening the cinch around Dolly's middle. To his surprise, Sophie moved closer, her eyes keenly focused on his movements. Realizing she was interested, he slowed down so she could follow what he was doing.

"Does it hurt him?"

"Her. This is Dolly." Forbes looped the end cinch through a metal circle, tying it off. "It doesn't hurt."

Sophie didn't look convinced. She put her finger between the horse and the leather strap. "It's awfully tight."

"If it were any looser, the saddle would slip from her back. You with it. You wouldn't want that?"

"No. But..."

"Trust me. I—" Forbes broke off, laughing at Sophie's sideways glance. He hadn't realized how often he asked for somebody to blindly believe in what he had to say. Until now, he had never been called on it. Or—to his knowledge—doubted with such veracity. "I know what I'm doing, Sophie. So does Dolly. If you don't believe me, you can count on her. She won't let you down."

"Okay."

Forbes didn't know why, but he found Sophie's acquiescence annoying. She trusted Dolly but not him? All he received were looks of either anger, weariness, or contempt. *Great. Just, freaking great.* The only thing that stopped him from abandoning the lesson, and telling Sophie where to shove it, was his promise to his father.

Despite Sophie's constant jabbing at his ego—Forbes had yet to decide if it was intentional—he could tell how excited she was at the prospect of learning how to ride. Forgetting him for a few seconds, she ran her hands over Dolly's neck, leaning close, breathing deeply. A slow smile formed on her lips.

Without a single word, Forbes understood.

Sophie had made the connection. That moment that passed between human and horse. Not every human did. An unspoken agreement to treat each other with respect. The way Sophie breathed in Dolly's scent. She didn't wrinkle her nose the way some girls of his acquaintance did. Rather than back away, she leaned closer, inhaling again.

Forbes knew from experience. Either one loved the way a horse smelled, or one didn't. It *wasn't* an acquired taste. Sophie's grin told him on which side of the debate she fell.

"Now that the two of you are on friendly terms, let's get going." Forbes laced his fingers, holding his hands for Sophie to step into. "Grab the pommel. That's right. Now put your foot in my hands and swing your leg over."

Sophie's tennis shoes were not ideal horseback riding footwear, but they would do for today. Forbes wouldn't take the pace beyond a walk. Boots would be required if the lessons went further, but that was something to worry about if or when it happened.

"I like it up here." Sophie took the reins from Forbes, her head turning from side to side.

"If you're looking for the best view, nothing beats what you'll see while riding a horse. Make me a promise?"

"That depends."

"Smart girl. Never agree to anything until you hear the terms."

Sophie nodded, her dark eyes telling him it was a lesson she had already learned. Briefly, Forbes thought about asking when? Where? How? Sophie was such a contradiction. One second she was wise beyond her years. The next, she seemed impossibly young and naïve.

She had a story to tell. Forbes was interested. Kind of. Getting anything out of her beyond a sentence or two would take time and patience. He didn't know if he cared enough to try. However, if they were going to move along to a point where Sophie was comfortable having a nice, long heart to heart, now was the perfect place to start.

"Don't pull on the reins," Forbes instructed. "Relaxed, but not too loose. That's right. Lightly, give Dolly a nudge with your heels. Good."

Sophie was a fast learner. Intent and interested, Forbes didn't have to tell her anything twice. It was natural for her to start off a little tense, but it didn't take her long to settle into the saddle, moving with Dolly's gait instead of against.

Satisfied that Sophie had a handle on the basics, Forbes continued to keep an eye on her but allowed himself to relax and enjoy the ride.

"Where are you from?"

Forbes thought it an easy, non-invasive kind of question. A good way for people who were—for all intents and purposes—strangers, to break the ice.

"Here and there."

"Name a here. Or a there," Forbes prompted.

When Sophie hesitated, Forbes patiently waited. He had all day. Or at least the duration of the ride. He couldn't understand why she treated his question with more thought than it deserved.

"We moved around a lot. Florida. Nebraska. Louisiana."

"I want to travel. Someday. Right now, I'm glad that I've gone to school in the same town with the same friends. Was it tough? Moving around so much?"

"Yes."

Sophie didn't elaborate. However, the one word—said with stark honesty—was illuminating. She had none of his advantages. Not the loving family. Not the tight-knit group of friends. Unless

81

her worn jeans and ratty sneakers were a fashion statement, money must have been tight.

Another tidbit his father had passed along answered part of that question. Joy had gained custody of Sophie quite suddenly—their mother's unexpected death meant the poor kid had been practically dumped in her sister's lap. Joy planned on using what little money she had to buy Sophie some new things. Then she met Newt. The rest had been such a whirlwind there hadn't been time to do more than pack their bags.

Forbes thought it sounded a little strange. More than a little. His father didn't agree. Basically, the conversation ended with, *because I said so*. Newt rarely fell back on such an old chestnut. Since Forbes had no real argument to present, he let it pass.

"Maeve told me that your mom and dad were in love. Do you remember what that was like?"

Out of the blue, Sophie's question caught Forbes off guard. He couldn't remember ever thinking about it. His parents—the way they felt about each other—simply was. Love? Definitely. Add affection. Respect. It had been a partnership. They had set a glowing example for Forbes to follow. Something to aspire to. He had been young when his mother died, but the memories were strong. If he ever got married, he would never settle for anything less.

"They were always touching. Not in a weird way," Forbes added. "A little brush of their hands when Dad passed by. Or Mom would set a hand on his shoulder for no particular reason. I don't think he realized, but it always made him smile. Every time."

"Sounds nice."

He noticed a wistfulness to Sophie's voice. Forbes nodded, feeling a little wistful himself.

"Tell me more."

Later, when he was alone in bed, Forbes realized how good it had felt to talk about the past. About his parents. Mostly shared things about his mother. Things he hadn't thought about in years. Sophie turned out to be a good listener. However—something else

Forbes realized in the dark of night—she was skilled at avoiding questions about herself. Whenever he asked, she adroitly turned it back on him.

Searching his mind, Forbes couldn't think of anything personal she had shared about herself. Or much on the impersonal side. In retrospect, it was… annoying.

Forbes rolled over. The pain that radiated from his side fast reminding him why it was a bad idea to try to sleep in that position. Moving to his back, he sighed with relief. He had football practice in the morning. To his surprise, his afternoon would be filled with giving Sophie riding lesson number two. And showing her how to use the weight room in the basement.

Smiling, Forbes pictured the scene.

Sophie had insisted on undoing the cinch from around Dolly's middle—it took some effort, but eventually, she managed. Taking off the saddle was another matter. It was heavier than she expected. Before Forbes could warn her—or rush to her rescue—Sophie ended up flat on her ass. A little bruised, she was no worse for wear.

"You need to build up some muscle." Teasing, Forbes made a wavy motion with his hand. "Spaghetti arms."

For a moment, Forbes worried he had offended her. Frowning, Sophie examined her arm. Her frown turned to interest. Then determination. Turning her head to the side, she looked at Forbes.

"Show me how."

*Interesting*, Forbes thought, staring into the darkened bedroom. It hadn't occurred to him to say no. At some point when he hadn't been paying attention, he and Sophie had discovered a fork in the road—so to speak. Where that path would lead was anybody's guess. But he no longer dreaded spending time with her.

Just maybe—though Forbes wasn't quite ready to admit it—he might be looking forward to Sophie's company. Considering where they started? That was saying a lot.

# CHAPTER SEVEN

FRESHLY SHOWERED AND looking forward to one of Maeve's big, rib-sticking breakfasts, Sophie had just left her room. Before she could take more than a step, Joy's hand landed in the middle of her chest. She gave Sophie a shove, slamming the door behind them.

"We have a problem."

Sophie figured it had to be serious for Joy to get out of bed this early. The question was, which problem was her mother referring to? Between them, they were teaming with them.

"You're going to have to be more specific."

"Newt wants me to register you for school."

*That wasn't a problem. That was a miracle.*

Sophie turned away before Joy could see the excitement in her expression. School. That meant they would be sticking around for a while. Good for Joy. Great for Sophie. How it would affect Newt and the rest of the Branson household, only time would tell.

"I'm game." That was putting it mildly.

"I don't care about you."

Alert the media. Sophie's thoughts dripped with sarcasm. Her face as she looked at Joy, was the epitome of bland.

"What do you need me to do?" Name it. If it meant attending a real school, Sophie would agree to pretty much anything.

"I've created a backstory. Newt buys it. Now it's up to you to help me sell it when the time comes."

"Okay."

"That's it?" Joy's eyes narrowed suspiciously. "You agreed awfully quickly. What happened to, *I don't like to lie*." Joy whined the words. "Where's that annoying conscience that crops up at the most inconvenient times?"

"Tell me what I need to know," Sophie said with all sincerity. "I'll back you one hundred percent."

Joy scoffed, shaking her head. "Now I see."

Sophie doubted it. Raising her eyebrows, she waited for Joy to explain her sudden revelation.

"It's because you have the hots for Forbes."

"What? You're crazy."

Sophie shouldn't have been surprised. Joy's mind traveled in one direction. Straight down the gutter. Her mother couldn't imagine any motivation that didn't involve a man.

"Oh, I admit you're a bit backward when it comes to such things." Joy stopped in front of the mirror—one of her top three places to be—to check her reflection. Licking the tip of her little finger, she smoothed it along the line of her eyebrow. "It was bound to happen. Forbes is a tasty piece of merchandise." She smiled to herself, licking her lips before slowly turning away.

"I don't think of him like that."

"Why not? It would be so easy. You're out riding horses." Joy shuddered, her mouth puckering unpleasantly as if she were sucking on a lemon. "There must be hundreds of secluded spots just right for fooling around."

"No." This time, *Sophie* shuddered. "Absolutely not."

"Do I have a budding lesbian on my hands?" Joy seemed to find the idea highly amusing.

Sophie wasn't interested in Forbes—or any other boy at the moment. But she knew that she was heterosexual. But gay or straight, the last person she would confide in was Joy. Sophie's sexuality wouldn't be fodder for her mother's nasty comments. Better she didn't know—one way or the other.

"What's the difference? I'm not interested in *fooling around* with either sex."

"You will be." Joy sounded so sure of herself that Sophie almost believed her. Almost. "This is a conservative part of the country, Sophie. You'll have a difficult enough time fitting in without the *gay* stigma."

Joy was on fire for such an early hour. She had managed to insult Sophie—*you'll have a difficult time fitting in*—and the entire gay community in a few short sentences.

"If I promise not to jump any girls in the bathroom, will that satisfy you? I think I can control my baser urges."

"Is that supposed to be a joke?"

"Of course not." Sophie's lips didn't even twitch. "I'm not clever enough, and you have no sense of humor. What would be the point of trying?"

Joy's eyes narrowed. Sophie's jabs usually didn't connect—ninety-nine percent of the time it was because she tuned out what her daughter had to say. That wasn't the case at the moment.

"You think I won't give you a slap." Joy sighed with regret. "And you're right. A pinch, on the other hand, doesn't bother me at all."

Before Sophie could react, Joy latched onto the flesh of her upper thigh, giving it a vicious twist. It took some doing, but Sophie managed not to yelp in pain. In her head, she called her mother a bitch. Then added a colorful assortment of other names she would never think of speaking aloud.

"That was satisfying. I don't know why I didn't think of it before." Joy brushed her hands together several times, signaling a job well done. "Back to the point. This afternoon, Newt will drive us to the high school for a meeting with Principal... I forget her name, but it doesn't matter. The adults will do the talking. All that is required of you is a smile and an occasional nod. Understood?"

"Don't you think the principal will want to ask me a few questions?"

"Perhaps." Joy gave it some thought. "You know what I told Newt."

About her evil mother keeping her isolated and uneducated? Since it was the truth, Sophie didn't think she would have any problem remembering the story.

"We're leaving at one o'clock. Sharp." Joy yawned. "I think I'll go back to bed. I don't know how anybody functions at this hour of the morning. One o'clock, Sophie. Don't make me come looking for you."

That wouldn't be necessary. The second Joy was out of the room, Sophie did an all-out, extended version of her happy dance. Hopping. Fist pumping. Feet thumping. Silent screaming.

The one-word song played in her head over and over again.

*School. School. School.*

Was there a more exciting, hopeful word in the English language? In Sophie's book, that was a big, fat no. For a chance at a formal education—surrounded by people her own age—it was a dream come true.

Sophie's smile slipped, her enthusiasm ratcheting down a notch or two. There would be a price attached to her happiness. And she was afraid Newt would be the one to pay.

Deep down—no matter what she tried to tell herself—she had known this moment would come. There would be no going back once she walked into her first class. To achieve her heart's desire, she would be stuck with the lies.

Would it be worth it? A week? A month? Perhaps an entire year of school? Selfishly, Sophie didn't have to search too hard to decide the answer was a resounding yes. She—and what was left of her crumbling conscience—would have to live with the consequences.

Whatever they were.

"THE CIRCUMSTANCES ARE unusual. But we have procedures in place for almost every contingency." Principal Doris Breckenridge tapped a series of keys on her computer. "Sophie is the victim in all of this. It's up to us—the education system—to make certain she won't be penalized again because of someone else's grievous errors."

"Sophie is a bright girl, Doris." Newt sent Sophie an encouraging smile.

"I'm sure."

Sophie wished she was as certain as Newt and Principal Breckenridge. An hour ago, her resolve was rock solid. As each mile passed on the drive to Cloverton, she felt her confidence slip. Bit by bit. Stepping into the high school for the first time, part of her wanted to turn and run. It was so quiet. Eerily so. The building bigger than she imagined.

Never dormant for long, her imagination began working overtime, clearly picturing the halls filled with sweaty, jostling teenage bodies. Sophie wouldn't stand a chance. They would trample her like so much trash, grinding her bones to dust.

What had she been thinking? Breaking out her never-before-worn shorts and making certain her hair was neatly combed had seemed like enough when she was getting ready. Now, she wondered why she bothered.

Sophie's heart felt like it was about to burst from her chest. Her mouth was dry. Her palms wet. Her stomach flipped, flopped, then twisted into a pretzel. Sophie swallowed, feeling slightly green around the gills. Maybe she shouldn't have eaten that second bowl of chili for lunch.

"The solution is simple. I will administer a standardized test to assess where Sophie is compared to her peers. Most students her age would be entering the tenth grade. Considering her... *situation*, I don't want anybody to expect too much." Principal Breckenridge sent Sophie a sympathetic smile. "The most important thing is to give you the best chance to succeed."

"Sophie is grateful for the chance. Aren't you?"

Afraid that if she tried to speak the best she could do was make an embarrassing squeak, Sophie nodded. It seemed to be all that anybody expected from her. Thank goodness.

"Fine. The test will take about three hours. I can set it up for any day this week."

"Tomorrow?" Newt asked.

Since it had worked so far, Sophie shook her head one more time.

"Wonderful. Did you bring Sophie's birth certificate?"

The ringing in Sophie's ears stopped. So did her breathing. *Birth certificate?* Watching intently as Joy took a piece of paper from her purse, Sophie struggled with the implications. For as long as she could remember, Joy claimed she didn't possess such a document. Sophie had lost track of the times she had asked. Where was I born? Who was my father? Joy would either shrug and not answer or coldly inform her that it didn't matter.

Well, it mattered to Sophie.

Principal Breckenridge read the document, a frown forming between her brows.

"Mother. Joy Lipton?"

"I was named after our mother. When she passed away, I found the birth certificate when I was cleaning out her apartment."

Joy was never without a plausible explanation, Sophie thought bitterly. She couldn't decide which she wanted most. Use her fingers to snatch the paper, or wrap them around her mother's throat. Wisely, she clasped her hands in her lap, refraining from either. She had waited this long. Besides, the document wasn't going anywhere. Neither was Joy's neck.

"You were born in Philadelphia?" Principal Breckenridge typed, preparing a file with Sophie's name on it. "What a small world. I did my undergraduate studies there."

"Sophie doesn't remember. Mom moved shortly after she was born."

Forty-five minutes later, and what seemed like an endless return trip to the ranch, a strange calm had settled over Sophie. She wasn't angry. Or distressed. Determined. That was the word she would use. Giving Joy a small head start, Sophie calmly made her way through the living room to the kitchen.

"How did things go?" Maeve asked, taking a chocolate Bundt cake from the oven.

"I'm taking a test tomorrow."

Sophie thought the kitchen smelled like heaven. Any other time she would have stopped to admire the dessert, imagining herself eating a hefty slice. Today, she didn't break stride.

"What kind of a test?" Maeve's gaze followed Sophie to the back staircase.

"Placement."

Before Maeve could waylay her, Sophie increased her tempo, her feet making short work of the climb. Turning left, she used her long legs to cruise down the hallway. Joy had taken the traditional route. With her usual leisurely pace, she beat Sophie by mere seconds.

"Stop."

"Go away." Joy didn't give Sophie a glance. She would have closed the door in her daughter's face if Sophie hadn't stuck the toe of her worn sneaker in the way. "Move it or lose it."

Joy had the haughty look and tone down pat. Sophie wasn't impressed. She had seen it a thousand times.

"We can have this out in your room. Or I can yell through the door. Where everyone can hear." Sophie had some attitude of her own. "Your choice."

Moving back, Joy opened the door enough for Sophie to slide through.

"Make it quick. I need a long bath." Joy sniffed at her arm, recoiling. "Ugh. I smell like public education."

Sophie had no idea what that meant. She doubted that Joy did either. It didn't matter. For once, she would push for some answers. Squaring her shoulders, she rose to her full height.

"I want to see my birth certificate."

"Is that what this is about? Help yourself."

As though it meant nothing, Joy tossed the purse on the bed. Was it some kind of trick? Had her mother somehow jerry-rigged an explosive device triggered the instant Sophie tried to open the bag? After years of guarding that piece of paper like it was the Holy Grail, suddenly it didn't matter?

It mattered to Sophie. She dumped everything on the lace comforter. It wasn't a large purse, but Joy had three different tubes of lipstick, two atomizers of perfume, a comb, a mirror, eyeshadow, rouge, nail polish—her signature bright red. A nail file which Sophie knew from experience could double as an effective weapon in a pinch. Tissue. Condoms. *Always be prepared.* Not exactly what the Boy Scouts had in mind, but it was the same principle.

Everything under the sun. But no birth certificate. Sophie turned the black leather hobo bag inside out, looking in every nook, cranny, and zippered pocket. Frustrated—and knowing she'd been had—she hurled the purse across the room.

"Oops. I forgot. I put it in my pocket."

Batting her eyes, a sly smile on her lips, Joy leaned against the dresser. In her hand was Sophie's birth certificate.

"Do you want me to beg?"

It was a silly question.

"Yes." Joy's laugh took on a different tone when there wasn't a man around. Not light. Or playful. Evil was the word Sophie would have chosen. "But I won't make you crawl. A simple please will do the trick."

Through gritted teeth, Sophie complied. "Please."

Easy as that, Joy held out the birth certificate. Snatching it, Sophie understood the implications. If the paper contained the answers she was looking for, her mother would have extracted a much higher price. Still, she had to know.

Scanning the document, Sophie found the line she was looking for. Reading the words, her shoulders slumped.

*Father*: *Unknown.*

Sophie felt a flush rise to her cheeks. Anger mingled with disbelief. It was classic Joy. Her expression was so smug. Filled with malevolence. Spiteful. Unrepentant. And loving every second.

It wouldn't do any good to rail or cry or plead. The last time she tried—around the age of five—Joy had walked out of the motel room without a backward glance, leaving a terrified Sophie on her own for hours.

No, tears had no effect on her mother. Sophie's only retaliation was to use the weapon Joy understood, appreciated, and had spent her entire life perfecting. Sheer nastiness.

Coolly, Sophie raised her eyes.

"Could you at least narrow the potential field to a baker's dozen?"

Sophie didn't know what she had expected, but it wasn't laughter—and applause.

"Nice dig." Joy clapped slowly. "You have a little backbone after all."

"I don't want your approval. I want to know who my father is."

"What would be the point? You were a mistake, Sophie. A one-night stand. Or was it two?" Joy sighed, obviously bored with the conversation. "Even at the time, it was forgettable. *He* was forgettable."

"Then why didn't you have an abortion?"

"I thought about it. Unfortunately, I was low on funds. By the time I raised enough cash, it was too late. I was stuck with you."

When Joy finally told the truth, she didn't hold back. Hearing the words stung a little. However, Sophie wasn't surprised by the revelation. Joy hadn't wanted her. Finding out what she had always suspected was hardly a newsflash.

"You could have put me up for adoption."

"Mm." Joy held out her hand, casually studying her nails. "Could have, but didn't. End of discussion. Leave, Sophie. I've had more than enough of you for one day."

"That's it?"

Joy began to undress. "There's nothing else to say."

Hardly. Sophie was certain that Joy knew who her father was. Keeping the name to herself was cruel.

"I always knew you hated me."

Turning, Joy shook her head. When she spoke, her voice was without emotion. "I don't hate you."

"You don't?"

"No. To hate somebody—or love them—you have to care. It takes a lot of time and energy." Pausing at the bathroom door, Joy flicked Sophie a look. "You just aren't worth the effort."

"I NEED ALL of your attention, Sophie. One hundred percent."

"Show me again. I'll get it this time."

Forbes hesitated. Something was clearly on Sophie's mind besides lifting weights. It wasn't any of his business. And he certainly didn't want to become the kid's confessor. However, he needed to get her to focus on the task at hand. If she were upset or distracted? Not paying attention was the fastest way to suffer a serious injury.

"Tell me what's wrong."

"Nothing."

When Sophie reached for the free-weight, Forbes waylaid her, taking her arm. She tried to pull away, but he was stronger. By a considerable margin.

Sophie stopped struggling, but the look she sent him was filled with frustration.

"If I were bigger, I would knock you on your ass."

"One day, if you concentrate and work hard, you might learn to do exactly that." Forbes sat her on the padded bench next to the triceps machine. He took a seat opposite. "FYI? Muscles and size are fine, but your technique is more important. I've noticed how quick you are. I can teach you to use it to your advantage. Drink some water." Forbes handed her a bottle from the built-in cooler. "Lesson number one. Stay hydrated."

"I thought lesson number one was concentrate. Work hard would be number two." Sophie unscrewed the cap. "That makes water number three."

Why was it the only time Sophie strung together more than a couple of sentences it was to give him lip? Around everybody else, she was polite. Quiet to a fault. The quiet part carried over when they were alone. Until something pissed her off. That something seemed to be him.

There was no figuring her out. He could either laugh or knock his head against the wall. Since he wasn't a masochist, Forbes chuckled.

"Are you worried about taking that test tomorrow?"

"No." When Forbes raised an eyebrow, Sophie caved—a little. "Maybe."

"I get it. You're fifteen. You want to go to school with kids your own age."

"I'll take the test. They'll put me where they put me." Sophie shrugged.

Surprised, Forbes could tell that Sophie meant it. She wasn't worried. He couldn't imagine surviving the embarrassment of getting stuck in the eighth grade when his peers were starting their sophomore year.

"Then what's wrong?"

"I—"

"Whatever you say stays between us, Sophie. I'm not a snitch."

For a moment, Forbes didn't think Sophie would answer. She frowned. Stared at him long and hard. Then sighed.

"Joy and I had words."

Once more, Forbes was struck by what an odd kid Sophie was. So much about her screamed immaturity. Smart, but socially unsure and awkward. Then with a snap of the fingers, she sounded mature beyond her years. She and Joy *had words*? Who spoke like that—outside of a book or a movie?

"Isn't it natural for sisters to fight?"

"*Sisters*? I suppose it is." Though Sophie smiled, with a tinge of somberness to it. Lurking in her eyes was something Forbes couldn't identify. "Joy and I are seldom on the same wavelength."

"She wasn't around much when you were growing up. With time, you're bound to grow closer."

Forbes couldn't speak from experience. But some of his friends had sisters. Some of his friends *were* sisters. They had a strong bond—one that wasn't easily damaged and almost impossible to break. Or so he understood.

"Time isn't the problem," Sophie muttered, more to herself than to Forbes. "Can we drop the subject?"

Forbes nodded. That was fine with him. For some reason, he found himself adding, "If you ever want to talk…"

"I've always kept my thoughts to myself."

"Why?"

"I got tired of talking to the walls."

The words tugged at his heart. Sophie met his gaze, her eyes a dark chocolate brown. This time it was easy to tell what she was feeling. Sadness. Stripped away was the attitude. For the first time, Forbes realized how lonely Sophie must have been.

Forbes found the idea hard to imagine. He had always had somebody. First his mother and father. Maeve. Mike. Jerry. The ranch hands who wandered on and off and back onto the Branson ranch.

As he grew older, making friends came easily. Aaron. His classmates. The guys on the football team. The list was too long to count.

Once Sophie started school, she would learn how to interact with other kids. Until then, Forbes would have to do. Friends with Sophie. Hard as it was to believe, he decided he liked the way it sounded.

Jumping to his feet, Forbes slapped his hands together. Time to change the energy in the room from maudlin to upbeat.

"Okay, spaghetti arms. Let's start building you some muscle."

"I have muscle." Sophie held up her arm. "Some."

Forbes lightly squeezed the area where Sophie's bicep should have been. "Spaghetti, kid. Limp and soggy."

Sophie laughed. Unreserved. Full-bodied. *Well, I'll be damned*, Forbes thought, grinning back. The way her face lit up. The sparkle in her dark eyes. Sophie Lipton was pretty.

If she did more of that, the boys at Cloverdale High School would take notice.

"Well, shit," Forbes said under his breath.

He knew what teenage boys were like. Because he was one. The only thing they liked better than a pretty girl was a pretty girl who was new in town.

*Fresh meat.* Forbes had used the term on more than one occasion without a second thought. For the first time, he agreed with Maeve. Men could be pigs.

Keeping an eye on Sophie would be a bigger pain in his ass than he originally anticipated. Briefly, he wondered if he could encourage her *not* to smile.

"What?" Sophie frowned, pausing in the middle of slowly lifting a five-pound dumbbell. "Am I doing it wrong?"

"Perfect form." Forbes had warned Sophie about not concentrating. He needed to get his head in the game. "Do ten reps. alternating arms. You'll be beating me at arm wrestling in no time."

"I don't know about that." Sophie watched as Forbes started with a *much* heavier weight. "Nobody will ever call *you* spaghetti arms."

"I've been doing this for a long time."

Considering his words, Sophie nodded.

"If I can get to the point where lifting a saddle doesn't knock me on my butt, I'll be happy. That and knocking you onto yours."

# *CHAPTER EIGHT*

"FORBES. MAY I speak with you for a minute?"

Sweaty and wanting a shower, Forbes held in a sigh when he found Joy waiting for him outside the exercise room. The politeness his mother had instilled in him since birth, coupled with the desire to make his father happy, prevented him from asking her if it could wait. They had lived in the same house for several weeks and from the looks of things, would continue to do so for the foreseeable future.

Couldn't the woman wait until he had his shower? From the determined look on her face, Forbes guessed the answer was no.

"Would you like to sit down?"

"That would be lovely. Thank you."

The entire basement had been converted into a place for men to hang out. Women weren't excluded, that's just how it tended to work out.

Besides the weight room, Forbes, his father, and their friends would gather to watch football or for a night of poker in a recreation room with a vintage pinball machine against the far wall. When sports weren't dominating the big-screen television, a flip of a switch converted it to the perfect place for marathon video game sessions.

Forbes led Joy to one of the leather chairs scattered around the room.

"Can I get you something to drink?"

Like in the weight room, Maeve made certain the mini-fridge was always stocked.

"Such nice manners. I'd love some water. If it isn't too much trouble."

Joy's smile was warm and admiring. When she crossed her legs, Forbes found his eyes drawn to them. The skirt she wore rode up—not too much. Just enough to show off an enticing amount of smooth, creamy skin. Realizing what he was doing, Forbes looked away, taking a quick peek to see if Joy had noticed. Noting that she seemed completely unaware, he mentally wiped his brow with relief. It would be embarrassing to get caught ogling his father's girlfriend. Even if it was completely unintentional.

"Would you mind pouring mine into a glass?" Joy asked when Forbes would have handed her the bottle of water.

"No problem."

Forbes didn't see the change in Joy's smile. The way it curved turned from friendly to sly. Her eyes glittered with female power—power she had honed on much tougher targets than Forbes Branson. He had no idea what was happening. And that was the way she wanted it. One day in the not-so-distant future, he would be doing a lot more for her than fetching a glass of water.

Joy licked her lips, enjoying the play of muscles in his arms as Forbes did her bidding. First the handsome father, then the young, studly son. Not yet. For the first time in her life, she could afford a little patience. When she had what she wanted from Newt—and wasn't he turning out to be the easiest target in history—she would find a way to discreetly enjoy what Forbes had to offer.

Boredom. Joy couldn't abide it. Surprisingly, ranch life turned out to be more interesting than she could have imagined. Newt had gone so long without a woman in his life—he was so starved for affection—that it had taken her no time to have him tightly wound around her little finger. He wholeheartedly embraced Joy's slightest whim.

Shopping. Dancing. Drinking. Late nights followed by late mornings in bed where Joy was happy to show her appreciation.

Cloverton wasn't exactly a hub of entertainment. But Spokane was within a few hours' driving distance. Newt had already promised Joy a long weekend in Seattle.

As Forbes turned, Joy's smile made another transformation. It proved that she could do sweet. When necessary.

"Thank you."

Joy took a sip of the water. My, oh, my, he was gorgeous. It had been a while since she had enjoyed anybody as young as

Forbes. The things she could teach him. Just the thought made her insides quake with anticipation. She had no doubt that if she played her cards right, he would soon be her lover and Newt would never have to know.

"Are you cold?" Forbes asked when Joy shivered, rubbing her bare arms. "It can get a little cool down here."

"I'm fine. Sit. I won't keep you long."

Unaware that behind Joy's benign smile lurked a scheming predator, Forbes did as she asked, taking the chair next to hers.

"What can I do for you?"

"It's about Sophie."

Joy had prepared this speech carefully. She wanted to come across as a caring, concerned sister. In truth, she wanted to nip her daughter's blossoming friendship with Forbes in the bud. Not because she saw Sophie as a rival—the idea was ridiculous. The girl was a pain in the ass. A necessary evil that through no fault of her own, Joy was stuck with. Most of the time—as she told Sophie—she didn't give the girl a lot of thought.

However, in the last few days, Joy had started to take notice. It had always been an effort to get the girl to move with any purpose. Now, she noticed a definite bounce in Sophie's step and Joy didn't like it. Joy knew that enjoying her daughter's discontent was petty and spiteful.

Truthfully? Joy had no problem with that.

"You're worried that Sophie will have trouble fitting in at school?"

*Hardly*, Joy thought. But what the hell. She could use school as a jumping off place.

"I know you'll do your best to help her." Joy smiled. "But I need to warn you."

Forbes frowned. "About what?"

"Sophie—because of how isolated she has been for most of her life—tends to grow attached to people. Quickly." Joy shook her head, her eyes filled with concern. "I'm afraid that is what's happening with you."

"I haven't noticed. If anything, Sophie pushes me away every chance she gets."

"That's at first. The more you're around, the more she'll start to cling." Joy looked away for effect. "Then the jealousy begins. Just this morning, she complained that I'm spending too much time with your father."

"Sophie doesn't seem to need anybody." The frown deepened on his brow. "She takes long walks by herself. Never asks for help unless absolutely necessary."

"Don't get me wrong. I love my sister. She's had a hard time." Joy could tell it was time to pull back. She had planted the seeds. That was enough for now. "This wasn't meant to be a knock against Sophie. She needs time to adjust. I simply wanted you to be aware of the situation."

With a friendly pat on Forbes' hand, Joy rose to her feet, leaving him to mull over what she had said. Feeling his eyes on her, she couldn't resist putting a something extra into the natural sway of her hips.

IF JOY HAD known what Forbes thought after their conversation, she wouldn't have been happy. As a woman, she never crossed his mind. Sure, he found her attractive. But in an abstract way. Aaron's mom was a looker. However, it would never occur to him to think of her in a sexual way.

Joy was pleasant. Had a nice smile. She was involved with his father and was Sophie's sister. That was the beginning, middle, and end of the way Forbes thought of her. *When* he thought about her. With his busy schedule, that wasn't often.

With football practice, his work on the ranch, and school starting in a matter of days, he had a lot on his plate. Yet he did find himself considering Sophie's situation. The seed that Joy had planted had taken root—but not in the way she had hoped. Instead of wanting to avoid all contact, he searched for a way to help.

The way Forbes saw it—if Joy was correct—Sophie needed to meet some people her own age. The more friends she made, the less dependent she would be on her sister. She could lean on him instead. Not that she had shown any inclination in that direction.

That was what niggled in his brain. Sophie came across as fiercely independent. Almost to a fault. With a shrug, he dismissed his doubts. After all, Joy knew her sister better than Forbes did.

"Hello. Forbes? Are you in here?"

Forbes looked around, tossing a salt-lick onto the back of the truck next to a half dozen others. The cattle needed the dark-pink blocks during the hot weather. Late summer was dry, and the forecast was for the heat—and lack of rain—to carry well into the fall. The foliage that contained essential nutrients was as sparse as the rain.

They replaced the dark-pink blocks several times a year. Now that he had them loaded, Forbes was headed to the southwest grazing areas. Later in the week, he would cover the northeast.

"Daphne?" Forbes took a bandana from his back pocket, wiping sweat from his face. "What are you doing here? It's pushing ninety in the shade. I thought you'd be getting in as much time at the lake as possible before school starts."

"You left a message that you wanted to talk to me. Here I am."

Like most of the kids in his class, Forbes had known Daphne Parks for most of his life. Blond, brown eyes. Head cheerleader. She was considered the prettiest, most popular girl at Cloverton High. Forbes couldn't argue.

"I told your mom there was no hurry. I was going to stop by tomorrow after football practice."

Smiling, Daphne laid a hand on his chest. She gazed up at him, whispering as if somebody other than the horses could overhear. "I thought I'd save you the bother."

FROM HER SPOT outside the far wall of the barn, Sophie couldn't see what was happening. However, she could hear every word.

Eavesdropping hadn't been Sophie's goal when she and Bailey set out for an after-lunch stroll. Taking the path along the river, they were ready to sit and enjoy a few minutes in the shade.

Leaning her back against the wall, the dog flopping down beside her, Sophie had drifted off to sleep until Forbes woke her when he drove into the barn. But since she hadn't felt like moving—and she had no reason to alert him to her whereabouts—she had kept silent. How could she have anticipated that company would arrive? *Female* company.

To speak up now would be awkward. Silently, Bailey laid his head on her lap. Sophie took that as his sign of agreement.

"WHAT CAN I do for you?" Daphne started walking her fingers down his chest.

Forbes laughed, squeezing Daphne's hand, he stopped it before it ventured any lower. He knew what she had in mind. It wouldn't be the first time they had fooled around. Neither of them looking for anything serious, it had always been fun and easy for them. Another time, another place, Forbes would have taken her up on what she offered.

"*That* isn't why I called."

Not the least bit offended, Daphne leaned against the truck, her tanned legs crossed at the ankles.

"Your loss."

"I'm well aware." Forbes set his gloves on the hood of the truck. Removing his baseball cap, he ran a hand through his sweat-matted hair. "I need a favor."

"Name it."

"Just like that?" Forbes narrowed his eyes. He knew Daphne never made anything that easy.

"I resent your tone." Flicking a non-existent piece of lint from her sundress, Daphne sighed. "We're friends. If you need something that is within my abilities to deliver, it's yours."

"Thank you."

"That said—"

"And the other shoe drops."

"But it's such a pretty shoe." She held out her foot, showing off the strappy sandal.

"What do you want, Daphne?"

"You first." Understanding that she could push Forbes only so far, she said, "I promise. My terms are practically painless."

"It's that part that has me worried. Our idea of painless might not mesh."

Daphne opened her purse, taking out a pack of cinnamon-flavored sugar-free gum. She offered some to Forbes.

"No, thanks."

Thoughtfully, she removed the wrapper, popping a piece into her mouth. "I tell you what. We'll each state what we want. Put it right out on the table. Either we both agree, or it's no deal."

Forbes had to give Daphne credit. She was a shrewd negotiator.

"I'll go first."

"Seems fair," Daphne said, executing a perfect bubble.

"I know there's gossip around town."

"That's like saying the sky is blue. You'll have to be more specific."

Daphne knew exactly what he was talking about. And she knew he knew. The little… Forbes let it pass. After all, he was the one who started this.

"Joy and Sophie Lipton."

"Your father's friend and her sister? That isn't gossip, Forbes. It's like a gift from the Gods. There hasn't been so much speculation since… Come to think of it, I can't think of anything coming close. If I head back to town with a scoop, people will be beating my door down."

"*That's* why you're here?" He was more disappointed than angry. "Jesus, Daphne. Doesn't friendship count for anything?"

"What did I do that was so bad?" Daphne reasoned. "As long as I don't make anything up, who am I hurting?"

Though purely a matter of semantics, Forbes wouldn't make a big deal out of Daphne giving into curiosity. She wasn't the first to casually "stop by" the ranch in search of information. Maeve didn't go into details, just stating that she had dealt with it.

"Sophie Lipton." Forbes would be as brief as possible. "She took a placement test the other day."

"I know."

Naturally. "How did she do?"

"I wish I knew." Daphne sent him a disgruntled look. "Mom invited Principal Breckenridge for dinner last night, but the woman was annoyingly closemouthed."

In spite of himself, Forbes laughed. You had to love a small town.

"Gifted. That's how she did. So well that she'll be starting the tenth grade even though she's had no formal education."

"Rumor has it she was kept chained to her bed. In the basement. And she has to wear sunglasses all the time because her eyes are sensitive to light. And she's so skinny because—"

"Bullshit."

"All of it?" Daphne sounded disappointed.

"Every word."

"That's too bad. New students are hard enough to come by. But when we do get them, they're always so… ordinary."

Forbes rubbed his shoulder, a slight smile curving his lips. "I don't know her very well. But the last thing I'd call Sophie is ordinary."

"Is she pretty?"

"I guess."

"Prettier than me?"

His head falling back, Forbes let out a long-suffering sigh. "You can relax. Sophie won't be a rival to your lofty position as queen bee. She's a kid who could use a break. Which brings me to the favor."

"I don't hang out with sophomores." Daphne's shudder made her horror at the idea perfectly clear.

"You don't have to. All I'm asking is for you to acknowledge Sophie. Say hello. Call out her name as you pass in the hall. Be nice, and the other kids will follow your lead."

"They do look to me for guidance," Daphne preened

Forbes swallowed his laugh. The only thing bigger than Daphne's heart was her ego.

"Then you'll do it?"

"Why not? I'll wave and say hello and steer all the gossip in the right direction. However," Daphne looked Forbes in the eyes. "If your new friend turns out to be a creep, she's on her own."

"She isn't a creep."

"Then there shouldn't be a problem. Now, about your end of the deal."

Forbes braced himself. "Let me have it."

"Take me to the homecoming dance."

"That's it?" He waited for more. When Daphne nodded, Forbes breathed a sigh of relief. "I was expecting something less... ordinary."

"Ordinary? Are you kidding? No girl has ever wrangled you into taking her to a school dance. Never. Not one. This will be my crowning achievement. When we walk into that crepe paper-covered gymnasium, I will be a legend."

"You're overselling, Daphne."

"Maybe. Just a tad. But it *will* be a minor coup." Sidling close, her hand returning to his chest, Daphne smiled like a little girl waiting for a treat. "Do we have a deal?"

"Why not?"

Forbes had never understood why a fuss was made over such things. He avoided the drama by going stag. It saved him the major pain in the ass of trying to fulfill some girl's weird fantasy of the perfect date and the commitment that seemed to go along with it.

One dance. One date. If it helped Sophie, it was a small—and relatively painless—price to pay.

"My dress is royal purple. Buy my corsage with that in mind."

"I can handle a corsage."

"Naturally, we'll be voted king and queen."

Knowing Daphne, Forbes didn't doubt she was right. He supposed it was part of that weird fantasy thing. What the hell. If she wanted her picture taken with a paper crown on her head, Forbes could smile for the camera.

"Is that all? I have work to do."

"For now. I'll fill you in on the details as we get closer to the big night."

That brought Forbes up short. "How many *details* are we talking about?"

"Minor. Miniscule. I promise."

"Fine. You take care of the details. I'll be there." Forbes had committed to taking Daphne. He wouldn't back out. If she wanted to turn it into a circus, he would rather be unpleasantly surprised.

"Don't frown. We'll have fun." Daphne's smile turned provocative, her hand sliding to the fly of his jeans. "Why don't I give you a sneak preview?"

"I don't have time." Forbes groaned when she squeezed his rapidly rising erection.

"From the feel of this," Daphne went to her knees. "It won't take long."

"Daphne." Forbes leaned against the truck, his eyes closing. "This isn't necessary."

"Which is why I want to." Daphne had his jeans around his knees before he put up another token protest. She licked her lips as if she were about to devour the sweetest lollipop ever made. "Believe me. It is my pleasure."

"FOR THE LOVE of—" Sophie whispered with disgust.

Eavesdropping on a conversation—especially one that concerned her—was one thing. Sophie drew the line at audio voyeurism. Putting her finger to her lips, she motioned for Bailey to follow. The dog didn't understand what his owner was doing on the other side of the barn wall, but Sophie thought he looked slightly embarrassed. She didn't blame him.

Once they were clear of all the moans and groans, Sophie quickly put that part of the Forbes and Daphne exchange from her mind. Sex was a tool. Thank God she had never been witness to any of Joy's many conquests—the woman did have some sense of right and wrong. However, Sophie didn't need to see what went on behind closed doors—or not so closed barns—to understood how it worked.

*Quid pro quo.* Apparently—even on a ranch in Eastern Washington—it was the same everywhere.

"Not me, Bailey. Never. If I have to starve. Naked. In the freezing cold. I will die before getting on my knees for any man."

Filled with a sense of self-righteousness, Sophie slipped into the house through the mudroom door. As had become her habit, she detoured through the kitchen, checking the cookie jar. Ginger snaps. Yum. Three should hold her until dinner.

The house was quiet as Sophie made her way to her room. That wasn't unusual for late afternoon. Maeve was in town grocery shopping. Joy was never around. If she couldn't talk Newt into taking her shopping, she disappeared in his SUV. With his credit card. Alone, she returned around six o'clock. If Newt was with her, they rarely returned before one or two in the morning.

Sophie didn't care what they got up to. She had found peace with her guilt over lying to Newt. He was an adult. Capable of making his own decisions. More importantly, he seemed genuinely happy. If it didn't last, it wasn't her fault. She wouldn't waste her time worrying when—for the time being—nothing was wrong.

"Sophie?"

Sophie jumped a foot. She had been so wrapped up in her thoughts—and so certain she was alone in the house—she hadn't noticed Newt walking down the hall.

"Did I startle you?" he asked, stopping next to her.

"I thought everybody was out of the house."

"Joy and Maeve went to town. I had some paperwork to catch up on." Suddenly, Newt looked uncomfortable. "Sophie."

"Was there something you needed me to do?"

"No." He smiled. "You're always up for doing chores. Why is that?"

"I like keeping busy," Sophie shrugged. "Any work on the ranch? It doesn't feel like work."

"I've never seen anybody take to it so quickly. Maybe you were a cowboy in a different life."

Sophie liked that. The cowboy part. But mostly the idea of a different life. She didn't like the one she had. Until now. Before she was born—if she had been given a choice—this was the one she would have picked.

"I have something for you."

Newt held out a box wrapped with a pretty red ribbon. The concept of receiving a gift was such a foreign one that Sophie stared at the package, unsure what she was supposed to do.

"Take it," Newt urged, solving her dilemma.

"I..." Sophie swallowed, searching for the right words. She held the box lightly, not wanting to dent the smooth, white exterior. "What is it?"

Newt reached around her, turning the doorknob. "Open it and find out."

Slowly, Sophie walked across the room, setting the present on her bed. She glanced at Newt. He stood half in, half out, waiting expectantly.

With great care, Sophie slid the satin ribbon to one side not wanting to mess it up. She lifted the lid from the box, then pushed aside a layer of delicate tissue paper.

"It's a dress."

"For your first day of school. I know some of the kids like to dress up a little. Joy picked it out." Newt rambled, watching Sophie closely. "What do you think?"

Sophie knew at first glance that it would be at least three sizes too big. *Thank you, Joy.* A non-descript brown cotton. At least it was soft. She took it from the box, moving to the mirror. It wasn't ugly. Or pretty. She decided it was the kind of dress a person wore if they wanted to blend into the scenery.

"Well?"

Tears filled Sophie's eyes, causing the expectant light in Newt's to fade. Quickly, it was replaced by worry.

"You don't like it. It's awfully big looking. I guess Joy made a mistake with the size."

Clutching the dress, Sophie took a hesitant step forward. Then another. She threw her arms around Newt's waist, burrowing close.

"It's perfect," Sophie said, her cheek against his warm chest. And she meant it. It wouldn't have mattered what was in the box. The fact that Newt had gotten it for her made it the most beautiful dress ever made.

Newt didn't hesitate to hug her back. To him, giving affection came naturally. He had no way of knowing it wasn't the same for Sophie. This was a first for her. To her surprise, it felt good. Right. Like something she could actually get used to.

"I wanted you to have something nice." Newt patted Sophie's back. "If you want to return it, I won't be offended."

"I wouldn't do that." Though it was tempting. The thought had come from Newt. Joy was responsible for the actual garment.

"Think about it." Newt brushed her hair from her face before stepping back. "The owner of the shop in town is a friend of mine. She'll be happy to let you exchange the dress for something else. And while you're there." He took an envelope from his back pocket. "Buy some other things. Jeans. Shirts. Shoes. Whatever you need. A girl your age should do her own shopping."

With one last smile, Newt closed the door behind him. Sophie wiped her eyes before opening the envelope. What she saw made her legs go all wobbly. She collapsed onto the bed. *Money*. With shaking fingers, she removed the bills. New, crisp twenties.

*Holy crap*. With a laugh, she fell onto her back, tossing the money into the air. She ignored the twinge of guilt. She hadn't asked. Newt wanted her to have it. A gift. Freely given. No strings attached. Sophie vowed to work hard on the ranch. Whatever needed doing, she would do it.

But for now? Sophie would buy what she wanted. Brand new. Never been worn. And all her own.

Sophie gathered up the money. She returned it to the envelope, hiding it where nobody—Joy in particular—would find it. It was almost too much to believe. New clothes. *And* school started on Monday.

Never mind what came before. As far as Sophie was concerned, her life began now.

# CHAPTER NINE

"THIS IS ALL your fault."

"I take full blame."

"Good. Now, move your butt. I don't want to miss the team running onto the field."

Sophie laughed, picking up the pace. Jogging next to her was her best friend, Tory Crandall. They were on their way to watch the Cloverdale Cavaliers play for the state football championship. A few short months ago, both ideas would have been impossible to conceive.

High school football. And a best friend.

It had all gone by in a blink. Yet Sophie could remember each moment—each first—with crystal-clear clarity.

The first day of school had been a rollercoaster of emotions. It began with her putting on the new skirt and blouse she had purchased. Surprisingly, Joy had let it pass when she found out about the money Newt gave Sophie. Her mother was too busy spending as much of his money as she could. She barely gave Sophie a second thought.

"Have a good time." Maeve had called out. She had done her bit by providing a huge first day of school pancake breakfast. "Forbes. You be sure to watch out for Sophie."

"You don't have to." Sophie followed Forbes into the garage.

"I don't have to what?" he asked.

"Watch out for me."

"You won't need me for long. In a week, two at the most, it will feel like you've been going to school all your life."

Sophie couldn't imagine that happening. She would settle for her nerves ratcheting down a notch or two. There had been no mention of what she overheard at the barn. Mostly because she

111

didn't want Forbes to know she had been witness to his sexual escapades.

Sophie had given the other part a lot of thought. At first, she was angry. Was she so pathetic he had to strike a bargain with his girlfriend? If Daphne didn't smooth the way, would she end up a social pariah? An outcast? Destined to eat her lunch alone, avoided like the plague? Sophie managed to work herself into quite a frenzy.

However, as she calmed down, Sophie could look at it more reasonably. Forbes wanted to help. It was thoughtful. Kind. She owed him her thanks, not her wrath. She knew it would be hard enough fitting in. Any help she could get was a good thing.

They wove past Newt's SUV and the medium-sized dark-blue sedan that belonged to Maeve. Sophie had never been inside the garage. It was huge. And oddly luxurious for a place they used to park cars. The walls were a creamy beige with wood trim. And the heather gray-stamped concrete floors were so clean they practically gleamed.

"How do you keep it so dirt-free in here?"

"Maeve. She has a polishing obsession—and an eagle eye. When we get home, we sweep any tracks we brought in with us."

Sounded fair. Sophie liked that Maeve was a stickler. It meant she cared. She took pride in maintaining the Branson home.

"Jump in. I'll drive you to school every morning. I'm afraid that when I have practice, you'll have to ride the bus home," Forbes told her apologetically.

Riding a school bus. Sophie refrained from rubbing her hands together in anticipation. Forbes would never understand, but it was another first that Sophie looked forward to.

Forbes stopped beside a dark-red car. Sophie knew nothing about such things, but she thought it looked old. Not rundown, but shiny as a new penny and not a dent in sight. Vintage. That was the word.

"What kind of car is this?" Sophie asked, sliding into the passenger seat.

"A Ford Mustang. 1964. The first year it was made. It belonged to my mother."

Sophie heard the pride in Forbes' voice. Pride tinged with sadness.

"I see pictures of your mother all over the house. She was beautiful."

The car's motor sprang instantly to life. Music—something Sophie didn't recognize—pulsed from the radio. Shifting gears, Forbes backed out of the garage.

"Mom was gorgeous. Inside and out," he said, once they headed away down the driveway. He stopped at the end, looking right, then left, before pulling onto the main road. "I miss her every day."

The idea was unimaginable. Not that she wanted Joy dead. But if she were gone—any place that Sophie wasn't—she wouldn't be missed. Finding out that Forbes felt the exact opposite about his mother made Sophie curious to hear more.

"Do you mind talking about her?"

"Not at all. I don't get a lot of opportunities. Be warned. Once I start, I might talk your ear off. Are you sure you want to take the chance?"

"Yes. Please."

Sophie listened intently. It wasn't the stories Forbes told—though he made her laugh with many of them—it was the look on his face. He loved his mother. Present tense. She imagined that no matter how many years passed, that would never change.

"I envy you."

Forbes glance at Sophie. "Don't you have any good memories about your mother?"

Without hesitation, Sophie shook her head. She couldn't think of a single good time she had shared with Joy. Not one. How sad was that? It would have been easy to resent Forbes. Instead, she was grateful that he was willing to share his mother with her. That was how it felt. That while they were driving along, as she listened intently, Ella Branson became her mother, too.

"Here we are. Cloverdale High School." Parking, Forbes turned off the engine. "Scared?"

"A little. What?" Sophie asked when he grinned.

"I was thinking how much has changed since we first met. You would have socked me in the eye before giving me the time of day, let alone admitting that you were frightened."

Because she knew it was true—and she didn't appreciate him reminding her—Sophie shot Forbes a dirty look. "I might still give you a punch if you don't watch it."

"That's what I was looking for. There is nothing like somebody riling you up to put some color in your cheeks. Rosy pink suits you much better than stark white."

Sophie raised a hand to her face. "Was it so bad you had to piss me off?"

"I probably could've found a different method. But it wouldn't have been as much fun." With a wink, Forbes left the car, rushing around to help her out.

"I've never seen anybody do this." Sophie took his hand, letting Forbes pull her to her feet. "Outside of an old movie."

"It's a special occasion. After today, you'll be on your own."

On her own. That was what she had been all her life, and what she expected when she stepped through the doors leading to Cloverdale High School. However, that wasn't what happened. Perhaps Daphne's acceptance was the key. Or the fact that Forbes personally escorted her to her first class. Whatever the reason, Sophie found fitting in easier than she had expected.

The sailing wasn't smooth. Forbes had predicted it would take her a week. Maybe two. A month was more like it. In that time, she figured out that the learning part of school was wonderful. Books. Teachers. Tests. Sophie absorbed it like a thirsty sponge. Even math. Thank goodness Forbes was a wiz in that department. He eased her through some initially confusing homework.

The social part turned out to be trickier. It took Sophie time to figure out how to interact with so many hormone-laden teenagers. They weren't as mysterious as she imagined them to be. Some were nice. Some were god-awful. And a lot were somewhere in between. Once she had that revelation, things became less confusing.

Tory Crandall helped. From day one, she took Sophie under her wing. Tory wasn't the prettiest. Or the most popular. She was an average student. Average height. Medium-brown hair. Medium-brown eyes. Average in every way. Until one got to know her. Tory had a wicked sense of humor—most of which she directed toward herself. She and Sophie clicked immediately, becoming the best of friends.

Sophie was the one who suggested they attend the first home football game. Tory hadn't been against it. Boring, was the word she used. Stupid jocks bashing each other in the quest of moving a weirdly-shaped ball up and down a field. *No, thank you.* But after one game, Tory was hooked. She became the team's biggest fan. Sophie was there to support Forbes. She enjoyed the camaraderie of cheering with her fellow students. For Tory, it became life and death. Her friend took it so far as to begin dating the Cavaliers' starting right tackle. With a great big grin, Tory claimed she did it for the good of the team. She helped him maintain his focus.

"Come on." Tory tugged on Sophie's coat. "Stop lagging behind. We're in the middle of a parking lot. In the middle of December. What could you possibly find to daydream about?"

Sophie shook off her thoughts, rushing through the packed stadium to take her seat beside Tory. They were in the Cloverdale High School booster section. Students. Parents. Anybody who loved the team. All were bundled in their school colors of blue and white, ready to cheer their boys on to victory.

Near the top of the stands sat a proud Newt. Next to him, sat Joy. To the casual observer, she looked like she was having a good time. But Sophie was an unwilling expert on the *Moods of Joy*. The signs were there if one knew how to interpret them. Her mother's interest began to fray at the edges. Just a little bit. The wear and tear weren't serious—yet. But if something weren't done immediately, her eye would soon wander to another man. And another. And another. She couldn't help herself. Joy liked who she was, and she didn't see any reason to change.

When it came right down to it, nobody could do anything. No amount of attention or money from Newt would help. If Sophie broached the subject, it would be like throwing gasoline on a badly banked fire.

As if sensing the attention, Joy met Sophie's gaze. Slowly, her lips moved into a sly, mocking smile. It seemed to say, *you knew this day would come. You've gotten as much out of it as I have. Maybe more. Be glad it lasted this long.*

"Here comes the team," Tory yelled, pulling Sophie to her feet. "We're going to bring that trophy home to Cloverdale. Just wait and see."

*Wait and see.* Sophie thought it was the only option she had.


"What a game!" Newt hugged Sophie close. "Forbes was on fire. MVP. There's a college scholarship in his future. No doubt about it."

Sophie nodded rather than shout over the still-buzzing crowd. The game had been close, but in the last few minutes, Forbes led his team down the field for the winning touchdown. Cloverdale had their state championship, just as Tory predicted.

"Would you and Tory like to ride back with us?"

"No, thanks, Newt. We want to go back on the bus with the rest of the students."

"I don't blame you. It's more fun to celebrate with your classmates than a couple of old-timers."

"Speaking of which, where *is* Joy?"

"She needed to use the bathroom." Newt gave a good-natured sigh. "I told her the lines would be brutal, but she couldn't wait. I'm going to meet her at the south exit."

Maybe it was undue paranoia, but Sophie had a bad feeling. Joy loved to take chances. It gave her a rush to fool around in a public place. The risk of getting caught added to the excitement.

Amid the whoops and hollers of a group of rowdy teenagers, Sophie made her way to the waiting bus.

Gazing out the window, she crossed her fingers that at that moment, all Joy was doing was taking an innocent pee. But when her mother was involved, it was rarely that simple—or innocent.

"I'VE ASKED JOY to marry me."

Forbes rubbed the sleep out of his eyes, shaking his head. His father announcing his upcoming marriage wasn't something a guy heard every day. At six thirty on a Sunday morning. The one day Forbes slept in. The news was difficult to assimilate when he was still in bed, half asleep and still a little buzzed from his first Saturday night party since football started.

"That's... great?" Forbes hadn't meant for it to come out as a question. Blame it on too much cheap beer.

"I know this must come as a surprise."

Propping himself up on his elbow, Forbes watched his father pace across the bedroom floor. Newt was still in his pajama bottoms, robe, and slippers. His hair, already mussed from a night's sleep, wasn't helped as Newt repeatedly ran an agitated hand through it.

"Joy has lived here for almost five months. If I'd given it any thought, I guess marriage seemed inevitable. I take it she said yes."

"It's crazy. I never thought I'd remarry. Your mother was the love of my life. Joy is..."

"You don't have to explain, Dad."

"I get looks from people in town. Friends. Acquaintances. None of them have found the nerve to ask. If they did, I don't know what I'd say." Newt took a seat on the edge of the bed. "It's love, Forbes. I wouldn't marry her otherwise. But it isn't the same as with your mother. It couldn't be. Ella will always be in my heart."

For a long time after his mother's death, Forbes wanted to believe it was a mistake. He sat at the funeral. He knew she had been buried. He watched as they lowered the coffin into the ground. But that didn't stop him from wishing it wasn't true.

Slowly, he found acceptance—if not peace—with the fact that his mother would never coming back. It took his father a lot longer.

"Nothing can erase Mom's memory. But she would want you to be happy."

"I think so too."

The silence that followed was brief, though not the least bit awkward. Newt was lost in his thoughts. Forbes waited, still absorbing the news.

"Joy has always dreamed of going to Paris."

"Sounds like a good place for a honeymoon," Forbes nodded.

"We thought we would leave today. Stop in Las Vegas. Get married. Then continue on to France."

"Wow." Forbes didn't know what else to say.

"Joy loves spur of the moment things. I'm all for skipping the planning and the guests and the big day. My only worry is you."

"Me? It's your wedding."

"You won't mind missing it?"

"I wasn't there the first time."

Newt smiled. "Seriously, Forbes. What do you think? We won't be here for Christmas. Or New Year's."

This time of year had never been the same since his mother's death. She was the one who loved to decorate and entertain. *She* made it special. Still, it would be strange not to celebrate with his father. Forbes would leave for college next fall. Depending on where he went, it might not be practical to make it home for the holidays. One more sign that he was becoming an adult. Now was a good time to prove it.

"We'll open presents when you get back."

"It won't be the same." Clearly, Newt wanted this, but he didn't want to hurt his son.

"Answer one thing. Are you sure?"

"Yes."

"Then get packing. Call the travel agent."

"I already did." Newt shrugged. "Just in case. Our flight to Vegas leaves at noon. We'll finalize the rest of the itinerary from there."

"I'm impressed." And slightly dizzy. "Have a good time, Dad. Take lots of pictures."

"We will." Newt sighed, his shoulders sagging. "Thank you for making this so easy for me."

Forbes shook his father's outstretched hand. "You don't have to worry about the ranch. Mike, Jerry, and I'll look out for everything."

"And Sophie."

"Sure. We'll keep an eye on the kid."

"I meant, she can help out. Sophie loves working on the ranch, Forbes. Make certain you include her."

The mention of Sophie reminded Forbes of the conversation he had with Joy just before the start of the school year.

"Does Sophie know about the wedding?" Forbes asked cautiously.

"Joy is telling her now." Newt patted Forbes on the shoulder. "Don't look like that. I'm sure Sophie will be happy for Joy and me."

Forbes hoped so. Sophie had grown up a lot. She was thriving at school. She had friends. But he had no way to anticipate her reaction to the news that her sister was getting married. If, as Joy had said, Sophie was prone to jealousy, this might set her off.

Things were good between him and Sophie. They didn't spend a lot of time together because neither had a lot of spare time. Their relationship had fallen into a brother/sister dynamic. Forbes didn't want to rock that boat. But if he had to, he was prepared to do whatever it took to make sure nothing endangered his father's future happiness.

"NEWT AND I are getting married."

"No."

119

"Yes."

Joy held out her hand, the overhead light catching on the facets of the biggest diamond ring Sophie had ever seen. Not that she had seen very many. But even to her untrained eye, the one that Joy sported was huge.

"You have to give it back."

Sophie continued to make her bed, her movements quick and sure. But her mind raced. She had played out a lot of possible ways for all of this to end. Joy and Newt married? *That* hadn't been one of them.

"Why would I do that? I've found my big, fat, easily manipulated, golden goose, little girl. And I'm holding on for dear life."

"If you don't call off the engagement, I'll tell Newt everything."

"You're bluffing." Joy took a seat. She crossed her legs, arranging the silky material of her black negligee. "Pull me down, and you go with me. You like your life too much."

Taking a deep breath, Sophie straightened, turning to face Joy. Her mother was right. If Newt knew the truth, everything would end. School. Her friends. The ranch. They would all be gone. She had no idea what would become of her. In all likelihood, wherever she ended up, it would be as bad, or worse, than before. It was a frightening proposition.

Sophie had pushed her conscience aside when Newt played the fool over his girlfriend. That was bad enough. But the thought of him making Joy his wife? That was the last straw. She could never live with herself if she didn't speak up.

"Newt won't listen to you, Sophie."

As much as she wanted to, Sophie couldn't argue. Newt was so far gone; his brain had turned to mush—at least as far as Joy was concerned.

"I'll go to Forbes."

Joy, with a smile that held more pity than worry, walked to the door.

120

"You may be *gifted* in the classroom. But my skills have nothing to do with brains." She had no need to elaborate. Sophie knew exactly what Joy meant. "Forbes is a man. In that arena, I will kick your ass every time. Think about that before you try something stupid. You'll be the loser. Not me. By the way, Newt and I are getting married today. In Las Vegas. Sorry you won't be there to catch the bouquet."

With a quiet click of the door, Joy exited the room.

One way or another, Joy always won. But why did it have to be that way? Sophie refused to let hopelessness close in on her. She would talk to Forbes. He would take her side over Joy's.

Wouldn't he?

MONTHS AGO, JOY had laid the ground work, just in case Sophie decided to stage a coup. Now was the time to reap what she had sown—so to speak. But how to get to Forbes first was the question.

As she walked down the hall, she met Newt as he came out of Forbes' room, and found her answer.

"How did it go?" Newt asked, taking her hand.

"Sophie was surprised. But happy for us," Joy told the lie without a second thought. "How about Forbes?"

"The same. It looks like you can start planning a wedding."

"Wonderful. Will Forbes be coming down for breakfast?"

Newt chuckled. "After a long shower and some aspirin. He tried to hide it, but I think my son overindulged a bit last night."

Good, Joy thought. The longer Forbes was in the shower, the more time it gave her to act on the plan forming.

"I should start packing."

"Don't worry about taking very much. I'll buy you whatever you need when we get to Paris."

*Damn straight you will.* Joy waved at Newt as he headed downstairs, her smile beaming. The second he was out of sight, she burst into action.

Heading to her room, she pictured the perfect outfit to wear. Something in a sympathetic black. And the perfect words to say. Emotional but not over the top.

If Sophie thought she could stop the wedding, she was in for a big surprise. Joy had waited a long time for a chance like this. Nothing—no one—would get in her way.

Once that platinum band was on her finger, Sophie could spill her guts until the end of time. It wouldn't make a bit of difference.


PULLING ON HIS right sock, Forbes ran a hand through his damp hair. He felt like a big breakfast—a sure sign that a hangover wasn't in his future. Dreaming of scrambled eggs, bacon, and jam-covered toast, he heard a knock on his door.

Eyes flashing with distress, Joy stood in the hall. She was dressed in black. Leggings. Suede ankle boots. A heavy cable knit sweater. Her hair was pulled back, held by a clip at the base of her neck. Her makeup—as always—was impeccable. Except for the trail of mascara down one cheek.

"I'm sorry to disturb you in your room. But I need to talk to you in private. May I come in?"

Forbes stepped back. He closed the door after Joy rushed in.

"Are you crying?" Joy and his father couldn't have argued already.

Her back to him, Forbes couldn't see Joy biting her lip, scrunching up her eyes, willing liquid to form. To her regret, Joy didn't have the talent that allowed her to summon tears at a moment's notice. Her eyes were perfectly dry. But Forbes wouldn't find out. Keeping her face averted, she sniffled. Loudly.

"Sophie doesn't want me to marry your father. She..." He heard a catch in Joy's voice. "She said some terrible things."

"What kind of things?"

"I don't want to repeat them. She told me that if I didn't break the engagement, she would tell Newt nasty lies that would turn him against me."

Forbes was torn. How could he dispute Joy's accusations? She obviously was distraught. Crying. However, he found it hard to believe Sophie would say such things. It went against everything he knew about her.

"Are you sure you didn't misinterpret Sophie's meaning?"

"I was there, Forbes. Her words were perfectly clear. Ugly, but indisputable."

"I'll speak with her."

"She'll lie." Brushing at her cheeks, careful to keep her head down.

"Leave it to me. You and Dad will be on that plane. Sophie doesn't have the power to stop you." Forbes gently took hold of Joy's arm, leading her across the room. "Go to your room. Splash some cold water on your face. And stop worrying."

"Thank you, Forbes." Joy gave him a tentative smile, her chin low. "I didn't want to tell your father. He's so proud of Sophie's achievements. I don't want to upset him unless absolutely necessary."

"I agree."

It wasn't until Joy was out of eyesight that Forbes realized he had a death grip on the doorframe. He took a deep breath. In and out. In and out. Trying his best to center his emotions. Confronting Sophie in anger wasn't a good idea. He didn't know what she would say or do. How she would react. Playing football had taught him how to stay calm in the eye of a storm. No matter what, he wouldn't lose his temper.

"I need to talk to you."

Forbes tightened his grip. It was the only thing that kept him from jumping out of his socks. Somehow, Sophie had snuck up on him. Holy shit. It felt as if they had picked that morning for a round of musical chairs. Only the players were moving from room to room.

"Come on in."

Sophie was dressed in jeans, thick socks, and a plaid flannel shirt. Forbes knew she ate regularly. He could bear witness to the fact that her stomach seemed to be a bottomless pit. Yet for some reason, she never put on any weight. This morning, standing in the middle of his bedroom, she seemed slighter than usual. Tall. Long legged. But delicate. Vulnerable. It made what he had to say all the harder.

"We have to stop the wedding."

"Jesus, Sophie." Forbes ran a hand over his face. So much for the slightest hope that Joy was mistaken. "It's going to happen. You don't have to worry. You won't lose your sister just because she's married."

"Lose my—" Sophie clenched her fists. "You've spoken to Joy."

"I don't know what you said to her. I don't care," Forbes interrupted before Sophie could launch her attack. "Joy was in tears. How does that make you feel?"

"Joy hasn't shed a genuine tear in her entire life."

Forbes tamped down his impatience. "I don't know what the problem is between the two of you. I—"

"What did Joy say?"

"That you cling to her. You don't want to share her with anybody."

Sophie snorted.

"And that you made up a bunch of lies to tell my father."

When Sophie didn't answer, Forbes couldn't resist taunting her. "Aren't you going to tell me that you never lie? That was your claim when we first met."

"I lie."

"Joy was telling me the truth?" Forbes wished that Sophie had an explanation. A viable excuse. "Why?"

"Please, Forbes. I know you can talk your father out of this. At least postpone the wedding. Your father has been so good to me. I'm sorry I let things get this far. But I'm sure Joy will show her true colors sooner than later. She's already—"

"Enough!" Forbes grabbed Sophie by the arm, giving her a shake. "You selfish little bitch. My father is happy. Joy is the reason. Stop trying to ruin it. Understand?"

The look of hurt and betrayal in Sophie's eyes almost weakened his resolve. Almost, but not quite. Forbes would put his father first every time—no exceptions.

"This isn't a game, Sophie?"

"Sure it is." Sophie pulled away. "And Joy wins every time."

"What does that mean?"

"You don't want to know, remember?" Sadness had replaced the hurt in Sophie's eyes, and, in spite of everything, it twisted Forbes' guts into a knot. She held his gaze. "I won't say another word. Not to you. Not to Newt. Especially not to Joy."

"Good. That would be for the best."

"Just one question? If you don't mind? Something for you to think about."

"Okay."

"What if I'm right?"

# CHAPTER TEN

CHRISTMAS CAME AND went. New Year's. January. Valentine's Day. As February ended and March came in like a lion with a major snowstorm, Sophie had no problem keeping her word to Forbes. She didn't speak a single word to Newt. Or Joy.

It was easy. They weren't around.

The Paris honeymoon had turned into a full-blown tour of Europe. France. England. Germany. Belgium. Spain. Portugal. One postcard after another with basically the same message.

*Having a great time. Glad you're not here.*

"What is that man thinking?" Maeve asked with a shake of her head, sliding a stack of pancakes onto Sophie's plate.

They were alone in the kitchen on a snowy Saturday morning. Mike and Jerry had finished their breakfast and had left to put out feed for the cattle wintering on the south range. Forbes was down at the barn, tending the horses.

"Newt must be having a good time," Sophie shrugged. After buttering each cake liberally, she added a healthy amount of warmed maple syrup.

"That woman has him bewitched, damn her." Maeve patted Sophie on the shoulder. "No offense, honey."

"None taken."

Sophie didn't add her two cents worth, but silently, she agreed with Maeve. Bewitched? She thought it as good a term as any. However, Joy's powers had always been of a temporary nature. Until Newt.

"Newt belongs back here. On the ranch. Forbes could talk him into returning, but that boy won't listen to a word I have to say on the subject."

"He wants his father to be happy. I can't blame him for that."

Sophie repeated the mantra to herself over and over in an attempt to find peace with what Forbes had said to her. She understood. And she wasn't blameless. She had lied by omission. Over and over again. But when he called her a selfish bitch? It hurt. Her tender feelings turned to anger. Though some of the red haze had faded, she couldn't entirely let it drop.

"This house is empty ninety percent of the time. My feet echo through the halls. If it weren't for you, I wouldn't have a reason to stay." Maeve diligently scrubbed the already-gleaming countertop. "Jerry and Mike appreciate my cooking, but they are more than capable of taking care of themselves. Between his social life and whatever sport is in season—I can never keep track—Forbes is never around anymore."

"I'm sorry."

"It isn't your fault, sweet girl."

That was the problem. It *was* Sophie's fault. Her happiness had come at a price she hadn't anticipated. Knowing she could have put an end to Newt and Joy before they got beyond the wild weekend stage sat like a solid lump in her stomach. One that grew with each passing day.

If Sophie could go back to the day she first met Newt— knowing what would happen—she wished she could say she would do things differently. How could she? Six months ago, she was starving. For food. For knowledge. For friends. For the tiniest bit of kindness and affection. Now, she had all of those things. Only a saint would have the strength to not only give them up but change the past, so none of it had happened.

Sophie was a lot of things. A saint wasn't one of them.

"I'm the reason Forbes is gone all the time."

Maeve gave a dismissive snort. "It's been getting worse with each passing year. Football. Basketball. Baseball in the spring. Around the time puberty hit, Forbes spent more time with his friends. Those kids drove to each other's house and back long before they had a license making it legal. You aren't the reason, Sophie. He's been stretching the apron strings for a long time."

"It's more than that," Sophie insisted. "We had a... disagreement."

Talk about your neon-emblazoned definition of an understatement. However, it was as much of an explanation as Sophie could manage.

"Is that why you started taking the bus every morning instead of riding with him?"

Sophie nodded, pushing the last few bites of her pancakes around the plate.

"That little stinker." Tossing the sponge into the sink, Maeve placed her fists on her hips. "If men are supposedly so tough, why are their egos so easily bruised? You should have said something sooner. I'll set Forbes straight the next time he bothers to honor us with his presence."

"No! Please, Maeve. Don't say anything to him."

Sophie didn't want Forbes to think she had put Maeve up to it. Not that the housekeeper could help. Things had gone from cool to cold, to downright glacial. For any kind of thaw, one of them would have to make the first move.

One of them *not* named Sophie.

"I'll keep my thoughts to myself. Lord knows I've gotten good at it since the day your sister arrived. Thank goodness you came with her." Maeve poured herself a coffee before joining Sophie at the kitchen table. "I was dreading when Forbes graduated in June. The way things stand, it feels like he's already gone."

Maeve had been good to her. Better than good. Sophie had been dropped in the woman's lap—unasked for and unexpected. Instead of treating her like an interloper, Maeve fed Sophie. She taught her to make cookies. To knead bread. And prepare a casserole out of leftovers that in anybody else's less-capable hands, never would have gone together.

Because of the housekeeper's kindness—and because she had come to genuinely like the woman—Sophie knew what she had to do. Though it was a mighty bitter pill to swallow.

"I'll talk to him."

"That would be best." Maeve smiled.

Suspicious, Sophie raised an eyebrow. "Have I just been played?"

"Don't feel bad. I've been doing this a lot longer than you. Would you like anything else?"

"No. Thanks."

Unlike when she first arrived, Sophie had her saturation point. These days, instead of ten or twelve, six pancakes were her limit. Of course, it helped to know another big meal was only a few hours away.

Maeve carried Sophie's plate to the sink, scraping the scraps into the garbage disposal. "You'll feel better once you and Forbes clear the air."

"I can't make any promises."

"I have every faith in you."

Sophie finished clearing the table, filling the dishwasher with the rest of the breakfast dishes. When Forbes was at home, he spent most of his time at the bunkhouse with Mike and Jerry. So, task number one? Get Forbes alone? Then what? Sophie let out a heartfelt sigh. She had no idea.


"WHAT THE HELL is wrong with you?" Forbes demanded when the baseball he lobbed at Aaron plonked his friend on the top of the head. "Ever hear the term 'keep your eye on the ball?' This is where it comes from."

"Ever heard the term 'stick it up your ass?' I have no idea where it comes from but probably from a situation a lot like this one."

Aaron retrieved the ball, whipping it back at Forbes. Walking across the gymnasium, he sprawled onto the bleachers, the whole time attempting to rub the sting from his head.

The March morning was cold. Unlike the pros down in sunny Arizona and Florida, the Cloverdale baseball team's version of spring training performed drills on the hardwood normally reserved for indoor sports. Practice had ended thirty minutes ago, but neither Forbes nor Aaron had felt like heading home. Each lost in their own thoughts, they tossed the ball back and forth.

"If you wanted to quit, all you had to do was say the word. Sometime before I plunked you would have been nice."

"I wasn't concentrating," Aaron mumbled.

"No shit." Forbes took a seat, stretching out his long legs. Sweats and t-shirts were their usual practice attire. In deference to their indoor location, they had swapped cleats for sneakers. "You want to tell me what's crawled up your ass. Whatever it is has been hibernating for over a week. I'd say the sucker could use some air."

Aaron snorted. It was as close to a laugh as his friend had produced in way too long.

"I'll spill if you will."

"Me?"

"Yes, you." Aaron slapped Forbes on the arm with his catcher's glove. "I'm not the only one with something lodged up my backside. Only yours has been there a damn sight longer."

Forbes swiveled until he was stretched out on the wooden bench, his hands behind his head. For several moments, he stared in silence at the florescent light-littered ceiling.

"When did life get so complicated?" he began. "I miss the days when my biggest problem was that summer vacation never lasted long enough."

"Summer was the best," Aaron agreed. "We could play outside for hours and hours. Swimming. Biking."

"Those were the days."

"Cindy broke up with me."

The nostalgic smile fell from Forbes' lips. He jackknifed to a sitting position.

"What? When?"

"About a week ago."

That explained a lot. Aaron's normally laidback disposition had headed south about then. It had been impossible to ignore.

"Now the tough one. Why?"

"I cheated on her."

Forbes rubbed a hand over his face. They could long for simpler times all they wanted, but lost love and infidelity were definitely grown-up problems. One more piece of evidence that there was no going back.

"Who with?"

Clenching his fists heavenward, Aaron let out a long, loud wail of frustration. "Why is that the first question out of everybody's mouth?"

"Cindy?" Forbes had to assume that Aaron's longtime—recently ex-girlfriend—was the other part of *everybody*.

Miserable, Aaron nodded. "It doesn't matter who. I told Cindy that it didn't mean anything."

"What if the tables were turned? Would you like to walk down the halls wondering which guy she had been with? Some fuckwad smirking because he had sex with your girl before you did?"

"Are you trying to make me feel lower than I already do?"

"I'm trying to help you see it from Cindy's point of view. She's hurting. *You* hurt her. Try not to rub any extra salt in her wounds."

"The girl I had sex with doesn't go to our school."

"There's still a chance that Cindy could—"

"They won't meet." Aaron rounded on Forbes, his eyes blazing. "Okay? They don't know each other."

"No need to bite my head off."

"Count yourself lucky. I feel like punching you in the face."

"Thanks a lot."

"It isn't personal. I've had the urge since Cindy kicked my ass to the curb."

"I won't ask why you did it."

"That was Cindy's second question."

"Please tell me you didn't put the blame on her."

"I'm not a complete idiot." Aaron frowned. "Though now that you mention it—"

Forbes knew he was supposed to have his best friend's back—part of an unwritten code. Any other time, his support would have been a given. However, he had known Cindy as long as he could remember. She was the sweetest girl he knew. Generous to a fault. With a smile that could light up the gloomiest of days. He wouldn't sit silently by while she was thrown under the bus.

"Cindy wasn't ready to have sex. You knew it. Accepted it. Claimed you were okay with waiting. If that changed—if you couldn't keep your dick in your pants—you should have broken up with her. Then you could have dipped your wick without any consequences. Except for a possible STD."

"I used a condom, asshole."

"That's something." Forbes gazed—unseeing—across the empty gymnasium. "You know it was a mistake. And it won't happen again. Right?"

"Absolutely not."

"Then why the hell didn't you keep it to yourself?"

Aaron hung his head, his hands clasped behind his neck. When he spoke, he no longer sounded angry. Tortured was the best word to describe it.

"I thought a confession was the right way to go. Now I realize that my main goal was to make myself feel better. Cindy is so understanding. So forgiving. I…"

"You thought she would take you in her arms and tell you everything would be okay."

*Jesus.* Forbes blew out a long breath. *The man lived in a deluded dream world.*

"She cried, Forbes. Quiet tears. They ran down her cheeks, her eyes staring at me as if I'd ripped her heart out." When he looked at his big, wide-palmed hands, they shook. "Maybe I did. I'd rather she had hit me with a sledgehammer. *That* kind of pain I could deal with."

"Do you want platitudes or the hard, honest truth?"

Aaron braced himself, giving Forbes a short nod. "Let me have it."

"You fucked up. Literally and figuratively. Cindy should roast your nuts over an open fire—with you still attached. She should forget you ever lived. Burn your memory from her consciousness. Find somebody better. At this point? That wouldn't be hard."

The only sound Aaron made was a whimper muffled by the fact that his face was buried in his hands.

"All that said, I believe—because she loves you and she is who she is—Cindy will forgive you. Eventually."

"You do? Really?"

Hope—even without any real evidence of its existence—was better than a double dose of Prozac.

"Give it time. And Cindy space. If you're lucky. *And* you keep your nose clean. I predict she'll be your date at our prom."

"It's going to be a long, lonely three months."

"That's what sports are for." Forbes flipped Aaron the baseball. This time, he caught it with ease.

Heading toward the locker room, Aaron slung his arm around Forbes' shoulders.

"If you were my girlfriend, how long until you forgave me?"

"Me?" Forbes grinned. "Never. I would hang your roasted nuts on my rearview mirror for the world to see."

For the first time all afternoon, Aaron laughed. "Gee, thanks."

Forbes chuckled. "No problem, buddy. That's what friends are for."


COLD DIDN'T BEGIN to describe the weather. So much worse. Arctic. Frigid. Half asleep and shivering, Sophie checked the end of her nose, expecting to find an icicle instead. Nope. But a near thing.

Snuggling deeper under the covers, she checked the digital clock near her bed. Or she tried. The screen was dark. Next, exposing as little skin as possible, she tried turning on the lamp that sat on the end table. Nothing. She wasn't an expert, but it didn't take an electrical engineer to deduce the problem. The power was out. Sophie felt her body temperature dropping by the second.

Bailey was curled at the foot of the bed. Snoring lightly, he seemed happily oblivious to the lack of heat.

She had several options readily available to her. She could stay as she was. In reality, the chances of her freezing to death before morning were slight to none. However, even if she survived, she didn't have to spend the rest of the night miserable and sleepless. Gathering extra blankets from the closet and heavy socks from the top drawer of the dresser, she would warm up. Eventually.

Rather than wait, Sophie rolled out of bed, bracing herself. Yikes. It had to be below zero. The house was equipped with an emergency generator. According to Maeve, it was supposed to automatically come on in the case of a power outage. Obviously, that hadn't happened. Hopping from rug to rug—avoiding the hardwood floor—Sophie made quick work of grabbing what she needed. The socks. Her fleecy robe. Her Christmas gift from Maeve, a hand-knitted hat and matching half gloves done in a cheery red yarn. Sophie considered changing her pajamas bottoms for sturdier jeans but didn't want to take the time.

"Are you coming with me?"

Lifting his head, Bailey sighed. Content where he was, he didn't understand all the fuss. But without Sophie, the bed just wasn't the same. The picture on the wall—a painting of the original homestead—rattled from the force of Bailey's paws hitting the floor. Wide awake, he trailed behind Sophie as she pulled a thick quilt from the closet, on her heels as she hurried from the room.

The house was pitch black. Using her memory, she kept one hand on the wall as she maneuvered down the hall, before carefully descending the staircase.

Maeve stayed the night at her sister's place in Cloverdale. Sophie hadn't seen hide nor hair of Forbes. He rarely spent a Saturday night at home. That meant in all likelihood, she was on her own.

Entering the kitchen, Sophie felt her way along the counter, finding the drawer by the sink where she knew Maeve kept a flashlight. She sighed with relief, clicking it on.

134

"If you're ever alone and the power goes out, report it right away," Maeve had told Sophie, showing her where to find the list of emergency numbers.

The phone was mounted on the wall near the refrigerator. Sophie dialed. Naturally, it was an automated system asking for her address and the reason for her call.

Sophie wanted to say, "The power is out, and I'm freezing to death, jerk. Why else would I be calling at this time of the night?" But she refrained. Barely. She left a brief message stating where she was located—and that the power had been out for at least an hour.

Almost the second she hung up, the phone rang. Sophie yelped in surprise. Bailey yelped in sympathy. Laughing, she patted the dog's head, picking up the receiver.

"Hello?"

"How you doing, kid?"

Jerry. She should have known one of the ranch hands would be in touch.

"Fine. Cold. The generator didn't come on."

"I know. There were some problems last time it ran. Newt planned on getting it fixed, but… Well, the reason doesn't matter."

Sophie didn't need Jerry to finish. But…? Who else but Joy. Newt had let a lot of things slip since getting tangled in her mother's web. The backup generator was the least of it. She appreciated Jerry's tactful attempt to spare her feelings. He didn't know that it wasn't necessary. When it came to Joy, Sophie was pretty much numb.

"I called the power company, and I was about to head into the living room to start a fire."

Jerry laughed. "I told Maeve you would have everything under control."

"Maeve called you?" Why not call Sophie and eliminate the middle man?

"Don't be offended. She was concerned. The snowstorm turned out to be bigger than originally anticipated, and the power is out all over. Maeve figured Forbes would stay in town. He didn't make it home, did he?"

"No."

Sophie always heard when Forbes arrived. He stepped on a squeaky floorboard directly outside of her room when passing, no matter the time. She was pretty certain he did it on purpose.

Sophie's knew it was her own fault. When they had been on better terms, she had mentioned that she was a light sleeper. Forbes seemed to get a lot of enjoyment from using that confession against her.

"Maeve was afraid you might be spooked all alone in the big house. I told her you were made of tougher stuff than that."

"I'm not alone. I have Bailey. We were about to build a fire and hunker down in the living room for the rest of the night."

Hearing his name, the dog pressed his large body against Sophie's leg, a look of adoration in his eyes. Smiling, she rested her hand on his head, giving him a scratch behind the ear.

"Sounds like you have everything under control. But I promised Maeve check on you. I can come over." Jerry paused for a beat "If you really want me to."

"How soon can you get here?"

"Well, I..." Obviously, Sophie's answer had surprised Jerry. "I have to get dressed. My truck is under a foot of snow, so I'll have to walk. Then—"

Sophie burst out laughing. She had grown fond of Jerry and Mike to the point she felt comfortable teasing them.

"Stay where you are. I don't need anybody to hold my hand."

"That's what I told Maeve." Jerry gave a relieved chuckle. "If anything happens, Mike and I are a phone call away. Hell, if push comes to shove, stick your head out the window and yell. One of us will hear you."

Sophie couldn't imagine needing anything, but it was nice to know the two men were there. Jerry. Mike. Maeve. For the first time in her life, she had people who cared what happened to her. People who worried about her wellbeing. Imagine that.

"Don't forget to pick me up in the morning before you head out to feed the cattle."

"Are you kidding? You've become my go-to driver. Not too fast. Not too slow."

Hearing Jerry's praise, a glow of welcome warmth spread through Sophie. Knowing what his answer would be, she couldn't help but ask.

"I could ride on top, cutting the bales of hay and tossing them to the cattle."

"The last time I told you why that wouldn't happen, you called me a chauvinist."

"I left off the pig part," Sophie reminded him.

"It was implied."

"Jerry—"

"Build up some more muscle. We'll talk again in the spring. Now, get that fire going and stay warm."

Hanging up, Sophie thought about the hours she had spent in the weight room. It might not show through her clothes, but the full-length bathroom mirror told her that the time she had dedicated to working out was paying off.

While her breasts would never be anything to brag about. And her hips were practically nonexistent, she certainly had some definition on her arms. On top of that, her stomach showed the beginning signs of a few ridges. One might say she was three cans short of a six pack.

Sophie flexed her budding biceps. Nobody—especially Forbes Branson—would ever call her spaghetti arms again.

The fireplace hadn't been used for several days. Too bad. It would be a lot easier if she could find some glowing embers to help her out. Sophie had never started a fire on her own. However, she had paid attention. Paper. Kindling. Wood. Picturing the order and method, she began.

In the end, it was easier than Sophie imagined. Of course, it helped that all the tools were right at her fingertips.

Sophie struck the match, setting it against a piece of crumpled-up newspaper. With a satisfied smile, she watched as the flames spread, catching the dry pieces of kindling. When she confirmed a steady and satisfying sound of wood crackling, she closed the screen.

"If push had come to shove, I would have managed to split the wood, Bailey. And carry it into the house. Don't give me that look. So what if there's a blizzard raging outside? And I've never lifted an ax in my life? How hard could it be?"

Bailey cocked his head to one side and waited.

"I didn't say it would have been easy. I'm glad there is plenty of chopped wood right here. And a reserve pile neatly stacked in the garage. All I said was that I *could* have done it."

"And cut off one of your fingers trying."

Sophie heard the man's voice only a few feet away and acted on instinct. Blindly—remembering a move she had recently witnessed—she made a backward kick, aiming a sock-covered foot at his most vulnerable area. Not a direct hit. But it was enough to send him to the floor, clutching his balls.

"What the hell, Sophie?"

Picking up the flashlight, Sophie moved the beam toward the shadowed, groaning figure.

"Forbes?"

"Of course it's me. Where did you learn to do that?"

"*Buffy the Vampire Slayer.*"

Sophie felt a smug satisfaction. Television might be a vast wasteland, but it had taught her a thing or two.

Bailey—always assuming some game was afoot—excitedly plopped his paw onto the same spot Sophie hit with her foot. When Forbes grunted, Bailey's doggy grin widened.

"So much for man's best friend."

"You didn't squeak," Sophie accused, not feeling the least bit sympathetic.

"I didn't what?" Forbes carefully extracted himself from Bailey. He gave the dog's ear a "no hard feelings" scratch before getting to his feet.

"The board outside my bedroom door? You always step on it when you pass by—especially when I'm sleeping." Forbes gave her a blank look. Hearing the words, Sophie realized how silly they sounded. All this time she assumed he had done it on purpose, hoping to wake her up. Finding out she was wrong bothered her more than she wanted to admit. Even to herself. Turning to stir the fire, she muttered, "Never mind."

"Then it *did* wake you up." Forbes sounded pleased. "You never mentioned it, so I wasn't sure."

"I knew it." Sophie resisted the impulse to bash Forbes with the fire poker. Part of her was mad. Part couldn't resist smiling. "That was a lousy thing to do."

"The first time was an accident."

"I'll bet."

"Honestly?" Gingerly, Forbes moved next to her, holding his hands out to the now roaring fire. "Pure luck. Once I remembered you were a light sleeper?" He shrugged.

"You decided to wake me up every chance you had."

"Guilty." Forbes didn't sound the least bit repentant.

Sophie gathered the quilt around her. "My mother told me to never tell the enemy anything that would make me vulnerable. It's my own fault that you had information to use against me."

"I'm not the enemy, Sophie. And no offense? Your mother sounds like she was a crazy-ass bitch."

"She had her moments," Sophie sighed. *Still did.*

Enjoying the fire, they stood side by side in silence. Sophie wondered when Joy's crazy would smack Forbes in the face. Sadly—if history was any indicator—it was only a matter of time.

"Dad and Joy will be home day after tomorrow. Barring any weather snafus."

Forbes sounded happy at the prospect. Sophie's feelings weren't as cut and dried. Like Forbes, she had missed Newt. However, the time away from Joy had been the happiest of her life.

After fifteen years, Sophie had been given three months of freedom. Unshackled from her mother's influence. One hundred and ten pounds of deadweight magically lifted from her chest. She couldn't go back.

"About what happened before they left?"

Sophie had come to terms with her part in letting it happen. It was either self-flagellation or acceptance.

"Newt and Joy are married. End of story."

"It's going to be okay, Sophie. You'll see. Dad and Joy had a great time. When he calls, he sounds happy."

Sophie could have said a lot. But nothing that Forbes wanted to hear. Silently, she nodded.

"If I tell you I'm sorry for calling you a bitch, can we end this ridiculous feud?"

Because Sophie desperately wanted to be friends with Forbes again—plus the promise she had made to Maeve—she refrained from reminding him that to be exact, he had called her a *selfish* bitch.

"*Are* you sorry?"

"Yes."

"So am I." Sophie didn't go into details. She was afraid her reasons would have started the fight all over again.

It seemed that was that. All was forgiven if not forgotten. Forbes pulled two upholstered chairs up near the heat of the fire.

"Sit. I'll be right back."

"Where is he going?" Sophie asked Bailey. Curled comfortably into a ball, the dog didn't raise his head, snorting in the way of a response.

It took a few minutes, but when Forbes returned, his hands were full. "Now that we've buried the hatchet—metaphorically, thank the Lord—I think we should seal it with a toast."

"I don't drink."

"Since you're fifteen, I should hope not. Careful, it's hot," Forbes warned, handing Sophie a mug.

Sophie wrapped her hands around it, sighing with pleasure as the heat suffused her skin. Tentatively, she sniffed at the contents.

"How did you manage to make hot chocolate? Or anything hot for that matter?"

"We have a bunch of camping gear stored in the basement. There's a battery-operated stove. Perfect for the wilderness—or a cold, snowy, powerless winter's night. I put the milk on to get hot right before you assaulted my... dignity."

Sophie grinned behind the rim of her cup. "How is your... dignity? Better?"

Forbes shifted in his seat, grimacing slightly. "I don't think you did any permanent damage.

"I thought I was alone. Any damage—permanent or otherwise—you brought on yourself. What made you avoid the squeaky board tonight?"

"After spending most of the day and night listening to Aaron cry in his beer, all I wanted to do was crawl into bed and conk out. Letting you sleep seemed only fair. I might have made it until noon if my room hadn't turned into a deep freeze."

"What happened? Unless it would be breaking Aaron's confidence."

"Since everybody is bound to find out, he wouldn't mind me telling you part of it." Forbes let out a sigh. "He and Cindy broke up. Or rather, *she* broke up with *him*. I can't share the details. Suffice it to say, she had good reason."

Sophie didn't know Aaron or Cindy very well. Giggly girls in the school bathroom described them as soulmates. The term made her roll her eyes. Soulmates? What did that mean? It certainly hadn't kept the couple together. Aaron had done something bad enough to get tossed to the curb. Forbes said the tossing was deserved.

"Did he hit her?"

141

"What?" Forbes' eyes popped open. "Of course not. Why would you ask such a thing?"

"In my experience—"

"What experience?" Forbes made a dismissive motion with his hand. "You've never even been on a date."

"I had a life before I came here." Sophie didn't know why she felt the need to defend herself. "And dating isn't the only way you gain experience. I've seen things you wouldn't believe."

"Like what?"

Things that would make his sheltered, country boy's hair curl. Sophie wanted to shock Forbes. She could have. However, all of her stories involved Joy, and that subject was off limits.

"This I know," Sophie informed him. "The two biggest reasons a woman cuts ties with a man are violence and infidelity. If Aaron didn't hit Cindy, then he cheated on her."

Sophie didn't ask for confirmation. Forbes' silence was all the answer she needed.

"Aaron is miserable."

"It's what he deserves." Sophie wouldn't placate Aaron. Or by association, Forbes.

"I agree—in theory. It was a stupid thing to do. But he's my best friend. I figure it's my duty to see him through this mess to the other side."

"*The other side*? As in, you think Cindy will take him back?"

"*Hope*. Aaron loves her. He couldn't do better than Cindy. As for her? She could do a hell of a lot better. I don't know." Aaron ran a hand over his face as if trying to scrub away the dilemma. "Let's change the subject."

Sophie didn't mind. She hadn't developed an overriding need for gossip that so many of her contemporaries seemed to possess. Perhaps she had been born without that particular gene—if such a thing existed. Or maybe living in the orbit of Joy's soap opera existence had bled out her need for salacious information.

"Have you decided on a college?"

It seemed like a safe, innocuous subject. Turned out, she was wrong.

"Can I tell you a secret?"

"Sure." *What was one more?*

"I don't know if I want to go."

"You're kidding?"

Since Sophie arrived at the Branson ranch, it seemed that half the conversations revolved around *'the day Forbes left for college.'* Newt. Maeve. Even Mike and Jerry. It seemed like such a big deal she assumed Forbes was as excited as everybody else.

"It isn't that I *don't* want to go. When my mother died, I was too young to think about it. But as the years passed, I knew that I had to stay close to the ranch. Dad made it clear that I could pick any college I wanted. But I knew he was hoping I would pick his alma mater. There's nothing wrong with Washington State University. Or any other college in the state."

"Where do you want to go?"

Forbes shrugged. "This is all I've ever known, Sophie. I love my life. But I want to see more of the world. Travel. Have some adventures. Does that make any sense?"

As far as Sophie was concerned, they were sitting in a little slice of heaven. However, if she sat back and looked at it from Forbes' point of view, it made all the sense in the world. He had options that were never open to her. If he left, he always had a cushion to fall back on. A warm, loving place to come home to. Given that, she understood completely.

"What's stopping you?"

"Nothing. Not now. Dad has somebody in his life. I won't feel as guilty leaving."

A lightbulb suddenly went on in Sophie's head.

"That's why you were so willing to accept Joy's marriage to your father. So you could leave with a clear conscience."

"When you put it like that it makes me sound like a selfish bastard."

"You said it, not me."

"If I didn't believe they were a good match, I would have said something."

Sophie believed him. Forbes loved his father. He wouldn't put his self-interests in front of Newt's happiness.

"Which brings us back to my original question. What college did you choose?"

"None."

"None!" Sophie frowned at Forbes. "How does that fit into your plans?"

"I'm going to take a year off from school. Work my way around the world."

"What kind of work?"

"Fishing." This time when Forbes sighed, there was a hint of excited anticipation. "Aaron's uncle has offered us jobs on his boat this summer. With that experience under my belt, I could get other jobs in other places."

"When are you going to tell your father?"

"As soon as he gets back." Thoughtfully, Forbes ran his thumb along the rim of his cup. "What do you think?"

"About your plan?"

Forbes nodded.

Sophie was surprised that Forbes would ask for her opinion. Surprised. And Pleased. Taking her time, she gathered her thoughts and carefully chose her words.

"You should do it. If not now, then when? You're young. Unattached. So what if you finish college a year or two later than originally planned? Twenty. Thirty years from now, what difference will it make?"

"You're right." Forbes looked pleased. "Maybe I should have you talk to Dad. I know what I want to say, but it never comes out sounding right."

"If you tell Newt what you told me, you'll do just fine."

"I hope you're right."

Forbes put another log on the fire. Sophie sipped at her not-so-hot chocolate, cataloging all the topics they had touched on. She stopped when she came to something she wanted to clarify—for his edification.

"I could have gone on a date."

Forbes tucked his feet under Bailey's belly, his sigh of contentment turning into a puzzled frown. "What?"

"When you said I'd never been on a date? I wanted you to know that I could have gone on one. If I wanted to."

"Okay." Forbes' lips curved into a half smile, one that Sophie thought looked a bit condescending.

"It's true," she told him, her eyes narrowing.

"I believe you. I'm glad you said no. You're too young to date."

"Rick Billingsley didn't think so."

"Rick—" Sitting up, Forbes stiffened, his abrupt movement disturbing Bailey. With a disgruntled snort, the dog moved several feet away. "Never, ever, agree to go out with Rick Billingsley. He's a jerk when it comes to the girls he dates. If you can call it that," he added with a mutter.

The logical part of her brain understood that Forbes looked out for her. But that didn't stop the illogical part from getting its hackles up.

"I didn't want to go out with him."

"Good," Forbes nodded with satisfaction.

"However, if I had, you couldn't have stopped me. Unless." Sophie continued before Forbes could stick his foot any farther into his mouth. "You *asked* instead of *told* me. And gave me a reasonable reason not to go."

The air seemed to go out of Forbes' righteous outrage. Shaking his head, he chuckled.

"Fair enough."

With that settled—at least for the time being—Sophie suddenly felt weary. Her eyes were growing heavy, and she covered her mouth when a large yawn snuck up on her.

"It's late." Forbes tipped his watch toward the firelight. "Or early, depending on your point of view. It's been an eventful day."

"I'm glad we're friends again." Sophie yawned again, snuggling into her chair.

"We were always friends, Sophie."

"It didn't feel like it."

"Friends have disagreements," Forbes settled in, his head turned toward Sophie. "Wherever I go. No matter how long I'm gone. You can always count on me to have your back."

Sophie had never had anything she could count on. Or anybody. She looked at Forbes, smiling when she realized he had already drifted off. Her friend. No matter what. He would never understand what that would mean to her. Or how much she wanted to believe it was true.

# CHAPTER ELEVEN

"WHERE IN THE hell did you come up with such a harebrained idea?"

"It isn't harebrained, Dad." Forbes didn't explain this properly. Where was Sophie when he needed her? Her words—so eloquently stated—popped into his head. "I'm talking about one year. Twenty years from now it won't matter that I graduated later than originally planned."

"That is quite possibly the stupidest thing you've ever said."

"You once told me that you regretted not seeing some of the world before you settled down to run the ranch. That's all I'm asking. A little time to travel—spread my wings—so I won't have to live with those same regrets."

"I don't remember saying anything of the kind. I met your mother. Had you. Ran this ranch. What is wrong with that?"

Forbes didn't know how the conversation had gotten so out of hand. When he had knocked on the door to his father's office, he hadn't expected an argument. What had happened to his normally reasonable father? They had always been able to talk—about anything. It seemed Forbes had found a subject that was the exception to the rule.

"I'm eighteen. If I want to leave, you can't stop me."

Such a cliché. Forbes couldn't believe the words had come out of his mouth. That it had been necessary to say them. The fact that he meant it was little comfort.

Newt rubbed his brow. He looked tired. The lines on his face were new and deep. Forbes frowned with worry, a pang of guilt tightening the inside of his stomach.

"Go away, Forbes. We'll talk about this later."

"Are you okay, Dad?" Forbes took a step closer.

"I'm fine." Newt didn't raise his head, his hand moving to the back of his neck. "Still settling in. Give me a few days. I'll be back to my old self."

Still frowning, Forbes let himself out of the office.

His father and Joy had been home for almost a month. Shouldn't he have *settled in* already?

The first few days after the honeymooner's return his father had been busy catching up on ranch business. During the day, Forbes was at school. The weather had finally cooperated, allowing the baseball team to spend some practice time outside. He rarely made it home in time to sit down with everybody at the dinner table. By then, Joy and Newt were usually gone, spending most nights out in Cloverdale with friends.

If he had wanted to press the issue, Forbes could have asked his father for some time alone. However, the truth was, he was relieved to have an excuse to delay the inevitable.

It was Sunday. Maeve was gone for the day. As usual, Joy was nowhere to be seen. An hour earlier, he and Sophie had ended up in the kitchen where they threw together a couple of sandwiches

"Newt is alone in his office," Sophie said, taking the last bite of her turkey and provolone on whole wheat. "Now is the perfect time for that talk you've been putting off."

"He's probably busy. I don't want to..." Forbes caught the look in Sophie's eyes and laughed. "Just stamp wimp on my forehead. I won't stop you."

"Talk to him," Sophie laughed, giving him a friendly shove. "You'll be glad you got it over with."

Sophie had been wrong. Forbes wasn't glad. He was... confused. What the hell was going on with his father?

"Oh!" Joy bumped into Forbes. Atomically, he grabbed her arms to keep her from falling. Breathlessly, she laughed, resting her hand on his chest. "I'm sorry. I wasn't paying attention to where I was going."

"Neither was I. No harm done."

When Forbes would have moved away, Joy curled her fingers into the fabric of his shirt.

"You look upset." She glanced towards Newt's office. "I hope nothing happened."

Unlike Sophie, Forbes didn't feel comfortable confiding in Joy. But he realized she might have some information that would shed some light.

"I don't want to pry." Forbes almost laughed. That was exactly what he wanted to do.

"You can ask me anything, Forbes."

"Dad seems a little out of sorts. Has something happened? He isn't sick, is he?"

"Healthy as a horse. As far as I know." With a sigh, Joy shook her head. "I've noticed a change in him, too. Day by day. Little by little. There's a growing distance between us, Forbes. I keep asking myself what I've done."

"I'm sure it's just your imagination." Forbes didn't want to hear the specifics.

"Newt is a wonderful man. But since we've been back, he's lost interest in the intimate side of our relationship. I need affection, Forbes."

Joy moved a little closer. Though she wore her ubiquitous high heels, she barely reached his chin. Tipping her head, she gazed upward.

Forbes wanted to believe the look he saw in Joy's eyes was completely innocent. If it were anybody besides his father's wife, he would have sworn she was coming on to him. He had to be mistaken.

Dropping his hands, Forbes took two steps back. Joy took two steps forward. When he hit the wall, she pressed her advantage, grabbing his head with both hands and gluing her lips to his.

Shock. It prevented him from pushing Joy away. But the feel of her tongue winding its way down his throat quickly galvanized him. With no consideration for her sex or the fact that he outweighed her by at least a hundred pounds, Forbes shoved. Hard.

Joy teetered on her spiked heels. But after years of practice, she easily maintained her balance. The predatory smile on her face—and the taste of her in his mouth—turned Forbes' stomach.

"What the hell?"

"Don't get all huffy. Admit it. You've wanted this for a long time." Dark eyes sparkling with the thrill of the hunt, Joy grabbed Forbes by the hand, guiding it toward her breast. He was stronger, but she was determined. In the end, a brush against her hardened nipple was her only reward.

"You're married to my father," Forbes spat out the obvious. Joy simply smiled, shrugging her shoulders.

"So? Newt doesn't have to know what we do when he isn't around."

"I would know."

"Your conscience might protest. But you'll get over it soon enough." Flicking her hair over her shoulder, Joy posed, one hip cocked in Forbes' direction. "Trust me. I'm that good."

*Trust me*. It made Forbes think of what Sophie had told him. Never trust a man who says trust me. Or a woman, it would seem. Then it hit him. *Sophie*! God, what would she think if she knew what Joy proposed? Is this what she had feared when she tried to talk Forbes into stopping the wedding?

Sophie had asked him a question at the time. *What if I'm right?*

"Son of a bitch," Forbes muttered. He should have listened.

"Relax." Joy lowered her voice to a coaxing purr as if she were speaking to a frightened animal. "Think of the fun we'll have."

"Listen carefully," Forbes ground out the words. "Not now. Not ever. Not if you were the last woman on the planet."

Joy licked her lips, moving closer. "You don't mean that."

That was it. Forbes didn't want to hear another word. Sending her one last look of disgust, he turned to leave. When Joy tried to stop him, sinking her claws into his arm, he jerked away. At that exact moment, the door to the office opened. Newt stepped into the hall, and Joy went to work. She gasped, staggering as if reeling from an attack that only she and Forbes knew was imaginary. Playing her part to perfection, she fell into a limp heap—directly at Newt's feet.

"Joy?" Newt knelt. When he tried to help her up, she clung to him, sobbing. Looking from her to Forbes, he asked, "What happened?"

"I—"

Whatever Forbes might have said—to be honest, he had no idea what would come out of his mouth—was blocked by Joy's tearful babbling.

"Forbes knocked me down," she sobbed, trying her best to burrow as close to Newt as possible.

Newt looked as perplexed as Forbes felt. His father didn't come right out and say he believed Joy, but the expression in his eyes— the doubt that said, just maybe, he believed Joy—was like a sucker punch to the gut. Feeling he had to defend himself, though he couldn't believe it was necessary, Forbes pulled his shoulders back, unwaveringly meeting Newt's gaze.

"She's lying."

As far as Forbes was concerned, those two words should have been enough. Forget the crazy woman on the floor. *He* was Newt's son. They had eighteen years of history. Characterized by mutual respect, caring, and—he would have bet his left nut— unconditional love. In a heartbeat, a trace of doubt had crept into what Forbes thought was a rock-solid relationship.

Holding his breath, he waited for Newt to say something. Anything.

"Come with me, sweetheart." Newt gathered Joy into his arms. Standing, he whispered words of comfort in her ear. "Let me get you to our room."

"Dad?" That was it? His father wouldn't defend Forbes?

"Later. Can't you see that Joy needs me?"

Stunned, Forbes watched as Newt strode away without a backward glance. It seemed sides had been chosen. And as hard as it was to believe, his father hadn't sided with him. Joy, her eyes as dry as dust, sent him a catty, satisfied smile.

Was her act payback for turning her down? Or insurance in case Forbes tried to tell Newt what really happened?

Forbes slumped against the wall, his face falling into his hands. Did Joy's reasons matter? She achieved her goal—a break between father and son. The beginning of a wall. And for the life of him, Forbes didn't know how to stop it from growing. Brick by agonizing brick.

THINGS HADN'T SEEMED as hopeless the next morning. After a restless night's sleep, Forbes stood under the blast of the shower, telling himself that he had to have a long talk with his father so they could clear the air. About Joy and his wish to spend the next year—away from the ranch. Experiencing some of what the world had to offer.

The Joy part would be tricky. Should he tell the truth? Or would it be best to let it slide? In two months, Forbes would be gone. A year away. Followed by four years of college. When he had to be around his stepmother, he would avoid any chance of them being alone. The more witnesses, the better.

Forbes saw no reason they couldn't fix what wasn't really broken.

Unfortunately, finding time alone with his father turned out to be harder than Forbes could have anticipated.

"Newt took Joy to Seattle for a few days. They left as soon as the sun was up." Maeve set a plate of bacon and eggs in front of Forbes. Under her breath, she muttered, "Bet it's the first time that woman has ever gotten up to see a sunrise."

Another delay. Forbes hated to wait, but he couldn't do anything else.

"You don't like Joy very much, do you?"

"Not my place to say one way or the other. But I'll tell you this—"

A yawning Sophie entered the kitchen, causing Maeve to break off what she was about to say.

"Good morning, slugabed."

"It's only six thirty," Sophie laughed, taking the glass of juice Maeve held out for her.

"That is like eleven o'clock for most folks."

With a shrug, Sophie took the seat opposite Forbes.

"Just toast, please."

Maeve frowned, sending Sophie a concerned look. "No eggs? Or bacon? Would you prefer something else?"

"No, thank you."

"Hot cereal? Pancakes? I'll heat up the maple syrup the way you like."

"Just toast. Dry."

Maeve put a hand to Sophie's forehead. "You don't seem to have a fever. Is your stomach upset?"

"I feel fine. Honestly," Sophie added when Maeve didn't look convinced. "Congratulations. You finally filled me up."

"Hmm." Still skeptical, Maeve popped two pieces of bread in the toaster. "I'm going to put in a load of laundry. Yell if you change your mind."

"Did you raid the kitchen in the middle of the night?" Forbes asked when he and Sophie were alone.

"Yes," Sophie admitted. "But that has nothing to do with it. I wanted to get Maeve out of the kitchen. Did you speak with your dad?"

"Yes."

Sophie's eyes sparkled with curiosity. "Well? Talk to me. What happened?"

Forbes found the idea tempting. More than anything, he wanted to tell Sophie. She would understand without passing judgment.

Unfortunately, Sophie was the last person he could confide in. She was Joy's sister. Though the relationship wasn't a close one, it wasn't fair of him to lighten his load by dumping it onto Sophie.

The fault for this mess lay firmly on him. He had to live with the knowledge that he might have prevented this mess if he had listened to her warning.

153

Forbes wasn't above admitting to Sophie that he was wrong. He could survive the direct hit to his pride. Getting knocked down a peg or two might be exactly what he deserved.

It would be selfish to tell Sophie the truth. And damned embarrassing. In keeping silent about what had transpired outside his father's office would be a blessing for both of them.

"Come on, Forbes," Sophie urged when he took too long to answer. "You told Newt that you're taking time off before starting college. What did he say?"

"Dad wasn't keen on the idea."

"Really?" Sophie's eyes grew thoughtful. "I suppose it came as a surprise. When you explained it the way you did to me, he had to understand."

*If only it had been that simple.*

"Dad needed some time to get used to the idea." It was partially the truth. "We'll talk about it again when he gets back."

"Back? He's only been home a short time." Sophie set down her half-empty glass. "Where did he go?"

"He and Joy left for Seattle early this morning. It's just for a few days."

Sophie's frown deepened. For a moment, Forbes thought she would say something. But when her eyes met his, he saw a flash of something. Pain? Worry? The words—whatever they might have been—didn't come. Instead, her gaze dropped his barely touched bacon and eggs.

"Are you going to finish that?"

To his surprise, Forbes felt his lips forming a genuine smile—something he wouldn't have thought possible. Sophie and her never-ending appetite. Shaking his head, Forbes pushed the plate across the table.

"It's cold," he warned. "Maeve would be happy to make you some of your own."

"No time."

Sophie grabbed her newly toasted bread, slathered it with butter, then piled on the scrambled eggs. She rooted in the refrigerator, emerging with some pre-sliced cheese and a jar of mustard. Forbes watched in amazement as she assembled a makeshift sandwich.

"What's the hurry?"

"I have a math test this morning." Sophie grimaced. Arithmetic was still her weakest—and least favorite subject. "I want to get in another hour of studying before we leave for school."

Tearing off a paper towel, she wrapped it around her creation. Sophie took a bite, sighing with pleasure.

"Think that will hold you until lunch?" Forbes teased.

"I doubt it." She said it in all seriousness. "That's why I keep a stash of snacks in my locker."

It was like looking at a different person, Forbes thought as Sophie and her long legs strode from the room. Was it only August when she arrived all bristles and surly attitude? Back then, getting a few words from her, let alone a smile, had been like pulling teeth from a fully alert wild tiger.

The change had been so gradual, Forbes hadn't stopped to think about it until now. Sophie brimmed with confidence and fun and... life. The edges were smoother, but just the right amount of snark remained.

*Shit*! It added to the list of reasons he had to keep his mouth shut. Blowing Joy out of the water would be infinitely satisfying. But at what cost? Sophie's newfound happiness? His father's peace of mind?

Forbes made a vow. He would protect Sophie and Newt from the truth at any price. Silence. It was the only way.


GRADUATION DAY AT Cloverdale High School wasn't any different than at thousands of other schools all over the country. Excitement tinged with nerves. *The Future is Now*. The senior class slogan was cheesy. Obvious. And pretty much said it all. Some had firm, set-in-stone plans. Others would play it by ear. Either way, they were leaving behind one life and stepping toward another. However, it turned out there was no going back.

"We made it, buddy." Aaron slapped Forbes on the back. They and their classmates were gathered, about to march across the gymnasium in front of friends and family. "Can you believe it?"

Forbes watched as Aaron tugged at the collar of his starched white dress shirt.

Forbes slapped Aaron's hand away when he would have loosened his tie.

"Knock it off. Your mom put a lot of effort into getting that thing just right. Don't mess it up. At least until the end of the ceremony."

Forbes had watched the entire process. Part of him had found the sight of Aaron's tiny mother making her hulking son bend down so she could lovingly put the tie around his neck hilarious. Part of him felt a tug of sadness that his own mother wasn't there to do the same for him.

*Jesus*, Forbes thought. He was only eighteen. How had he managed to get weighed down with so many regrets so early in his life? Some had been out of his control. Some were of his own making. Either way, he couldn't wait until today was over.

If things went as planned—fingers crossed—the new start that Forbes desperately needed was only a few hours away.

The beginning strains of *Pomp and Circumstance* had Mrs. Fletcher clapping her hands to gain everyone's attention. She was a strict taskmaster and a damn good English teacher. Out of respect—and a healthy dose of fear—the group quieted without her having to ask twice.

"Aaron Green. Shouldn't you be standing next to Trish Gladstone?"

"Yes, Mrs. Fletcher," Aaron muttered, moving to his proper place.

After a brief inspection, Mrs. Fletcher nodded to one of the underclassmen whose job it was to man the gymnasium doors. "Shoulders back. Smile. And good luck. It has been a pleasure to have you in my class. Well, most of you."

The comment—directed at nobody in particular—received the expected round of laughter.

Forbes felt a sense of calm. After weeks of anxiety, it felt strange—yet welcome. Since his run in with Joy, he wasn't sleeping well. His appetite was almost non-existent. Home had become a relative term since he spent little time there anymore.

School and baseball. Using a crazy schedule as the reason, he had all but moved in with the Greens. Forbes didn't believe for a second that Aaron's parents bought the lame excuse. They must have spoken with his father. But it was never mentioned. Not by them, and not by Newt.

Aaron didn't ask. They were best friends. He was there if Forbes wanted to talk. Or not. On the weekends, he helped out on the ranch. Spring was a busy time. But all communication took place between him, Mike, and Jerry.

Hardly a surprise. Forbes and his father had stopped talking. Beyond a few terse words and a grunt or two, it felt as if they were strangers. Worse. Enemies. The tension between them bordered on hostility. The one time Forbes tried to breach the divide, Newt's cold rebuff cut him to the core.

Mike and Jerry kept quiet—which never happened. Maeve always seemed on the verge of tears. Sophie? Often stoic, the young woman made it impossible to tell what was going on inside her head. She was smart enough to understand the tensions had to do with Newt and Joy. However, she held firm to her promise that the subject was off limits. Forbes wouldn't lift the moratorium. As a result, the few times they spoke, little of substance was said.

The ceremony passed in a blur. Lost in his thoughts, Forbes didn't realize his name had been called until the person next to him jabbed their elbow into his ribs. Standing to a round of continuous applause, he walked onto the stage, shaking Principal Breckenridge's hand, automatically taking his diploma.

Forbes glanced at the audience beyond the blinding lights. Mike and Jerry were out there. Maeve. Sophie. Newt—no matter what—would be sitting with them. He felt a familiar tug of sadness. Until he thought of Joy. Was she here? It was a silly question. The one positive he could find about not living at home wasn't having to worry about her ambushing him.

Anger replaced sorrow when Forbes thought of Joy playing the dutiful wife and stepmother. *That* was the sticking point. The reason he hadn't tried harder to reach out to his father. Newt chose Joy without once asking his son to give his side.

As a result, Forbes didn't think he had a choice. Nothing— short of his father taking him aside for a much-needed heart to heart—was changing his mind.

Without telling anybody close to him, Forbes was leaving with Aaron for Alaska. First thing in the morning.

FORBES LIFTED HIS duffle into the back of the truck. Aaron—snoring away the effects of too much after-graduation partying—was strapped into his seatbelt, his head resting against the passenger-side window. Forbes hadn't been in the mood to celebrate, making it easy for him to lay off the alcohol.

It was two in the morning. A cool breeze had come up off the river, prompting Forbes to pull on his jacket. When he had insisted they get an early start, Aaron had grumbled. Early was one thing. This was the middle of the night. However, dragging his friend away from the party hadn't been difficult. The bitter chill between Aaron and Cindy showed no signs of warming. After trying all evening to break the ice, Aaron gave up. Like Forbes, he was ready to get out of Cloverdale.

Aaron's truck would take them to Seattle. From there, a plane to Alaska. This was the beginning of Forbes' longed-for adventure. The circumstances weren't great. Hell, they were downright shitty.

Despite what Forbes left behind, a world of possibilities called to him. He didn't know what was waiting for him. But now that the time was at hand, he couldn't wait to find out.

Forbes had said his goodbyes to Bailey, promising it wasn't forever. The dog seemed to understand. Non-judgmental. His eyes, filled with unconditional love.

Just as Forbes was about to climb behind the wheel, he caught movement out of the corner of his eye. On the far side of the road, a shadowed figure wound through the trees heading up the side of the mountain. Close behind the two-footed creature came one traveling on four.

*Sophie and Bailey*? Forbes frowned. *What the hell were they doing out at this time of the night?*

"I'll be right back." Forbes shut off the truck engine.

Aaron's answer was a muffled grunt.

Taking the keys from the ignition—just in case Aaron decided it was a good idea to test his drunk-driving skills—Forbes took off after Sophie.

The moonlight helped as Forbes found a well-worn path that wound around the trees. This part of the trail wasn't steep, making a gradual upward progression. It wasn't an obstacle-free trip. Fallen branches, large rocks that over time had made their way from the top of the mountain to hide under an outcropping of innocent-looking brush.

Forbes cursed as the toe of his boot clipped a particularly large boulder. He stumbled, just saving himself from a nasty face plant. Forbes worked on two things. Keeping upright and the scathing speech he would give Sophie when he caught up to her. She shouldn't be out here alone. What if she fell and hurt herself?

Picturing her broken, unconscious body lying in a bramble-filled ravine, Forbes picked up his pace, going from a quick walk to a fast jog.

Forbes stopped to look around, wondering how Sophie could have gotten so far ahead of him. Almost three in the morning, the tall pines blocked out much of the moonlight, making it difficult to see more than a few feet in any direction. Since spotting her with his eyes wasn't working, he closed them and listened. An owl. The rustling of the wind in the trees. And…? There it was. Sophie might move like a whisper. Bailey wasn't as light footed. An enthusiastic runner, the dog never worried about letting the entire countryside know of his arrival.

Moving to his left, Forbes danced around a sticker-laden bush but didn't quite manage to avoid scraping the back of his hand. It didn't hurt. And Lord knew he had suffered a lot worse. But damn it. He should have been ten miles down the road, the ranch in his rearview mirror. Instead, he chased after a crazy girl and her loopy accomplice.

Forbes let out a self-deprecating laugh. He supposed that made him just as crazy as Sophie.

The path suddenly widened, leaving behind the trees and bushes. In their place was a bluff that provided a spectacular, panoramic view. A long ribbon of glistening water, the river bordered the backend of the scene. The main house. Bunkhouse. Barn, corral, and various storage sheds. They sat in a row, sandwiched on one side by water, and on the other, field after field of green alfalfa.

"We made it, Bailey." Sophie, her back to him, stood with her hand on the dog's head. "The truck is still there. I don't see Forbes."

"That's because he's right behind you."

To Sophie's credit, she didn't yell. Nor did she kick out *Buffy* style. However, just to be safe, Forbes didn't get too close until she knew it was him.

"You have to stop sneaking up on me." Sophie let out a whoosh of breath.

"It's only sneaking if that is your intent," Forbes said, moving next to her. Sophie was right. From here, Aaron's truck was plain as day.

"What are you doing up here, Forbes?"

"Following you. Running around on these trails at night isn't safe."

Sophie shrugged. "I do it all the time."

Jesus. Forbes wished he had known sooner. Or maybe not. There wasn't a spot on this ranch that Sophie considered off limits. It had turned into her playground—one explored over and over again with complete freedom. He could explain the dangers until he was blue in the face. Short of locking her in her room at night, there was no stopping her. He doubted even that would work.

"If you knew I was leaving, why didn't you simply say goodbye?"

"I figured you wouldn't want me to." Sophie didn't look at him, keeping her eyes on the view.

Forbes heard the hurt in her voice. Cutting Sophie out of his life hadn't been deliberate but a byproduct of everything else that happened. It seemed to be a pattern. Just as they started to build a friendship, something would come between them.

"I'm sorry."

"Okay."

"Just like that?"

"If I asked for an explanation, would you give me one?"

"I can't."

"Then I'll settle for your apology." Turning her head, she met his gaze. "You're going to Alaska?"

Forbes nodded. "A year on my own."

"Do me a favor?"

"If I can."

"Have a good time."

That was it? Forbes had expected her to ask for something personal. Letters. Perhaps the occasional postcard. Sophie was hard to figure out. She certainly wasn't like any other girl he had ever known.

"I'll do my best."

Forbes didn't know why, but he took Sophie's hand. It was something he had never done. For a moment, he thought she would pull away. Instead, she curled her fingers around his. Something happened with that brief touch. A connection. An intimacy that he had neither the time nor inclination to analyze. The need to sneak away in the middle of the night had already heightened his emotions. That was his only excuse for what he did next.

Forbes brushed his lips across Sophie's. Surprise flared in her eyes. But she didn't punch him. So, he kissed her again. A little longer. There was nothing sexual in the gesture, though he felt a familiar stirring in his blood. Raising his head, he smiled, touching her cheek ever so lightly with the pad of his thumb.

"Well, I'll be damned," he breathed, backing away.

Sophie didn't speak. Or move. She looked confused, a frown furrowing her brow. Her first kiss. Forbes was sure of it. There were a hundred other firsts she would share with other men. But this would always be his.

Forbes turned when he reached the trees. He waved, taking one last look at his home—at Sophie—before disappearing into the dark.

# CHAPTER TWELVE

## TWELVE YEARS LATER

"FIRE!" SOPHIE YELLED at the top of her lungs, though nobody could hear her except for a startled dog and whatever creatures came out after the sun went down. She didn't stop to worry about who was around. Instead, she ran—straight for the burning barn.

Heart racing, Sophie didn't take the time to assess the severity of the blaze. With one hand, she grabbed a fire extinguisher—one of many placed strategically around the ranch building. A fairly new precautionary measure, up until now they mercifully hadn't needed to use. Holding the red canister between her legs, she pulled the metal ring from the top. With her other hand, she took out her phone.

"What?" Mike's groggy voice answered after the third ring. It was the middle of the night. Anybody with a lick of sense—like the ranch hand—should be sleeping.

"One of the barns is on fire," Sophie said, the calmness of her tone belying the adrenaline pumping through her body. Tucking the phone under her chin, she pointed the fire extinguisher at what looked like—fingers crossed—something they could contain before too much damage was done. "Grab Jerry and anybody else who is available and get down here as fast as possible."

Sophie didn't wait for an answer, trusting Mike to recognize the urgency of the situation. If she didn't have help in the next two minutes, she would chow down on her favorite horse blanket. Without a water chaser.

The blaze was small—thank God. However, the barn was filled with stacks and stacks of dry—extremely flammable—bales of hay. Left unattended, it wouldn't have taken long for it to turn into a pile of soot. Considering the price of feed, it would be cheaper to burn a stack of money.

However, hay could be replaced. The fifteen horses that were housed in the nearby stable couldn't. Several were expensive thoroughbreds. Others would be cow ponies. And a few needed extra care after suffering abuse. The animals represented an investment of time, hard work, and years of planning.

A big portion of Sophie's dreams rested on their handsome heads. If just one of them was injured under her watch—by fire, no less—it would be a huge stain on the reputation she had built with so much care.

The sound of a truck screeching to a halt was like music to Sophie's ears. Doors slammed, followed by the thud of booted feet hustling in her direction.

"What the fuck?" Jerry exclaimed.

If the cowboy had arrived with only a curse on his lips, Sophie would have kicked his ass. Luckily, he had always been a multitasker. He carried with him the rubber hose they kept connected to the waterspout on the far side of the barn. Jerry planted his feet near hers, turning the nozzle on full force. Mike and two other ranch hands joined them with shovels and two wheelbarrows filled with dirt.

"Where did those come from?" Sophie asked. The men were efficient, but she didn't think they'd had time to pull that together.

"Maeve wanted us to put in some flowers along the driveway," Mike explained as he doused the remaining fire with shovels of the dark soil. "Had this ready to use first thing in the morning."

"Handy."

Mike grinned, putting his back into his job. Sophie took a breath for what felt like the first time since discovering the fire. With the arrival of reinforcements, it was almost out. She lowered the empty extinguisher, setting it aside.

"I won't ask how you caught this so fast since I already know the answer," Jerry said as he kept the water running on the smoldering hay.

Sophie had nothing to say. Her habit of taking nocturnal walks wasn't a secret. She functioned just fine on a few hours' sleep. The direction she took depended on her mood. After a long, easy stroll across the open fields, she had felt ready to turn in when a light in the barn—a light that shouldn't have been there—caught her eye.

"Your insomnia finally paid off," Mike teased, directing the ranch hands to begin pulling down the charred stack.

Just because they found no visible evidence of glowing embers didn't mean they weren't lurking in the bales. More dirt and more water. They didn't want to take the slightest chance of the fire sparking to life.

"Once you've soaked the hay thoroughly, load it all into the bed of the truck," Sophie directed. "Then drive it to the dump."

By the time the last of the cleanup was completed, the sun's first light peeked over the eastern horizon. Sophie felt ready to drop, her mind as weary as her body, but she took the time to make another inspection before declaring the area fire free.

"Get some sleep," Jerry told her. "You saved the day—or rather the night. We'll take care of the morning chores."

"Do you smell that?" Sophie asked, ignoring the need to do as Jerry suggested. She knew her limits. She still had a little left in her tank.

"I smell smoke and wet hay."

"Try again."

Frowning, Jerry took a deeper breath. Then another. "Is that...? *Son of a bitch*! Gasoline."

Sophie nodded. She had caught the distinctive smell as soon as she entered the barn. This hadn't been an accident. Somebody had deliberately set the fire.

"We need to call the police," Mike said, removing his gloves. Like the rest of them, his face was covered with sweat, soot, and dirt. Returning from giving the ranch hands some last-minute instructions, he overheard the end of the conversation. "You could dismiss the other things as coincidence. The downed fences and opened gates that led to stray cattle we had to spend our days rounding up. Three times over the past month."

"It's your job," Sophie reminded him.

"Don't forget the missing equipment." Jerry piped in.

"That's why we carry insurance."

"The company jacked the premium," Mike reminded her. "You had some choice words about that."

"Fine." With a tired sigh, Sophie leaned against a post near the entrance to the barn. "Somebody is targeting us. What good will it do to call the police? All we have at our disposal is a bunch of inexperienced deputies and the acting chief. Eli Stover is a bumbling fool. Basically Barney Fife with a beer gut."

Jerry snorted. Mike's lips curved into a tired smile. He couldn't argue with Sophie's spot-on assessment of the current state of the Cloverdale police department.

Sophie wiped her face, grimacing when her hand came back covered with gritty soot. "I need a shower. Look, guys. Until a replacement is found for Chief Didier, we're on our own. Come on, Dandi. It's past your breakfast time."

Dandelion—Dandi—for short, left her spot in the corner of the barn to trot after Sophie. The tan-colored dog had an even, unexcitable temperament making her perfect for herding cattle— and staying out of the way in an emergency. While the humans took care of the fire, she stayed patiently waited until Sophie told her it was time to leave.

Mike followed Sophie, exchanging a guarded look with Jerry. "Sophie—"

"I'm going to take your advice." Sophie yawned, stretching her arms over her head. "A couple hours shut-eye is just what I need."

"Sophie…" Jerry hesitated.

"What?"

"Well. You see. I… We," he motioned to Mike. "We need to tell you something. What with the fire, we haven't had time until now."

"I'm listening." Sophie waited, her curiosity piqued. Jerry and Mike never hesitated to speak their minds.

"Cloverdale has a new chief of police. The mayor is going to make the announcement this morning."

166

"That's great news." When neither man answered, Sophie felt a niggling tickle of concern. "Isn't it?"

"Yes," Mike piped up.

"Absolutely," Jerry agreed. "It's just..."

"For the love of Pete. What's the problem?"

"The new chief?"

Why were they dragging this out? Sophie sighed, motioning for one of them to get on with it.

"It's Forbes."

THE TOWN OF Cloverdale hadn't changed in twelve years. Not in any significant ways. Homes with fresh paint in a different hue plus a new building here or there. An empty lot on one corner where the old Nesmith place used to stand. But overall, it looked like the same place.

Forbes parked outside the mayor's office, near the pole that sported the American flag, unfurled in all its glory. He left hoping for adventure. Dreaming of seeing the world. He hadn't anticipated just how much he would do and see. There had been no shortage of excitement—to put it mildly. Forbes' smile didn't quite reach his deep-blue eyes. The things he had experienced. The memories he brought back with him. Most were good. Some, not so much. The rest? He wouldn't wish them on his worst enemy.

One thing Forbes knew. Leaving had been the right decision. What he regretted was staying away for so long.

Flipping down the visor, Forbes checked his reflection. Not out of vanity. He had a meeting with the mayor, the press—whatever that amounted to these days—and any member of the public that cared enough to show up. He hardly anticipated a throng. However, it wouldn't hurt to get off on the right foot whether he stood in front of two people or twenty.

There hadn't been a lot of time for primping. When Cloverdale's mayor called, Forbes was in a hospital in Germany. The job offer was the last push he needed to make a decision he had toyed with for months. Two days later, Forbes was on a plane headed for the United States. He didn't carry a completely clean bill of health. But close enough. He had worked through a hell of a lot worse.

With a grimace, Forbes touched his side. The stitches itched— a good sign, he supposed.

In all honesty? Forbes knew he looked like ten miles of bad road. He had bags under his eyes. He needed eight hours of uninterrupted sleep. The idea of clean, soft sheets almost made him weep.

At least he had managed a shower, taking off the funk that twelve hours in a military transport plane will put on a body. The pilot—a buddy of long standing—had taken pity on Forbes, letting him use the officer's quarters at Fairchild Air Force Base to clean up and change his clothes.

A crisp white button-up shirt, a sport coat, and a faded, but clean pair of jeans would have to do. Until recently, Forbes had spent most of his time in areas of the world where there hadn't been a lot of call for anything dressier.

An hour after landing, Forbes drove off the base in a brand-new, shiny Ford truck decked out with every bell, whistle, and ridiculously useless accessory available. A phone call was all it had taken to have the truck delivered and at his disposal without delay. Because of who he was and who he knew, He had many strings at his disposal to pull when needed.

Without the engine running, the air in the cab quickly turned from pleasantly cool to sleep-inducing warm. The longer Forbes sat, the heavier his eyelids grew. A loud rap on the window had his head shooting up with a start.

"Forbes! Stop napping and get your ass out here."

Shaking himself, Forbes looked out the window. When he saw who it was, he grinned, opening the door without delay.

"Aaron." The men hugged, holding on tight, slapping each other on the back. It had been too long. Too damn long. "You look good."

It was true. Aaron had slimmed down since high school. The tailored suit he wore showed off a leaner, trimmer version of the once-hulking football player. Though still imposing, he no longer had the look of somebody who wanted to rip his opponent's head off and dine on his carcass.

"I'd say the same about you." Aaron gave Forbes one last pat before stepping back. "Unfortunately..."

"I look like hell. I know. For the sake of my ego, would it have killed you to lie?" Forbes laughed, easily falling into their old, familiar rhythm. "You're a politician now, *Mr. Mayor*. Fabrication is supposed to come naturally."

"Sorry, old buddy. My wife has me on a strict truth-only diet."

"Is Cindy still putting up with your shit? The woman is a saint."

Slinging his arm over Forbes' shoulders, Aaron headed them toward the courthouse entrance. "Cindy passed sainthood long ago. Owns a successful business. Somehow keeps up with three children. And doesn't look a day older than when we were in high school. I'm a lucky man."

Cindy finally forgave Aaron for cheating on her. It took time. Patience. And a lot of groveling. But in the end, one thing mattered. She loved him. It gave her the strength and faith to believe his promise that he would never do it again.

After watching the way Aaron suffered through the breakup. The way he never looked at another woman that summer in Alaska. Forbes believed to his core that his friend kept his promise.

"All kidding aside," Aaron said, shutting the door to his office. "It's good to have you home, Forbes. I'm not the only one who thinks so. The news that you were taking the chief of police job leaked yesterday. The town has been buzzing ever since."

"Is that good or bad?"

After everything that had gone down after he left town, Forbes wondered if the name Branson was still held in high esteem. Or was it tarnished—by association?

"You were a football hero, Forbes. You were a big reason Cloverdale won State our senior year. The team tries, but they haven't sniffed at a championship since."

"That was a long time ago, Aaron." A lifetime.

"Obviously, you've forgotten the power of football in small-town America. Why do you think I was elected? Nobody cared about my stance on recycling or jumpstarting the Cloverdale's economy."

"Your ability to knock running backs on their asses got you votes?" Forbes laughed at the thought until he realized Aaron was serious.

"*I was there the night Cloverdale won it all. You have my vote.*" Aaron recited the words with a *sing-song, rah-rah* tone to his voice as he moved to a sideboard that sported a fancy coffeemaker. Without asking, he filled two cups. "If I heard it once, I heard it a thousand times."

Gratefully, Forbes took the mug, breathing in the aroma. The fumes alone made his eyes widen, telling him that he and Aaron still liked their coffee done the same way. Unadulterated and strong enough to wake the dead.

"People are crazy." Forbes took a sip of the steaming liquid, sighing with pleasure.

"Amen." Aaron agreed. He motioned for Forbes to sit, unbuttoning his jacket before taking his chair behind the desk. "However, if crazy got me elected, I won't complain. Now that I'm here, I plan on working my ass off. Under my watch, I plan on making Cloverdale thrive. With some help from my friends."

Forbes smiled, recognizing a pep talk when he heard it. Though he didn't know how much he could do to help. Cloverdale had never been a hub of criminal activity. Chief Didier had spent most of his time running down petty thieves and filling out paperwork. Deciding to take the job had been a major decision. Though—in the end—a surprisingly easy one.

For almost ten years, Forbes had lived life on the edge. Between assignments, he rarely had time to do more than take a breath—sometimes not even that. He was ready for a change. Right now, slow and uncomplicated sounded like heaven.

"I'll do my part, Mr. Mayor," Forbes said, ending with a jaunty salute. "Though, unless things have taken a drastic turn for the worse, Cloverdale isn't exactly a hub of criminal activity."

"Things are always changing, Forbes."

Not exactly ominous. But the tone of Aaron's voice sent a warning prickle down Forbes' spine. He knew and trusted that feeling. In the field, it usually came just before the shit hit the fan.

"What did you say when you offered me this job?" Forbes set his empty cup on the desk. "That I should come home to rest and relax. You made it sound like I'd spend my time with my feet up and reading *People* magazine. I don't recall any mention that *things had changed*. Want to elaborate?"

"*People* magazine? Really? I thought you were more of a *Sports Illustrated* man."

"I may not be in top form. But I can still kick your ass. Tell me what's going on, Aaron."

"Nothing major." When Forbes sent him a warning look, Aaron held up his hands. "Honestly. There's been an uptick in minor crimes. We want to nip it in the bud before it goes any further. Combined with the trouble they've been having at the ranch, I thought—"

"What the hell is going on at the ranch?"

The prickle along Forbes' spine ramped up several notches, his thoughts instantly turning to Sophie. He hadn't seen her in twelve years. Hadn't spoken to her or exchanged a single letter, email, or text. Yet—for reasons that wrapped themselves around each other in a pattern of complicated twists and turns—she was the person he thought about. First, last, and—no matter how much time passed—always.

"You didn't know?" Aaron frowned. "I assumed someone would have told you."

"Obviously not."

171

Forbes spoke with Mike and Jerry on a regular basis. And Maeve about once a month. Not once had they mentioned anything was wrong.

"Again. The trouble is minor. Probably kids causing mischief."

Forbes wanted details before he decided if the situation was minor or not. Before he could ask—or demand—Aaron to fill him in, the office door opened.

"I hope the two of you are finished reminiscing because I couldn't wait another second. Welcome home, Forbes."

"Cindy." Forbes stood, welcoming her embrace. "Now, *this* is what I call a welcome. Not only are you prettier, but you also smell a lot better than your husband."

The best way to describe Cindy Green was to say she sparkled. Always had. Her honey-blond hair. Hazel eyes. Her smile. Cindy was bright as a new penny. Aaron said she was as pretty as her high school days. In truth, she was prettier. The girl had become a woman. Still young and vibrant, the added maturity suited her.

"I'm so sorry about your father," Cindy whispered.

When Forbes received the news that Newt had died, it had been a shock. Then came the pain far worse than anything he had ever known. It lessened, but he had been left with a dull, constant ache that he was certain would never completely go away.

Giving Forbes another squeeze, Cindy stood back, looking him up and down. "You need some fattening up. And some rest. But even with those bags under your gorgeous blue eyes, you are still the best-looking man I've ever seen."

"Excuse me?" Aaron pushed an imaginary dagger into his heart. "Is that any way to talk when your husband is in the room? Or when he isn't, for that matter."

Cindy laughed, taking Aaron's hand and lifting it to her lips. "Forbes is gorgeous. But you, my love, are now, and will always be, the sexiest man alive."

Watching Aaron and Cindy together warmed Forbes' cynical heart. Happily ever after might not be the norm. But it was possible with hard work and a little luck. Most of all, finding the right person was the key. His friends were that rare, perfect match that—in his experience—mostly existed only in books.

"I can step outside if the two of you need to be alone."

Color rose in Cindy's cheeks. Forbes found it amazing—and a bit charming—that a married woman with three children could still manage to blush.

"Don't be silly." Cindy brushed a kiss across Aaron's lips. Forbes received the same gesture—on his cheek. "You'll come for dinner as soon as you've settled in. That isn't a request. It's an order."

"Yes, ma'am."

"Good," Cindy said with a decisive nod. "Don't be long. The crowd has been gathering for a couple of hours, and they are getting restless."

"Crowd?" Forbes sent Aaron a puzzled look.

"I told you the town was buzzing about your return. In a good way," Aaron rushed to assure him. "Don't worry. This will be short, sweet, and relatively painless. I promise."

As Forbes knew from bitter experience, painless was a relative term. Often, it was a matter of perspective. In this case, Aaron was far off base. Standing in front of a crowd of people had never been his favorite activity. It was different when he had a football in his hands. Or a baseball bat. In those moments, Forbes had found it easy to narrow his focus, blocking out everything but the play on the field. Today, he stood on public display. The crowd—at least two hundred of them if his quick headcount was close to right— had come with the express purpose of sizing him up.

"I don't see any torches or pitchforks."

They stood on the first-floor balcony that ran along the back of the courthouse. A podium and microphone were set up in the center, near the railing.

Suppressing a chuckle, Aaron straightened his tie. "That was a long time ago. And you had nothing to do with what happened."

"I'm my father's son."

173

"Nobody placed the blame for what happened on Newt. He never lost the respect or love of this community."

Forbes nodded, hoping it was true. He had never wanted his father to suffer for his mistakes, but that was exactly what happened. Newt had married Joy of his own free will. But no one could have anticipated what a disaster it would be. Or how many people would suffer as a result.

Hindsight. Turned out it was a mother-fucking bitch.

Aaron stepped to the podium.

"Ladies and gentlemen." The crowd quieted. "Every day I come to work honored and grateful that you've trusted me to be your mayor. However, there are times that go beyond the everyday. Ever since our beloved chief of police announced his retirement, we've searched diligently for the right person to take over the job. You'll note that I didn't use the word replace. Ernie Didier was—and is—one of a kind. For over thirty years, he served Cloverdale, remaining at all times fair and dedicated. However, time moves on. Today we're here to welcome a new chief of police and at the same time, welcome home one of our own. Give a rousing round of applause to Chief Forbes Benson."

FORBES SPENT THE next hour shaking hands and listening to grievances. He was still learning his responsibilities, but he was pretty certain he *wasn't responsible for the mating habits of the local cat population.*

"Try keeping your Tiddles in at night, Mrs. Truman. Or you could have him neutered. A lot of people consider it the responsible thing to do."

"Isn't it dangerous?" the elderly lady asked, clutching her wicker purse with gloved hands.

"Not a bit," Forbes assured her. "A simple trip to the veterinarian and Tiddles will no longer be tempted to wander. So to speak."

"Well, done," Aaron said. "You've sent Mrs. Truman away a happy lady."

"I wonder if Tiddles will be as grateful." Forbes made a snipping motion with his fingers.

Aaron grimaced. "Better Tiddles than me."

"Amen, brother."

Chuckling, Forbes turned his head when he heard somebody call out his name. Seeing who it was, he opened his arms.

"Hello, Maeve."

"It's been too long."

A little older, a little rounder, Maeve still gave the best hugs in the world. For the first time, Forbes felt the tug of home.

"I didn't expect to see you today," Forbes said.

Maeve pulled a tissue from her purse, dabbing the tears from her eyes.

"Nothing could have kept me away. Mike and Jerry drove me."

"Hey, kid." Mike grinned from ear to ear. Hair slicked back, he held his special occasion Stetson in his hand. "Good to have you home."

Jerry pushed Mike aside to slap Forbes on the back. His hat was still on his head, but the familiar scent of the cologne he only broke out for something important filled the air. "Chief Branson. Has a nice ring to it. By the way, I have a speeding ticket that—"

"Don't start that," Maeve warned, though it was said with a smile. "Forbes won't be showing any favoritism. Isn't that right?"

"Absolutely. The letter of the law and nothing but," Forbes assured her. Surreptitiously, his gaze kept wandering to the crowd. Naturally, eagle eyed as ever, Maeve took note.

"Sophie couldn't make it. But you'll see her at dinner."

"It's a busy time," Jerry added. "Can't have everybody off the ranch at one time."

That was a load of crap. Jerry knew it, and so did Forbes. If Sophie had wanted to be there, she would be. Not that he was surprised. Disappointed, but not surprised.

"I've missed your cooking, Maeve."

"I can tell." Maeve huffed. "You're skinny. Never had that problem when I fed you."

Almost twenty pounds under his normal weight, it had come off while Forbes was in the hospital. To stop her from worrying, he had deliberately kept the news of his injury from Maeve. Jerry, Mike, and Aaron were the only ones who knew—at least the part he could share with them.

Unfortunately, he was flat on his back fighting a nasty infection when he received the news of his father's death.

"About Dad's funeral, Maeve. I—"

"Funerals are for the living, Forbes. Your father would have been the first one to understand why you weren't there. You and Newt made peace a long time ago. That's all that mattered to him. It's all that should matter to you. Okay?"

Maeve had always known just the right thing to say and now was no exception. The guilt Forbes had carried around for weeks lifted—a little.

"Are you through for the day?" Mike asked.

The crowd had thinned. Aaron and Cindy had left to pick their oldest daughter up from her piano lesson. Technically, Forbes' first day on the job would be Monday. But he wanted to stop at the police station to look around.

"I'll see you all at home."

Home. It had a damn fine sound to it. Forbes had laid his head in a lot of places, but none had come close to being a home. He walked with Maeve, Mike, and Jerry to their car, waving as they pulled away.

"Hello, stranger."

"Daphne."

Forbes barely had time to say her name before she was in his arms, her mouth glued to his. The kiss was short and kind of sweet. When Daphne pulled back, she gave him a smile that he remembered well.

"I might not be the first to welcome you home, but I hope I made my version memorable."

More than memorable. Daphne had surprised the hell out of him.

"I didn't think you'd want to talk to me."

Daphne looked genuinely puzzled. "Come on, Forbes. It would be ridiculous to hold you responsible."

"Joy was my stepmother." The words left a bad taste in his mouth. "It might not make any sense, but I feel like I owe you an apology."

"The bitch broke up my parents' marriage. There. I said it. Believe me, I cried more than a few tears over it. And wished that woman to hell—and worse. But it never had anything to do with you."

"I appreciate you saying that, Daphne."

"I didn't want our first meeting to be awkward." Daphne grinned. "I think I took care of that. Look. I have to run. But promise we'll get together soon so we can catch up."

"That sounds good."

Funny how easy he found it to forget how many years had passed. When Forbes pictured Cloverdale and everyone who lived here, they were frozen in time. That wasn't the case. Obviously, Daphne had come to terms with what had happened. He wondered if the same could be said for the rest of the townsfolk. Forbes' return was bound to stir up talk. Gossip never really died. Joy had left her husband to be with someone else. Two marriages had been torn apart. That was a juicy story on its own.

What took the story to another level was that the man Joy ran off with wasn't a man at all, but a woman. Daphne's mother.

# CHAPTER THIRTEEN

FORBES HAD FINALLY come home, and everybody had known. Everybody but Sophie. The people who she thought were her friends—her family—had deliberately kept her out of the loop. And it hurt. A lot.

Out of frustration, Sophie gave into an impulse—something she rarely did even when she was alone with no witnesses. Picking up a pillow, she buried her face and screamed. Loud. Long. All the while stomping her feet. Her version of a temper tantrum. But she was twenty-seven years old with a reputation to maintain.

Cool, composed, and in charge. Sophie liked it that way. She was running a business dominated by males. It hadn't been easy. She had been sixteen years old. Forbes had left. Then Joy. Deathly afraid that Newt would throw her out, she kept her head down, hoping he would forget she was there.

It turned out, Sophie had nothing to worry about. Newt didn't care about her. Or anything else. He fell into a deep depression accompanied by a lot of alcohol. No one could talk to him, though his friends tried. For their effort, he threw them out and told them to stay away.

Mike and Jerry did their best to keep the ranch going, but there was more to it than mending fences and branding cattle. Someone needed to be at the helm. There were salaries to see to. Paperwork to complete. Feed to order. Buyers. Distributers. The list went on and on.

After a few months of watching everything—and everyone—around her falling apart, Sophie knew she had to do something. Perhaps it was all the years of dealing with a crazy mother. To survive, she had learned to adapt to whatever was thrown at her. That had always meant staying out of the way. She would figuratively curl into the smallest ball possible to ride out the latest storm.

But an invisible Sophie wasn't what Newt needed. So, she adapted.

Learning came easily to Sophie. The problem was getting Newt to teach her. After a couple of huge stumbles, she finally hit on the right recipe for success. The secret was catching him first thing in the morning. Before she had to leave for school and before he had his first drink. And questions. Hundreds of questions. Newt soon realized that the only way to get Sophie to leave him alone was to tell her what she wanted to know. In a few weeks, she had a rudimentary idea of how things worked. In a few months, had taken over the business—in the office. After that, she fell naturally into running every part of the ranch.

Not that it had been easy. However, from the very beginning— when her insides had the consistency of a bowl of JELL-O— Sophie refused to blink. She knew she had to hit the ground running, and established her position of power. She made it clear. Her way or the highway. More than one cowboy had quit rather than take orders from a *girl*. However, the ones that stuck around discovered she was tough, but fair to the bone.

Sophie had one rule carved in stone. *Do the work*. They found times when a day ended at noon. Other times, they were pushing cattle at one in the morning. Working beside them whenever possible, she led by example. She gave one-hundred-percent effort and expected the same from the men who worked for her.

After a year, Newt finally hit rock bottom. He entered rehab. Then began the process of rebuilding bridges. They were glad to have him back. Not exactly the man he had been before, but close enough.

However, if anybody thought things around the Bronson ranch would return to the way they had been, they were in for a shock. Newt took back the reins, but not all of the responsibility. As far as he was concerned, Sophie had earned her place—and no one argued.

Sophie flopped onto the bed, adjusting the pillow under her head. Without the support of Mike and Jerry, she would have failed—miserably. They made it known that they had her back. When she gave an order, they never questioned her in front of the other ranch hands. If they disagreed or had a suggestion, they waited until they could speak to her alone.

Maeve gave Sophie a shoulder to lean on and listened when she needed to vent. When Sophie was at the end of her rope, clutching at the frayed ends, Maeve was the one who propped her up.

Mike, Jerry, and Maeve. They had become Sophie's friends and her family. They had been through so much. Why hadn't they told her that Forbes was coming home? It felt like a betrayal. Like they were already choosing sides, and she was getting pushed aside in favor of the blood heir.

Over lunch, Maeve had done her best to explain.

"Forbes made the decision quickly. Yes, he had been thinking about coming back for a while. But it wasn't until Aaron offered him the chief of police job that he made up his mind."

"His father's death wasn't reason enough?" Sophie took a bite of her sandwich. She felt a lump in her stomach, but, as always, nothing could kill her appetite. "Or three months ago, when Newt was alive and would have appreciated spending time with his son."

"Sophie—"

"If you plan on defending him, I don't want to hear it. I'm happy that Newt and Forbes reconciled. The phone calls and FaceTime. Fantastic. And wasn't it great of him to fly his father to New York one Christmas. And Paris one spring. And all the other places. A week here or there. What a freaking saint."

Sophie knew how she sounded. Like a bitter, petulant child. Didn't she have the right? Twelve years, damn it. Forbes had reached out to everybody. Newt. Maeve. Mike and Jerry. Everybody but her. Why? She had asked herself that question a million times.

Only one thing made sense. Forbes blamed her.

The whole ugly truth had come out after Joy ran off. Sophie had poured her heart out to Maeve, confessing her part, ready for the punishment she deserved. Instead of going to Newt—who in retrospect had been in no condition to listen—the housekeeper had cursed the woman who wrecked so many lives.

"Joy is the villain, Sophie. Would it have helped if you'd told the truth? Maybe. Maybe not. Your sister—I mean mother." Maeve had sighed. "It's going to take a little while to get used to that one. From the moment she met Newt, her claws took hold. And Newt let her. Believe me, I'm not giving him a total pass. But you?" Maeve had gently smoothed a hand over Sophie's hair. "Just the thought of what that woman put you through makes my blood run cold. I understand why you kept quiet and I don't blame you one bit."

When Newt learned the truth, he felt the same as Maeve. As had Mike and Jerry. They were so kind and understanding, Sophie wanted to cry. Which she did as soon as she was alone in her room.

No one had blamed Sophie. Except for Forbes. And it seemed that hadn't changed. The jerk.

As Sophie pulled off her clothes, she wondered if she made too much of it. Maybe Forbes didn't blame her. Maybe he never had. Maybe he simply didn't care about her one way or the other. Not hate or affection. Not blame or forgiveness. Nothing.

Sophie had spent the whole day gearing up for when they came face to face. She would be polite. If he spoke to her, she would respond in a civilized manner. Cool, calm, and collected. Mature. She was no longer a girl. They were on equal footing. Satisfied with how she would handle the meeting, she had almost been looking forward it. Then he didn't show up.

True, Forbes had the courtesy to call Maeve. Some old friends had insisted on him joining them for a drink. Probably more than one. Rather than hold everyone up, he told her to go ahead without him.

Maeve had taken it in stride. As had Mike and Jerry. Sophie had fumed in silence.

Sophie slipped a t-shirt over her head before heading for the bathroom to brush her teeth. Looking at herself in the mirror, she sighed. It had been a long time since she had ridden an emotional rollercoaster and had forgotten how exhausting it could be. After the fire this morning and a full day riding fences, she was ready to shut down her mind and her body. There would be no late-night walks this evening.

"I'm not really upset with Maeve. Or Jerry and Mike. This morning, their silence regarding Forbes felt like a betrayal. Tonight." Sophie frowned. "Disappointed is a better word. We've been through too much. I will not let Forbes cause a rift. Even a temporary one. He will not get in my head, Dandi. You have my word on it."

Already settled on her bed in the corner of the room, Dandi raised her head inquiringly when she heard her name.

"I know what you're thinking. He's already there. Even when I'd go a week or two without giving him a thought, he lurked in a dark corner of my brain. You might be right."

Dandi stared unblinking as if to say, *Of course, I'm right. Aren't I always?*

"It was only natural," Sophie continued her one-sided argument. "Forbes kissed me. I was bound to think about him after that. Do you think he did it on purpose?" Sophie nodded, punching her pillow. "Me, too. Jerk."

Reaching over, Sophie turned off the bedside light. There had been many, many more kisses. Good ones. A few that were great. And a couple that bordered on spectacular. So what if the one she shared with Forbes had been the sweetest? And yes, if she were completely honest, the most memorable? She was no longer a clueless fifteen-year-old girl. Whatever Forbes had to throw at her this time around, she was more than ready.

The thought put a smile on Sophie's lips, staying there as she drifted into a deep, dreamless sleep.

THE FAMILIAR SQUEAK of the floorboard woke Sophie. However, it had been so long since she heard the noise, she wondered if it had been her imagination. The string of curse words that followed moments later gave her the answer.

Definitely not her imagination.

Throwing back the covers, Sophie rushed across the room. When she pulled open the bedroom door, she was greeted with the sight of a man—feet bare, shoes in hand—tiptoeing down the hall.

"You're still about as quiet as an avalanche. I guess some things never change."

Forbes stopped. With a sigh, his head fell back.

"It was an accident," he said.

"I've heard that before."

Slowly, Forbes turned to face her. As crazy as it sounded, Sophie found herself holding her breath as if expecting... What? He wasn't *that* much older. How much could he have changed?

What Sophie realized the instant she looked into those oh-so-familiar eyes, was that she had asked the wrong question. Forbes had changed, but that wasn't it. It was her. *She* was different.

The kiss Forbes gave her just before he left hadn't magically sparked Sophie's hormones into action. A year passed before she was interested in going on her first date with a very nice boy who gave her a very nice kiss good night.

If over the years she occasionally thought about how Forbes' lips had felt against hers, so what? It didn't mean anything. The last time she saw him, it wouldn't have entered her mind to think of him as anything but a friend. She hadn't been ready.

Now? Sophie looked at Forbes. Had he always been so handsome? Her eyes moved from feature to feature. A strong, straight nose. Killer cheekbones. Full lips and a chin that seemed to beg her to knock him down a few pegs. Her heart rate had accelerated. Her skin felt hot. Apparently, her twenty-seven-year-old hormones worked just fine.

"Well, crap," Sophie muttered.

"Excuse me?" Forbes' lips twitched.

"Are you smirking? Really?" Sophie placed her hand in the middle of his chest, giving him a shove. "Think again. This time around, I'm the one with her feet planted firmly on the moral high ground."

Sophie knew Forbes could argue the point—and rightfully so. She didn't give him a chance.

"Did you have very much to drink?"

Forbes frowned, obviously confused by the way she abruptly moved on to a completely unrelated subject. But Sophie knew something he didn't. She worked her way up to something, wondering with each word if she would have the guts to follow through. That was the problem with giving into an impulse. When she didn't have a plan, it was a lot easier to fall on her face.

But now that Forbes was home, she wanted to make it clear from the start that things had changed. She wasn't the inexperienced girl he remembered. She was a woman. Strong. Decisive. And in charge.

"No. A couple of beers is all."

"You're in possession of all your faculties?" Sophie asked in a matter-of-fact tone. Calm on the outside. On the inside, every nerve in her body was on high alert.

"I'm dead on my feet, but otherwise? Sure. I'd say my faculties are just fine. What's this all about, Sophie?"

"I'm going to kiss you, and I want to make certain you know exactly what's happening." Sophie stepped closer until her bare toes almost brushed against his.

Forbes swallowed. Sophie gave him plenty of time. He could have gone into his room, shutting the door in her face. Or brushed off her suggestion with a laugh. Instead, his gaze dropped to her mouth—and stayed there. The hall was bright enough for her to notice that the color of his eyes had darkened to blue so intense it took her breath away.

"I only have one question."

"What?"

Rising up on her toes, Sophie leaned close, her voice dropping to a husky whisper.

"Yes? Or no?"

184

In the way of an answer, Forbes shuffled his feet, eliminating the fraction of an inch that separated them. Sophie gasped, surprised at how erotic the simple brush of one set of toes against another could be.

"You like that."

Forbes wasn't asking. He stated a fact—and sounded smug while doing so. If he thought the balance of power shifted his way, he was seriously mistaken.

"I liked it," Sophie nodded, her hands sliding up his arms. "But not as much as you're going to like this."

Holding Forbes' gaze until the last second, Sophie covered his mouth with hers. It wasn't sweet or tentative or searching. She wanted hot and fast. A statement kiss. One he wouldn't likely to forget anytime soon.

Just as Forbes angled his head, when his arms would have pulled her closer, Sophie ended the kiss as quickly as it started. Satisfied by the glazed expression in his eyes, she backed away. Pausing at her bedroom door, she smiled.

"Welcome home, Forbes."

# CHAPTER FOURTEEN

"CAN I GET you a cup of coffee, Chief? You look like you could use a pick me up."

"Thanks, Olly," Forbes nodded. "Black. No sugar."

"Be right back."

Forbes stood, stretching his legs by taking a slow walk around his new office. Pretty standard fare. City-issue furniture consisting of a sofa that had seen better days. The dark-brown leather had faded in spots to more of a light tan, with long cracks in the cushions and along the armrests. The old metal file cabinet in the far corner was dented as if someone had more than once taken out their frustrations on it, leaving one side decidedly concave. However, after a brief inspection, it seemed to be more for decoration than function. The drawers contained exactly three files. One was empty. The other two held a few papers but the cases mentioned were from before Forbes was born.

Officer Olly Wabash was the station's jack of all trades. He was their go-to tech guy, secretary, victim liaison, and shoulder to cry on. The office was his purview. He rarely went out into the field unless it was an emergency, and Cloverdale being Cloverdale, that pretty much amounted to never.

Yesterday when Forbes dropped into the station, Olly had sprung to his feet, rushing to greet the new chief as if jabbed by an electric probe. Nearing forty, below average in height, paunchy but not exactly fat, his light-brown hair thinned quickly. A fact he tried unsuccessfully to disguise with an unfortunate combover.

Pumping Forbes' hand with an overenthusiastic handshake, he almost tripped over his tongue, letting it be known that he was available if Chief Branson had any questions. Day or night.

Having seen the type before—many times—Forbes recognized the man for what he was. Olly Wabash was a brownnoser. Luckily, he seemed to be damned good at his job. Forbes had met the officers under his command—all six of them—and had been briefed on the open cases on the books. Not bad for his first morning.

Ten years ago, the Cloverdale Police Department had finally modernized their system, transferring all their records onto computers. Why Chief Didier kept the old file cabinet was anybody's guess. Sentimental reasons? Or perhaps he hadn't thought about it one way or the other. It had probably occupied that same corner for the better part of the *last* century.

Furniture wasn't high on Forbes' priority list. Except for the chair behind his desk. With a frown, he rotated his stiff shoulders. The thing had all the back support of a wet noodle. Not to mention the complete lack of a cushion. The ex-chief must have had as ass made of steel.

"Here you go, Chief. Black and hot." Olly sat the cup on the desk. "You have a lunch meeting with the mayor in twenty minutes. Is there anything in particular you want to go over this afternoon?"

"The report on the thefts at the Branson ranch?" Olly nodded. "I want to study it closer. And I have some notes to add. A fire broke out in one of the barns yesterday morning."

Olly frowned. "Nobody reported it. Do we think there was something suspicious about it?"

"That's what I'm going to find out."

With a nod, Olly left him alone.

Forbes had spoken with Mike and Jerry that morning before leaving for the police station to get their take on the thefts. That was when he found out about the fire. And that they believed it had been set on purpose.

"You should talk to the boss," Mike had suggested.

"The boss?" Forbes asked, momentarily confused. Newt was dead. A fact that he hadn't completely come to terms with.

"Sophie," Mike reminded him with a pointed look.

"Right." Forbes hadn't forgotten. However, like the loss of his father, some things around the Branson ranch would take some getting used to.

With a shake of his head, Mike had a look on his face that seemed to say that some air needed clearing between Sophie and Forbes. And it should happen sooner than later.

Forbes agreed. But after last night, he wasn't sure how to begin. The Sophie he had spoken with in the hallway wasn't what he had expected. The gangly, cute kid had turned into a stunning woman. Not beautiful in the classic sense of the word. But she made a man want to take a second look. And then some. The sudden awareness had been surprising. The way she acted had been... Forbes wasn't sure how he felt.

Sophie still took things head on, Forbes was glad to discover. That in his face, 'nothing intimidates me' attitude had always been one of the things he liked about her most. He hadn't meant to step on that stupid board outside her bedroom. She could have ignored it. He probably would have. But instead, she called him out. From her tone, it sounded like she wanted to call him an asshole.

In retrospect, Forbes wished she had. He would have gladly taken Sophie's lip, and given some in return. Her lips on his? That was another matter. Not because he objected to the idea of kissing her. Just the opposite. It was the way she did it. It had been jarring. Like she tried to be someone she wasn't. Forbes knew a certain amount of change was inevitable. But not that much.

Yes, Forbes had played along. Brushing her toes with his was something he wouldn't mind trying again under different circumstances. Hell, he was only human. Given a little encouragement, he might have deepened the kiss. But Sophie didn't give him a chance. She ended it just as quickly as it began, leaving him wondering what the hell had happened.

Picking up the cup of coffee, Forbes moved to the office window.

Who would have guessed that Forbes Branson would grow up to be chief of police? Certainly not him. When he left for Alaska, he dreamed of adventure. Something different and exciting. Whoever coined the phrase *be careful what you wish for* knew what he was talking about. The past twelve years had been a never-ending, no time to breathe, by the seat of his pants thrill ride.

Forbes laughed. Talk about going from one extreme to the other. Moving aside the curtain, he looked down from his second-story location onto the quiet, peaceful town. This was home. No matter where he traveled or how long he was away, that had never changed. Now, it was his to protect and serve.

The town. The surrounding area. The people who lived here depended on him to keep them safe. That included Sophie. He would find out what was happening. On the ranch. And with her. Whether she liked it or not.

"DO YOU WANT ham and cheddar, or turkey and Gruyere?" Tory asked as she opened the insulated hamper. When Sophie didn't answer, she nodded. "I know. Silly question. You want both. Which is why I picked up three sandwiches at *Rodney's* instead of two."

The friend's lunch was set up outside the tack room near a row of stalls currently filled to capacity. The horses—unconcerned with what the humans were up to—contentedly munched on their daily snack of vitamin-enhanced oats.

Sophie and Tory made a point of having lunch together at least once a week. The location varied depending on their schedules. Today, they had decided to meet on the Branson ranch.

Tory—always wanting things to be as pretty as possible—spread out a lavender blanket. Kicking off her shoes, she was on her knees unpacking the treats she had purchased before leaving Cloverdale. She was only one of two lawyers in the area. To say her clientele was varied and colorful would be putting it mildly. She loved the work, but getting away for an hour or two was something she looked forward to.

Accepting one of the sandwiches, Sophie took a bite, chewing slowly.

"I kissed Forbes."

189

This time, Tory remained silent. Tossing her hands in the air—but keeping a firm hold of her lunch—Sophie fell backward onto a pile of loose hay.

"Say something," she demanded. "Anything."

"Other than wow?"

"Wow is a start. Care to elaborate?"

"I'm processing." Tory arranged the skirt of her summer-weight business suit, so her legs were in a ladylike position, curled to the side. "*Why* did you kiss Forbes? Not that I blame you. I was at the courthouse yesterday, and all I can say is yum. Still, you never said you were pining for him."

"Because I wasn't. Not like that." Sophie sat up. "The kiss wasn't about sex."

"So, you found it was like kissing your brother?" Tory shuddered.

"No." Definitely not. "I didn't plan it."

Sophie explained what had led up to the kiss. The squeaky floorboard. Her state of mind before she had fallen asleep.

"You were pissed."

"I was," Sophie agreed, liking how Tory always boiled things down to the bone.

"Things got out of hand. It was only a kiss, Sophie. Stop worrying. Forbes is a big boy, he'll get over it."

"You don't understand. The kiss didn't result from anger. It was a power play." Sophie swallowed. God, this was hard. "That wasn't me, Tory. It was Joy."

"Come on," Tory scoffed. "That's ridiculous."

"No, it isn't. I spent fifteen years watching how Joy operated. When she wanted something, she got it by using her body. I wanted Forbes to understand that I'm in charge. So, what did I do? I channeled my mother."

"Sophie—"

"That move I made last night was vintage Joy."

190

The thought of it made Sophie sick. It had taken some time, but maybe her bad blood finally bubbled to the surface.

"Stop. Right now." Tory grabbed Sophie's arm. "I can see the wheels turning in that brain of yours. You are the smartest person I know, but sometimes you overthink things. You. Are Not. Your. Mother. Not close. And if you say it again, I will kick your ass."

"There isn't another explanation, Tory."

"Besides the fact that you were upset? And angry? Give yourself a freaking break, Sophie."

"But—"

"If somebody who works for you makes a mistake, you always give them a second chance. You do your best to help them make it right. You have the same philosophy with your friends. Try giving yourself a break sometimes, Sophie." Tory squeezed Sophie's hand. "The only person who expects you to be perfect is you."

For so long after Joy left, Sophie worried about her place on the ranch. She made herself indispensable. Nobody could argue with a job done perfectly. Even after her place was secure, she continued to hold herself to a higher standard. A way for her to show her gratitude.

Newt had been the closest thing to a father Sophie would ever know. Making him proud had meant the world to her.

"I don't know how I'm going to face him." In true cowardly fashion, that morning Sophie made sure she was gone before Forbes came down for breakfast.

"Forbes is the one who owes *you* an explanation. Not the other way around. Keep reminding yourself of that, and you'll be fine. Just one piece of advice."

"What's that?"

"Don't kiss him." Tory grinned, popping a grape into her mouth. "At least not right away."

# CHAPTER FIFTEEN

SOME THINGS NEVER changed. Thank the Lord.

As Forbes entered the kitchen—the way he had hundreds of times in the past—he stopped to breathe in the familiar scent of Maeve's baking. What she made never mattered as much as the comfort he found in simply knowing she was there.

Closing his eyes, Forbes smiled. Fresh bread. Hopefully out of the oven and ready for him to sample.

"Hello, beautiful." Forbes kissed Maeve's cheek.

"Come here." Maeve wiped her hands on her apron, holding out her arms. She pulled Forbes close, swaying back and forth.

Forbes chuckled, hugging her. "Not that I object, but didn't we do this already?"

"I have a lot of hugging to catch up on," Maeve said, clearing her throat. "Indulge an old woman."

"Old my—backside." Forbes caught himself at the last second, remembering Maeve's dislike for any form of cursing. Considering the company he had kept over the past decade, curbing his language—every time—would be a challenge. "For you, time has stood still."

"I appreciate the thought." Maeve gave him a big squeeze before letting go. Without asking, she took the cooling loaf from the rack and sliced him a thick piece. "How was your first day on the job?"

"Uneventful. Which is fine with me," Forbes said, slathering the bread with butter. He took a bite and sighed with pleasure.

"Good?" Maeve asked.

"Yes, ma'am." Forbes polished it off, wondering if he could talk Maeve out of another piece.

"Dinner is in an hour." When it came to food, Maeve was a master mind reader. "Have an apple if you can't wait."

Wasn't that a blast from the past? When Forbes was growing up, Maeve tried her best to push him toward fruits and vegetables when he wanted a solid diet of candy and potato chips. She hadn't changed, but he had. He grabbed the apple, enjoying the crunch and the tart sweetness.

"Is Sophie around?"

"She always catches up on paperwork before dinner. Forbes." Hesitating, Maeve frowned. "I know that you and Sophie have a lot of things to talk out. But..."

"But what, Maeve?"

"Sit down. Please?"

Puzzled, Forbes did as Maeve asked. Obviously something troubled her.

"Sophie wouldn't thank me for telling you this. However, that young woman doesn't always know what's best." Maeve took a seat next to Forbes. "There is no way for you to imagine what Sophie went through after Joy took off. Two married women running away together? They created a scandal the likes of which I've never seen—and hope never to see again."

Forbes listened intently. Though he knew what happened, the details were still a mystery. His father had never spoken of it, and Forbes would never have asked.

When the news about Joy and Talia Banks had finally reached him via Aaron, it had come as a shock. To put it mildly. The measures he had taken to protect his father from the truth about Joy had been a big, fat exercise in futility. It turned out that Joy had been intent on blowing up her marriage to Newt whether Forbes was around or not.

"For quite a while after Joy left, Sophie became little more than a ghost. She made her own meals when I wasn't around. Slipped out of the house in the morning and back in at night. To be honest, we were all in such a state of shock, I didn't pay her much attention. I'm not very proud of that fact."

Forbes covered Maeve's hand with his in a silent gesture of support.

193

"A couple of weeks passed before Sophie finally came to me. The girl was shaking, Forbes. Clearly, she wasn't sleeping. And what little weight she had put on since coming to the ranch had melted off. Skin and bones on top of a bundle of nerves." Maeve's voice cracked with emotion. "The truth about Joy being her mother spilled out in a rush. I half expected her to collapse in a heap, but that isn't Sophie. She has a backbone made of pure steel."

"You didn't blame her." Forbes hadn't meant his tone to be quite so harsh, but he felt like he was experiencing Sophie's distress as it happened, wishing he had been here to help her through it.

"Of course not. You wouldn't believe what Joy put that girl through." Maeve rubbed her arms, shivering at the thought. "It's criminal. And, I suspect Sophie didn't tell me half of it."

"What—?"

Maeve stopped him. "Ask Sophie. She'll tell you if she wants you to know."

Forbes nodded, wondering if he really wanted the details.

"What Sophie never shared with me were the things she went through away from the ranch."

"At school?" Forbes knew how thoughtlessly cruel kids could be. Even worse when they took the time to plan their attacks. The crap with Joy would have made Sophie an easy target.

"I heard from a few of my friends who work at the high school—after the fact. Some of Sophie's classmates—mostly the ones who were friends with Daphne Parks—were relentless. They called her names. Left rotten food in her locker. There were rumors of a fight. I don't know any of the details—or how much of it was true."

"Did you ask Sophie?"

Maeve's eyes were sad. "Sophie didn't report the bullying to anybody. By the time I heard what was going on, the worst of it had died down. Luckily, Tory Crandall stood by her. And on occasion—again, this is strictly hearsay—in front of her."

"Fucking Joy," Forbes muttered.

For once, Maeve didn't reprimand him for his language. She simply nodded, her expression turning cold.

"The Christian in me wants to forgive. However..."

"I hope the bitch rots in hell."

"Yes." Short and to the point. "Sophie was a victim, Forbes. Though whatever you do, don't use that word around her."

The corner of Forbes' mouth ticked upward. "Thanks for clueing me in, Maeve."

"One more thing." When Forbes would have stood, Maeve stayed him, putting her hand on his arm. "I told you because I didn't know how you felt about Sophie. If you blamed her for... Well, for any of it."

"Dad didn't blame her. You didn't. Neither did Jerry or Mike. But you thought I did?" Forbes didn't know how he felt about that.

"You cut Sophie out of your life, Forbes. Not a word. What were we supposed to think? What was *she* supposed to think?"

That he was an idiot with issues? That while Sophie's secrets were out in the open, Forbes hadn't decided if his should ever see the light of day? Twelve years later, he didn't know what he should—or shouldn't—tell her. He would have to play it by ear.

"Sophie is safe with me, Maeve. I promise. The last thing in the world I would do is deliberately hurt her."

Satisfied, Maeve nodded. "Sophie is in her office."

"Her office? Where is that?"

"The only one in the house."

"You mean Dad's office?"

Maeve shrugged. "It's the one they shared for years. When Newt passed away, why wouldn't Sophie continue to use it?"

"No reason at all," Forbes assured her.

Sophie was in charge of the ranch. Legal and binding. Laid out in Newt's will in easy to understand black and white. According to the document, Sophie was co-heir. Half of everything belonged to her.

When the changes were made—three years before Newt's death—it was done with Forbes' knowledge and blessing. At the time, he was still gung-ho about the job he was doing. Saving lives. Serving his country. Convinced he was helping make the world a better place.

Forbes knew he would eventually come home. But in ten or fifteen years. He hadn't been ready for a change. Besides, Sophie had earned her right to the ranch. More than earned it. From everything he heard, she had become the place's heart and soul.

As he left the kitchen, Forbes paused, watching as Maeve opened the oven to check the progress of the roasting beef.

"Sophie was lucky to have you, Maeve." Thinking about his father, Forbes added, "And all of you were lucky to have her."

THE DESK AND its contents were organized down to the last paperclip. It had taken some time to organize things to her liking. Newt's system had been a bit haphazard—to put it mildly. As Sophie began to work with him, he gladly allowed her to organize his system. Her first project was to get rid of the clutter.

The desk had been in the Branson family for generations. Maeve kept the mahogany gleaming, but when Sophie opened the drawers, she wondered if they had ever been cleaned out. She found papers—everything from illegible scribblings to out-of-date invoices—crumpled in every corner. Some were dated from over sixty years ago. Historically interesting, but of absolutely no practical use. Sophie gave Newt the assignment of deciding which to save—for posterity—and which to junk. By the end of the day, they needed a bigger trash can.

Sophie found packages of stale cheese crackers, several candy bars that had solidified to the consistency of granite. And what looked like part of a sandwich that was so old, it had fossilized.

Remembering Newt's embarrassed expression as she mucked out the years of mess—and forgotten meals—Sophie smiled wistfully. She missed him. Every day. In so many ways.

Hitting the send button, Sophie closed the laptop. Paying the bills always gave her a sense of accomplishment. Luckily, money had never been an issue—even when Newt had been at his lowest point and had let things slide. The Branson ancestors had left behind a sizable and diverse fortune. Sophie relied on trusted advisors to help her keep the coffers robust. But nothing was done without her approval and signature. She watched each investment with an eagle eye. Read every contract. Twice.

Years from now when the next generation took over, Sophie would make certain they inherited a thriving business. One that was even stronger and more robust than when she was handed the reins.

"Done for another month." Sophie swiveled the chair until she faced the window. On the second floor, she loved this view of the river. "Benjamin Franklin was right. A place for everything and everything in its place. This is my place. It's where I belong."

"I agree."

The only thing that stopped Sophie from jumping a foot were her fingernails digging into the arms of the chair. *Forbes*. He still had a way of sneaking up on her. And it still pissed her off.

"Try knocking next time." Sophie took a deep breath before swinging the chair around. "This is my office. For future reference, the closed door means I don't want to be disturbed."

Forbes ignored her less than welcoming words, moving to the corner where Dandi calmly watched the proceedings.

"Hello." Forbes went down on one knee. He held out his hand for the dog to sniff. "I knew this couldn't be Bailey. Who are you?"

"Her name is Dandi."

"I'm Forbes," he said, running a hand over the dog's head. He looked at Sophie. "Why Dandi?"

"She loves to eat dandelions."

Sophie frowned when Dandi leaned into Forbes' caress, her eyes closing with pleasure. Women had always fallen at his feet. Human or animal. It seemed that hadn't changed.

"Sounds reasonable."

197

Sophie had rehearsed what she would say the next time she saw Forbes. While taking care of the horses—brushing their coats, combing their manes—she had carried on the one-sided conversation in her head. She picked her words carefully, delivering them with a cool, measured confidence. Now that the moment was at hand, she drew a blank.

"Let's get a few things straight right off the bat." Forbes' long legs covered the distance across the room before Sophie could blink—or protest—he took the chair across from the desk. "I don't blame you. For anything. I don't hate you. Or resent you. Or wish you were anyplace but where you are right now. That is your chair. This is your office. On paper, the ranch belongs to us both. But you're the boss, Sophie. And that's the way it should be."

Sophie felt as if Forbes had crawled inside her head, plucking out what she had wanted to say—almost word for word. However, he didn't deliver her speech with a cool, measured confidence. He did it with eloquent emotion that she heard in his tone and saw in his eyes. Sophie's throat tightened.

"I don't know what to say." Forbes had pretty much said it for her.

"Don't get me wrong," Forbes continued. "I want to be a part of it. I'll work the ranch when I can. For my own enjoyment *and* to help. I'm used to giving orders, so I'm afraid overstepping my authority on occasion is an inevitability. When I do, let me know."

"How are you at *taking* orders?" Sophie inquired.

"Not so great," he admitted. Forbes sent Sophie a grin she remembered well. A little cocky. A little self-deprecating. And all Forbes. The weight that had deposited itself on her shoulders began to lift.

"I can be a strict taskmaster."

"When I respect my superior—when I trust she knows what she's doing—I do just fine."

"Why the Army?"

Sophie didn't know where the question came from. Though she was curious, it certainly wasn't at the top of her need-to-know list.

However, now that she had asked it, she was curious to hear the answer.

Forbes laced his fingers together, tapping one against his chin. His blue eyes turned thoughtful, meeting Sophie's.

"You sure this is where you want to start? We have a lot of backstory to get through."

"Are we on the clock?" The next question Sophie asked *was* near the top of her list. "Are you planning on taking off anytime soon?"

"I'm home for good, Sophie. Unless..." Forbes thought about it then shrugged. "As far as I'm concerned, my traveling days are over."

Rolling her shoulders, Sophie felt the rest of the weight fall away.

"You never mentioned a desire to join the military."

"I suppose, like a lot of people, after 9/11, it was always in the back of my mind. But when I left for Alaska, fishing was the only thing I thought I'd be doing."

As far as Sophie knew, Forbes hadn't shared his motivation with his father. Or anyone else on the ranch. Fascinated to discover the answer, she sat forward, resting her elbows on the desk.

"What happened?"

"It turned out that Aaron's uncle wasn't the successful fisherman he claimed to be. He was able to eke out a living— barely. We were lured up there as what amounted to cheap labor. Clean the fish. Pump the water from the boat. In exchange, he provided a place to sleep and three meals a day. Fish as a steady diet gets old fast. We lasted a month. Aaron headed home. That wasn't an option for me."

"Because you wanted to see the world?"

"That was part of it." Forbes hesitated. "I'll tell you everything, Sophie. But it will be easier if I take it section by section—so to speak. You asked about the Army."

Now that they had begun, the questions zinged around her brain. Fast, furious, and in no logical order. Forbes was right. Keeping to one subject at a time would be the smart way to go.

"Join the Army, see the world?"

"Sounds good on the recruitment posters. Mostly? I saw dirty barracks, ate crappy food, and walked. A lot. It wasn't perfect, but because of the men and women I met and served with, I will never regret my decision." Forbes looked over his shoulder. "Are there any beers in the fridge?"

"Help yourself."

For a while—after Newt came back from rehab—Sophie removed all traces of alcohol from the office. After his death, she decided to restock the refrigerator and bar for when she entertained business associates.

"Can I get you something?" Forbes asked, twisting the cap of a long neck bottle.

"Water. Thanks." Sophie wasn't much of a drinker. The occasional glass of wine was about it.

"I signed up for two years." Forbes continued after taking a sip of beer. He settled into his seat, stretching out his legs. "Did you know that really means eight?"

"Eight years? I don't understand."

"I didn't either. When a recruit signs on the dotted line, he agrees to two years of active duty. After that, it's two years with the National Guard. Then four on what's called inactive service."

"What does that mean?"

"Active duty is a possibility. In the case of an emergency."

Sophie wondered how often it happened. A man or woman settled into civilian life. Then out of the blue—two or three years later—they get recalled. She couldn't imagine such a thing.

"That's kind of scary."

"Honestly? My hand shook a bit when I signed the papers." His chuckle made Sophie smile. "It isn't so bad once you know what you're dealing with. I stuck for six years." Forbes lowered his voice to whisper "Military intelligence. And before you say it, I've heard

200

all the jokes. Yes, it is an oxymoron. I can attest to the fact. Still, I learned more than I would have in the trenches. Some good. Some— You don't want to know."

"What if I said that I did want to know?"

"You don't want it in your head, Sophie. And I don't want to put it there." The blue of Forbes' eyes darkened to a midnight blue. Sadness and pain. "Even if I did, I couldn't. Classified up the wazoo."

Sophie didn't push. Though she really wanted to. Whatever Forbes had been through, it had helped mold the man he was today. Not that he had changed that much. He was older. Harder. A little more reserved. The smile didn't come as easily, but when it did, she recognized the boy she used to know.

"What made you leave the Army?"

"Somebody made me an offer I couldn't refuse."

Feeling the story was about to get juicy, Sophie leaned closer, anxious for details. Before she could urge Forbes to continue, Maeve knocked on the office door.

"Dinner's ready. Wash your hands."

"To be continued," Forbes said, getting to his feet. He opened the door, gesturing for Sophie to precede him.

"After dinner?"

"Tomorrow."

"But—"

"After dinner, I want to hear about the problems you've been having around the ranch. You can fill me in while you show me where the fire started."

"Mike and Jerry." With everything that happened, the fire had slipped Sophie's mind.

"Mike told me to speak with the boss," Forbes said matter-of-factly.

It seemed they were settling into their roles. Sophie still expected a bump or two. However, Forbes had made it clear that though they were equal partners, he was fine with her taking the lead. On the ranch. When he put on his badge? *That* would be a different story.

# CHAPTER SIXTEEN

THE FIRE CAUSED minimal damage to the barn and its contents. If Sophie hadn't seen it when she had, it could've been worse. A lot worse.

Forbes had given the charred area a cursory examination that morning. It hadn't taken him long to determine it had been deliberate. Though the scent of charred hay overrode everything else, when he had picked up a handful of loose straw, the scent of gasoline filled his nose.

This evening, Forbes knelt next to a pile of bales that had been removed from the barn. Dandi pushed her nose against his shoulder. He and Sophie's dog were still getting acquainted, but he understood what she wanted. While he examined the evidence, he laid his hand on her head, scratching behind her ear. Dandi let out a happy sigh before finding a spot to lie down.

Between the initial fire and the water and dirt that was used to put it out, not much was left. However, after closer examination, he noticed a blackened ring in the middle of one bale. He recognized the familiar pattern—an indicator of where a flame had been put to the accelerant.

First thing in the morning, Forbes would have the bale picked up to be analyzed. They didn't have the proper facilities in Cloverdale. That meant calling in an outside contractor. That kind of expert didn't come cheap. But since he would be using his own money, Forbes wasn't concerned that someone might accuse him of overstepping his authority as chief of police. If a fuss were raised, he would calmly tell them to shove it up their asses. Or words to that effect. This was his home. He would do whatever it took to keep it—and the people on it—safe.

"Do you think there's anything to find?"

Forbes straightened, turning his head to meet Sophie's pensive gaze.

"The crime scene isn't exactly pristine." That was putting it mildly. They found footprints on top of footprints in a big pile of dried mud and soot. "The chance of finding anything helpful is slim to none. But important clues sometimes pop up in the least likely places. I know some people who are experts at finding something out of nothing. I'll get them to look over the area."

"Will it be like something out of *CSI*?

Forbes lips quirked. "Hollywood and real life rarely mesh. What my people do is a lot less flashy, and they almost never solve a case in one commercial-packed hour."

"*Your* people?" Sophie asked, her eyes sparkling with interest. "How many do you have? Why do you need them? Are they still yours now that you're Cloverdale's chief of police?"

Leave it to Sophie to zero in on that particular nugget of information.

"The number varies. I need them for jobs like this. And, yes, they are still mine."

"Why are they still yours? If—"

"I'll explain later."

"Part of, the "*to be continued*" you mentioned earlier?

"Exactly."

Sophie had a quick, nimble brain. A trait Forbes had admired when they were younger. Now? He found a beautiful woman with a brain and the sense to put it to good use. It was sexy as hell.

*Not the time or the place*, Forbes reminded himself. Though he couldn't be blamed for noticing the way the evening sun encased Sophie in its glow. Had her hair always contained those warm, eye-catching auburn highlights? He remembered a less spectacular color running along the lines of plain old, run-of-the-mill brown. And how was he supposed to ignore the way the sleeveless shirt she wore showed off her sleek, toned arms. Apparently, she was still making use of the basement weight room.

Forbes' eyes moved lower to the gentle slope of her breasts, imagining how they would look if he slowly peeled away the thin layer of cotton that shielded them from his gaze.

"Hey!" Sophie snapped her fingers in front of his face. "Earth to Forbes."

*Shit*! Forbes blinked. *What the hell*? He never let his mind wander when on the job. Giving himself a mental shake, he focused on Sophie's face instead of her other assets.

Forbes cleared his throat. "Sorry. What did you say?"

"It doesn't matter." Frowning slightly, Sophie put a hand to his forehead. "Are you feeling okay? You look a little flushed."

Forbes gave himself a moment to enjoy Sophie's cool touch before taking a step back.

"I'm fine."

"Maeve is worried that you've lost weight." Sophie tilted her head, looking him up and down. Her frown deepened. "You could use to put on a few pounds. Have you been ill?"

"No." Technically, it wasn't a lie. A gaping knife wound wasn't the same as an illness. "It was work related. A few weeks of meals like the one Maeve served up tonight, and I'll back to my fighting weight."

"But—"

Not liking the turn the conversation had taken, Forbes firmly moved it back toward the original subject.

"You didn't see anything suspicious? Besides the fire in the barn."

Thankfully, Sophie followed his lead. However, the look she shot him said she knew what he was doing. He could dodge and weave all he wanted. Eventually, she would get her answers.

"It was the middle of the night. I didn't see anybody. And there's no way I would've missed a vehicle driving away."

"Since you caught the fire before it spread very far, whoever set it had to have arrived on foot. You had more important things to worry about. He—or she—could have been hiding in the shadows, slipping away while your back was turned."

"You think the person was still here when I arrived?" Sophie swallowed. "That possibility hadn't occurred to me."

Forbes wasn't exactly thrilled at the idea either. He didn't want to frighten Sophie. Nor did he want to keep her in the dark. Better she was aware of any potential danger. That way she wouldn't be caught unaware.

"My guess is no. This has amateur written all over it. That said." Forbes made certain he had Sophie's full attention. "You have to take this seriously."

"I am." Sophie rubbed her arms, a shiver coursing through her in spite of the seasonably warm temperature. "It's my horses that I'm worried about. Their building has locks, but that's no protection against fire."

"The security around here is non-existent. That wasn't a criticism," Forbes assured Sophie. "I'll take some pictures and send them to my tech experts."

"More of your people?" Sophie teased, leading the way.

The hay barn and the original horse stalls were part of one large, long building. Forbes had kept up with ranch business and knew of Sophie's growing reputation dealing with troubled horses. She kept a low social media profile. She didn't have a website advertising her services. Her business had grown over the last five years by word of mouth. Sophie Lipton had a calming touch. Not a *horse whisperer.* She didn't like labels. Her methods were her own. Whatever she did, it worked.

Success meant they needed to expand. Now, the stable could house as many as sixteen horses at any given time. As of this afternoon, after another satisfied owner picked up her newly gentle-as-a-lamb gelding, all but one stall was occupied.

"Newt was the one who encouraged me." Sophie tapped out the code on the keypad. When the lock disengaged, she pulled open the door. "He recommended me to my first client, practically sealing the deal before I could back out." Sophie smiled. "I loved that man, Forbes. I miss him."

"Me too."

In theory, Forbes knew how Sophie felt. She hadn't saved Newt and the ranch because she expected a reward. She did it because she cared. Deeply. But hearing her say the words—the emotion in her voice—brought it home to him how all of this was to her.

"Thank you for being here, Sophie. Dad loved you like a daughter. All the years you had together. Every time I saw him, he spoke of how much you meant to him."

"Are you trying to make me cry?" Sophie sniffled, rubbing her eyes. "Enough mush. Get your pictures. As long as I'm here, I might as well do a quick check on the horses."

Setting up security cameras in all the buildings and around the perimeter was the easy part. The barn's distance from the house was the biggest problem.

"How do you feel about security guards?" Forbes took the last picture, returning his phone to his back pocket.

Frowning, Sophie gave the last horse a pat before closing the door to the stall. "Are you talking theory or reality?"

"In this case, they're one and the same. With all the wild animals that run around at night, movement-sensitive sensors would be going off every five minutes. The best deterrent would be actual bodies paroling the area. The bigger, and better armed, the better."

"I like the idea of big. Armed? Not so much." Sophie left the barn. When Forbes joined her, she locked the door. "I know it's necessary. But..."

They fell in step with each other, walking back to the house. The sun low in the western sky, the light provided a perfect backdrop for a leisurely stroll, Forbes measured his stride to match Sophie's.

"They will only use their weapons if they have no alternative." When Sophie nodded, Forbes continued. "One more thing. No more late-night walks. It's never been safe—even without this current threat."

"I disagree." Sophie let out a sigh. "However, for now, I'll do as you ask."

"That was easier than I expected. First, you agree on the armed guards, now this? What's the catch?"

"Don't be so suspicious." Smiling, she shot him a sideways look. "We'll find plenty to argue over. I'm saving my ammunition for when *I* want something from *you*."

When Sophie smiled at him like that, Forbes was tempted to tell her she could have anything she wanted. It wouldn't happen, but he was tempted.

"I want to apologize for last night."

Forbes didn't ask what Sophie was talking about. Their encounter in the hall. The kiss. As far as he was concerned, he didn't need an apology. However, an explanation would be nice.

"I wish I had a reasonable explanation." Sophie looked up, down. To her right. Anywhere but at Forbes. "I was tired. Worried about the fire. You showed up out of the blue. I was angry."

"At me? Or the person who set the fire?"

"Both." Stuffing her hands into the front pockets of her faded blue jeans, Sophie sighed. "When you stepped on the board outside my room, I should have ignored it and you. Instead, I acted rashly."

"I was surprised," Forbes admitted.

"Really? Is that all? I was horrified."

"Good God, why?"

"Wasn't it obvious? When push came to shove, I became my mother."

"The hell you say." Forbes stopped dead in his tracks. Grabbing a startled Sophie, he gave her a shake. "If you ever again suggest that you are anything like Joy, I will turn you over my knee. Understood?"

"You must have seen it." Sophie tried to pull away, but Forbes held tight. Jutting out her chin, she met his gaze head on. "Kissing you. The tone of my voice. The way I shimmied my hips. I didn't recognize myself. But I sure as hell recognized Joy."

"Do you want me to tan your backside?" Sophie raised her chin an inch higher, her eyes turned a dark chocolate brown. For a moment, Forbes thought she would argue. But in the end, she simply shook her head. "Here is why I know you're nothing like

208

your mother. First. You have a conscience. The fact that you're worrying over this proves it. Second. Newt survived Typhoon Joy because you cared enough to repair the damage she caused. Third—and as far as I'm concerned, it's the most telling fact—The thought of even touching Joy makes me sick to my stomach. But you? I want to do a hell of a lot more than touch you, Sophie."

Sophie's eyes widened. "You do?"

Moving closer, Forbes softened his grip, his touch turning into a caress. "I wouldn't lie about something this important."

"Are you planning on kissing me now?"

"No."

"Hm." Sophie resumed their walk. "You say you want this hypothetical kiss."

"There is nothing hypothetical about it. I want it. You want it. Right?"

"I suppose," she said.

Obviously, Sophie was unwilling to concede the point quite yet. But with a spring in her step, it was clear she no longer worried about her actions bearing any resemblance to her mother's. Forbes felt a stir of satisfaction. Mission accomplished.

Forbes chuckled. "The kiss will happen. Soon. Many, many kisses—if you decide you like the first."

"What if *you* decide you don't? Like it, that is."

"I've kissed you twice. The first time was an impromptu moment. A goodbye. The second was..."

"A mistake?" Sophie asked, her gaze filled with interest.

"Never that. Like the first, it was unexpected. But I remember thinking I wanted more."

"I like the sound of that." Sophie burst out laughing. "I feel better. But you have to admit this is an odd conversation."

Thinking about it, Forbes smiled. "I can't think of a better subject. Except for ice cream. A big bowl of whatever Maeve has in the freezer."

"Mocha Almond Fudge and Raspberry Cheesecake Swirl."

"Can't argue with those choices." Reaching the house, Forbes held the mudroom door for Sophie. "Care to join me in a bowl of the flavor of your choice?"

"I have to choose?"

How had he forgotten? Sophie could eat a boatload of lumberjacks under the table without gaining an ounce. As she took two bowls from the cupboard, Forbes admired her from behind. She hadn't put on weight, but she now had some interesting curves where they hadn't been before.

"Well?" Sophie asked, opening the freezer door. "What will it be?"

*I'll take you*, Forbes thought. A never-ending helping. He didn't know where it had come from. Or how he felt about it. To go from talking about kissing to discussing flavors of ice cream to wanting Sophie... he swallowed. Forever? It seemed like a crazy idea. He swallowed. Wasn't it?

"What are you having?"

"A scoop of each. To start."

Some ice cream and a little Sophie. To start. Forbes breathed easier. "Sounds good to me."

# CHAPTER SEVENTEEN

FORBES STARED AT the ceiling, forcing himself not to look at the clock. Why bother? How much time could have passed? A minute? Maybe two? Not a hell of a lot when it was pitch black outside, and dawn was hours away.

With a sigh, Forbes turned onto his good side—away from the clock.

How often—when he had nothing but the hard ground to sleep on and an even harder rock for a pillow—had he dreamed of this bed? More times than he could remember. His business had taken him to some shit holes—literally. In the middle of blood, guts, and crap, his mind easily turned to home and all its comforts. Now that he was here with his body relaxed on the soft mattress and clean, fresh as spring rain, sheets. His brain wouldn't follow suit.

After a week at home, Forbes had discovered that the idea of slowing down was easier than the reality. He knew it would take some time before he stopped listening for things that went boom in the night.

Not that he was complaining. Forbes was back in his childhood home. Surrounded by old friends. Each day, he went to a job that was important to the community. Where he could make a difference. Not earth shaking by most standards, but he was right where he wanted to be.

The only thing that would make it better was if his father was around. However, Forbes felt Newt's presence in every corner of the house. Oddly, it was comforting.

Then there was Sophie. They had fallen into a familiar rhythm like the one they had as teenagers. With the added bonus of sexual tension. They knew the kiss was coming—and more. Still, neither was in a hurry to take the next step. It felt like an unofficial courting period. They had a lot of catching up to do. A lot of tales to tell. A lot of questions to ask and answer.

In the mornings, they would eat breakfast before he helped with the chores. That was when Forbes continued his story. With Sophie's help.

"Why did you leave?" Sophie asked. Early, it was the morning after they checked out the fire. "And why did it take you so long to come back?"

Jumping right in before he had a full cup of coffee in his system hadn't been Forbes' plan. However, Sophie seemed determined. She wanted to begin at the beginning? So be it. Like ripping off a Band-Aid, he told her the worst in one long run-on sentence.

"I left because Joy hit on me and convinced Dad that I was the villain. After that, he pretty much shut me out."

Holding his breath, Forbes had waited for Sophie's reaction. Once again, she surprised him.

"I figured it was something like that," she stated calmly. When she met his gaze, her eyes were heavy with sadness.

The idea of telling Sophie had filled Forbes with dread. He wished he could have spared her another crappy piece of news concerning her mother. "Why aren't you surprised?"

"The first day we arrived, I saw the way Joy looked at you. Like a prime piece of meat dangled in front of a predatory cat."

"Nice imagery."

"I'd seen it before. Many times." Sophie continued using her pitchfork, adding hay to each stall. "I didn't know you or Newt. All I was worried about was myself. I hoped Joy would wait to take a bite out of you until I was able to enjoy the best playground ever. In other words, I was a selfish bitch."

"Sophie." Forbes stopped. Leaning against his pitchfork, he shook his head. "No."

"I could have ended it all right there. Instead, all I could think about was myself."

"I could have forced my father to listen to me. Instead, I ran away. In the middle of the night. Knowing what Joy was, I left him to fend for himself. What does that make me?"

"The answers seem so easy now. I know what I should have done. Back then, it seemed impossible."

"Because it was." Forbes resumed his work. "We were kids, Sophie. Joy's talons were in deep before you arrived at the ranch. Dad made his choices. I don't know if anything we did would have changed how things turned out."

*If only... I wish... What if...?* Forbes had asked himself these questions a thousand times. Eventually, he stopped. What was the point? He found a kind of peace. Reconciled with his father. Though it was never the same between them.

The trust and closeness had been altered irrevocably. When he and Newt were together, their conversations never delved deeper than friendly, gossipy news about the ranch. Forbes kept the details about his job light and breezy. He would always be grateful for the time they had together. But it was sad when he remembered how it used to be.

"You could have returned after Joy left."

"I wasn't ready. I blamed my father for taking her side. For choosing that woman over me. By the time I let go of my anger, I was living a different life."

"Filled with excitement and adventure."

Forbes smiled. "Something like that. I had commitments. A thriving business that I couldn't walk away from. More than that, I didn't want to walk away."

As the week continued, Sophie asked her questions. And Forbes answered them to the best of his ability. Starting with his decision to leave the Army.

Six years in, Forbes had been tired of the bureaucracy. The paperwork and trying to figure out who was in charge on any given day. It seemed they were always taking one step forward followed by two steps back.

Forbes would always be grateful for the first-class education in everything from electronics to surveillance to crime scene investigation. However, he had known it was time for a change.

When an ex-Army buddy offered him the chance to get in on the ground floor of a fledgling security business, he weighed his options, checked it out, and then jumped. He invested the money he had inherited on his twenty-first birthday, making him a full partner. It was slow going at first. But things took off fast when they received their first government contract. Then another. And another.

The business grew by leaps and bounds, expanding so fast they barely had time to take a breath. They earned a reputation for getting the job done. Quickly. Efficiently. And most of all, quietly. In and out. Little fuss. No publicity. They handled the messes nobody else wanted. And were paid extremely well for their trouble. Forbes made back his investment ten times over.

The lack of publicity wasn't just about discretion. Many of the team's assignments were top secret. Strictly need to know. If something went wrong, they were on their own. Contacting the US government for assistance would be futile; as far as the government was concerned, they didn't exist.

Gingerly, Forbes touched his wounded side, his thoughts on his last mission. It had started out fairly routine. Extricate the kidnapped son of a wealthy, high-powered businessman. He had his own opinion on the idiocy of the guy's decision to leave the relative safety of Dubai for a trek into the desert where he was captured and held for ransom.

As always, Forbes kept his thoughts to himself. His job wasn't to judge. He and his team flew in. Did what they were paid to do— returned the stupid party boy to his overly indulgent daddy—and collected their huge fee.

That was the plan. A plan that usually worked with little drama. Forbes had received his share of bumps, bruises, and scrapes over the years. One time, he broke his left arm when it connected with the club wielded by a particularly stubborn bad guy. The last mission—Forbes' last mission period—hadn't ended well.

Oh, they completed their mission. Idiot boy returned to the bosom of this family, money in the bank. One catch. The gaping knife wound delivered to his right side.

It wouldn't have happened if the victim—the twenty-year-old they were there to rescue—hadn't turned out to be a mass of quivering jelly. Fifty yards from the waiting helicopter, the fool decided to have a hissy fit. Forbes was forced to knock out the screaming ninny, hoisting him onto his shoulder. That was when it happened. A kidnapper they hadn't accounted for sprang out of nowhere, the knife he wielded hitting its target. Forbes managed to get the kid to the helicopter before collapsing from the rapid blood loss. It hadn't killed him. But it had been a close call.

Two weeks later, Forbes woke up in a German hospital. He learned his father had passed away and he decided it was time to leave active duty. He still believed in what they were doing. But he'd had his fill of risking his life to fix somebody else's mistakes.

Forbes was still a full partner. However, from now on, his duties were strictly on the consulting side.

The basics, he had shared with Sophie. Most of it, he couldn't have told her if he wanted to. Telling her about his wound had been a last-minute decision. Downplaying the severity hadn't worked for even a second.

"You could have died." Sophie set down the curry comb, stepping away from the horse who had been enjoying her ministrations.

"But I didn't." Knowing it was a lame response didn't stop Forbes. He had no reasonable explanation. Besides, it was all he could come up with.

"What about missing Newt's funeral?" Sophie crossed the space that separated them, getting in Forbes' face. "I thought you put business before your father. Some pretty nasty thoughts floated through my head. All the while, you were fighting for your life."

"By that time, the fight was over. I won. However, I was weak as a newborn kitten, so traveling was out of the question."

215

Sophie's eyes narrowed. Forbes could see the storm brewing behind them. He remembered that she had a temper, though he had never experienced its full wrath.

"Where exactly are you hurt?"

Not liking the tone of her voice—all calm and reasonable—Forbes pointed toward his side."

"Asshole!" Sophie jabbed his shoulder—the left one on the opposite side of the wound. "You should have let us know."

"Well..."

"Who knows?" Forbes opened his mouth to answer, but Sophie beat him to it. "Mike and Jerry," she said with a huff. "Not Maeve. She would have told me. Aaron? Of course."

"What was the point of worrying you and Maeve?"

"Me? You mean Maeve. Period. Don't include me. I've been off your radar for twelve years. Any information I learned about you was secondhand at best. Old news." Sophie frowned, shaking her head. "That discussion is for another time. I have to ride some fence, and you need to get to work. Show me."

Automatically, Forbes' hand went to his side as if hiding his injury was still an option.

"It isn't that bad, Sophie."

"Sure. A mere scratch kept you in the hospital for how long?" Sophie swatted his hand away.

"A month. Give or take."

"Give, if my guess is right.

Forbes watched as Sophie bent closer, carefully lifting the edge of his t-shirt. Her gasp told him what he already knew. It didn't look good. Though the doctors had done a stellar job saving his life and stitching him up, they weren't miracle workers. It looked red and puffy. Better than a week ago, but not as good as it would after a few more months of healing.

The scar would be a doozy. About six inches long and just jagged enough to let anybody looking know that it hadn't been put there with the care of a surgeon.

"Does it hurt?" Sophie's touch was light as a feather, her index finger tracing the line of stitches. When Forbes let out a groan, she would have moved away if he hadn't caught her hand, holding it where it was.

"It hurts a little. More of a dull ache. There have been a few times when the itching has been so bad, I wanted to rip at it with all ten fingernails. But your touch is so cool and soft, it makes me forget everything else."

The groan turned into a hiss, making Sophie chuckle.

"You kissed me."

"I kissed your injury." Sophie straightened. "I don't have any personal experience, but rumor has it a kiss will make it better."

Interestingly, Forbes thought it worked. Or Sophie's lips distracted him. He was fairly certain it was the latter.

"I thought you were mad at me."

"I guess it goes to prove that anger doesn't preclude me hating the thought of your pain. Whatever I can do to help, I will."

"I have a few suggestions."

Shaking her head, Sophie had scurried away before Forbes was able to pull her back.

That had been yesterday.

With a sigh, he gave up and left his bed. It hadn't been the time—or the place—for him to kiss her the way he wanted. If it felt as good as he anticipated, they wouldn't stop with just a kiss.

Naked, Forbes considered heading to the kitchen for a glass of juice. As he reached for a pair of sweats from the dresser, a flash of light outside the window caught his eye. Frowning, he moved quickly, standing to the side, out of sight so he could get a good look at the area two stories down.

At first, he saw nothing but black. No moon, the night was filled with shadows and not much else. He knew a guard patrolled the area. One here, two at the barn. The cameras were operational. Plus, lights came on at the slightest movement, illuminating the grounds like a baseball field at game time.

The guard never carried a flashlight. It made him a target. The men relied on their natural ability to see in the dark—and the best night-vision goggles available—when on their rounds. That meant whoever was out there—if Forbes hadn't imagined it—was probably up to no good.

There it was. A burst of light, then darkness. Smart. Instead of a steady beam, the person used the flashlight only when needed. Forbes could pick out a figure dressed in head-to-toe black moving toward the side of the garage.

*Why the hell hadn't the motion-sensitive lights come on?* He would ream out the guy who installed them, but that was for later. Right now, he had something more important to deal with.

Slipping on the sweatpants, a black t-shirt, and a pair of sneakers, Forbes took his gun from the end table drawer. Checking to make certain it was loaded, he hurried from the room, grabbing the com-unit as he went. He called to the guard. Twice. Nothing but silence. *Shit.* That wasn't good

Quick and quiet. Forbes knew it was his best chance to catch the prowler. Hopefully before the person perpetrated whatever mischief was on his or her agenda.

Halfway down the stairs, Forbes stopped when he saw he wasn't alone. Ahead of him by half the length of the living room was Sophie—fully dressed and carrying a baseball bat.

Forbes took the remaining steps three at a time, catching up in a few strides.

"What do you think you're doing?"

"Son of a—" Sophie spun around. "How many times do I have to tell you to stop sneaking up on me? What if I'd smashed in your head? Or worse?"

"Worse than a smashed head?" Forbes maneuvered himself in front of Sophie, taking the lead. He wouldn't waste his time by telling her to go back to her room. Nor would he ask what she was doing up and dressed at this time of the night when she had promised to curtail her nocturnal wanderings. He wasn't letting it go. But at the moment, they had more important issues at hand.

"There is almost always something worse," Sophie informed him, trailing close behind.

"I guess you're right." They were near the side exit. Pausing with his hand on the doorknob, he looked over his shoulder. "Is there any chance I can convince you to stay in the house?" Sophie snorted, giving Forbes his answer. "Then, please. I beg of you. Keep behind me. Gun beats baseball bat every time. And if I say hit the ground? Do it. No argument. No hesitation."

"You're the expert."

It would have been nice if Sophie had thought of that sooner—before she left her room. But again, not the time.

Cracking open the door, Forbes listened. A faint noise to his right. And the smell of...? The fumes from an aerosol can? Before he could decide, the faint noise turned into the sound of somebody running—away from the house. One of the floodlights finally engaged. It happened just in time for him to see a body slip from the light into the dark.

Forbes took off at full speed, shouting, "Stay here, Sophie. I mean it. And lock the door."

In his high school football days, Forbes had been known as a quick and agile quarterback. As an adult, he was just plain fast. However, in this case, fast wasn't good enough. Before he had the chance to catch up, he heard the slam of a door and the roar of a vehicle taking off. Skidding to a halt, he didn't have the chance to get a visual through the cloud of dust kicked up by the spinning tires. Coughing, Forbes squinted. Taillights. Nothing more.

Diesel, by the sound of the engine. In all likelihood, that meant a truck. Mind working possibilities, Forbes started back. Raising the com unit, he hit the send button.

"Moncrieff? Drysdale? Do you copy?"

"Copy, boss," Drysdale answered immediately.

"Copy, boss." Moncrieff gave his reply seconds later.

"Any sign of trouble?" he asked the men patrolling the barn area.

"Negative. It's been quiet," Drysdale informed him.

"Any word from Pike?" Forbes still couldn't reach the other guard.

"Negative, boss." Moncrieff paused. "Do we have a man down?"

"Too soon to tell. Give me ten. Over."

Forbes scrolled through the numbers on his phone. The truck left tire tracks. Deep ones if the dust they left behind was any indication. Forbes' first instinct was to call his usual forensics team, then stopped. Pictures and casts of the tracks. It didn't take specialized equipment. As chief of police, he had to start trusting the Cloverdale officers under his command. His thumb pushed the button before he could change his mind.

"Chief?" Ollie Wabash sounded surprisingly alert for this time of the night.

"There's been more trouble at my place, Ollie."

"Anybody hurt?"

"No. A prowler. I'll write a report when I get to the office. For now, here's what I need you to do."

Forbes hung up, checking the time. Three thirty. All things considered, it would be an hour, maybe more, before the Cloverdale P.D. arrived. By then, the sun would be up—or close to it. The adrenaline rush started to wear off, and that bed he hadn't been able to sleep in sounded pretty good about now.

"Forbes?" Sophie met him by the garage.

"Damn it, Sophie! I told you to stay in the house."

"Since that was my plan, I'm going to let that tone of male arrogance in your voice slide—this time. Just as I was shutting the door, I heard a groan."

"Naturally, you had to investigate."

"Naturally. Do you want to stand here and argue? Or can I finish my story?"

"Your story. By all means." In spite of himself, Forbes felt his lips twitch. "We'll pick up the argument later."

"Jackass." Sophie turned away, but not before Forbes saw a smile. "I found your missing security guard. Come with me."

Forbes followed Sophie into the house. Maeve, in her robe, slippers, and a head full of curlers, stood beside one of the bar stools, a bottle of peroxide and bandages on the counter. In the chair sat the guard, Kyle Pike. Dried blood ran from his hairline, down his cheek. On his temple was the beginning of a nasty bruise. Seeing Forbes, Kyle lost what little color remained on his face, his skin going from sickly gray to stark white.

"I have no excuse, boss," Kyle said. Back rigid, it looked as if he would shoot to his feet, ready to stand at attention. Maeve kept him in place with a firm hand and a warning look any drill sergeant would covet.

"I agree," Forbes said, crossing his arms over his chest.

"The man is injured, Forbes." Maeve shook her head as she cleaned the gash on Kyle's head. She had become an expert at fixing all kinds of nicks and scrapes that were an inevitable part of ranch life.

"I messed up, ma'am. My patrol. My responsibility." Kyle raised his chin. "I officially tender my resignation, sir."

"We'll talk about that later." Forbes believed in second chances—especially since Pike was the only one hurt. But he wasn't giving the ex-soldier a pass until he heard some details. "What happened out there?"

Kyle shook his head. "I was making my rounds. Everything seemed normal. I was about to report in with Drysdale and Moncrieff when I heard what sounded like a wounded animal. I flipped down my goggles to get a better look and then..."

"Go on," Forbes urged impatiently. Though it didn't take a genius to figure out what happened next.

"Somebody hit me from behind." Pike raised a hand to his head. "Or the side, I guess. Next thing I remember, Ms. Lipton was kneeling next to me."

Maeve applied the last piece of adhesive tape. Removing her disposable gloves, she tossed them into the garbage. "Get yourself to a doctor right away, young man. Head injuries are nothing to take lightly."

"Thank you, Ms. Kincaid."

"Maeve is right, Pike. I'll get Moncrieff to drive you to Spokane."

"He's on duty. I can—"

"You can't do anything but take orders. Understood? I have reinforcements on the way." Forbes gave Pike a pat on the back. "Don't worry. Your job is safe. It could have happened to anybody."

Five minutes later, Pike and Moncrieff were on their way.

"You don't believe that," Sophie said. She stood beside Forbes, watching the black SUV disappear from view.

"What don't I believe?"

"That it could have happened to anybody."

"Sure I do." Forbes smiled when he saw the doubtful look Sophie shot him. "Anybody but me."

"That's what I thought." Shaking her head, Sophie rubbed her arms.

If Forbes had a jacket, he would have played the gallant card, draping it over Sophie's shoulders. Or he could have suggested he share some of his body heat with her. Holding her close, his hands rubbing slowly up and down her back sounded like a good idea. Until he remembered where they were and what was happening. Lately, *another time* seemed to be his mantra—at least when it came to Sophie.

"It's chilly out here. Let's get inside."

"I need to show you something first." Sophie let him back the way they had come walking past the door. "I smelled something in the air the first time we came outside."

Forbes had forgotten. "I smelled it too."

"It seems our prowler had a purpose." Sophie pointed to the side of the house.

"Well, shit."

"My thoughts exactly."

The penmanship was sloppy. Obviously, the author hadn't been able to finish. However, sprayed in big, black letters, the message was clear.

SOPHIE DIE

# CHAPTER EIGHTEEN

SOPHIE WAS CONTENT to leave the *maybe it was, maybe it wasn't* a death threat to Forbes, his hired guns, and what looked like the entire Cloverdale police department. She was a busy woman. Too busy to dissolve in a fit of vapors or hide behind closed doors. Or whatever Forbes seemed to think was appropriate behavior. He tried to argue her out of business as usual. But she wouldn't hear of it.

Running a working ranch meant no one had a day off. Animals needed tending. Not to mention the myriad of matters that couldn't be put off if she wanted to keep her well-oiled machine operational. In an emergency, Sophie would allow for some leeway. A few hastily spray-painted words didn't qualify. Was she a bit unnerved? Absolutely. She wasn't a fool. The secret wasn't to think about it. Most of all, she wanted Forbes to think the incident hadn't phased her in the least.

Forbes had spent the past hour supervising his officers to make certain they knew what they were doing. He seemed satisfied that they could work on their own long enough for him to stop for something to eat. After washing his hands, he joined Sophie at the counter.

"Maybe they were going to write Sophie Diet," she reasoned, smiling her thanks when Maeve set a plate in front of her that sported a hot, crispy waffle.

His cup of coffee halfway to his mouth, Forbes hesitated. The look he gave her was a cross between incredulous and exacerbated. Sophie knew it was ridiculous. But she would rather laugh than cry any day.

"You think somebody snuck onto the ranch with the purpose of letting you know you needed to lose weight? In what crazy world are you fat?"

Sophie knew she was lucky. Her metabolism ate up the calories as fast as she could pour them in.

"It isn't about losing pounds but eating better. Sometimes I don't make the healthiest food choices," Sophie explained, drowning her waffle in maple syrup.

"It isn't about your eating habits, Sophie." Though his words belied his wince when she added another layer of butter. "For your safety—and my peace of mind—it would be better if you stayed inside. Until I can get you a permanent bodyguard."

"That isn't happening." Sophie held up her fork. "I don't need a professional when the ranch is filled with willing and able cowboys. There is always somebody around, Forbes."

"A professional would—"

"Be a waste of manpower." Sophie found it easier to finish Forbes' sentence than present her case after the fact. "Wherever I go, I'll take a big, able-bodied ranch hand with me."

"I could assign somebody to you without your permission." Forbes seemed to like the sound of it.

"Save him—or her the embarrassment. First sniff of a bodyguard and I'll saddle my horse and head for the hills. Think one of your tenderfoots can keep up?"

Sophie could navigate every inch of the ranch with her eyes closed—and Forbes knew it.

"Maeve?" Forbes turned to the housekeeper for backup.

"Do you promise you'll be careful?" Maeve spoke to Sophie, ignoring Forbes.

"Yes." Sophie jumped to her feet, giving Maeve a hug.

"One sniff of trouble and I'll move my vote to Forbes' side of the ledger," Maeve warned.

"Sounds fair to me."

Sophie deposited her dishes in the sink. On her way by, Forbes laid a hand on her arm. "You have your phone with you?"

Casual affection had never been Sophie's thing. She didn't object. More like it didn't occur to her for the simple reason that she hadn't been raised that way. Her mother didn't believe in wasting her hugs on Sophie. And if one of her gentlemen callers had tried such a thing, she would have kicked his balls so far up into his body, it would have taken a month of Sundays for them to fall back into place.

However, with each passing day, wanting to touch Forbes had become a pressing need that was harder and harder to ignore. For the first time, Sophie acted without thinking. As she passed by, she laid her hand over his.

"I'll be fine. If it will make you feel better, call me a couple of times during the day and check in."

"Or, you could call me. Every hour." Forbes smiled to let Sophie know he was kidding. Mostly.

Sophie chuckled, giving Forbes' hand a squeeze before grabbing the keys to her truck and heading out the door.

Opening the cab door, Sophie waited until Dandi jumped in before grabbing the steering wheel. She pulled herself up. Sitting for a minute, she looked around the driveway thinking of the day she first saw it and the ranch. Love at first sight. Though she hadn't known it at the time because she had no frame of reference, the moment she set foot on Branson land, Sophie was home. It had taken her a while to understand what she felt, but the sense of belonging had never left. This was her little corner of the world. Nothing or no one would change that.

"I'm scared, Dandi. Whether it was a prank or something more serious, I refuse to let anybody paralyze me with fear."

Dandi wagged her tail. Wise, adoring eyes seemed to say the dog was on Sophie's side—no matter what.

"Women power," Sophie nodded.

As Sophie drove down the road, she kept one hand on the steering wheel and one on Dandi's head. Already, her thoughts had veered away from her personal problems to the Appaloosa waiting for her at the barn. The owner purchased the horse as a gift for his daughter's eleventh birthday. If Sophie didn't work her magic, who knew what would happen to the animal. She had one month to turn the animal from skittish to friendly.

So far, Sophie had a perfect record. But this wasn't about her ego. The horse's future was in her hands. Failure wasn't an option.

"HAVE YOU CONSIDERED moving into your father's old bedroom?"

"No." Starting to lag from lack of sleep, Forbes poured himself another cup of coffee. With the long day he had ahead of him, the more caffeine he pumped into his system, the better. Taking a drink, he looked at Maeve. "Dad shared that room with Joy. An exorcism and a ton of burned sage wouldn't get me to set foot in there."

"It's just a thought." With her back to him, Maeve returned a plate to the cupboard. "It might be better if..."

"If? Something's bothering you, Maeve."

Setting down the dishtowel, Maeve turned to face him.

"Sophie touched your hand. Not a big deal unless you've known her as long as I have. She's more affectionate than she used to be, but not when other people are around."

"You're making more of it than you should."

"Perhaps. Except, I saw the way you looked at her. It hadn't occurred to me before. But now, I think a little separation wouldn't hurt."

If it weren't for Maeve's earnest expression, Forbes would have laughed.

"Sophie and I were always in the same wing—just down the hall from each other. It didn't seem to bother you when we were teenagers."

"Sophie was a child in so many ways. That's how you thought of her. But she's grown up. Unlike then, mentally and physically, she's on the same level. And you've noticed."

Forbes couldn't argue. When he looked at Sophie, he saw a beautiful, desirable woman. It was only natural for his thoughts—and body—to respond accordingly.

"We live under the same roof. If Sophie and I want to..." Forbes felt odd discussing sex with Maeve, so he shrugged. "The point is that my moving to the other side of the house won't make any difference."

"I know that. But…"

Teasing, Forbes winked. "Whose virtue are you worried about? Mine or Sophie's?"

"Honestly." Maeve put her hands on her curvy hips. "Virtue has nothing to do with it. Though you lost yours long before it was seemly. That's right," she said when Forbes showed his surprise. "I know everything that goes on in this house. As did your father. If he was fine with you sneaking girls into your room, it wasn't my place to say anything."

Looking away, Forbes rubbed the back of his neck. Wondering if his father and Maeve had known was one thing. Having proof positive to the affirmative was something else altogether. He was embarrassed as much as… Fine. He was embarrassed. Almost thirty years old and he felt like a kid caught with a stash of dirty magazines. Only his centerfolds had been flesh and blood.

"However, that has nothing to do with you and Sophie. You're adults. I wouldn't dream of telling you how to live your lives."

"But…?" Forbes knew one was coming.

"If you act on this attraction, what then? Have you given any thought to what happens if it doesn't work out? I know you wouldn't intentionally hurt Sophie. Nor she you." Maeve's expression softened. "Sophie is happy. She's found her place."

"I know that."

"I hope that you're home for good?"

"Yes," Forbes said emphatically.

"Then my advice is to take a step back and really think about what you want. Is it Sophie? Or is she simply an itch that needs scratching?"

Maeve held Forbes' gaze for several beats. With a sharp nod of her head—a signal that she had said what needed saying—she walked out of the kitchen, leaving him to his thoughts.

As far as Forbes was concerned, Maeve's words didn't change anything. Yes, he wanted Sophie. That was a given, and it wasn't going away. But it wasn't an itch. That implied something easily taken care of and quickly forgotten. Sophie was neither. She never had been. Never would be.

Still, Forbes needed to take Sophie's feelings into account. This attraction was new on both sides. What he wanted—now and in the future—might not be the same for her. The idea brought him up short. He had never worried about it before. A one or two-night stand between consenting, properly protected adults had been his M.O. for longer than he cared to remember. Now that he wanted more, wouldn't it be ironic if Sophie thought of *him* as nothing but an itch?

"SOMEBODY BUSTED THE lights, boss."

"Excuse me?" Forbes' hearing was excellent, but he couldn't believe what Drysdale told him. "Somebody broke our practically indestructible, expensive-as-hell flood lights?"

Ian Drysdale was a man of medium height—a half-foot shorter than Forbes. But he was strong with arms like bulging steel. He wore his hair military short, never changing the style after leaving the Marine Corp.

Forbes and the security guard/bodyguard/ex-soldier/tech expert stood inside the shed that had been set up as command central. About ten yards from the horse stalls, the equipment monitored all the buildings from the main house to the bunkhouse, to the corrals, storage sheds, and hay barns. Not to mention the surrounding fields. They had a cot in the back for a quick nap, a fully stocked refrigerator, plus a coffee pot that never ran dry. At the moment, a newly arrived addition to the team—Moncrieff's replacement—made the rounds, his movements easy to trace on one of the monitors.

Drysdale showed Forbes the box filled with chunks of glass. "This is what's left of the four floods that we had placed at the front of the house."

Forbes shook his head. "Great. Just fucking great."

"I think I know how it happened," Drysdale, said, his expression grim.

"Well," Forbes urged. "Don't leave me in suspense."

"I haven't been able to contact Moncrieff. He dropped Pike at the emergency room three hours ago. Since then, he's been off the grid."

"You checked his phone?" Modern technology made tracing a person's whereabouts ridiculously easy.

"One of our guys found it in a garbage can outside a gas station on the outskirts of Spokane. I can't find any record of Moncrieff using a credit card. My guess is he filled up his tank and paid with cash."

"What about the SUV?" The car was owned by the company, which meant it—like all their vehicles—was equipped with a tracker.

"Dumped—just like the phone. This time at a truck stop about fifty miles south of the city. We have ears and eyes all over, boss. We'll find him."

Maybe. Forbes hadn't personally trained Moncrieff, but he had a big hand in the curriculum. He and his partners were rigorous in their efforts to hire only the best. Either a recruit passed the program with flying colors, or they didn't pass at all. Moncrieff had been one of their best. Until now, Forbes would have sworn he was loyal.

"If he slips up, we'll get him. Otherwise…" It pissed Forbes off too much to think about. "If Moncrieff is behind this, there must be a good reason. What was going on with him?"

"Money problems," Drysdale stated, his face deadpan. But anger burned in his eyes. A member of his team had gone rogue, and it didn't sit well.

"Gambling?"

"Ex-wife and three kids. Plus, his new girlfriend has expensive tastes."

They paid their people well. Very well. However, a salary—no matter the size—only went so far. Moncrieff had decided to play above his means, and now they all paid the price.

"You should have told me." Drysdale shrugged, and Forbes growled. "I know. Brothers in arms. I'm all for it, Ian. Up to a point. You don't have to rat out your buddies over every little bump. But this was a potential fucking sink hole. If anything had happened to Sophie—" Forbes took a deep breath, refusing to fill his head with images of something that hadn't happened. "You'd be out on your ass, and I'd personally run Moncrieff to the ground."

"I've met Ms. Lipton. I'd be right by your side.

"You have a job to do." Forbes shot Drysdale a warning look. "Sophie is not a perk. Understood?"

"I get it," Drysdale nodded. His expression remained stoic, but his lips twitched—just a little. "There's no rule against admiring the view."

Briefly, Forbes considered the possibility. Deciding it would be impossible to police, he reluctantly let the idea pass.

"If Moncrieff took a bribe, there has to be a trail."

"Already on it, boss. If I can't find the money, Renly will."

Drysdale was right. When it came to his computer skills, Silas Renly was a legend. He was Forbes' business partner and someone to be trusted without question. If Moncrieff let off the slightest cyber ping, Renly would find it.

"Keep me posted." Halfway out the door, Forbes hesitated. "And Drysdale?"

"Boss?"

"This should go without saying. But tell the rest of the men. Sophie is off limits."

Drysdale didn't laugh often. Not unless he found something off-the-charts funny. It seemed Forbes' warning qualified.

"I didn't mean it as a joke," Forbes muttered.

"Sophie Lipton must be something if the mighty Branson has fallen," Drysdale said, still grinning.

"This isn't about me." Of course it was, but Forbes wasn't about to admit it. When Drysdale snorted, he kept walking. "Tell the men to do their jobs, that's all."

Slamming the door, Forbes took his sunglasses from his pocket. The mighty Branson hadn't fallen. However, it wouldn't take much to push him over the edge. A few words from Sophie— the right words—and he had the feeling he would tumble willingly. Enthusiastically.

Funny. Forbes had yet to kiss Sophie. Not a real, I mean it, mutually consensual, adult kiss. They had circled each other for the past week with a sense of growing attraction. And need. He couldn't forget his body's constant reminder of how much he wanted Sophie. Yet, the non-physical side of their relationship occupied his mind as much as wanting to feel her naked body next to his.

How did that saying go? Women learned to desire the men they loved. Men learned to love the women they desired. Or something like that. The point was that Forbes always bought into the idea. From a man's point of view, it made sense. Sophie—beautiful, funny, thick-skinned, marshmallow-hearted, Sophie—had turned the notion on its head. In a way, he had always loved her. The desire had come much later.

Forbes checked his watch. He didn't have time for daydreaming. Jumping in his truck, he aimed the vehicle north.

The problems on the ranch weren't Forbes' only responsibilities. Though he was just a phone call away, as chief of police, he wanted the people of Cloverdale to know he was committed to his job. For that to happen, he had to do more than occasionally show his face at the office whenever he wasn't too busy with something else.

Hitting a button, Forbes told the in-dash computer to call the station.

"Chief."

"I'll be there in thirty minutes. Anything I should know?"

"The evidence from the ranch has been bagged, tagged, and sent to the lab. There have been a few minor instances around town. Nothing out of the ordinary."

"Have the reports on my desk." When his stomach rumbled, Forbes realized he hadn't eaten since breakfast. "Is *Rick's Diner* still around?"

"Going strong. Thursday is meatloaf and mashed potato day."

The road ahead was flat and clear for the next few miles. Swearing he could smell the meat and gravy, Forbes hit the gas.

"Add another thirty minutes to my ETA. I haven't eaten lunch, and that meatloaf is calling my name."

"Roger that, Chief. You won't be sorry. And if there's any left, don't pass up on the blackberry cobbler. If you want, I can call over and have them save you some. I know the cook personally."

"Girlfriend?"

Ollie paused. "Boyfriend. Is that a problem?"

"Not on my watch. Make that call. I'm a big fan of blackberries."

"Will do. Thank you, Chief. Drive safe."

Smiling, Forbes ended the call. They lived in a different world. Some of the changes were good. Some, not so much. However, the change in attitude concerning a person's sexuality swung way onto the good side. He imagined Ollie and his boyfriend received their share of crap. But not from him. If anybody else in the department had a problem, they damn well better keep it to themselves.

AS SOPHIE LAY awake, listening, she felt like she was fifteen again. Only then, instead of wondering when Forbes would return home, she had fallen asleep the second her head hit the pillow, hoping he would have the common courtesy to miss the squeaky board outside her bedroom door—for once.

Tonight, Sophie's feelings were the opposite—in every way. She cared about Forbes' arrival. She wanted to know the second he passed her door. And she hoped that he made certain she knew. That he cared enough to put his foot on that stupid, pesky, wonderful board.

"He fell asleep in his office, Dandi."

Sophie rolled to her back, turning her head to look at the dog. On her bed in the corner, Dandi's response was to lift one eyelid, snort, and let out a huge sigh before going right back to sleep.

"You're right," Sophie continued, looking at the ceiling. "Forbes has a lot on his plate. After last night, he probably thinks that sleep is at a premium around here."

Around dinnertime, Ollie Wabash called to inform her that Forbes was sleeping soundly and had been for about an hour. Since Ollie was about to go off duty, he wondered if he should wake the chief.

"Let him sleep," Sophie had said without having to think about it. "Tell whoever is on duty to leave him be unless there is something they can't handle on their own."

That *something* came around eight thirty. Several somethings. A car was reported stolen. A fire broke out near the high school. And a fight at *Smokey's Bar* resulted in several arrests. Not a lot in some cities, but for Cloverdale, it was practically a crime wave. As Forbes said when he called at ten o'clock, when it rained, it poured.

"I don't know when I'll be home. *Smokey's* sounds like a mess. The fire is under control, but I want to swing by and take a look. Luckily, the stolen car was found at the end of Main Street undamaged. Some kids probably took it for a joyride. That's what Mr. Greely gets for leaving his keys in the ignition."

Sophie smiled at the exasperation in Forbes' voice. Mr. Greely taught math at the high school and had for as long as anybody could remember. "Did you tell him that?"

"I did. Do you know what his response was?"

It wasn't hard to guess, but Sophie let Forbes deliver the punchline.

"No, what did he say?"

"After he reminded me that I once received a B-minus on one of his Algebra tests, he laid into me over my lack of leadership. *What kind of town are you running, Forbes Branson? I've left the keys in that car every day for thirty years. Nobody took off with it*

234

*before.* Then he asked why I wasn't wearing a uniform. As if that was relevant."

"It's a fair question," Sophie said. "Why don't you wear a uniform?"

Forbes rolled his eyes. "I wore a uniform in the Army. When I took this job, it was with the understanding that a full uniform wasn't my style. A dark-blue cotton shirt, Cloverdale P.D. insignia on the sleeve. It should arrive tomorrow."

"Okay," Sophie nodded. Satisfied with Forbes' answer, she shifted back to the original topic. "I like Mr. Greely. He was very helpful when math was still my enemy."

Mr. Greely had taken the time to help Sophie. As a result, she had the confidence to take calculus during her senior year. And passed the class with a solid B average.

"I liked him, too. Still do." Forbes chuckled. "I saw a definite twinkle in the old coot's eyes while he bawled me out."

"Call me before you leave for home."

"It's going to be well after midnight. If you have any trouble—anything, Sophie—buzz Drysdale."

"I will," Sophie promised. It was nice that Forbes had called. Nice to know she was in his thoughts. "Call me."

"Okay."

Forbes had been right about the time. He called at half past two, letting Sophie know he was on his way. He sounded worn out.

"Are you sure you're up for driving?" Sophie asked. If there was any chance of him falling asleep at the wheel, he should stay in Cloverdale.

"I'm fine," Forbes assured her. "Tomorrow is my day off. I don't want to start it in my office on that lumpy old couch."

Sophie understood his point. However, it didn't stop her from worrying.

"Roll down your truck windows and play some music. Something loud. With plenty of percussions."

"How about the *1812 Overture*?" She heard a teasing note in Forbes' voice.

"Perfect."

Laughing, Forbes hung up. That had been almost thirty minutes earlier. Sophie would give him another ten. If he weren't home by then, she would go out looking for him.

Sophie sat up. She hadn't heard a squeak, but the sound of Forbes deliberately avoiding the board so he wouldn't wake her. *Honestly*. Did the man think she would sleep a wink until she knew he was safe, sound, and in his own bed? Apparently not.

With a sigh, Sophie padded across the room, opening the door to the hall.

"We have to stop meeting like this."

Forbes' head fell forward. Without turning, he looked at her over his shoulder.

"Nice line. What movie is it from?"

"Dozens." Sophie kept walking until she stood in front of him. "Most were in black and white. Maybe Bette Davis? Definitely Myrna Loy."

Up close, Forbes looked worse than he sounded. Not merely tired. He was ready to drop.

"How did that *1812 Overture* work for you?" Turning the doorknob, Sophie took Forbes by the arm, leading him into his room.

"I went with Led Zeppelin. Heartbreaker could wake the dead."

"I'll take your word for it." Removing his jacket, Sophie stared at the gun she found underneath. Considering her options, she decided to let him take care of it. "Remove that thing. Please."

"Are you undressing me?" Forbes released the harness, letting it—and the gun—slide free.

"Looks that way." Under Forbes' eagle eye, Sophie set the gun aside. She grabbed the hem of his t-shirt. "Lift your arms."

Forbes followed her instructions, watching as she tossed his shirt onto a chair. "I like where this is heading. However, when I pictured this moment, you were naked. And I had a lot more energy."

"Men. Why do your minds always go to sex?"

"A beautiful woman is taking off my clothes." On his own, he toed off his boots. "Do you really need me to explain why my mind works the way it does? I don't think my body is up to it—no pun intended. Give me a few hours' sleep. I'll be ready, willing, and more than able."

As Forbes yawned his way through the speech, Sophie shook her head. Unfastening his jeans, she hid her smile at what she found. Mentally, he was exhausted. However, it seemed his body was flying on autopilot.

Forbes raised an eyebrow, pleased when he noticed the bulge between his legs. "Well, what do you know? And they say a man hits his sexual peak at nineteen. Ten years later and I can still go under adverse conditions."

"Go, maybe. But something tells me I would have to do all the work." Sophie gave Forbes a push. He toppled back onto to the bed like a felled tree. "Timber."

"And yet the mighty oak remains standing."

"Down, boy." Sophie took hold of his jeans, tugging them past his wiggling hips, taking his socks off with them. "I'd say keep it in your pants, but your boxers will have to do."

"I like to sleep naked."

"I'm not stopping you." With Forbes' help, Sophie rolled him to his side and under the covers. "Need a lullaby?"

Forbes yawned again. "No."

With Forbes settled, Sophie smoothed a hand over his tousled hair. "You're pretty adorable, you know that?"

"I'd prefer sexy, but at this point, I'll take adorable.

Sexy dripped from every pore in Forbes' body. Considering the situation, Sophie chose to keep that observation to herself.

"Good night."

"Where are you going?" Forbes took Sophie's hand, keeping her from leaving.

"Back to my room." Sophie tugged, but Forbes wouldn't let her go. "Go to sleep. I'll see you at breakfast."

"Stay."

"Bad idea."

"Please?" When Sophie hesitated, Forbes pushed his advantage. "Just to sleep."

The idea was a tempting one. Which surprised Sophie. She didn't sleep with men. Sex? Sure. But she wasn't comfortable with another body lying next to hers. She found herself listening to his every breath. She would tense every time he shifted his body. The longest she made it was an hour. Eventually, she found it easier to leave right away than try to sneak out later.

If Sophie attempted to sleep with Forbes, she had one advantage. She wouldn't need to drive home in the middle of the night. Her bed was just down the hall.

Silently, Forbes patted the empty spot beside him. A man didn't need to speak when he had eyes like that. Deep blue. Electric. A little wild. Yet infinitely tender. They coaxed Sophie under the covers without a word.

"Okay," Sophie said, scooting close, her back to Forbes' chest. "We'll give this a shot." Then she remembered. "What about your wound?"

Forbes' arm snaked around her, holding her tight. "It's become less of a wound and more of an annoyance. The stitches come out on Monday. However, if you want to kiss it again, I won't object."

"Nice try." Sophie took a deep breath. Then another.

"Sorry," Forbes said, his chin nuzzling the top of her head. "I've had a long day. Should I hop in the shower?"

"No." Taking another deep breath, Sophie rubbed her cheek against Forbes' shoulder. "You smell good. Don't laugh?"

"Where would I get the energy?"

"You smell manly."

"That deserves a little chuckle," Forbes said. Against her hair, Sophie swore she could feel his lips curving upward.

"Sleep."

"Yes, ma'am."

Forbes dropped off immediately. For Sophie, that wasn't as easy. She liked the feel of his body next to hers. He felt warm. And she felt... safe. A strange word, all things considered. But there it was.

Sophie's muscles loosened. Her eyes grew heavy. Amazingly, her body was able to relax. Forbes' breath against her neck wasn't an irritant, but soothing. She doubted she would sleep, but a restful night would be nice.

It was her last thought as she drifted off. Deep and dreamless.

# CHAPTER NINETEEN

AS ALWAYS, SOPHIE was up with the sun. The difference was that this morning when she opened her eyes, Forbes' arms were around her. And for the first time that she could remember, she was tempted to snuggle closer, forgetting the responsibilities that awaited her around the ranch.

Indulging herself, Sophie brushed her lips against Forbes' arm. If he had stirred, she would have given in to her impulse. Turning her head, she looked at his face. And what a nice face it was. Handsome didn't begin to describe the way every feature fit just so, complementing each other perfectly. Forbes would make a wonderful subject for a sculptor. The strong bone structure almost begging to be immortalized in marble.

Sophie smiled. Without touching, her finger traced the outline of Forbes' lips. She knew how they would feel. Warm. Strong, yet wonderfully soft. When he opened his eyes, the intense blue was startling. Breathtaking. While in repose, he was beautiful. However, a cold piece of stone could never capture the qualities that made Forbes unique. To understand, a person had to look into those eyes. Feel the life force that drove him and the energy that made others want to inhabit his orbit.

Carefully, Sophie slipped from the bed. As tempting as it was, she didn't want to disturb him. He needed his sleep—and his energy for what she had planned for him.

"We'll find our moment," Sophie whispered, sending Forbes a last look as she gently closed the bedroom door. "Soon."

"I OPENED MY eyes, hoping to find a beautiful woman in my bed. Imagine my surprise when the warm body next to me wasn't the one I expected."

Sophie continued piling lunch meat onto a piece of sourdough bread. She kept her expression neutral. However, inside, she was laughing. Loudly.

"Dandi is beautiful. Though her breath often leaves something to be desired."

"So I discovered when she decided to cover every inch of my face with her saliva."

Holding it in became too much of an effort. Sophie sputtered, breaking out into a full-fledged chuckle.

"I gave Dandi the choice of coming with me or keeping you company. I couldn't fault her choice."

Forbes took a seat at the counter, his dark blond hair still damp from his shower. Dressed in a faded shirt and jeans, his feet were bare. Reaching across the granite top, he snatched a piece of sliced pastrami.

"While I appreciate her show of affection, next time I'd prefer a nice hand-to-paw shake."

"Most of the time, Dandi exhibits amazing control over who and when she licks. The temptation of your face so close to hers got the better of her."

"Mm." Forbes didn't sound convinced. Moving to the refrigerator, he removed a pitcher of iced tea. He set two glasses near Sophie. From behind, his arms slid around her waist. "When did you get up?"

"Early."

Sophie had already eaten breakfast, done her chores, and worked several hours with her horses. Feeling the need for fuel, she had returned to the house intent on a mid-morning snack. Finding Forbes once more amongst the living was a nice bonus.

"I didn't notice when you left. Or when your replacement joined me." Forbes nuzzled Sophie's neck. "Dandi is nice, but you smell a hell of a lot better."

"Thanks. I think." Sophie moved her head, baring more of her neck to Forbes' mouth.

"Where is Maeve?"

"Shopping. We were out of milk and... I don't know. A ton of things. I tuned out as Maeve read them off." With affection in her

241

voice, Sophie shook her head. "I don't know how she can get so enthusiastic about going to the grocery store."

When Forbes found a spot that made Sophie moan, he stayed there, alternating between kissing and nibbling. His hand slid into her hair, fingers massaging her scalp.

"To each her own. How long will she be gone?"

"Most of the day. She plans on stopping at her sister's for a visit.

Taking a long butcher knife from a wooden block on the counter, Sophie expertly sliced her sandwich in half.

"What's on your agenda for the rest of the day?" Forbes breathed, his tongue taking a swipe at the curve of her ear.

Sophie knew where Forbes' thoughts were headed. If the timbre of his voice hadn't given him away, the interesting bulge brushing against her backside would have done the trick. As she arranged her snack on a plate, she kept her tone casual.

"I have a horse ready to return to its owners. They will be here at three o'clock to pick her up. Until then, I thought I'd putter around. There is always something that needs fixing or cleaning. Before, and after, I plan on eating."

"That's hardly a revelation." Sophie sighed as his arm tightened, his hand brushing the underside of her breast. "Any chance I can tempt you into skipping food—for now. We have the house to ourselves. I changed the sheets on my bed."

"Are suggesting we take a nap," Sophie teased.

"We can do that. After."

"Just to be clear. You want to have sex. With me. Now."

"Yes." Forbes kissed Sophie's ear. "So, you want exact terms?"

Sophie nodded.

"Very well. I want to have sex with you, Sophie. I want you naked. Under me. Over me. My mouth on yours. On your breasts. Your stomach. On every inch of you. I want to be inside of you. Again and again. I want it now. I'll want it tonight. Tomorrow. Next week. In my dreams and out. I can't imagine there coming a time when I won't want you."

Good thing Sophie had her palms flat on the counter. Without their support—and Forbes at her back—she would have slid to the floor; her legs turned into a couple of wet noodles.

"I'm supposed to choose between you and food?"

The fight wasn't fair. Not even close. But Forbes didn't know that.

Letting out a disappointed sigh, his hold loosened. "If you want to eat, I can wait."

"Well, I can't."

Galvanized by the thought of losing Forbes' touch, Sophie spun around. She took his face between her hands. One look into those deep blue eyes was all the encouragement she needed. Sinking into his embrace, she pressed her lips to his.

"Stop." Forbes spoke the word with this mouth against hers.

Sophie groaned. "No means no. Is that what you're saying?"

"Hell, no." To prove his point, Forbes grabbed the counter on each side of Sophie, boxing her in. "You want it. I want it. But I want to clarify one thing. For me, this isn't just sex."

Heart racing, Sophie breathed deeply. "What is it?"

"More." Forbes dropped his forehead onto Sophie's. "A lot more. I don't want a fling. As far as I'm concerned, there will be no *housemates with benefits*. Is that what *you* want? One and done?"

"No." That was the last thing Sophie wanted. However, like Forbes, she wasn't ready to put a label on what she *did* want.

"Then let's call this the first step toward—"

"Toward more," Sophie finished. She kissed the end of Forbes' nose. "Sexy and sweet. Lucky me."

"About that." Moving his hands to Sophie's hips, Forbes walked backward from the kitchen to the living room, taking her with him. "Between my last mission, the month I spent in the hospital, and this thing with you and me—. Well, you know. It's been a while."

Sophie matched her footsteps to Forbes. For balance, she ran her hands up his arms, coming to rest on his shoulders.

"Believe me, I know."

As they reached the bottom of the staircase, Forbes came to a stop.

"You too?" he asked, kissing Sophie's left cheek, then her right.

"For different reasons. Obviously. The ranch takes up most of my time. When a man asks me out—which happens quite often, by the way."

"If it didn't, I'd be worried about the intelligence of Cloverdale's male population."

"Mm." Sophie's brain clouded over for a second when Forbes' lips moved to her neck. It had always been a sensitive area, but he found happy spots she hadn't known existed. "What was I saying?"

"You're a busy woman. Sex isn't a priority."

"Right." When Forbes lifted her into his arms, Sophie gasped. "I have a feeling that is about to change."

Forbes took Sophie's mouth with his. The kiss wasn't friendly. Or about a play for power. This was about a man and a woman. No question where they were headed—only hope over where they would end up. She wound her arms around his neck, tilting her head. His tongue ran along her bottom lip as if to request entrance. She didn't hesitate. Yes. Please!

"Damn," Forbes said, lifting his head. His breath came in harsh puffs as he looked over Sophie's shoulder at the sofa. "It's a long way up those stairs. Any reason we need a bed?"

"No." Sophie laughed. "Unless you want to give Mike or Jerry a show. Or one of the other cowboys who like to drop in unannounced throughout the day to raid Maeve's baked goods."

Without a word, Forbes changed direction. He took the stairs at a jog, passing her room.

"Mine is closer," Sophie pointed out.

"My bed is bigger," Forbes countered. He easily shifted her weight, using his free hand to open the door. "As long as we're up here, we might as well have plenty of room to play."

"I thought you were too impatient to play."

"Oh, we'll play." Forbes set Sophie on her feet. "Eventually. Just not right now."

Sophie's shirt came off first. With a gentle push, Forbes had her on the mattress, removing her boots and socks.

"Purple toenails. With sparkles. I never would have guessed."

"There is this spa in Spokane. Tory drags me there every month or so. I like my pedicures." Sophie licked her lips, her eyes narrowing with pleasure as Forbes gave each toe a kiss. "I pick a different color every time."

"Very nice." Forbes bit her big toe, before pressing his lips to Sophie's instep. With impressive efficiency, he unfastened her jeans while his mouth explored the inside of her denim-covered thighs. "What else do you get done at this spa?"

"This and that."

"I like this." One more caress of her foot, Forbes pulled off her jeans and panties in one motion. With a slow smile, the look in his blue eyes heated. Ever so lightly, he touched her flat stomach, slowly moving lower. "And *that*. So much smooth, bare skin."

The air in Sophie's lungs came out in a slow sigh. "It was an impulse. I like the way it feels."

"I agree. Wholeheartedly."

To prove his point, Forbes caressed Sophie's upper thighs—with his fingers and his eyes. Leaning close, he followed the same path with a trail of kisses. Soft, but deliberate. Sophie watched—eyes wide—not wanting to miss a second. However, when his mouth reached its destination, she gasped with pleasure, her head falling back as her eyes closed. It didn't take long before she clutched the sheets, her body tensing as waves of pleasure coursed through her.

"Lovely," Forbes whispered, standing.

Over the ringing in her ears, Sophie could hear the sound of Forbes removing his clothes. She wanted to look, truly she did. But that would have taken too much effort. Heart racing, skin tingling, she was happy to watch the fading light show playing out on her closed eyelids.

"Should I thank you or apologize?" Sophie asked as she felt the mattress dip.

"Since I enjoyed it as much as you—"

"That seems highly unlikely."

Chuckling, Forbes kissed Sophie's shoulder, slipping off her bra strap. "Maybe not from your perspective. From mine? I loved every minute. Or should I say every second? It didn't take as long as I hoped."

Sophie smiled, letting Forbes manipulate her body from side to side until her bra joined the rest of their clothes on the bedroom floor.

"I confessed that it had been a while."

"And I thought it was my expertise that had you screaming my name to the rafters."

"I didn't scream. And we don't have any rafters. At least none I can see." Sophie met Forbes' gaze "However if it feeds your ego to hear my confession, that's never happened so quickly. And never in that way."

Forbes looked amazed. "What's wrong with the men you've dated? Savoring the way a woman tastes is one of life's great pleasures."

"I didn't say they weren't willing to try." Sophie wondered how the conversation had taken this turn. And wished she could have a do-over, stopping before she began. With a sigh, she pushed on, wanting it to end as soon as possible. "A few have tried. Valiantly. Since it didn't do much for me—and because I like so many other things—I assumed *that* wasn't my cup of tea."

"And now?"

Laughing, Sophie asked, "What do you want me to say?" She knew, but she wouldn't make it easy for him.

"All I ask is the truth," Forbes said, placing his hand over Sophie's breast. His thumb brushed her nipple, bringing it to an instant peak. "I succeeded where other men failed."

"You make it sound like you were the first man to conquer Everest. It's called an orgasm, Forbes. A very nice one. But come on, you didn't invent the thing."

Forbes' attention was focused on Sophie's breast, his tone casual as if he were speaking about the weather. "Oral manipulation. Sounds easy—in theory. When done correctly, it's art. Those other men obviously had no idea—"

"Would you stop referring to those *other men* as if their numbers were legion?"

"How many?"

Forbes surprised Sophie with the question. That he would actually ask.

"How many women have you been with? And I'm aware that you asked first."

Thinking for a moment, Forbes shrugged. "I haven't kept track."

Sophie didn't care how experienced Forbes was. As far as she was concerned, who, where, why, and how often could stay a mystery until the end of time. What mattered was the here and the now.

Sophie turned to face Forbes, cupping his face with her hand. "I want to be with you. Only you. Do you feel the same?"

"Yes," Forbes said, kissing her palm.

"Are there any health issues I should know about?"

Blue eyes sparkling with humor, Forbes shook his head. "They ran a shitload of tests when I was in the hospital. My blood—to quote the doctor—is pristine."

"Pristine?" Sophie shot him a look dripping with skepticism. "Really?"

"Words to that effect." Forbes leaned over Sophie, opening the end table drawer. Settling back beside her, he held up a condom. "Safety first, last, and always."

"And so ends the get to know our sexual history part of the program. Thank God."

"Awkward," Forbes agreed. He used his teeth to rip open the packet. In a flash, he rolled the contents into place. "But necessary. I would never put you in danger, Sophie. I'd defend you to my last breath."

*Wow*! Sophie had never considered herself much of a romantic. She survived her childhood by adopting a pragmatic view of the world. Yet, Forbes' declaration made her heart flutter—just a bit. He hadn't made the statement to impress or seduce. His words weren't flowery or embarrassingly over the top. The statement was made without preamble. Simple. Straightforward. Sincere.

That said, Sophie didn't want to think about Forbes taking his last breath—for any reason. Putting her hands on his chest, she pushed him onto his back.

"Let's promise each other something," Sophie said, straddling Forbes' waist. "No acts of heroism unless absolutely necessary. We're going to stay alive. For a long, long, time."

Forbes slid his hands up Sophie's legs, to her hips, finally settling on her backside. "This long life? Are we spending it together?"

"Would you mind?" It hadn't been Sophie's intention to make a declaration. Or to extract one from Forbes. Then again, the path that had led them here was unique—to put it mildly. Why should a moment this important be any different?

"When I imagine the rest of my life, I see you. Right beside me. All the way."

Words failed Sophie. She looked into the deep blue of Forbes' eyes, seeing something she never thought to find. A man she could trust. With her life. With her future. With her heart.

The kiss began sweetly. Sophie wove her fingers into Forbes' dark-blond hair as she opened her mouth, her tongue teasing his. Sweet sparked to hot. Forbes' fingers bit into her skin. He growled his approval when Sophie's teeth sank into his bottom lip. And that was it. Hot morphed into unbridled.

Her blood already singing, Sophie felt the world tilt only to find herself flat on her back, staring up at Forbes.

"I can't wait, Sophie." Forbes' chest rose and fell in rapid succession. "Are you with me?"

"Yes."

*Always. Forever.*

Forbes entered her with one smooth, strong thrust. The veins on his neck stood out from the effort of keeping his instincts in check. Sophie could see what he wanted. No. Not *wanted*. *Needed*. Hard. Fast. She was right there with him.

To make certain Forbes understood she was ready, Sophie twined her legs around his hips. Her muscles held him tight, firm and strong from years of working on the ranch.

"Don't hold back," Sophie urged.

"You're sure?"

At the breaking point. Sweat covered his body. His arms shook with the effort of preventing his weight from crushing her. And still, Forbes was able to take a moment to tease her. The man was unbelievable. Sophie took two fistfuls of hair, tugging him close.

"Now, you idiot."

Sophie pressed her lips to his. And Forbes turned into a wild man. Had she thought it would be hard and fast? That didn't begin to describe the ride he took her on. She felt herself soar. Up. Up. Up. Higher than she thought possible. The air seemed thinner as breathing became more and more difficult. For a second—right at the end—Sophie wondered if she would pass out. But she needn't have worried. Forbes held her head in his hands, willing her to look into his eyes. They were in this together. He wouldn't let her miss a moment.

Sophie crashed over the edge, Forbes toppling right behind. A burst of light. A rush of heat. Followed by the feeling of floating back to Earth. Slowly. Gently. Landing softly in Forbes' arms.

"Whoever said that anticipation is the best part was a freaking idiot." Forbes pulled Sophie close, his lips brushing the top of her head.

"Amen," Sophie sighed, adding a silent hallelujah and praise the Lord.

"I need water. And food. And sex. After the water and food."

"Sounds like a plan I can get behind," Sophie nodded. "If I could move."

"Give me a minute. Or ten," Forbes said, making Sophie smile. "I'll take a run to the kitchen for provisions." With a groan, he lifted his head. "It's just after twelve. Plenty of time until you have to say goodbye to one of your babies."

"It is hard not to get attached to the horses," Sophie admitted. Forbes had only observed her working with them a couple of times. Yet somehow, he understood how she felt.

"You work magic, Sophie. To do that, you need to bond with the horse. You have a big heart. Big enough to send a little of it with them when they go."

"Thank you." Sophie felt humbled by Forbes' words.

"Water, food, and sex." Forbes gave Sophie a quick kiss before rolling out of bed. "I suppose I should put something on."

"Not as far as I'm concerned." The sight of Forbes naked would never grow old. "But as I said, the kitchen is open territory during the day. How many clothes you wear—or don't wear—depends on your sense of modesty."

"In the Army, there is no such thing," Forbes said, pulling on his jeans. "In case Maeve returns. It's been over twenty-five years since she last saw my bare backside. I'd rather keep the streak alive."

"YOU COOKED," SOPHIE said, looking at the tray of food Forbes set on the bed. In addition to the sandwich she left on the counter, he added a few more items.

"Scrambling a few eggs and toasting a couple of slices of bread doesn't equal cooking."

"It does in my book."

"I'd love to read your book sometime. Cover to cover."

"It would bore you to tears. I live a clean, industrious life." As far as Sophie was concerned, her story began the day she arrived on the ranch. The first fifteen years were filler. She burned the pages long ago. Ridding herself of the memories wasn't as easy. But she tried her best not to think about them—succeeding most of the time.

"No more secrets?" Forbes asked, dropping his jeans, kicking them across the room.

Sophie shrugged. Though she wasn't comfortable with the subject, she had nothing to hide. Not anymore. "A secret is something a person wants—or needs—to hide. I don't enjoy talking about the past, but if there is something you want to know, ask."

"I can think of a few things. Just for clarification." Forbes fed Sophie a grape. "Later. For now, let's enjoy our lunch.

Comfortable with his nudity, Forbes joined Sophie, sitting cross-legged. Seeing the direction of her gaze, he kept a straight face. However, his blue eyes twinkled brightly.

"You put on my t-shirt. Should I cover up?"

"I was chilly." Sophie made no bones about studying all Forbes had to offer. Why not? He was gorgeous. Top, bottom, and everything in between. "Apparently, you aren't."

Forbes took a bite of toast, letting his silence—and strangely adorable smug look—speak for him.

"Which horse is leaving this afternoon?

As Sophie ate, she told Forbes about the black and white pony. Abused, starved, and abandoned, she was rescued by a wonderful couple who took care of animals others left behind.

"When Jem arrived, she was nothing but a rack of trembling bones. The gashes on her back had healed, but it was easy to see where and how often she was abused. Paul and Lynnette Shields— they have a ranch in Wyoming—took her in after a neighbor was arrested for animal cruelty."

The Shields ended up with dogs, cats, chickens, goats. The list went on and on. They found homes for most, keeping the others to add to their ever-growing menagerie.

"Jem needed special care. I'd worked with Lynnette last year. We belong to a national organization that helps fund what she and Paul are able to do for free."

"How long has Jem been here?" Forbes handed Sophie a napkin, drinking down the last of his coffee.

"Four months. Longer than most, but I've had some up to a half year. Jem's progress was slow. Gradually, I earned her trust. Now, she is the sweetest horse I've known. Gentle and loving." Smiling, Sophie set the now empty tray on the floor. "She will be perfect for Paul and Lynnette's younger grandchildren. But most of the time, Jem will laze around the fields, playing with the other horses."

"Sounds like a good life." Forbes took Sophie's hand. He ran his thumb over the back, his eyes looking into hers. "You could have kept Jem."

Sophie shook her head. "If she didn't have a good home to go to, I might have considered it. However, I can't let myself become so attached that I lose sight that—first and foremost—I'm running a business."

"And doing a damn fine job of it." Stretching out on the bed, Forbes tugged Sophie down by his side. "I looked at the books when I was in the hospital. Not my forte, but I understand them well enough. You've increased the value of the ranch and its assets every year since you took over."

"Newt guided me."

"At first, sure. I know for a fact that Dad handed most of it over to you long before he died. He was damn proud of you, Sophie. So am I."

Forbes' words sent a burst of warmth through Sophie. Plus a whole lot of unease. She didn't doubt her abilities. Ranching was still a world dominated by men. She had learned quickly to stand up for herself. When it came to making a deal, she could go toe to toe with the best of them.

For all that, the one thing she hadn't discovered was the secret to gracefully taking a compliment. Praise from Forbes—especially regarding her handling of the ranch—was welcome. It also made her want to change the subject—as quickly as possible.

"Want to go for a ride before dinner?"

"Sure." Forbes scooted down until his face was inches from hers. "I really want to make a joke, but..."

"If it involves me using you like a horse and ends with ride em', cowboy. Save yourself the embarrassment. I've heard them all."

"Men and their lousy pick-up lines," Forbes sighed dramatically. "Pigs. That's what we are."

"Only the ones who won't stop when I make it clear I'm not interested." Sophie lifted her arms, happy to let Forbes pull the t-shirt over her head.

Forbes frowned. "Does that happen often?"

"No. Most of the ranchers I've met are good men—and a few women. They welcomed me like a daughter—and an equal, once I showed them that I knew my stuff. However, there are always the ones who get handsy after a few too many drinks. Sometimes I wound their pride. Once..." Sophie trailed off. She saw no need to burden Forbes with the gory details. "Let's just say I can take care of myself."

"I want a name."

Sophie almost laughed. Except she found nothing funny about the deadly serious tone of Forbes' voice. In a blink, the blue of his eyes had turned from warm to icy cold. It was her first glimpse of the soldier. The man who lived on the edge, courting danger for a living. She hated violence, but she couldn't help the thrill that ran up her spine. Forbes called men pigs? Women—at least this one— were suckers for a man with a dangerous edge. It didn't hurt when the man had the body of a warrior and the face of a movie star.

"If I kiss you, will you forget about doing bodily damage to a man twice your age?"

"Twice my age?" Forbes mulled over the scrap of information. "That describes three-quarters of the possibilities."

Sophie smiled. She knew what she was doing. Forbes wasn't getting a name. Nor was she about to tell him about her new—and surprising—weakness for his tough-guy side. Better she kept both a secret—for the sake of all concerned.

"Fine," Forbes huffed. Under his breath, he muttered, "For now."

"For good. It happened years ago when I was green, and he was beyond three sheets to the wind. Since then, nothing. It's settled. Okay?"

"Do I still get that kiss?"

"And many, many more," Sophie promised.

But first, they had some unfinished business. A question that needed asking. One she couldn't put off any longer.

"Why the frown?" Forbes touched his index finger to the spot between her brows, rubbing lightly.

Sophie took a deep breath. "You reconciled with your father. Spoke with Jerry, Mike, and Maeve. But never me. Why?"

"The big question," Forbes' frown matched Sophie's. "I wondered why you didn't ask it sooner."

"I was afraid the answer would hurt. Or piss me off." Rolling to her back, Sophie kept her hand where it was. On the bed. Next to Forbes. When his fingers laced with hers, she felt herself relax a little. "Since you didn't volunteer the information, I let it slide."

"Me, too."

"Despite what you said, was it because of my..." Sophie didn't want to say Joy's name. Here. After what they had shared, it felt wrong. "Was it all the lies?"

"No." Resting on his elbow, Forbes leaned over Sophie. "The truth is, I didn't have a reason. So many times I thought about calling you. Before I could dial, something stopped me. A feeling that I couldn't explain. Until now."

Forbes smoothed back her hair, brushing his lips across hers.

"I loved my life. It was exciting. I felt I was making a difference. Small, but substantial. When I thought about you, I felt a tug toward home. For a long time, this was the last place I wanted to be. I think—somewhere deep inside—I knew the only thing that could make me want to come back was you."

Sophie touched Forbes' cheek, her eyes—and heart—drinking in what she saw in his expression.

"I wanted you to come home," she said. "But never would have asked."

"You wouldn't have had to. It was easier to stay away, to cut you out of my life completely. I know it was selfish."

"It wasn't. You weren't ready. Neither was I." Sophie felt giddy. As if champagne had replaced the blood in her veins. "This is our time, Forbes. Right here. Right now."

"I think you're right." The side of Forbes' mouth ticked upward. "I'm glad we waited for each other."

Sophie wound her arms around Forbes' neck, breathing in. He always smelled so good.

"I didn't know it at the time," she told him. "But looking back, the wait was worth every second."

# CHAPTER TWENTY

FORBES READ THE report detailing what happened at the ranch. He poured over the pictures of the broken flood lights, the words painted on the side of the house. Dozens of tire tracks left from the vehicle that sped away before Forbes could get a look at it or the driver. For some inexplicable reason, there were several pictures of Sophie's dog Dandi. She was cute as hell but had nothing to do with the investigation. Forbes made a note. Give the photographer a crash course in what is and isn't relevant at a crime scene. And schedule a longer forensics seminar for the entire department.

After all of thirty minutes, Forbes had discovered nothing new. The type of getaway vehicle had been confirmed but in the vaguest terms. The tires—almost new—were the kind one would find on a pickup truck. Mid-sized. Generic tread. Information Forbes had already deduced.

If this were a television show, Forbes' expert team would have found a clue. Miniscule. Something nobody, in reality, could have detected. However, this was real life—and his team was anything but expert. A fact that was now his responsibility to correct.

"These are online courses set up by my company to train our employees." Forbes sent a secure link to Ollie's computer. "Beginning immediately, I want every man and woman employed by the Cloverdale P.D. to take them and pass them."

"Everyone? Or just the uniformed officers?" Ollie set a cup of coffee on Forbes' desk. With one of his own, he took a seat.

"Everyone. These programs are for in-office use only. Understood?"

Ollie nodded. He took a drink of his coffee, set aside the cup, and began taking notes.

"Find a private room where you can set up two computers. Use one of the interrogation rooms. God knows why we need three.

Make a rotating schedule for during working hours. One or two at a time depending on what we're dealing with from day to day."

"What if somebody finds the program too...?" Ollie shrugged. "Challenging?"

"The courses are bare-bones basic. Theoretically, what every man and woman out there should already know." Forbes knew a small-town police department couldn't compete with the kind of operation he was used to, but he saw no reason they shouldn't up their game. "I expect everybody to pass, Ollie. If somebody can't, or struggles to barely get by, they should reconsider their choice of profession."

"Yes, sir."

"Do you think that's too harsh?" Forbes asked, hearing the tone of disapproval in Ollie's voice.

"May I speak freely?"

Forbes met the other man's gaze. "Always. I might not always agree. Take my word as gospel when I say the last thing I want— or need—in this office is a yes man."

Ollie nodded. "The last chief was good at his job. But he wasn't as vigilant in his hiring practices as he could have been."

"Are you saying there is some dead weight out there?"

"That might be a bit harsh." When Forbes shot him a steely look, Ollie sighed. "Okay. Yes. From time to time, Chief Didier indulged in a bit of cronyism."

Forbes' fingers flew over the keyboard, pulling up the department's employee files. He had deemed the process of reviewing each one important, but something he could get to in stages over the next few weeks. That was when he thought this job would be a cakewalk. Evaluating his staff just moved up his to-do list.

"Give me the names."

Ollie tugged at his collar, obviously uncomfortable with Forbes' request.

"Shouldn't you observe everybody for yourself? Make your own unbiased decisions?"

"Your loyalty is admirable, Ollie." A quality Forbes valued above almost anything else. In the field, it moved to number one. "This isn't about ratting out your fellow officers. I don't have the luxury of getting to know everybody in a leisurely manner. Your opinion will help guide me. However, it will be only a small part of my final decision. Every man and woman will be judged on their own merit and performance. That includes you."

"Start with Eli Stover," Ollie said. He found an empty page in his notebook and began writing.

Forbes wasn't surprised to hear the name. Stover had been acting chief after Didier stepped down. From all accounts, the man had spent his two months in office strutting around town showing off his shiny badge. Or filling up on free coffee and donuts. Though Stover hadn't come out and said so, it was clear he resented Forbes taking over as chief of police. His attitude came off a bit surly, but he did his job—with a minimal amount of effort.

When Forbes looked at the list Ollie handed him, he nodded. Just as he suspected. Norm Freemont and Win Bodine. They always seemed to be in Stover's orbit. Slightly behind and to the side.

"They'll claim I have it in for them," Ollie stayed on his feet, back ramrod straight. "Last year when I came out, Chief Didier didn't blink. Most of the department supported me. With a few exceptions."

"Stover, Freemont, and Bodine?"

Ollie's chin rose another inch. "Yes, sir. Not that they overtly made their feeling known. A few dirty looks. Some whispered comments."

"Did you report their behavior to Chief Didier?"

"I can handle their brand of intolerance. It's pretty mild compared to some of the things I'd dealt with before I moved to Cloverdale."

In Forbes' experience, tolerance was an impossible concept to teach. Either one possessed the ability to accept the differences in others, no matter one's moral or religious beliefs, or not. The secret was finding a way to co-exist.

"Any kind of harassment—verbal or physical—will not be tolerated in this department, Ollie. Do I need to assemble everybody and remind them?"

"No," Ollie said emphatically. "Stover and his pals had their fun for a week or two. It died down quickly."

"So, the problem isn't their bigotry. It's their incompetence as police officers."

"As you said, that's for you to decide, Chief."

"So it is." Forbes liked the man's style. Taking his gun from the desk drawer, he secured it in the holster at his waist. "I have a meeting with the mayor. As always, call if you need me."

On the way out of his offices, Forbes stopped to give himself the once over. His new, dark-blue shirt—the one with the Cloverdale P.D. insignia and the shiny badge pinned perfectly straight—gave him a proper air of authority. Hanging neatly in his closet were five identical garments. When Forbes took one off after work, Maeve laundered it before expertly removing every crease and wrinkle with her trusty iron. His jeans received the same treatment.

When Forbes told her it wasn't necessary, she scoffed. She may have no control over how his clothes looked when his shift ended, but she would make certain they started out clean and spiffy.

Taking out his sunglasses, Forbes walked out of the police department, turning right toward the courthouse. He hadn't taken three steps when he was greeted by a passerby.

"Morning, Chief," a woman he didn't recognize called out with a big smile as she pushed a stroller in the opposite direction.

"Morning," Forbes called back, almost wishing he wore a hat—of the cowboy variety—so he could tip it in her direction.

The same scenario played itself out as he walked four blocks and crossed the street. Some people he knew. Some he didn't. But all of them made him feel welcome. Like he was part of the community. That was something he hadn't felt for a long time.

"Hello, Bree."

"Morning, Forbes," Aaron's secretary's expression brightened.

Bree Saunders was somebody Forbes remembered well from their high school days. She used to anchor the girls' basketball team with a mean hook shot that rarely missed its target. From what he understood, Bree's daughter was just as gifted.

*God,* Forbes thought. How was it possible for one of his friends to have a kid on the cusp of junior high school? Before, he hadn't thought much about the passing years. Now that he was back in Cloverdale, he was reminded of it every time he turned a corner. Or ran into an old friend.

"Is the mayor free?"

Bree laughed. "As his secretary, I know I shouldn't admit this. But it still cracks me up. Aaron Greene. Mayor. And Forbes Branson. Chief of police. If we could go back and tell our teenage selves what was coming, do you think they would believe us?"

"No," Forbes said without hesitation. "However, if you come across a time machine and decide to make the trip? Don't look me up. If I knew what was coming, I might hide in a dark room and never come out."

There had been some major bumps along the way, but Forbes liked where the journey had taken him. Back to his hometown. And Sophie. He didn't know if she was his reward or his salvation. Maybe a little of each. One thing was certain. She was the best thing that ever happened to him.

Forbes rapped his knuckles on the door of Aaron's office.

"Come in."

"Ready for me?" Forbes asked. Without waiting, he entered, strolling to the chair in front of Aaron's desk.

"One second." Aaron signed an official-looking document. Setting it aside, he leaned back in his chair. "Done. What's new with the Cloverdale P.D.?"

The weekly meeting had been Forbes' idea. First, it made sense. Keeping Aaron up to date meant there would be no surprises later on. If a member of the community came forward with a complaint about the police department, Aaron would already have the cases and the fa0cts at his disposal. An open-door policy was the best way to prevent accusations of corruption—on either side.

Second, it gave them a chance to catch up. Their lives were busy and finding time to hang out like in the old days wasn't easy. An hour without interruptions was a good way to keep in touch.

Forbes gave a concise rundown. There wasn't a lot new to tell, so it didn't take very long.

"Sounds like you have things under control."

"I'm settling in," Forbes said.

"Good." Smiling, Aaron rested his elbows on his desk. "Now that we've covered all the official business, let's get personal. Dinner. Tuesday night. Cindy's mother is taking the kids. Grownups only. She's even breaking out the good china and silver."

"Grownup indeed."

"I need to warn you. Cindy has decided to try her hand at matchmaking. Her cousin Flora will be joining us."

"Aaron—"

"I know," Aaron held up a hand before Forbes could protest. "Blind dates suck. But you don't have to marry the woman. Think of it as dipping your toe in the Cloverdale dating pool."

"I'm not looking for somebody to date." *Talk about your understatements.*

Aaron sighed. "Are you still on that old kick? Casual sex and no commitments are fine when you're a kid, Forbes. Don't you want something more?"

"Sure I do." Forbes hadn't planned on mentioning Sophie but now was as good a time as any. "In fact, I've already found it."

"Really?" Aaron said, surprised. And pleased, if his smile was any indication. "I'll tell Cindy. Though her cousin will be disappointed—as will every single woman in the area. From what my wife tells me, quite a few of them have plans to lure you in."

"That sounds disturbingly unpleasant." And potentially painful.

261

"Probably." Aaron took a bottle of water from the mini-fridge by his desk, unscrewing the cap. "Want something? Coke? Root Beer? Juice?"

"I'm good thanks."

"Spill. Who is the woman?"

"Sophie."

Aaron spat his mouth full of water over the surface of his desk. The trajectory was impressive. Forbes didn't think a single piece of paper avoided the deluge.

"Sophie?" Aaron wiped his mouth. "Sophie Lipton?"

"Of course, Sophie Lipton. I get the surprise. But your reaction is a bit over the top."

"It's just that I didn't realize you... I mean," Aaron ran a hand over his head. "I don't know what I mean. You and Sophie Lipton. It's going to take me a minute to wrap my thoughts around the idea."

"You don't like her?" Forbes had never considered the idea. If Aaron had a problem with Sophie, their friendship was in trouble.

"What's not to like?"

"My thoughts exactly," Forbes agreed. "So what's up?"

"Shit." When Aaron looked at Forbes, his eyes were troubled. "It isn't Sophie. It's her mother."

"Joy?" The answer confused Forbes even more. "Jesus, Aaron. Join the club. Half this town has reason to hate that woman. You can't hold what that woman did against Sophie."

"I don't." Aaron surged to his feet, tipping over the bottle of water. Ignoring the mess, he turned his back on Forbes and took a deep breath. "Back in high school? When I cheated on Cindy?"

Forbes was getting impatient. Then the truth hit him. Straight between the eyes. "You have to be kidding me. You fucked around with Joy?"

"Yes."

It was inconceivable. Yet, Aaron had no reason to lie about something so vile. Forbes had to swallow the bile, willing himself not to be sick all over the office floor.

"My father's wife." It was all Forbes could think to say.

"I know. I wish I could explain what would make me betray so many people. Newt was like a second father to me. You were—are—my brother. And Cindy. The fact that she eventually forgave me doesn't erase what I did."

Aaron looked as sick as Forbes felt. A pasty yellow with a shimmer of green patina.

"Sit down before you fall," Forbes told him.

"You can hit me." Aaron collapsed into his chair. "I won't stop you."

"If I wanted to hit you, you couldn't stop me." Sidestepping the pool of water that had formed beside the desk, Forbes took another bottle from the fridge. He tore off the cap, downing the contents in a series of deep gulps. With a surge of anger, he slung the empty container across the room. "Just when I think that woman's ghost has finally been exorcised, she finds a way to haunt us from the goddamned past."

"I had to tell you, Forbes." Aaron's color had improved, but he still looked shaky. "If you're dating Sophie—"

"We aren't dating," Forbes ground out. "It's more than that. A lot more."

"Okay." Aaron wiped the sweat from his upper lip. "What about us?"

"My father—man more than twenty years older than you—fell under that bitch's spell. What chance did you have?" Joy had screwed them all in one way or the other.

"I can't explain how it happened."

If Aaron was looking for some kind absolution—a way to get the last of the guilt off his chest—Forbes couldn't help.

"Please, buddy. Spare me any of the details. I understand why you needed to tell me. And I'm fine with it."

"Really?"

Aaron sounded skeptical. Rightfully so. Forbes smiled, realizing he must be feeling better. The urge to toss his cookies had faded to a slight churning in his stomach.

"Give me a day or two. By Tuesday night, we should be golden. That is if the invitation to dinner is still open. And I can bring Sophie."

"Of course." Aaron groaned. "Christ. Sophie. Are you going to tell her?"

"We've finally cleared away all the lies and misunderstandings. I won't keep anything from Sophie. Not now. Not ever again."

"Smart way to start a relationship."

"For us to work, it's the only way." Forbes wouldn't let anything ruin the best thing that had ever happened to him. Especially not Joy.

"The trouble you've been having at the ranch." Aaron frowned with concern. "Do you think Sophie is in any real danger?"

"I hope not." Forbes' eyes narrowed dangerously when he thought about anyone or anything hurting Sophie. "But you can sure as hell bet that I'm not taking any chances."

FORBES STOPPED BY *Rick's Diner* on his way back to the station. The plan was to pick up something to go that he could eat at his desk while he took care of some paperwork.

Nodding a hello to Ollie's boyfriend, Forbes grabbed a menu. Perusing the contents, he picked up the scent of a floral perfume just before he felt a hand slide up his back.

"There you are. I've been trying to track you down all week." Daphne moved in for a hug.

"I'm always around. Somewhere." Forbes returned the embrace, moving back when Daphne would have clung a little longer than he found comfortable.

"I'll take your word for it. Now that I have you, I'm not letting you get away. Let me buy you lunch." Taking his hand, Daphne tugged him across the room.

"I really don't have time, Daphne."

"Don't be silly. You need to eat. And you did promise we would get together and catch up."

Forbes let Daphne lead him to an empty booth. He could have stopped her, but he didn't want to make a scene in front of the packed diner. Besides, she was right. He had to eat. Why not do it in the company of an old friend? The paperwork on his desk wasn't going anywhere.

They ordered. Forbes chose the today's special—chicken fried steak. Daphne decided on a small chef's salad. Thanking the waitress when she set down their drinks, he looked around the diner.

"A lot of new faces in town. I guess that's a good thing."

"I suppose," Daphne tapped one red nail on the table, flipping her hair over her shoulder. The color seemed lighter than Forbes remembered. More platinum than honey blond.

"What are you up to these days, Daphne?" Other than Aaron and Cindy, Forbes hadn't kept up with his friends.

"I work at *Pollard's Realty*. If you ever want to sell the ranch, I'm your girl." Daphne winked, letting Forbes know she was kidding.

"Are you married? Kids?"

"Divorced. My ex-husband was—is—an ass. Considering the way things turned out, it's best we didn't have children. He cheated. Practically from day one."

"I'm sorry," Forbes said. He wondered if Daphne was as cool and emotionless about her ex-husband as she appeared.

"Since I married him for his money, it doesn't matter. I received a decent settlement. Not huge." Daphne gave a philosophical shrug.

*What was he supposed to say to that*? Luckily, Daphne continued. Apparently, Forbes' participation in the conversation wasn't necessary.

"After Dad had his heart attack last year, I decided to move back home to make sure he slowed down. My brother and sister live within a five-minute drive, but Dad can't count on them.

Worthless. They always were." Daphne sighed. "When I left, I never thought I'd see Cloverdale again. Especially after Mom ran off. The memories aren't the best."

"No. I don't imagine they are." Memories could be a bitch. "Have your brother and sister been here the whole time?"

"Unlike me, they all toughed it out." Taking a sip of her iced tea, Daphne stared out the window. "Mom was the one with money, you know."

Forbes hadn't known.

"She took it with her." Daphne continued, her tone bitter. "After that, all we had was Dad's income from his law practice. A country lawyer doesn't make a fortune. To say our lifestyle changed would be putting it mildly. I grew up rich and pampered. Able to buy anything I wanted without a second thought. Finding myself on a budget came as a shock. Worse than my mother running off with another woman. I suppose that makes me sound terribly shallow."

Daphne said it with another sigh. Long and drawn out. This time when she flipped her hair, it was with disdain—and a bit of a sneer. For what? Her mother? Her family's lack of money? That anybody would dare consider her attitude shallow? Forbes had no idea.

The entire conversation seemed bizarre and made Forbes uncomfortable. It was one thing to catch up. It was another to spill personal information to somebody you hadn't spoken to in over a decade.

Surreptitiously, Forbes glanced at his watch, wishing he had stuck with the original plan and gotten his food to go.

"Enough about me." Daphne brightened. Smiling, she pulled her shoulders back. Leaning toward Forbes, she led with her chest. "I've heard all kinds of rumors about you. Were you really a spy? Or was it a mercenary for hire? Did you seduce a world leader then help overthrow her government? Somebody said you discovered the cure for a rare disease while in the jungles of South America. I thought that one sounded a bit farfetched."

Forbes laughed. This was the Daphne he remembered. Bright and flirty. He didn't know which version was the real deal, but if she settled on this side of her emotional schism, he could enjoy her company—and his lunch.

"Sorry to disappoint you. The truth isn't nearly as exciting."

"Oh, I doubt that." Daphne smiled slowly, reaching for his hand. Her move was thwarted by the arrival of their food.

"Here you go, Chief. Daphne."

Their waitress, Paula Flagg was another graduate of Cloverdale High School. Same class, same social circle. She had put on a few pounds, and they looked good on her. Forbes thought Paula looked good period, with an air of happiness around her. The life of a married woman with three children seemed to suit her.

"Thanks, Paula." Forbes smiled, picking up his fork. The smell of the gravy and mashed potatoes made his mouth water. "Looks good."

"The special has been flying out the door. Or is that out of the kitchen?"

Paula laughed at her own joke. Forbes joined in. Daphne looked impatient. The women exchanged looks that told him that the less-than-friendly rivalry that had existed between them in high school had morphed into outright dislike.

"Enjoy," Paula said.

"That woman has an awfully superior attitude for somebody who makes a living serving food." Daphne frowned, following Paula with a narrowed gaze.

"It's honest work, Daphne. Paula is helping to provide for her family."

Forbes tucked into his food, anxious to finish and get back to work. When they were growing up, there had been so much to like about Daphne. She had been fun and easy to be with. The sex had been satisfying and uncomplicated. Unfortunately—like now—she had the tendency to be a petty, stuck-up bitch.

As if she suddenly realized how it sounded, Daphne wiped the frown from her face, dropping the disdain from her voice. "It's been a tough morning. I'm trying to sort out Mom's estate. Though calling it that is a stretch. She had almost nothing left. She and that bitch ran through most of the money Mom's father left her. The rest went toward her care. What little there is will go to my lawyer and taxes."

"Your mother passed away?" Forbes wondered why he hadn't heard. It was the kind of juicy gossip a small town thrived on.

"Last month." Daphne picked at her salad, pushing it around the bowl instead of eating it. "It didn't come as a shock. She had been in a nursing home for the last few years. Early-onset Alzheimer's."

"That must have been tough for you and your family." A tragic end to a selfish woman's life.

"The tough part was getting over Mom's initial betrayal. Dad never did. Do you know he always expected her to come back? He would have forgiven her. Welcomed her with open arms." Daphne's fingers tightened on her fork, her voice vibrating with anger. "The bitch took off when the money began to dry up. After that, Mom lived alone in Florida until she entered the nursing home. Do you know how I found out?"

"How?"

"After I moved home, I found a drawer full of letters in Dad's office. He and Mom had been corresponding for a long time. You should have read them, Forbes. She didn't show an ounce of remorse—not even in the early ones. All chatty and friendly. As if she was writing to a pen pal instead of her husband. Did you know they never divorced? Can you imagine? Dad loved her to the end. The stupid old fool."

As Forbes listened while Daphne vented her anger, he couldn't help but wonder about Joy. Not because he cared what happened to her. Rotting in the lowest depths of hell would suit him just fine. But like it or not, she was Sophie's mother. Just because she hadn't been in touch, didn't mean it couldn't happen. As long as the woman lurked in some corner of Earth, the chance of her rearing her ugly head was always a possibility.

Knowledge was power. Forbes never left on a mission until he knew everything about his target. The best way to protect Sophie from her mother would be to discover Joy's current location and what she was up to. He kicked himself for not thinking of it before. As soon as he was back in his office, he would get his best people on it. ASAP.

"What do you think?"

"I'm sorry?" Forbes looked across the table at Daphne's expectant expression. "I was thinking about work. What were you saying?"

"I thought we could drive into Spokane and make a night of it. Drinks. Dinner. Dancing. I'll book us a room at the *Davenport Hotel.* That way we won't have to worry about driving home." Daphne placed her hand over his. With nothing suggestive about the squeeze, her intentions were as clear as a freshly washed glass. "I have some new lingerie that I can't wait for you to see—and remove."

Deliberately, Forbes retrieved his hand. He didn't want to hurt Daphne's feelings. However, he wouldn't leave any doubt in her mind about his total lack of interest.

"We were always friends, Daphne. Let's keep it that way."

"Friends—and more," she reminded him.

"It was nice. However, we aren't teenagers anymore. You deserve more than a casual hookup."

"Is there any reason we can't be more to each other?"

"I've already found it." Forbes knew it would sting, but Daphne would find out soon enough. It might as well come from him. "With Sophie."

"You're kidding," Daphne laughed, obviously expecting Forbes to join her. When he didn't, his eyes cool, her mouth fell open. "Are you crazy? After what *her* mother did to *your* father?"

"That had nothing to do with Sophie."

"Right," Daphne scoffed. "The poor baby was blameless. Do you know how many times I've heard that? You weren't here, Forbes. Sides were taken. *I* was born here. *I* was the victim. But more often than you would believe, people defended Sophie. They actually called me a bitch for not feeling sorry for her. She was hardly an angel, you know."

"I never thought she was." An angel was the last thing Forbes wanted. Sophie had faults and edges and could be a royal pain in his ass. He wouldn't change a thing.

"What about your inheritance? Well?" Daphne's voice rose unconcerned with the attention she was attracting. "Sophie got half of everything. How? On her back. Like mother, like daughter. Only Sophie had the patience to stick it out until your old man kicked the bucket."

"That's enough!" Forbes was only willing to give so much leeway. Daphne hadn't crossed the line. She obliterated it. "Sophie doesn't need me to defend her. But my father is another matter. He made his share of mistakes, but he thought of Sophie as a daughter. Suggesting otherwise is sick and malicious."

Forbes took out his wallet, tossing enough money on the table to cover the check and a healthy tip. Getting to his feet, he pinned Daphne with a withering stare. When he spoke, he made certain his voice carried to every person in the diner. He didn't want anybody to have the slightest doubt of his opinion on the subject. "As for my inheritance. I wouldn't have one if it weren't for Sophie. She convinced my father to enter rehab. She kept the ranch running with a combination of brains and hard work. Still does. She deserves half of it. Hell, as far as I'm concerned, Dad should have left her everything."

Forbes didn't stomp from the diner. Or rush out in an angry huff. He walked with an easy swagger. Like a man who knew the truth and didn't give damn about anybody else's opinion.

Stopping outside the diner, Forbes breathed deeply, lifting his face toward the sun. After taking in Daphne's crap for the past hour, the fresh air was a relief. Sliding on his sunglasses, he jogged across the street.

How much of that had Sophie heard over the years? Daphne came right out and said what she thought, but most people hid behind whispers and innuendo. No matter how strong she was, words could hurt. And folks were bound to talk once word spread about the two of them.

Taking out his phone, Forbes pulled up Sophie's number. For some crazy reason, he felt a surge of pleasure when she answered after the first ring—as if she were anxious to hear his voice.

"Hello," Sophie said. Forbes pictured her smiling.

"Do you care what people say about you?"

"I used to. Right after Joy took off. But not anymore." Sophie paused. "Do you?"

"Nope. I care about what you think. The rest of the world can go to hell."

"Well, then." Sounding pleased, Sophie laughed. "That would put us firmly on the same page."

"I can't think of anyplace I'd rather be."

Saying goodbye, Forbes' expression grew pensive. Hitting a couple of keys, he raised the phone to his ear.

"Kia. I need you to find somebody."

"Got a name?" The woman on the other end didn't ask Forbes for an explanation.

"Joy Branson." Just saying her name left a bad taste in his mouth. "The bitch used to be my stepmother. At this point, she could be going by any name. Last known location, Florida."

"Got it. What's the priority?"

"Top of the list. I want all the information you can find. Her location. Activities. Associates. You know the drill."

"Anything and everything. You'll know the second I do."

"One more thing." Walking through the police station doors, Forbes glanced at the diner. "Dig up all you can find on Daphne Parks."

# CHAPTER TWENTY-ONE

SOPHIE LAY ON her side watching the bathroom door. Or rather, the light under the door. Finding herself in Forbes' bed felt strange enough. Anxiously waiting for him to join her was... Well, it simply wasn't like her.

Not that she didn't like the changes in her life since Forbes' return. Just the opposite. Sophie embraced them wholeheartedly. However, finding herself waiting for a man—any man—was a new experience. It would take some time to get used to it.

The light turned off just as the door opened. Sophie smiled when Forbes exited. Freshly showered. And naked. No need to adjust her thinking there.

"A beautiful woman in my bed. Smiling. How lucky am I?"

"That depends," Sophie said, laughing as Forbes stopped her from scooting over by lying on top of her. "Would you be happy with any beautiful woman—as long as she was smiling?"

"At one time? Sure." Forbes kissed her shoulder before settling himself at her side, pulling her close. "Quite recently, my taste has become more discerning. I want *your* beautiful face and *your* welcoming smile."

"If that were a pick-up line, you would score—big time."

Forbes grinned. Sophie sighed. The man wasn't short on ego. Or charm. Or sex appeal. And he was smart. Kind. Gentle—with just the right amount of edginess to prevent any chance of boredom. What chance did she have against a man who was the total package? No. Check that. The question was, why was she wasting time worrying about it? She liked where she was. Where *they* were. The last thing she wanted was the past to ruin the here and now.

"I don't want you to look for Joy." Since Forbes had filled her in on what he was doing, Sophie had felt a growing sense of unease. She remembered it well. The feeling had been her constant companion back in the days when Joy dragged her from pillar to post. "She's been out of our lives for a long time. Poking around, whether she finds out or not—is just courting trouble."

"There's no harm in knowing where she is, Sophie."

"I don't want to know," Sophie insisted. "She's a plague. Getting rid of her the last time was hard enough. Once I convinced Newt to file for divorce, it took five years for it to become final. Joy refused to sign. Undoubtedly, she thought she would keep her claws in the ranch as a nest egg for her old age."

Five years. That was how long it took to legalize the divorce on the grounds of abandonment. Or the Washington state equivalent. Finding Joy. Trying to serve her with the papers. It had been a nightmare. Eventually, the court ruled in Newt's favor without the need for Joy to sign on the dotted line. Because the time they lived together as man and wife had been blessedly brief—and the fact that she left of her own free will, there had been no alimony or settlement. Joy received nothing.

"I understand what you're saying. If it weren't for you, I don't think Dad would have filed for divorce. You saved his ass—all our asses—as usual. Because you pushed him to follow through and stick with it, there is nothing for Joy here."

"Exactly."

"Nothing except you." Forbes sounded grim. "She can't hurt us, Sophie. Unless we let her. Discovering where she is. Knowing what she's doing. Think of it as another layer of security."

Sophie didn't like it, but for now, she would bow to Forbes' expertise on the subject.

"What about Daphne?"

"She pissed me off. And again, better safe than sorry."

Forbes had shared his run in with Daphne Parks. Sophie couldn't say she was surprised. Not by Daphne's remarks about her, or the fact that the woman made a play for Forbes. They had a history. Both were single. And Forbes was freaking gorgeous. Finding a man like him wasn't easy in any part of the world. In a small town like Cloverdale, it was a miracle.

*Too bad he was already taken.* To herself, Sophie smiled smugly.

"I haven't had very much interaction with Daphne since she's been back. Not that I would expect to. I'm not her favorite person. That's hardly news."

"A rational person would have gotten over it by now," Forbes reasoned. "Daphne doesn't have to be your best buddy."

"Thank the Lord for that."

Forbes chuckled. "The bitterness in her voice wasn't normal, Sophie."

"Do you really think she set the fire? Or spray painted the house?"

"No. I'm certain the person I chased was a man. By his build and the way he ran. It wasn't Daphne."

"Then...?"

"It's a feeling." Forbes shrugged. "I've learned to trust my gut. There may be a connection to Daphne. Maybe not. I'd like to know—one way or the other."

"Another layer of security?"

"Something like that."

Sophie kissed Forbes' flat stomach. "I like your gut. But I hope it's wrong."

"So do I. Daphne and I were friends once. I wouldn't hesitate to do it, but I'd hate to have to put her in jail."

"Maybe because once upon a time, the two of you were more than just friends?"

Sophie remembered the time she overheard Forbes and Daphne's encounter in the barn and Daphne ended up on her knees. With her mouth on his... The idea hadn't bothered Sophie at the time. Darn. She shouldn't have brought it up.

"We fooled around a little. But—" Forbes frowned, shooting Sophie a puzzled look. "How do you know what Daphne and I did—or didn't do?"

"I made a good guess?" And had a big mouth.

"Try again."

Sophie decided to go on the offensive. It was a lot less embarrassing than confessing the truth. "You were no choirboy. Chances are in my favor that Daphne was one of your teenage conquests."

"You're keeping something from me," Forbes said, his eyes narrowing. "No more secrets, Sophie."

Well, crap. Sophie sighed. "It isn't a secret—exactly."

Forbes simply raised an eyebrow and waited.

"Fine. It's silly. Ridiculous, even."

"Good. I could use a laugh."

*Like a dog with a bone.* Forbes just wouldn't let it go. With a huff, Sophie told the story. Careful to point out that she hadn't been spying. She innocently stopped by the barn to enjoy the shade. By the time she realized something intimate was about to happen, it was too late.

"I snuck away as soon as I could. It wasn't a big deal. At least not for me. Bailey looked a little embarrassed."

"Bailey was with you? Of course, he was," Forbes said, answering his own question. "I suppose I should be grateful you kept it to yourself at the time."

"As if I would have said anything." Sophie was horrified at the thought. Then she thought about why Daphne had been with him in the first place, and her insides turned slightly mushy. "If I *had* said something, it would have been to thank you. You asked Daphne to smooth my way at school. It was a terribly sweet thing to do."

"It was my attempt at an unselfish act." Touching Sophie's cheek, Forbes' eyes were a warm, melting blue. "You weren't supposed to know."

"I know."

Forbes, flat on his back, pulled Sophie onto his chest, her long body stretched over his. "You weren't traumatized by the experience?" he teased.

"I rolled my eyes, lamented how easy men were, and pretty much forgot about it until tonight."

"Me too. Forgot about it, that is."

"I'm glad to hear it." Sophie kissed Forbes. More and more, she found herself craving his lips against hers. Indulging her need, she savored every second. Reluctantly, she lifted her head. "I have an idea."

Slowly, Forbes smiled. "What did you have in mind?"

"Start with my mouth here." Sophie brushed a kiss across Forbes' chin. She moved to his neck. Then his chest. "Are you following my progress?" she asked, looking up. Before Forbes could answer, she swiped her tongue over his nipple.

"Jesus, Sophie," Forbes groaned. Sliding his hands into her hair, he followed her progress with his eyes.

With a lingering detour to the nicely healed wound on Forbes' side, she continued her journey. Lower. Lower.

"I can stop if you want," she said, her breath caressing him as her mouth hovered.

"Do I look like a crazy man?" Fingers flexing against her scalp, it was clear Forbes neared the end of his rope. "I'm not proud. Do you want me to beg?"

Sophie bit her lip. It was that or laugh with delight. She didn't want Forbes to beg. Knowing he wanted her enough to do so was all she needed to hear.

"Just lie back." Sophie's voice lowered provocatively. "We're about to make a memory neither one of us will forget."

SOPHIE RARELY CUSSED. But at that moment, she could have spewed enough curse words to make a sailor blush.

They were finishing breakfast. Ham and eggs with wheat toast. When she noticed that Forbes wouldn't finish his piece, Sophie snatched it before he could take his plate to the dishwasher. As she swallowed her last bite, the phone buzzed, signaling an incoming text. As she read, anger coursed through her body.

"Trouble?" Forbes asked when he heard Sophie's muffled growl.

"Mike and some of the guys were planning to clear a bunch of dead trees from the edge of the lower field first thing this morning. The tractor was already down there. When they arrived, ready to get to work, they found the tires had been slashed."

"What?" Forbes slammed shut the dishwasher.

Sophie handed Forbes her phone, not happy to find her hand shaking. "Mike is waiting for instructions. Since it's now a crime scene, I figured you'd want to tell him what to do."

"Shit." Jabbing the screen with his index finger, Forbes held the phone to his ear. "Mike? Tell me what happened."

"Like I said in the text. The tractor tires are slashed. I checked the rest of the tractor. The son of a bitch did a number on the engine. And the inside of the cab is trashed."

"Don't let anybody move or touch anything. I'll be right there."

"I'm coming with you."

Ready for an argument, Forbes surprised Sophie by nodding. "I need to make a call. And grab my gun."

"I need to brush my teeth. What?" Sophie asked when she saw the look on Forbes' face. "I brush after every meal. Why should I let some idiot vandal change my routine? If my teeth rot, I'll have to live on oatmeal. And soggy bread."

"You could get dentures," Forbes said as they walked up the stairs.

The thought made Sophie shudder. "Nope. Not going to happen. I like my teeth, and I plan on keeping them."

Forbes stopped by Sophie's door, taking her into his arms.

"I love the fact that, in a blink, you can go from royally pissed to worrying about your oral hygiene."

Sophie tipped her head, meeting Forbes' gaze. "I'm still angry. But I can't change what happened."

"It's my fault." With a sigh, Forbes laid his chin on the top of her head. "Whoever is behind this wouldn't stop. I blocked the house and the barn. He moved to a different part of the ranch."

"How is that your fault? There's no way to keep an eye on every inch of the place. It's too big."

"You're right." Forbes gently pushed Sophie into her room. "There's only one solution."

"What's that?"

Forbes' eyes turned steely blue. "Catch the asshole."

"FINDING YOUR STEPMOTHER was a snap. Unlike most of the people you ask me to locate, she wasn't trying to hide."

"That's ex-stepmother." Forbes felt it important to emphasize the distinction. Leaning on Sophie's desk, he crossed his arms. "Kai. This is Sophie Lipton. Sophie, Kai Northam."

"Nice to meet you," Sophie said.

"Back at you."

According to Forbes, Kai was a computer genius. They had met in the Army. A year after Forbes left for the private sector, he offered her a job. If the money and benefits hadn't been enough of an incentive, Kai had just come off a mission that had gone horribly wrong. She blamed her commanding officer. The upper brass wasn't interested in her opinion. So she walked away without a backward glance.

Kai's features were delicate. Exotic. Drop dead gorgeous was the way anybody with eyes would have described her. Dark hair streaked with purple highlights and lipstick to match, it was obvious that she was a woman who walked her own path and to hell with what anybody thought.

"Lipton." Kai glanced at one of the multiple screens that littered her desk. "That would make you the daughter. Sorry. Is there another, less offensive term, you'd prefer?"

"Smartass." Forbes' lips twitched.

"I own the relationship," Sophie said. "Though I try to think about it as little as possible."

"From what I was able to dig up, I can't say I blame you."

"Kai!" Jesus. The woman had absolutely no filter.

278

"It's okay," Sophie assured him. She looked at Kai. "I have fifteen years' worth of memories I'd rather forget. Spare me the updated version of Joy's life. Or at least as few of the gory details as possible."

"Sordid is a better term. Though there was an incident where a woman tried to commit suicide. Joy—and her affair with the husband—was right in the middle of that mess."

If Kai had been in front of him instead of three thousand miles away, Forbes would have kicked her in the butt. "What part of spare Sophie the details did you not understand?"

"Sorry."

Sophie looked sad. Though Forbes knew she wouldn't fall apart, the less she had to deal with Joy's shit, the better."

"Start with telling us Joy's location."

"Las Vegas. She's working as a dealer in one of the less glamorous casinos. Should I leave out that she's screwing the owner? Too much information?"

"Yes."

Sophie laughed, taking his hand. "I appreciate that you want to shield me. But I suddenly realized that it doesn't matter. Nothing will shock or surprise me. Besides, I have you. She has a seedy casino owner. I win."

"Ah," Kai batted her thick eyelashes. "That's sweet."

"Shut up, Kai."

"Shutting up, boss," Kai snickered. "I'll shoot you a copy of my report. This is only preliminary. What I could find with a general sweep. Give me a few more days for the real dirt. I'll include the stuff on Daphne Parks. Spoiler alert? *Boring*. The chick makes Wonder Bread look interesting."

"Do you want to read this?" As soon as Kai signed off, Forbes downloaded the files she had sent.

"I might as well." Sophie appreciated his offer. And the concern she saw in his eyes. To reassure them both, she walked into his arms. "I love a good horror story before bedtime.

SOPHIE WAS FIFTEEN again. It didn't matter that, subconsciously, she knew it was a dream. Or that she knew why her mind had taken her back to this place and time. Too much Joy. Reading about the last twelve years of her mother's crazy life stirred up memories she rarely thought about anymore.

It was the night Joy ran off for good. Sophie wasn't sure why she knew that. Except that dreams didn't have to make sense. She felt a hand on her shoulder, shaking her awake.

"Get up. We're leaving."

"What?" Sophie sat up, frowning. "Is the house on fire?"

"Your ass will be on fire if you don't get it out of that bed. Now. Get dressed. Take whatever you can fit into one suitcase. Leave the rest."

Groggy, two things struck Sophie as odd. That she actually had enough clothes to fill more than one suitcase. And that Joy didn't look her usual pulled-together self.

Disheveled, her hair stuck out in odd directions from a hastily fashioned French twist. She wore makeup, but the layers of perfection were missing. A bit of mascara. Too much blush. And lipstick that looked as though it had been applied with a less-than-steady hand. The buttons of her blouse were in the wrong holes, the ends tucked in willy-nilly.

Strangest of all. Joy had on flats instead of her ubiquitous four-inch heels.

"Is the world coming to an end?"

"Why is everything a question with you these days?" With a put-upon sigh, Joy didn't wait for Sophie and began packing. "You were always a pain in my ass, but at least you kept your mouth shut ninety percent of the time. I blame Newt. He's the one who encouraged your goddamned independent streak." Joy pushed back a stray piece of hair. "Jesus Christ, Sophie. Move. Your. Ass."

"No."

Sophie didn't know who was more surprised. Joy. Or her.

"I don't have time for this. Newt is passed out—as usual. That stupid housekeeper is gone for the night. I want to be gone before any of that changes."

"Then go. With my blessing. But I'm staying."

Joy turned, hands on her hips, her mouth compressed into an unflattering thin line.

"What do you think will happen when Newt discovers I'm gone? You don't mean anything to him. He'll throw you out on your ear and then where will you go?"

This was the moment Sophie had always wished for. Her true moment of independence. It felt right. Exciting. Scary as hell. But she would never back down. Inside, she trembled. Outside, she met Joy's gaze, her voice steady and cool.

"It doesn't matter what happens. Or where I go. As long as it isn't with you."

For the second time in Sophie's life, Joy hit her. Hard and true. A ringing slap across her face. She knew it was coming—probably could have avoided it. Instead, she suffered it gladly, the pain bolstering her resolve.

"You want to stay? Fine. Ungrateful bitch," Joy sneered. The spittle in the corner of her mouth gave her the look of a rabid dog foaming at the mouth. "I should have left you in that last shithole hotel. Or the one before that."

"Why didn't you?" If this was the last time she saw her mother—*please, let it be the last time*—Sophie wanted one question answered.

For a second, it appeared that Joy would give Sophie the usual silent shrug. Then the expression on her face changed. Her lips curved upward into an anticipatory smile.

"I suppose it doesn't matter now. In fact, I want to tell you. You should know how little you were wanted. By me. Or your father and his family. Sure you want to hear this?"

Sophie tensed at the mention of her father. Was this going to be another of Joy's lies? Or for once would she tell the truth? Either way, Sophie had to know.

281

"Go ahead."

"Your father wanted to marry me. To do the right thing. His family wanted me to have an abortion. Normally, I wouldn't have objected. It certainly wouldn't have been the first time. Does that shock you?"

"No." Sophie wasn't the least bit surprised. She knew of at least one other time Joy had gotten rid of an unwanted pregnancy. The fact that she had carried Sophie to term? *That* was the surprise.

Joy looked disappointed by Sophie's response, but she continued.

"The family had money. Not a lot, but more than I'd ever seen. Your father was the oldest son—and the favorite. It gave him some leverage. So they caved. The wedding was planned. Then the idiot got himself killed in a boating accident. A stag party gone wrong. I was almost ready to pop you out, so getting rid of you wasn't an option."

If Joy could have found a doctor willing to take care of the problem, Sophie had no doubt she wouldn't be here.

"After you were born, I left."

"You should have stayed gone."

"That was my plan." Joy crossed her arms, her hip cocked in Sophie's direction. "However, a little over three years later, your father's younger brother tracked me down. He had married, and his dutiful little wife had given him a son. An heir. He didn't want you around to muddy his inheritance."

"Why not put me up for adoption?"

"And have you look them up when you turned eighteen? No, he wanted you out of the way. I agreed. For a monthly fee, I made sure you never found out who your father was. In retrospect, I should have held out for more. But I was young. Any amount of money seemed like a fortune back then."

Sophie's one hope that somewhere people cared if she were alive or dead was dashed. It hurt. But she was hardly devastated. That was what living with Joy for fifteen years had done. Her skin was just tough enough to survive almost anything.

"Money. I should have known."

"Don't you dare scoff. That money kept a roof over your head and food in your belly."

"I was always hungry!" Sophie raised her voice for the first time. "*Always.*"

"Thin is in," Joy said blithely with a dismissive wave of her hand. "You should thank me. My family ran toward fat. I ran in the other direction."

Sophie didn't join in when Joy laughed at her own joke.

"God, how did I raise such a humorless stick in the mud?" Getting no response, Joy shook her head. "I saved your life, little girl. Not once have you shown me an ounce of gratitude."

Classic Joy. Somehow it seemed fitting that their last conversation should end with her mother's ego exerting its presence. Sophie was done. She had her answer—nasty as it was. Time to end this life-long farcical tragedy. Once and for all.

"Isn't your ride waiting?"

"No tears? No begging me to stay?"

Sophie shook her head.

"That's cold, Sophie." Joy gave her one last glance. "You know what? For the first time in your life, I'm proud of you."

*Sophie? Sophie!*

With a gasp, Sophie's eyes flew open. Forbes leaned over her, a concerned look on his face. She raised a hand finding warm, solid flesh. *Not a dream.*

"I'm not fifteen," she said, still a little disoriented.

"Thank God. That would make me a sick pervert. Here." Lifting Sophie, Forbes handed her a glass. "Take a drink."

Grateful, Sophie downed the entire contents. "Where did that come from?"

"I was in the bathroom getting some water when you began tossing and turning. Then you cried out. I brought the glass without thinking."

"I'm glad you did." She set the glass on the bedside table, the air slowly leaving her lungs.

"Bad dream?"

"The worst kind of nightmare. Joy was the star."

Forbes took her into his arms, smoothing back Sophie's tangled hair. "Want to tell me about it?"

Sophie nodded. It was one more piece of the puzzle. The only part she had yet to share with Forbes. She had no real reason to hold back except maybe she didn't want to throw out another example of how screwed her family was. Every single member.

"Why go to all the trouble of tracking Joy down?" Angry, Forbes shook his head. "If all he cared about was keeping you from staking a claim to the family money, your uncle could have paid a family to raise you with the same conditions."

Over the years, Sophie had spent long hours considering a hundred different scenarios that would have put her childhood in the hands of anybody except Joy. "I thought of that. Seems like a logical solution. Then I realized something. From day one, none of it was logical. My mother. My father's family. They seem to go with the first idea that pops into their head, the hell with it making sense."

Forbes opened and closed his mouth, searching for something to say. Finally, he threw up his hands.

"It's unbelievable."

Sophie had to agree. "Apparently, I come from a long line of self-involved idiots."

"Two traits you didn't inherit," Forbes said emphatically.

"Maybe I was switched at birth." Another notion that had crept through her head late one night. "That's a different can of worms I'd just as soon keep the lid on. With my luck, who knows what kind of sociopaths I might find."

"So, Joy has you and a steady income. What the hell did she do with the money?" Forbes scoffed. "Stupid question. When you arrived here, your clothes were a little better than rags. While Joy looked like she stepped out of an expensive bordello. Smelled like it, too."

"How much experience do you have with bordellos? Expensive or otherwise?"

"Little to none. Don't change the subject."

"You paid for sex?" Sophie found the idea surprising. And fascinating. "That is a much more interesting topic than my messed-up childhood."

"Maybe from your perspective."

"But—"

"Later," Forbes promised. "If you're still interested."

"Oh, I'll be interested all right." Sophie could wait. Forbes wanted to hear the rest. And she needed to tell him. "Joy always put herself first. I'll give her props for making an effort to drag me around all those years."

"That woman doesn't deserve any credit, Sophie. You raised yourself."

She hadn't thought of it that way. "I had a strong survival instinct. Quiet and unobtrusive. Nobody can bother you if they don't realize you exist."

Forbes gave Sophie a puzzled look. "That is hard for me to imagine. You were kind of quiet when we first met, but that didn't last long. Bossy with an attitude. That's the Sophie I remember."

"I never had a place where I belonged. I never had a place— period. The second I saw this, I could finally breathe freely for the first time in my life. I wasn't free to be myself. Rather, I discovered who I was." Sophie relaxed against Forbes. "I always thought it was Newt who gave me a home. But it was you. Your acceptance. Your friendship. Knowing I belonged gave me the strength to stand up to Joy."

"I left knowing you would be here when I returned. The idea that there was even the slightest chance of you leaving... "

Sophie felt a shudder run through Forbes. She tightened her arms, burrowing closer.

"But I didn't. I never will."

"I believe you." Forbes took Sophie's hand, placing it over his heart. The beat was fast and true. "What does that feel like?"

Replacing her hand with her cheek, Sophie whispered one word. "Home."

# CHAPTER TWENTY-TWO

"A NIGHT AWAY from here is exactly what we need."

Sophie took a sleeveless dress from her closet, amused when she realized the price tag was still attached. Thinking back, she tried to remember when she purchased the knee-length, floral-print summer dress. A year ago? Maybe two? Laughing, she gave up.

It wasn't that Sophie had a problem with showing off her legs. They were long and shapely. And a certain tall, muscular blonde seemed to find them irresistible. She liked dressing up. On occasion. When she had the time and wasn't too tired to do more than eat dinner and fall into bed.

Tonight was one of those times. Sophie was in the mood for a crowded bar filled with noise, alcohol, and plenty of dancing. Now all she needed to do was get Forbes into the party mood.

"You've been on the go non-stop since dawn. Wouldn't you rather cuddle up on the sofa with an old movie and a ton of popcorn?"

"Most nights? Absolutely. Not tonight. Come on."

Sophie tossed the dress onto her bed. Wearing nothing but two pieces of skimpy lace underwear—the color of sunflowers—she swayed her hips to a silent beat. Crooking her finger, she invited him to join her.

"This isn't the way to make me want to leave the house." Moving from where he sat on the edge of the bed, Forbes placed a hand on each of her hips. "Or the bedroom."

"You're so tall," Sophie sighed, batting her lashes. "Strong and handsome. Can't blame a girl for wanting to show off her arm candy."

Forbes' lips twitched. "Is that what I am? A pretty toy?" he asked, getting into the rhythm of her impromptu dance. He wasn't bad. Not bad at all.

"I want you for your brain." Sophie crossed her heart, her fingers lingering on the edge of the lacy bra. "Your ass isn't bad either."

"Funny."

When Forbes tried to pull her close, Sophie danced away. "Sorry. I'm saving my moves for the dance floor. Do me a favor? Go get prettied up. Wear that brushed cotton shirt. The one that matches your eyes."

Shaking his head, Forbes headed out of her room and down the hall. "You know I'll retaliate later when we're alone."

"Is that a threat?"

"Sweetheart, that is a set-in-stone, take it to the bank, promise."

A tingle of anticipation ran down Sophie's spine. Forbes had a wonderful imagination. Whatever he thought up as *punishment* was bound to be as fun as it was exciting.

Humming, she finished dressing, slipping the dress over her head and a pair of sandals on her feet. Sophie wiggled her toes. After her shower, she had changed the color of her nails. *Pink Passion*. It matched perfectly the spray of flowers that bordered the flirty hem of her dress.

The only jewelry she bothered with were a pair of stud earrings—a gift from Forbes. Pretty and practical, the topaz stones hid a tiny tracking device.

"Don't argue," Forbes had told her when he opened the small box. "Phones can be iffy—especially when you're rounding up cattle or riding fence. Even if one accidentally falls out, the other will tell me where you are."

"Will they record what I do in the privacy of my own bathroom?" she had asked, slipping studs into her ears.

"No," Forbes laughed. "They won't record anything. Tracking only."

"Then why would I argue?"

That had been a week ago. Sophie wore the earrings all the time, except in the shower. In a velvet case in the top drawer of her dresser sat a matching necklace and bracelet. Glamorous electronics for every occasion. But for tonight, she wanted to keep it simple.

Sophie picked up her purse, checked its contents, and headed out. She stopped short when she found Forbes waiting at the top of the stairs.

"That was fast."

"Blue shirt, per your request. Boots." He did a nice foot model pose, showing off the polished leather. "Wallet. Done."

Forbes held out his arm, escorting Sophie toward the living room. She liked the way his slightly damp hair curled around the collar of his shirt. Every now and then, he talked about getting it cut to a more chief of police-appropriate length.

"Don't cut your hair." Sophie ran her hand through the thick, silky strands.

Moving his head just enough to kiss the palm of Sophie's hand, Forbes raised an eyebrow. "Doesn't my position of authority demand a shorter length?"

"Has the mayor—or anybody else—complained?"

"Not that I'm aware."

"Then you should wear it the way you want." Sophie laughed when Forbes raised both eyebrows. "Okay. The way *I* want. But if you don't like it long, you shouldn't listen to me."

"Truth is, I've been too lazy to bother with it. However, if you think it's sexy this way—"

"Did I say sexy?" Sophie kept a straight face—barely.

Wrapping his arms around her waist, Forbes nuzzled Sophie's neck. "I recognize that sultry tone of voice.

"Sultry?" Sophie liked the sound of that.

"Mm. It drives me crazy."

"Are the two of you planning on leaving? Or should I take Dandi and give you some privacy?"

"We're on our way," Sophie said, beaming at Maeve. "Keep Forbes here for thirty seconds. Then send him out for his surprise."

Stopping, she gave the housekeeper a hug. "Are you sure you don't want to come with us?"

"Spend my evening in a smelly, sticky-floored bar?" Maeve shuddered at the thought. "I have a DVR filled with Chopped episodes. That and some popcorn and I'll be perfectly content."

"Told you popcorn was a good idea," Forbes called after Sophie.

"You're too young to be sitting at home every night." Taking his face in her hands, Maeve kissed each cheek.

"What was that for?" Confused, Forbes smiled.

"A thank you and an apology. I've never seen Sophie this happy. I was wrong, and I'm happy to admit it." Maeve blinked several times, unable to hide the moisture that formed in her eyes. "The two of you remind me of your Mom and Dad way back when. Remember how much joy and laughter they brought to this house?"

Forbes swallowed, feeling a lump in his throat. "I do," he nodded."

"It's been so long—so much bad has happened since—I'd almost forgotten what it was like to have a young, happy couple brightening up the rooms in this old place. When I heard you and Sophie just now... well," Maeve wiped at her cheeks. "It feels right, Forbes."

As Forbes hugged Maeve, he kissed her damp cheek.

"You think Mom and Dad would approve?"

"I believe they are together, the way they were always meant to be. Happy, and smiling down on you and Sophie."

"Careful," Forbes laughed, squeezing Maeve once more before pulling back. "What will it do for my manly image if you make me cry?"

"Trust me, a few tears won't hurt. Not with me. And especially not with Sophie."

"Speaking of the lady. What was all that about a surprise?"

"Find out for yourself." Maeve nodded toward the front door.

With no clue what he would find, Forbes turned the knob, stepping onto the front porch. The late afternoon sun hit him in the eyes, blinding him for a second. As his vision cleared, he shook his head, slowly walking down the steps, certain the image in front of him had to be an illusion.

"It can't be."

"Surprise."

A beaming Sophie stood beside a car. Dark red. In pristine condition. A classic. But not just any. His classic nineteen-sixty-four Ford Mustang.

Dazed, Forbes ran his hand over the hood. Not only was it a beautiful machine, it was a connection to his mother. "I thought it was gone forever. Where did you get it?"

"After you left, Newt went a bit off the rails."

While Forbes appreciated Sophie's attempt to sugarcoat it, he knew from Mike and Jerry that his father hadn't been *a bit* angry. Livid was more like it.

"Newt told Maeve to get rid of your car. He didn't care how."

"Was there a mention of selling it for scrap?"

Sophie shrugged, obviously uncomfortable with tossing Newt under the bus—even at this late date. As Forbes finished his slow walk around the vehicle, he stopped on the side opposite Sophie. "You saved it."

"I was certain Newt would regret his decision once he calmed down. So, I conspired with Maeve to find a place to store it. Just until you came home." Sophie's lips twitched. "Little did I know it would take you twelve years. However, your baby was well cared for."

"I can tell." Forbes grinned, almost feeling eighteen again. "Want to go for a ride?"

"I thought you would never ask." Sophie opened her hand, showing him a set of keys. "Catch."

As Forbes opened the passenger side door, he took Sophie's hand, raising it to his lips. If his heart weren't already in his throat, her smile would have put it there.

"Thank you."

"Will you let me drive on the way home?" Forbes nodded, grinning at the excitement that filled Sophie's eyes as she took her seat. "Then consider us even."

*Even? Not by a long shot.* He could never repay Sophie for the car—for everything. However, he thought, starting the engine, he would for damn sure try. Every day. And if Forbes had his way? For the rest of their lives.

A NIGHT OUT in Cloverdale. Sophie didn't have a lot to compare, but she supposed one small town was pretty much like all the rest. The chance to let loose with friends after a long day. A few drinks to help relax. In some cases, a lot of drinks. Loud and rowdy was a good way to describe the crowd at *Smokey's Bar.* And it fit Sophie's mood to a T. She felt like cutting loose. Celebrating. With Forbes at her side, she planned to do just that.

Forbes guided her to an empty table near the back, big enough for all the friends they expected to join them.

"I can't believe we're the first to arrive." Sophie scanned the crowd. Most of the faces were familiar, but she didn't find any she was looking for. "Tory's new boyfriend is driving in from Spokane, but he's going to meet her here."

Just as Sophie spoke, a text came in on her phone.

"Trouble?" Forbes asked, seeing the frown on her face.

"Minor. The boyfriend had car trouble on the way, and Tory is going to pick him up. Unless there is another delay, she expects to be here in about an hour."

"Aaron and Cindy had to wait for the babysitter," Forbes told her after checking his phone. "Mike and Jerry were right behind us as we left the ranch. Brent and Truck are coming, too."

Brent and Truck Unger were new to the ranch this season. Brothers, they came highly recommended. On top of that, their father was an old friend of Jerry's. Two weeks in and Sophie was happy with their skills as cowboys, work ethic, and genial personalities.

"Good. I'm thinking of adding a couple more full-time hands. Brent and Truck seem like good candidates. They're young and eager. Meeting some people will give them a nice foothold in the community if they decide they want the jobs. What do you think?"

Sophie wanted Forbes to know his input was important. Though she ran the day-to-day operation, they were full partners.

"I like them." Forbes signaled the waitress. "As long as you think they'll be a good fit—and Mike and Jerry—agree—I trust your judgment."

Forbes said it in such a matter-of-fact manner. He would never truly realize how much his absolute support meant to her. Sophie already knew it was there, but when he reinforced his faith in her, without pause, it left no doubt in her mind that this thing between them would work.

"What can I get for you?" the waitress asked, chomping her gum. With a layer of heavy makeup and teased-out bright red hair, her age could have fallen anywhere between thirty and fifty.

"I'll have a club soda with a squeeze of lemon."

"Do you have a bottled lager?"

"*Brooklyn* okay?"

"Make that two." Aaron clapped Forbes on the back, holding a chair out for his wife. "And a whiskey for the lady. Neat."

"You look nice," Cindy said to Sophie.

"So do you."

An awkward silence followed. They had always been friendly more than friends, and this was the first time they had met since Aaron's confession to Forbes. What was Sophie supposed to say? *Sorry my mother seduced your boyfriend?* It was true, but she was afraid it would come off sounding trite and insincere.

"I hate your mother," Cindy said so that only Sophie could hear over the other voices and the blaring jukebox.

"Me, too," Sophie said, relieved that Cindy had broken the ice with a resounding whack. "We belong to a big and varied club."

"Please. No t-shirts," Cindy laughed. Her eyes when they met Sophie's were kind. "Just so we're clear. I never hated you. That woman shoulders most of the blame. The rest sits firmly with Aaron." She shrugged. "I've loved him since grade school. I guess that's why I was able to forgive."

"But not forget?"

"Good luck with that. Anybody who say it's possible is full of crap." Cindy looked at her husband. "I believe Aaron loves me. That he will never hurt me again or do anything that would damage our family. I refuse to let one past mistake color the rest of our future."

Joy thrived on other people's misery. Every time one of her victims found happiness, it was a blow against a woman whose hobby was ruining lives. Someday when they were able to talk without interruption, Sophie would explain to Cindy that finding happiness with Aaron was the best revenge possible.

The drinks arrived followed by the four cowboys. Mike offered to brave the bar rather wait to be served. Three beers was the order. And whatever snacks he could rustle up. Ten minutes later, he returned. Chuckling, he set down a full tray, before taking the empty seat next to Jerry.

"What's so funny?" Forbes inquired, handing around the beers.

"The new bartender?" Mike pointed toward the attractive middle-aged woman who was busy filling glasses with practiced ease. "Pretty, isn't she? Name is Larissa."

Sipping his beer, Jerry shook his head. He knew his friend better than anybody. "What line did you feed her?"

"I told her about the ranch. That I'm a cowboy. Seemed real impressed. Then she asked if you and I went *Brokeback Mountain*."

"Well, shit." The grin dropped from Jerry's face. "Why did she pick on me?"

"Guess she thought we would make a nice-looking couple."

Exchanging looks with Forbes, Aaron could barely contain his laughter. "What did you say?"

"Told her that *if* I leaned that way, I could do a hell of a lot better than Jerry."

"The hell you say." Jerry punched Mike on the arm. Hard. "I'm way prettier than you. Maybe I'll take a run at that filly myself."

"Too late. I'm taking her out to dinner on the next night she has off."

As the good-natured insults flew between the old friends, Forbes stood, taking Sophie's hand. "There's a nice slow song. Let's dance."

Sophie noticed the glances coming their way. Stopping on the dance floor, she took Forbes' hand. Placing the other on his shoulder, she followed his lead, moving to the gentle beat.

"We are officially out as a couple."

"I didn't know we were hiding," Forbes chuckled, his hand at her waist, pulling her closer.

"More like we were keeping to ourselves," Sophie corrected. "Until now, all our activity as a couple has taken place on the ranch. Tonight, we're putting it out there for anybody who wants to look."

Forbes glanced around, his lips quirking. "We're drawing some attention. But I don't think it's because of our romantic situation."

"No? What is your theory?"

"My dazzling dance moves."

To prove his point, Forbes twirled Sophie in a circle, ending with an impressively executed dip—and a long kiss. A smattering of applause followed—and one or two *way to go, Chief* cat calls.

"You're a hit."

"*We* are a hit," Forbes whispered the words against Sophie's ear. "You and I are a team."

If it were physically possible, Sophie's entire body would have let out a long, happy sigh. They stayed on the floor for the next dance. As a third song began, she heard a muted buzzing.

"Sorry." Keeping one arm around her, Forbes took out his phone. He showed Sophie the screen before answering. "Kai. What do have for me?" He listened for a moment, frowning. "Give me five minutes. I'll call you right back."

"Has Kia found out something important?" Sophie asked.

"I don't know. Maybe. She wants me to look at some files. I need to go to the police station."

"I'll come with you."

Forbes shook his head. Moving his hand to the small of her back, he guided her to their table. "This shouldn't take long. Stay with our friends. If I'm delayed, I'll call."

She had no reason to worry. Yet as Sophie watched Forbes disappear from the bar, stopping to send her a wave, she felt a niggling sense of worry. She saw his face during the brief conversation with Kai.

Sophie leaned toward Aaron. "Forbes won't be alone at the station, will he?"

"There is always somebody on duty," Aaron assured her.

Mike patted her hand. "Don't worry. This is Cloverdale. What could happen?"

A dozen things sprang to Sophie's mind—none of them good. But she didn't share any of them. Everybody was having a good time. The last thing she wanted was to bring them down.

The waitress came by, taking orders for another round.

"Another club soda," Jerry asked.

Sophie nodded. "Order for me. I'll be right back. Nature calls."

The bathroom was at the back of the bar near the exit. She knew from experience that the ladies room consisted of exactly two stalls and a sink. Which—on a night like this—meant there would be a line.

Five women stood outside the door. Not bad, Sophie thought, taking her place toward the rear. She recognized everybody and would have struck up a conversation. However, since all were either on their phones—talking or texting—she waited in silence, the exit right at her back.

The door opened, letting in a burst of fresh air. Before Sophie could do more than take a shallow breath, an arm went around her waist, a hand holding a cloth clamped over her mouth. Her scream came out a muffled yelp, but it was enough to get the attention of the women closest to her.

"Hey!" She cried out. "What are you doing?"

"Stay where you are," a male voice commanded. Out of the corner of her eye, Sophie saw a ski mask—and the flash of a gun. "If you move, I'll shoot. Understand?"

Sophie did her best to fight. But the fumes from the cloth made her groggy. It wasn't like in the movies. She didn't lose consciousness. Instead, her body felt unwieldy. Out of her control. She wanted to kick. Scratch. Anything to stop her assailant. But moving her arms became impossible. They hung useless.

The man dragged her from the bar while the other women watched. Wide eyed, helpless, and horrified.

At the lowest point in her childhood, Sophie had never felt this helpless. With her body useless and her mind fogging over fast, she struggled to find some foothold. Something. Anything.

Focus, Sophie urged herself. She couldn't see the man's face, but she did notice other details. He was average height. Against her back, he felt bulky. Fat? Maybe. But strong. He didn't seem to have a problem dragging her dead weight into the parking lot.

"Throw her in the trunk and get in the car. Now!"

With little concern for the fact he carried a live human being, the man followed orders, dumping Sophie unceremoniously, before slamming the lid. The engine jumped to life, the tires squealing as the car shot forward.

Sophie swallowed, breathing in and out. She knew that voice. The harsh, domineering tone. It had been a long time. But not nearly long enough. She had no doubt who it was. Or who was in charge.

The woman was none other than her mother.

# CHAPTER TWENTY-THREE

FORBES READ THE files, his expression grim. The pieces were all over the place. A bit here, another there. Like a row of dominos, they fell into place. And the picture they formed was a twisted, convoluted mess.

"Money, sex, and power." Forbes' eyes narrowed as he continued to read the words on the computer screen.

"The big three," Ian Drysdale said, chiming in on speakerphone.

Drysdale had called just as Forbes arrived at the station with news that toppled another domino. They finally caught up with Moncrieff. The man had made it to the Mexican border, but no farther. Broke, he had taken a chance, using a credit card to withdraw some money. The second the transaction went through, Forbes' people had him, picking him up just as he left the rundown motel where he had been holed up.

"You didn't need to bring in the big interrogation guns, boss. Moncrieff crumbled the second our guys grabbed him. Cried like a baby, from all accounts."

Deep in debt, Moncrieff had sold out Forbes for a small amount of money with the promise of more sometime down the road.

"He claims he had no choice." Drysdale didn't try to mask the disgust in his voice.

Forbes couldn't have cared less about Moncrieff's motives. He wanted names.

"Who hired him?"

"Your gut was right. Moncrieff identified Daphne Parks."

"Son of a bitch."

Forbes didn't feel any satisfaction. Daphne used to be his friend and her actions stung.

298

"That's the only person Moncrieff identified. They will keep at him, but I don't think he's holding anything back."

"Stay on the line," Forbes told Drysdale. " has some information. I have the feeling it ties into this somehow."

"Your instincts have been dead on so far."

Forbes connected with Kai as he turned on his computer.

"What have you got for me?"

"Guess where one of your deputies went for his last vacation?" Kai asked.

"Kai..." The computer whiz loved guessing games. Forbes wasn't in the mood.

"You're becoming a grouch, boss man." Kai sighed. "Eli Stover spent two weeks in Las Vegas. Where most nights he could be found playing blackjack. His dealer was—"

"Joy Lipton." It might be a coincidence. But Forbes didn't think so. "Any idea if that was where they met?"

"That's a big fat no. According to Stover's phone records, they spoke several times a week for close to six months before his trip. I dug a little deeper. Joy initiated the relationship by contacting Stover online. *Shit*!"

Muscles tensing, Forbes sat forward. "What?"

"My contact just texted me. Joy missed her shift at the casino tonight. She hasn't been seen for almost a day."

"I thought we had eyes on her twenty-four seven."

"Somebody fucked up," Kai ground out. "I'm sorry, Forbes. I fucked up."

"Kick yourself later. I need your brain working overtime, not dealing with misplaced guilt. Got it?"

Forbes heard the sound of Kai taking a deep breath. "Right." She exhaled. "Okay. Joy didn't leave town by plane, train, or bus. I would have received an alert. By car, she could get here in sixteen hours. Maybe less if she drove straight through. But why would she? There's nothing for her here. It isn't logical."

Sophie's words when speaking of her mother popped into Forbes' head.

"There is no logic when it comes to Joy. That's what makes her dangerous."

Needing to hear Sophie's voice, Forbes grabbed the landline on his desk, dialing her number as he picked up the receiver. *Straight to voicemail.* Forbes cursed. Dialing Aaron, he checked his gun, making certain the clip was full.

Aaron answered after the first ring. "Forbes. Thank God. I was just calling you."

Forbes' fingers dug into the side of his desk. "Where's Sophie?"

"Somebody grabbed her. She's gone, Forbes."

"GET HER OUT of there and into the house. Put her in the back room and make certain she's tied up. Tight. After that, move the car someplace where nobody can see it."

Sophie must have lost consciousness. How long she was out, she couldn't say. Maybe minutes. Maybe hours. Pretending she was still unconscious, she opened her eyes just enough to get a peek at what was happening. It was still dark. The moon brightened things considerably, illuminating the man's face as he bent to pick her up.

Eli Stover! What was he doing with Joy? Sophie stopped herself from laughing aloud. Stupid question. When Joy was around, a man couldn't be far behind. But Deputy Stover. Even for her mother, it was dragging the dregs of the barrel. She preferred her conquests to either have money or looks. Stover possessed neither. Unless… She needed something from him.

Strong. Not too bright. And a police officer. Sophie realized that in his way, Stover was exactly Joy's type.

"I think one of those women recognized me." Stover's voice quavered. Out of breath, he puffed as he carried Sophie into the house. "I need to get out of town. Right away."

"The fastest way to look guilty is to run." Joy was out of Sophie's line of sight, but the click of her heels on the wooden floors couldn't be missed. "Don't lose your head and you'll be fine."

"But—"

"Eli." Changing tactics, Joy lowered her voice to a purr. Bossy wasn't working, so she switched to her specialty. Seduction. "I need you. That stupid Daphne couldn't keep her mouth shut. I told her if this would succeed, she had to keep a low profile. But no. Her blathering made Forbes suspicious. When he started checking up on me, I had no option other than to accelerate our timeline."

*Daphne and Joy. Working together*? Sophie couldn't believe her ears.

Before Sophie could process the implications, she felt Eli's grip loosen. Unceremoniously, he dropped her onto the floor, her fall cushioned—barely—by what felt like a paper-thin mattress. Her face smashed into the material, she wrinkled her nose at the musty smell. It had been a long time, but she would never forget how many times she had fallen asleep with the sickening scent in her nose. Stale cigarettes, sweat, and several mystery odors she was happier not identifying.

The room was lit only by a thin beam of moonlight from a small, curtain-covered window. However, if she squinted, Sophie could make out Stover's substantial shadow. He reached out, pulling Joy into his arms for a noisy kiss.

"There's my big bear," Joy laughed, patting his cheek. "Finish up in here. If you're fast, there might be time for a little fun before you leave."

Sophie had always been repulsed by the way Joy used her sexuality to maneuver and manipulate. However, this time, she found a reason to be grateful for it. In his haste to enjoy *a little fun*, Eli wasn't as careful tying her hands as he should have been. She was able to keep a fair amount of space between her wrists so that when he finished, the rope wasn't as tight as Joy had directed him to make it.

The second Eli scampered away, shutting the bedroom door, Sophie gave a tug. *Yes.* Slowly, she worked her way free, her mind running over the information she had gathered by eavesdropping on Joy and Eli's conversation.

Whatever plan Joy had fashioned must involve money. Which made this a true kidnapping. A public, witnesses present, kidnapping. Forbes would know. And unless both of her earrings somehow fell off, he would have her location. The cavalry was on the way.

Sophie gave another tug at the rope. Forbes would get here as soon as possible. But she wasn't waiting for him to rescue her. Joy sounded frazzled. She was the brains of this operation, and though she was smart, she tended to act on impulse. She wanted money. Sophie wouldn't give her a dime. When she figured that out, who knew what she would do.

Twelve years ago, a desperate Joy could be vindictive. Petty. She lashed out with words using her tongue to cut deep and painful wounds. She lied. Cheated. Stole from her lovers when she was certain she could get away with it. But she had never been a flat-out criminal. To sink to kidnapping, Joy must have hit a new low. Which—as Sophie could attest—would be saying a lot.

The air in Sophie's lungs released in a burst of relief as her hands came free. First thing, she grabbed her earlobes. Oh, thank God. The studs were still there. Just to be safe, she tightened the backs and said a little prayer that she could open the window without having to break the glass. Not that she would hesitate if necessary. But she wanted to get away causing as little noise as possible. Hopefully she'd find some trees nearby. Or other buildings. Someplace she could hide out until Forbes arrived.

As Sophie was about to roll to her knees, the bedroom door opened. A second later, Joy strolled in, accompanied by the sound of her heels on the hardwood. Click. Click. Click.

*Okay,* Sophie thought with a shrug. Change of plans. Instead of sneaking out the window, she would barrel straight out the front door. If she had to take the bitch down with a solid punch to the face? So be it. Sometimes a woman had to do what a woman had to do—and love every second of it.

"Have a nice nap?"

The smug tone to Joy's voice made the idea of hitting her all the more appealing. Until Sophie saw the gun. Though shadowed, the outline was unmistakable. Especially when Joy raised it slowly, using the barrel to caress her cheek. As if pausing for dramatic effect, she posed, then flipped the light switch.

Sophie turned her face away, giving her eyes a few seconds to adjust. Joy retrieved a chair from the corner—the only piece of furniture in the small, square room—and set it a few feet from the mattress.

"It's been a long time."

"Not long enough." Sophie kept her hands behind her back, hiding the fact that they were no longer bound.

"I agree." Gracefully, she took a seat, crossing her pant-covered legs. "Here we are nonetheless. Aren't you going to comment on how I look?" Joy gave Sophie a long, unblinking stare. "Better than you. That's nothing new, is it?"

Joy looked good. Her long honey-colored hair was perfectly blown out, flowing in a silky cascade over one shoulder. Her figure was trim. Admittedly, her face sported quite a few more lines and creases. Once, she had easily passed for Sophie's sister. Now? She looked like what she was. A beautiful woman on a quick slide toward fifty. Like somebody adrift in the middle of a huge, endless sea whose survival depended on one tiny piece of driftwood; inevitably, she would lose the battle.

Joy had always been a master at deluding herself. However, even the best plastic surgeon could do just so much to stop the progress of time.

"Considering the way you staged this little reunion, I don't think you brought me here to stroke your already overblown ego."

Joy's eyes narrowed, her mouth tightening with displeasure. Leaning forward, she waved the gun. Part threat, part reminder of who was in charge. In other words, Sophie had better watch her mouth.

"We're going to be here until I get what should have been mine a long time ago. Ask me what I mean."

Sophie knew this game. Joy had played it with her often enough. She expected Sophie to play along—tossing out questions while pretending she was interested. *Not this time*. Sophie wasn't in the mood.

"You want money."

"You always were a stick in the mud, Sophie." Joy sighed. "I deserve a share of Newt's estate. After all, I am his wife."

"Ex-wife."

"I didn't sign any papers."

The way the woman's mind worked was unbelievable.

"This isn't an argument you can win." Sophie adjusted the way she sat. The second Joy dropped her guard she would take her down. "You already know that, or you wouldn't have kidnapped me."

"It isn't a kidnapping."

"Let's see. Your goon grabbed me—at gunpoint. Drugged me. Stuffed me into the trunk of a car. He tied my hands—per your instructions. And now, you're waving that same gun around in what can only be called a threatening manner." Sophie felt she had covered the pertinent facts. "If that isn't kidnapping, I'd like to know what it is."

"This is simply a friendly negotiation between a mother and daughter. In the morning, you'll call your bank and authorize the transfer of five million dollars into an off-shore account. After that, you can go home."

Sophie's mouth dropped open. "Five million... Years of hairspray abuse has damaged your brain. Even if I were willing to give you the money. And let me make it perfectly clear, I am not. But if I were? Where did you get the idea I had access to that much?"

"Don't play stupid, Sophie." Joy sat back, crossing her legs. The gun rested near her knee with the barrel pointed toward the window. "I kept my eye on you over the years. You may not be much to look at, but you did inherit my brains. My sources tell me the ranch is thriving. The land alone is worth a fortune."

Arguing with Joy had always been an exercise in futility. Though for once, she was right. The ranch land and other assets were worth a fortune. If Sophie wanted to raise five million dollars, she could do it. It would take three or four days, but it could be done quite easily. However, she wouldn't admit that fact to Joy.

Sophie knew better than to try to change the subject. But that didn't mean she couldn't shift it slightly. "This source you mentioned. By any chance would her name be Daphne Parks?"

"You were only pretending to be passed out," Joy accused.

"I don't understand. Why would Daphne help you in any way?"

"Why else? Money. It is a universal balm that heals all wounds. We're both in need of a large influx of cash. So we joined forces. Getting in bed with the enemy is so much easier when it means a big payday." Joy smiled slowly. "Daphne was behind that fire at the ranch. And all the other things. And before you ask, the answer is no. I had nothing to do with any of that. Petty vandalism is hardly my style."

Sophie agreed. Still, if Joy had wanted to create a bit of chaos, getting somebody else to do it was exactly what she would have done.

"If what you say is true, what was Daphne's motive?"

"I suppose it was her way of letting off steam. She didn't like that you had money when she didn't—I can relate to that. Daphne used sex to manipulate a police officer into doing the dirty work for her."

Another thing Joy could relate to, Sophie thought. It seemed the two women had more in common than they could have imagined.

"The police connection is how I found out. Eli and Daphne's lover are friends. He told me. I used it as an in. At first, she was reluctant to work with me. But as I said..."

Sophie was angry. Livid. But she couldn't help the wave of sadness that washed over her. Joy, she understood. Money had always been the driving force in her life. But Daphne? She wasn't destitute. She had a home. Family. And yet she was willing to put it all at risk. And for what? The ability to buy a nicer pair of shoes? It was crazy.

"The fact that you're sleeping with Forbes didn't endear you to Daphne." She noticed an edge of bitterness in Joy's voice. "He never had any taste. But what is wrong with the man?"

Forbes had rejected Joy's advances. A fact that obviously still stung. Smiling, Sophie couldn't resist rubbing a little salt in Joy's wounded ego. "I've seen Forbes up close. Every inch of him. And I can state without reservation that there is nothing wrong with him. Not a single, solitary thing."

"You little bitch. Do you really think you can hold onto a man like Forbes? He'll tire of you soon enough. And then what?"

Joy flicked her hair over her shoulder—a gesture she used as a show of superiority and disdain. Unwisely, she used the hand holding the gun. The moment Sophie had been waiting for. Tightening her fingers into a fist, she reared back and swung.

WITH NO LIGHTS on in the house—no movement to be seen—it was quiet. Too quiet. Frustrated, Forbes grabbed Eli Stover by the shirt, giving him a bone-rattling shake.

"You're sure Sophie isn't hurt?"

"She was fine when I left," Eli whined. Turning his head, he spat out a mouthful of blood. "I think my front teeth are loose."

Aaron took Eli by the arm, shoving him onto the ground. With his hands cuffed, his balance was non-existent. As he toppled over, his face smacking into the dirt, he let out a cry of pain.

"You were stupid enough to take the first swing. Be grateful Forbes didn't break every last tooth in your mouth and shove them down your throat." Aaron took Eli by the collar, propping him up against a tree. "Now sit there and shut the fuck up."

Ignoring what was going on behind him, Forbes raised a pair of night-vision goggles. The small, dilapidated house, was the only building for miles. It sat in a hollow surrounded by trees. If it weren't for the tracking devices in Sophie's earrings, the chances of him finding her would have been been slim to none.

The thought sent a shudder through Forbes' body, and just as quickly as it came, he shoved it aside. Now wasn't the time to worry about what ifs. He had to concentrate on making certain nothing went wrong. Sophie's safety—her survival was the only thing that mattered.

Thank the Lord for modern technology. The second after Forbes received Aaron's call, he pulled up the tracking app on his phone. Finding Sophie's location was simple. Calming himself down so he didn't run off half-cocked took some effort.

First, he contacted Ian Drysdale. Giving the man a brief rundown of the facts, Forbes told him to gather the necessary weapons and equipment—plus the three security guards patrolling the ranch. They needed to head out ASAP. Ian had the tracking app, so he knew where to go.

Next, Forbes sent Ollie to the bar to interview witnesses. He didn't expect much help there, but it had to be done.

The hidden lockbox behind the seat in Forbes' truck was already loaded with everything he needed. As he started the engine, he took a deep breath, saying a silent prayer that Sophie was all right and would stay that way. Just as he shifted into drive, the passenger side door opened, Aaron, Mike, and Jerry piling inside. A thunk in the back had him looking in his rearview mirror. Brent and Truck sat in the bed.

Forbes didn't have time to argue. Not that he would have. These men cared about Sophie. He would have been surprised if they hadn't shown up.

"Where are we headed?" Aaron asked, his hand braced against the dash as Forbes took the turn outside of town at a dangerous speed.

"Northeast." The screen on the truck's built-in computer showed the tracking device as a moving red blip. Wherever they go, we follow."

Nobody said another word for the next twenty minutes. Forbes had one eye on the road, the other on the screen. Aaron, Mike, and Jerry sat in grim silence. Then, the red dot stopped moving.

"Where the hell is that?" Aaron asked "I don't know of anybody who lives out there."

"GPS will take us there."

"It's part of the old McHenry place." Mike knew the area around Cloverdale as well as anybody. "The family moved away almost twenty years ago. The land was broken up into separate plots. Now it's mostly rented out as grazing land."

Forbes took a left as directed. "Is there any kind of building? A house?"

"More like a shack. Wasn't much even then. But those old places were built to last. Chances are pretty good it's still standing."

The last road Forbes turned onto was little more than a deer path. However, the flattened weeds were evidence of another car having passed this way. They were close. Less than a mile away. Taking another turn, he was momentarily blinded by an oncoming set of headlights. Forbes hit his breaks, the other car swerved, hitting a tree.

Forbes ran from the truck, pulling open the car door. He found Eli Stover struggling with the airbag.

"You son of a bitch." Forbes pulled the deputy from the car. "If you have harmed one hair on Sophie's head, you won't live to see the sun come up."

"She's fine," Stover swore, raising his arms in self-defense. "I swear."

"Aaron, grab the handcuffs from the glove compartment and—
"

Forbes didn't know what prompted Stover to take a swing. Stupidity coupled with desperation? But it felt damn good to have a reason to punch the bastard in the mouth.

"Where is Sophie?" Forbes ground out, towering over the other man. "How many people are guarding her? Are they armed?"

Stover realized he was going to jail. Wisely, he figured out that if he didn't want to get there via a hospital stay, he needed to talk.

"There's an old house, in a hollow, just around the next curve. She's in the bedroom. Tied up. But that's all I did to her. I swear. After the chloroform."

"Don't kick him." Aaron put a hand on Forbes' arm. "You're the chief of police. It won't look good if you beat up an unarmed man."

"That's right," Stover piped up.

"Let me plant a knife on him first."

Stover scooted back, his eyes wide. "What the hell? You're the mayor."

"Exactly. When these other witnesses and I testify that you came at Forbes with a deadly weapon, nobody will even blink." Aaron tossed Forbes the handcuffs. "Now, answer the questions."

"The only other person in the house is Joy. And she has my gun."

Forbes had almost hit Stover again. He might have if Ian Drysdale hadn't arrived at that very second. It reminded him to focus his energy on Sophie, not the scum who helped kidnap her.

"What's the situation?" Drysdale asked, exiting his truck. Instantly, he was flanked by three other men.

"Grab your gear and follow me. I'll fill you in as we go. And have one of your men bring in the trash."

Drysdale listened as they jogged down the road, stopping on a hill just above the house. The men did a quick scout of the area, declaring it clear.

"What do want to do?"

Forbes lowered the goggles. "I'm going to check out the house to make certain Stover told us the truth. Unless I signal, do not approach. There is no telling what that bitch is capable of. Sophie is my first priority."

As he slid down the embankment, Forbes kept an eye on the house. His feet landed on solid ground just as a light went on. Crouching low, he ran the short distance, stopping by the window. A curtain blocked most of his view, but a small crack gave him a perfect angle. What he saw made his blood chill. Sophie with her hands behind her back, sitting on some kind of a cushion. And Joy, her back to Forbes, holding a gun.

Sophie looked to be in good health. She was listening to whatever Joy had to say, her expression ranging from disbelieving to exacerbated. She wasn't afraid or intimidated. Not his Sophie.

Forbes wished he could tell her that he was there. That she wasn't alone. She had to know he would come for her. For now, that had to be enough.

A few minutes passed, Sophie and Joy, exchanging words. It seemed almost casual if it weren't that one of them was bound and the other held a gun. All of a sudden, Sophie shifted her body— just a fraction. Her expression grew angry. Something was about to happen. Forbes felt it in his gut.

As Joy raised the gun, he tensed, taking aim. Sophie acted first. Fast, like a striking cobra, her fist connected with Joy's chin. The bitch crumpled into an ignominious heap. And that was it. Game over.

Always thinking, Sophie scrambled to pick up the gun. Smart. She would have made a great field agent. It was an odd thought. Then again, this was an odd situation.

Breathing for the first time since Sophie was taken, Forbes holstered his weapon. Using his knuckles, he tapped on the glass, gaining Sophie's attention and causing her to jump a foot. Cautiously, she lifted the curtain. In a flash, she pushed back the lock.

"So much for riding to the rescue," Forbes said, climbing through the open window. "Looks like you have everything in hand."

"Just your average mother and daughter reunion. Take this, please." Sophie handed him the gun which he unloaded, putting the bullets in his pocket. "Who would have guessed? Joy has a glass jaw. She's out cold."

"Remind me to pass the word to her future cellmate." Better safe than sorry, Forbes slapped a pair of handcuffs around Joy's wrists. Lips curving, somehow he was able to chuckle. "I know this isn't the most romantic setting. But..."

Sophie took a step closer. "But?"

"I love you, Sophie. I think part of me always has."

"I love you, Forbes. I didn't know what that meant when we were kids. But I do now. Always. That about sums it up." She sighed, her body drooping now that the adrenaline wore off. "It's finally over, isn't it?"

"For Joy? Yes. For us? This is just the beginning."

Forbes opened his arms. Without a backward glance, Sophie jumped.

# *EPILOGUE*

## *EIGHTEEN MONTHS LATER*

ROLLING OVER, SOPHIE looked at the time. Almost nine o'clock. She never slept this late. But instead of a surge of panic, she snuggled under the covers, closing her eyes.

It was December. Snow blanketed every inch of the ranch. The animals needed feeding. A few repairs needed taking care of. This afternoon she would see to her horses. But for now, she was content to stay right where she was and for once, let somebody else take care of the chores.

Letting her mind drift, Sophie thought what Forbes had told her in that old house the night of her kidnapping. That their dealings with Joy were finally over. And he had been right. Up to a point.

Joy had been arrested. As had Eli Stover and Daphne Parks. Win Bodine, another Cloverdale deputy and friend of Stover's— and the man who had taken care of Daphne's dirty work for her— had been picked up on his way out of town. It seemed he was the one who tipped off Joy that Sophie was at the bar—and when she got up to use the bathroom.

Daphne ended up getting off lightly. She served a month in the county jail. After which she was given three hundred hours of community service—to be carried out in Spokane, not Cloverdale. For her family, it turned out to be the scandal that broke the camel's back. They left town. Settling in Tacoma.

Stover and Bodine were still in prison. Sophie couldn't have cared less when they were scheduled to get out. They weren't coming back to Cloverdale. That was the only thing that mattered.

Then there was Joy. There hadn't been a trial. Besides the kidnapping charge, it turned out she had embezzled a good chunk of money from her boss in Las Vegas, and he wasn't a forgiving man. When faced with multiple charges—and little chance of leniency from the court—she made a deal. She pleaded guilty. For the next ten years, she would be the guest of the state. After that?

312

There was no rushing justice. It had taken almost twenty-nine years. But finally, Joy was out of her life.

"Still in bed? This must be some kind of record."

Forbes. The best part of Sophie's day. Morning. Noon. Night. She fell asleep in his arms. Woke with them around her. She rarely felt the need to wander alone in the dark. But when she did, he was right there by her side. For somebody who hadn't believed in love, she couldn't imagine her life without it. Without the man who filled every corner of her heart—her soul.

"You offered to do the chores with Mike and Jerry."

"And I was surprised when you agreed."

The red on Forbes' cheeks was proof he had spent the last few hours in the freezing-cold morning air. He was dressed in jeans, a plaid cotton shirt, and thick socks. Sophie, on the other hand, wore nothing but her birthday suit. However, that didn't stop her from lifting the covers, welcoming him in.

Happy to oblige, Forbes lost the socks. And the jeans. By the time he joined her, he was as naked as she was.

"Your hands are nice and warm."

"I stopped in the kitchen for a cup of freshly perked coffee." Forbes lay at her back, his lips nuzzling Sophie's ear.

"And you didn't bring one for me?"

"You, my love, have been off the coffee lately. Besides, I expected to find you dressed and ready to join me for breakfast. Sleeping late and you haven't had your first stack of pancakes." Forbes touched her forehead, his eyes concerned. "Are you feeling all right?"

Sophie felt wonderful. Never better. Tired, which wasn't like her. But that would soon pass. Or so she was told.

"I know Christmas isn't until next week, but I have an early present for you." Sophie took Forbes' hand—the one with the platinum wedding band that matched her own—and placed it over her stomach. "Actually, this is for both of us."

The catch in Forbes' breath was unmistakable. As was the feel of his lips on her shoulder. His fingers spread wide, covering the slight swell.

"When?" he whispered, his tone reverent.

"Early June."

"Are you happy?"

Sophie turned. She laced her fingers with his, her eyes looking into the deep blue of his.

"I love you. I love this baby. Happy doesn't begin to describe how I feel."

"I love you, Sophie."

As Sophie raised her lips to meet Forbes' kiss, she sank into the heat of his touch—the warmth of his love. This was home. Always and forever.